Look What They'

Mark Blackaby was born in 1962, and was educated in Stockholm, Croydon and at Oxford University. He is a journalist and lives in London with his partner and sons. His first novel, *You'll Never Be Here Again*, was shortlisted for the Authors' Club First Novel Award and won the Betty Trask Prize.

MARK BLACKABY

Look What They've Done
to the Blues

*IN*DI*GO*

First published in Great Britain 1997
by Victor Gollancz

This Indigo edition published 1998
Indigo is an imprint of the Cassell Group
Wellington House, 125 Strand, London WC2R 0BB

A catalogue record for this book is
available from the British Library.

ISBN 0 575 40091 9

Printed and bound in Great Britain by
Guernsey Press Co. Ltd, Guernsey, Channel Isles

98 99   10 9 8 7 6 5 4 3 2 1

Look What They've Done to the Blues

One

'Are most of the women you sleep with married?'

Some you see coming, some you don't. No shame in that – everyone has blind spots. Even Ali had a problem with left hooks. Cooper and Frazier both caught him. But remember what happened next. In the fifteenth against Smokin' Joe at Madison Square Garden, he got hit by a left just about as hard as any man ever got hit by anything and he was up in three. If you want to be a contender, it helps to be able to come back from the dead.

'They don't say.'

As a bid for immortality, it wasn't up to much. As an answer to Helen, it could have gone either way. This time she just smiled and checked her hair in the mirror.

'Does it matter?' I added, pushing myself up on one elbow.

She drew a couple of soft curls round one ear. 'Maybe not. I was just curious.'

I listened to the rustle of expensive fabric as she tucked and smoothed and buttoned. I couldn't see the labels, but I could guess.

'I liked you as you were.'

She smiled. 'Thanks. I could tell. But I'm off to fetch Matthew from school. I'm not sure as I was would be entirely appropriate.' She looked away from the mirror, out of the window. The soft light warmed her face.

'You know what I always associate these afternoons with? The sound of sirens.'

The Japanese cover version of the Simon and Garfunkel classic. I listened to the police wail and decided I liked sirens. They were a sign that someone else was having a harder time than I was.

'This is a rough area you live in. It's not good for me. When I'm lunching with the girls in Chelsea and I hear sirens, I start to blush. It's embarrassingly Pavlovian.'

'Maybe you could have a tape made for—'

The look told me I was pushing it, so I stopped. She came over and sat on the edge of the bed.

'I hope you don't think I'm here just for sex.' She traced a slow line across my chest with one of her fingernails, which rather confused the message. 'As it happens, Malcolm and I are just fine in that department.' She made it sound like one of her Sloaney stores. 'He's very gentle with me. Kind. Less aggressive than you are. And a lovely father.'

He sounded a sweetie. I was obviously sleeping with the wrong half of the couple.

I thought about Malcolm for a while. But it wasn't as much fun as thinking about Helen. My mind slipped back through the years, like a stream over smooth pebbles.

'You had them all at your feet.'

It took her a while to follow me back.

'I had some of them at my feet. I don't recall you being there.' Her hand moved lower.

'Maybe not. But I was everywhere else. Especially that first week when you wanted to stay a virgin. I had my head between your thighs, my prick between your breasts, my hands—'

'Thank you. I remember. But you're talking to a married woman now. Who's about to collect her young son from school. Who's settled and respectable.'

'I'm talking to a married woman who makes love on

8

summer afternoons with someone who isn't her husband. In a shabby flat a long way from the King's Road. I just wonder why.'

She trailed her fingers back up across skin that was still damp. Her nails found all the nerve endings and set them off like land-mines. I wanted her to stay. But asking would have broken the rules.

'For the good times, I suppose,' she said quietly. 'Because you were the first and I loved you. As simple as that. I loved us. We were pretty. We were special. We were young. What more d'you want?'

'I don't want anything more.'

She looked down at me and smiled. 'You don't, do you.'

I put my hand over hers, feeling the ring and the small bones.

'I've got a photo somewhere,' she said. 'Of all of us. All the first-years. It gets stranger every time I look at it.'

'D'you still see anyone?'

'A few people. I used to work with Becky. And I was always talking to David and Simon on the phone. Now I'm part-time I don't work on the big cases. But we keep in touch.'

Big cases. Serious work. Important lives. 'I wonder what I'd be doing now. If I hadn't left.'

'You had to leave. You hated it. I'm surprised you lasted a year. Anyway, it was a long time ago. What does it matter?'

Not much. Probably less than whether most of the women I slept with were married. But it still hurt sometimes.

'How long were you travelling, anyway?'

'Two years, just over. With another year to get back.'

'Three years. And not one letter.'

'I'm not the writing kind. If I had been, I would have stayed at college. And I didn't want to find out who'd taken my place.'

'No one took your place. That's why I'm here.'

'So you are.' I held her hand against my chest. 'I still didn't want to find out who you were sleeping with.'

'Almost everybody, at first. Then nobody. Then it sort of levelled out.'

She stood up and smoothed her skirt. 'I'm glad the people opposite are always out. Don't you ever draw the curtains?'

I smiled. 'I'm too eager. And they're not out. One old woman has the house to herself. That's her sitting-room. I expect she watches us and knits. She's very friendly when she sees me in the newsagent's. She probably feels she knows me.'

Helen reached into a soft leather handbag for her keys. 'One day they're going to come for you.'

'Let's hope I'm out.'

I swung myself out of bed and stood up. My dressing gown was crumpled on the floor, from when I'd been lying on it and Helen had been lying on me. I was grateful for the gown. The rug was thin and getting thinner. We'd still ended up in bed, though. Maybe that was age. Maybe our floor-show days were over.

'Tell me some more about your gentle husband.'

For a while I thought she wasn't going to answer. She certainly took her time.

'Malcolm isn't gentle. Not with other people. It's a hard firm and he's a hard man. That's why it's touching how kind he is with Matthew and me.' She smiled. 'Not that he has pictures of us on his desk or anything. Just a sign: "Winning isn't everything – it's the only thing." I think he means it.'

'So did Magruder.'

'Who?'

'Jeb Magruder. Part of Nixon's underground. He directed the Committee to Re-elect the President and dragged America towards its biggest constitutional crisis since the civil war. He had the same sign on his desk. I wonder if Malcolm knows that.'

'I don't expect he does.' She snapped her handbag and

looked around the room for anything she'd forgotten. 'What strange things you remember.'

'When are you coming again?'

She came over and kissed me. 'I'll ring.'

'I mean, not that it's anything to me. Don't get me wrong. I just want to know for the old lady opposite. It's only fair to warn her. She has a nap some afternoons and would hate to miss any—'

The door clicked shut. I sighed and let myself fall back on the bed, where I lay staring at a cobweb until I'd thought of some music that I could play loud enough to hear in the shower.

The 1812 Overture. Cover version by the Ramones.

Two

The girl was on the corner again. Sitting on the broken brick wall in front of a house on the other side of the road. The For Sale sign above her head looked as if it applied to her.

I pulled the front door closed behind me. Most of the afternoon had gone. Most of the summer, too. It was beginning to feel cold. I bunched my hands into my pockets and thought about buying a pair of cheap gloves. It was tempting after last winter. But if the cold snap didn't last, it would be wasted money.

At least I had a coat. The girl didn't even have that. Just a prickly-looking woollen shirt and some faded corduroys. And some heavy, mannish boots. The same clothes she was wearing the last time I saw her.

I crossed the road, heading for the corner. Usually I went the other way, towards the car. This time I was going to Ramon's.

The girl watched me walking towards her. She had a level stare – unfrightened and empty. When I got closer, I noticed she had her arm round the post of the For Sale sign. I guessed she was going to ask me for money. I felt in my pockets for change. There wasn't much.

She didn't ask for anything. She dropped her gaze down to the road and hunched up a little more into her shirt. The hand clutching the post was pink with cold, but the cuffs of her shirt were turned up a couple of times away from the wrist.

I hesitated, wondering whether to give her money anyway. After a couple of paces, I decided against. If she wanted it, she'd ask. And there was always tomorrow.

'Is your name really Gideon?'

I was already past her, so I had to turn round. She was looking at me without much interest.

'What kind of a name is that?'

'It's from the Bible. He was a judge.'

'A judge with a wig?'

She had me there. 'I don't know. He was a warrior judge. He fought people called Midianites. The wig probably slipped off at some stage.'

She thought about it. 'So you believe in the Bible?'

'It doesn't follow.'

'Then how come you've got that little gold cross dangling from your ear?'

That was a hard one to answer. A Rod Stewart album cover had shown me the way. But some truths are not for the young.

'It was a present. Like the name. If you want to know where that came from, ask my mother. Most people call me Charlie.'

I sat down carefully on the other end of the broken wall. The girl carried on watching.

'Aren't you going to ask how I knew your name?'

'I wasn't planning to. It's no secret. But tell me anyway.'

She pointed over to the other side of the street. 'The postman dropped a letter by the gate. It said "Gideon Lucas" and then number eighty-two. So Gideon had to be you or the black guy. I guessed it was you.'

That made sense. 'What happened to the letter?'

'What d'you think happened to the letter? I put it through the letter-box. I'm not a thief.'

I tried to guess how old she was. Whether she was playing

truant from school or had left as soon as she could. Or been expelled.

'I didn't mean: Did you steal it? But Luther sometimes borrows my post. I like to keep tabs.'

'Luther borrows your post?'

I couldn't believe how surprised she sounded. Half her friends were probably pregnant or strung out on crack, and she was stunned that Luther read my mail.

'Why does he do that?'

I hadn't really thought about it. 'I guess he likes letters. And he doesn't get many of his own. So he reads mine.'

'And you let him?'

'Why not? He passes them on when he's finished. Where's the harm?'

She shook her head. 'Weird.'

I couldn't decide whether it was or not. While I was still thinking about it, she asked: 'Whose house is it?'

'Luther's. I rent the top flat. Where do you live?'

'Round the corner. Luke Street. With my nan and grandad. But I prefer this road. Especially this wall. It's comfortable.'

It didn't feel comfortable to me. And I was getting cold. I stood up.

'Are you going now?'

I nodded. 'I'm meeting someone.'

'Can I use your flat?'

I wasn't sure I'd heard right. 'Can you what?'

'Use your flat.'

'For what?'

'Just to be in.'

There was no embarrassment. I recognized the tone. If you never get anything, you may as well ask for too much.

'I don't like being shut in with my grandparents. They're OK, but I like to be on my own sometimes. And I'm cold.'

That made two of us. I stood on the pavement, wondering

what to do. The girl began to scuff one of her boots along the wall.

'What about your friends?' I said, a little desperately.

'They're at school. I hate school. I can't wait to leave. I bet you didn't like it, either.'

She looked up curiously. I hadn't given her a straight 'no'. That was almost as much of a surprise as Luther reading my mail. And she was right about me and school.

'I won't touch anything. I promise. I only want somewhere I can be by myself and not be cold.'

I fingered the keys in my pocket and wondered why everybody saw me coming. I tossed them towards her and she caught them quickly, left-handed.

'I don't know when I'll be back. Leave the keys with Luther. And ask him for that letter you saw the other day.'

Ramon's was dark. The blinds were down.

It wasn't really Ramon's, but Jeff's. He hadn't bothered to change the sign. Mind you, even when it was Ramon's, it wasn't really – it was Tel's. Jeff got a good deal on the lease, because Tel only lasted five months. Which was a surprise to me. I thought he'd go in three. We weren't tapas people round our way – yet.

Jeff owned a couple of antiques shops. Other people ran them. He was also a one-man import–export company, dealing in electrical components. I sometimes wondered about those components, because Jeff wasn't well up on voltage. I'd done some wiring up at his place once. Anything more complicated than three-core and he was nowhere.

Jeff bought the bar because he could never resist a deal and he hated watching game shows. His wife worked part-time as a lab technician and he was hopeless on his own.

Jeff was the richest person I knew. After myself, of course. Most of my work was for him.

I squeezed between the tables and took a stool at the bar. The place was musty and warm. Jeff poured a coffee.

'No booze – you may be driving tonight.'

I wrapped my hands around the mug. In the mirror behind the bar I could see three builders drinking in a corner and a couple of women with carrier bags having a quiet half.

'What's going on? The place is packed. I thought it was meant to be a tax dodge.'

'It was. It is. Why else d'you think I leave the blinds down and all these poxy flamenco posters on the walls? I thought it would be my friends who came here. I can't believe these people have nothing better to do with their lives.'

'Why not? We haven't.'

This was unfair. Jeff was the barman. And he did have thirty-two other moneymaking schemes ticking away behind the scenes while I sat on my bum and sipped coffee.

'We have. I told you. You're going to be doing some driving.'

One of the workmen came up with a repeat order for spirits and beer. I slipped round the other side of the bar and took care of the spirits. The guy doing the ordering chatted away to Jeff, telling him the scaffolding hadn't arrived, so that was that for the day. He sounded understandably pleased.

When we'd finished serving, Jeff pulled out a pad and pencil and scribbled an address.

'It's not too far. You'll need the van. He's closing down – well, being closed down. He reckons they're coming for his stock first thing tomorrow. Said if I could get a van up today, he'd give me a price on the good stuff. Save it being picked up by cheapskates at auction.'

'Where's it going?'

Jeff wasn't sure. 'I need to look at it first. If there's anything . . . ah . . . special, it'll have to go over to France. Otherwise, Michael and Colin can handle it.'

I finished my coffee and folded the address into my wallet. 'OK. I'm gone. Yorkie man hits the road.'

The van was round the back, with the keys in the ignition. Jeff wasn't sure if it was the biggest I could drive with an ordinary licence, in which case we were fine, or the smallest I had to have an HGV for, in which case we weren't. He'd read somewhere that they'd changed the law. There were some overalls in the back for me to look the part.

I put them on over clothes that didn't deserve much protection and started crawling through shopping streets towards the motorway. There wasn't much to keep me amused. The radio seemed incapable of picking up any English stations. The glove compartment yielded one dog-eared soft-porn magazine and half a cheese and pickle sandwich in damp clingfilm. The sandwich was marginally more erotic. When I reached the motorway, it started to rain.

The only break I got was finding a folded piece of paper in one of the overall pockets. It was a poem. Well, sort of. A couple of verses in spidery longhand, including the promise 'always to be true to your eyes of sparkling blue', along with some more tortured yearn and burn stuff.

I guessed the poem was Michael's. He ran the less successful of Jeff's shops. A morose bloke with a beard. He did most of the driving in the van. If the porn mag was his as well, I thought I could fairly conclude that Michael had problems with women. Though probably not as many as they had with him.

It was a long day, and not a good one. Jeff wasn't going to be pleased. The big truck was almost empty: a couple of sofas, a fireplace, a *chaise-longue* and some lamps. Not enough to wedge together – everything had to be tied separately. It took ages.

The guy who was being closed down was a mopey little runt called Steve. He wasn't much help with the ropes and I certainly didn't fancy spending the evening with him. I walked around, looking for somewhere to eat, then gave up and ducked into an ugly, fake-beamed pub called the Crown.

It was hot inside – and clean. Shiny wood, gleaming brass, patterned carpets and mock gas lamps. I took a slow look around. The barmaid was chatting to a friend of hers, a blonde Rolling Stones' girlfriend type with lots of lipstick and not much skirt. Eyebrows were twitched in my direction. The friend half looked round, casually. I thought about it as I walked up to the bar.

The barmaid pulled the pint and took the money.

'You're not from round here, are you?'

'London.'

'Thought so. I was just saying to Linda, it's hopeless at the moment. Dead. No interesting people at all. What d'you do?'

'Antiques. I've just been collecting some stuff.'

They asked what sort of stuff, and I told them. They knew Steve's shop, but had never been in it. They weren't keen on old stuff, because it was ever so expensive. They wondered what sort of prices I charged in my shop in London. I hadn't a clue what most of Jeff's woodwork went for, so I made up some suitably daft figures and let them marvel at the gullibility of rich southerners.

The barmaid wandered off to refill one of the few other punters in the place, winking none too subtly at Linda, who blushed into her whatever-and-lemonade. I wasn't sure about the blush. It didn't go with the skirt.

There was a blast of cold air as three blokes bundled through the end doors. Linda tensed and moved a couple of feet away from me.

'That's my brother,' she murmured. 'Ray.'

I guessed she meant the leader of the little pack – a good-looking and deeply co-ordinated thug with slicked brown hair and a same-shade bomber jacket. He sauntered forward while his mates propped themselves up at the bar. I wondered if there was going to be trouble. I looked around and didn't like the odds. I couldn't even remember if my knife was in my jacket. And it wouldn't look cool to rummage. Sometimes I worried about going soft.

But at least I was tall. When Ray came over and stared into my face, he had to look up. I hoped that would give him something to think about. I hoped he'd get a crick in his neck.

'Pete can't make it,' Ray said. He was talking to Linda, but looking at me. Linda's friend the barmaid was keeping a very low profile.

'Thanks,' Linda said. 'I worked that out for myself.'

'He's working on the car. He says he's sorry.'

Linda didn't rush to accept the apology. She turned back towards me.

'He will be,' she said pointedly.

That pushed me further centre stage than I was comfortable with. I checked over Ray's shoulder. His two mates were slouched over the bar, dreaming of beer. They didn't look much use to anyone. I hoped Ray knew his back-up team was a mess.

'Who are you?' he said toughly. Hoping for a none-of-your-fucking-business answer.

'Gideon,' I said blandly.

He thought about it, then decided he didn't know me.

'So what are you doing with my sister?'

'Talking.'

We were two feet in front of him. He could see what we were doing. Why do people ask such stupid questions?

I had a few of my own that were much smarter. Like who was Pete in all this and what was the big-deal car he was working on? And why doesn't anything last? It couldn't have been so long ago that Pete would have given up any number of under-the-bonnet evenings for the chance to hitch Linda's skirt up and pull her knickers down. I would have laid money on it. Instead, it looked like I was going to lay Linda. So it goes.

Ray switched his attention back to her.

'You want a lift home?'

'I haven't finished my drink.'

The two mutts stirred in the background. The mention of drink reminded them they hadn't had any.

'So what do I tell Pete?' The aggression in Ray's voice gave way to real concern. When push came to shove, sisters could get shafted by strangers, but mates were mates.

Linda shrugged. 'Tell him what you like. Or don't tell him anything. I'm seeing him tomorrow anyway.'

There wasn't much to say after that. Ray gave me a final glower, squared his shoulders in his leather jacket, turned and swaggered off towards the door. His friends were slow to notice he was on the move. They tried to get it together enough to stare hard at me, take a last look as far up Linda's skirt as they could, and fall into the right formation. It was one too many. Their eyes crossed, they lurched into each other with a smack of low foreheads and one of them got his feet caught up in a stool. They were a shambles. Ray's exit was ruined. Wisely, he didn't look back.

Linda finished her drink. 'Poor little brother. You shouldn't have scared him like that.'

This seemed unfair. 'I hardly said anything.'

'You didn't need to. Take a look in a mirror some time.'

It was redundant advice. I knew what I looked like. For a while in the kids' home they called me Damien. I didn't like it much, but I could live with it. Later on, I found it had its advantages. But I still didn't like it.

I finished my beer. 'I'll drop you home.'

I half expected to see the leather gang waiting for us when

we left the pub, but there was no one around. Linda held on to my arm in case they were watching.

'How come that place was so empty?' I said.

'It's new. Just been done up. Julie only started working there last week. The drinks are more expensive because it's smart. Everyone goes to the King's Arms instead.'

I couldn't remember how much I'd paid for my beer. But if the price included Linda, I hadn't been ripped off. Of course, it was humiliating to be so blatantly used as a pawn in the battle between Linda and her grease-monkey boyfriend. But sometimes you've just got to take the blows.

The pavements were wet and her shoes weren't sensible. She clung on tight to stop herself from slipping. We walked down two roads of identical houses. Most of the curtains were drawn. Where they weren't, you could see the square blue light of a television.

When we reached the truck, I opened up the back, saying I had to check the furniture was tied properly. Which was almost true, given Steve's knots. Either he'd never joined the Scouts, or he'd spent all his time being seriously interfered with by Akela.

I pulled Linda up and managed to find a torch in the back of the van. The batteries were running low, so it didn't give out much light. I was glad there wasn't much stuff to ram my shins into.

'My place,' I said, pulling down the roller door. 'I think it needs a woman's touch.'

Linda picked her way round carefully.

'Try the sofa. Your last chance before a dim southerner pays a fortune for it.'

I balanced the torch on the fireplace. Linda sat down on the sofa and slipped off her shoes.

'You're sure this is tied securely?'

One of Steve's specials. I was pretty surprised it was still in the van at all.

'There's one way to find out.'

Which was by joining Linda on the sofa and starting to take off her clothes. She wasn't wearing many. But those she was wearing, she wanted to keep on, because it was cold. So we compromised. She got to keep them on, but I got to rearrange them. Which meant rearranging her sweater so it was above her breasts and rearranging her bra so it was below them. A little later it meant rearranging her skirt so it came up to where her bra had come down to. I was glad the torch batteries were just about holding.

The only things that came right off were her pants. By request. I was reaching over into my jacket pocket, as we've all been taught to do these days, when the switchblade spilled out. It was there, after all. She wanted to see it. She flicked the blade out a couple of times and pushed it back. While she played, I slid my hand up between her thighs. But the knife was making me uneasy. It wasn't the sort of toy I wanted lying around.

Linda had other ideas. 'Use it,' she said. 'Cut them off.'

She flicked open the knife and handed it to me. I hesitated, then slid it carefully up the outside of her left thigh, under the tiny elastic strip of her pants. When I turned the blade, the fabric snapped. I was pleased at how sharp the knife was. But the pants stayed more or less where they were. I switched hands and used the knife on the other side. Slowly, so I could see the elastic fraying, thread by thread.

Driving back was all about watching the windscreen wipers and trying to stay awake. I hit a few cones going through a contraflow, but nothing else happened. Most of the big trucks had pulled over into laybys. I envied their snug mattresses and portable televisions and whatever else they carried these days. Probably BSkyB receivers and pool tables. Me, I'd have settled for a radio that worked.

It stopped raining on the outskirts of town. I bought a pint of milk from an all-night garage and drank it down. Breakfast. I reckoned I had an hour to go.

More like an hour and ten. The streets were drying and it was light when I pulled into the yard at the back of Ramon's. I locked up the van and pushed the keys through the letterbox. Then I walked home.

I was just thinking it hadn't been such a bad trip when I remembered I had no keys. I bunched my fists and swore loudly, sending a scrawny cat scuttling into a hedge. I couldn't believe I'd been so stupid.

I thought about hammering on Luther's door, but he was a bit sensitive about dawn visits ever since Plod had roared up to bust his son Royale for supplying the neighbourhood with most of its grade-A blow.

I shoved my bunched hands into my pockets and blew out angry blasts of cold air. Then I vaulted the front wall, avoiding the creaking gate, and slipped quickly behind the tree on the left side of the house. The boundary wall was three times the height of the front one, and still wet. I hoped the neighbourhood watchers were sound asleep, because I wasn't in the mood for hassle.

I thumped my kneecap into a protruding brick and cut my hand as I hauled myself up. That was about my average for breaking and entering. And I clipped one of Luther's precious plants when I finished tightrope walking and finally dropped down into the garden. That was a worry. Luther liked his plants. I took out my knife and sliced cleanly through the broken branch, which I hid behind a bush a few yards up.

The shed smelled of woodshavings and creosote. It went the entire width of the garden. Luther hated it. He said as soon as I left he'd bonfire the whole thing and make a rockery. But for the moment it stayed. I used it to do my carving. And occasionally to sleep.

I cleared a couple of chisels off the old sofa and kicked off my shoes. Then I put the radio on low and lay down with my coat over me. The music was R. & B. I was asleep before I heard the B.

'You're a disgrace to the neighbourhood. Sleeping in a shed like an old hobo. What's the matter with you?'

Luther was doing his hard-man act. Unfortunately, he'd also brought a mug of tea, which told its own story.

I squinted and tried to sit up. 'What time is it?'

'Almost midday. I've been out here for hours, waiting for you to wake up. And don't think I haven't noticed you've been smashing up my plants. There's no point hiding a branch behind a tree if your footprints lead straight to it.'

I reached out and took the tea. 'I'm sorry about the plant. It was late. Early. I was tired.'

'You're a crazy sonofabitch. Sleeping in the shed. You're lowering the tone. I give you a shed to work in, I give you a flat to sleep in. You got two good rooms up there. And if you got any complaints, say 'em, because there's plenty of other people want to rent that place.'

'Is that sugar?'

Luther was holding some white stuff in a polythene bag.

'Bonemeal. Feel free.'

I passed on the bonemeal and rubbed my neck where it was stiff. I'm not really worth much in the mornings.

'You're a good man, Luther. For bringing me tea after I jumped on your plant. I don't deserve you.'

Luther just stood there, shaking his head. 'Where were you last night?'

'Driving Jeff's truck. I had to get some stuff for him. It was a long way. When I got back, I didn't have my keys.'

'Of course you didn't. How could you? You gave them to young Missy Thing – that little stray who's always on the corner. I just hope you know what you're doing, boy, because this is my house and my shed and there's certain things I don't like going on, you hear me?'

I heard him loud and clear. And if I could only wake up, I could muster some heavy indignation and reclaim a little lost ground.

'Luther, she was cold. That's all. I never even talked to her before. She asked for the keys because she wanted to be on her own in the warm. End of story. You've got a twisted mind.'

'And you've got a reputation.'

It sounded great, the way Luther said it. Rep-you-tay-shun. Definitely the thing to have. Except when it prompted suspicions of rampant paedophilia and general shed-dwelling degeneracy.

'Give me a break. It's not that kind of reputation.'

I hoped.

Luther said 'Hmph' and stroked his moustache. He was a good-looking guy, was Luther. Getting on a bit, with wiry grey-white hair and slightly tired eyes. He looked distinguished. I decided I'd be happy to look like Luther when I got to his age. But I didn't rate my chances.

I hauled myself up on my elbows and thought about the day ahead. Stumbling up to my flat for a bath struck me as a truly fine idea. Especially if I could take my tea.

'There's another thing.' Luther sounded serious. I wondered what I'd done now and hoped he wasn't raising my rent. I tried to concentrate.

'It's Opal. I think she wants to come back.'

I took a deep breath and wondered if that was the thing I most or least wanted to hear. It wasn't hard to figure out.

'I'm not interested. You know that.'

Luther was shaking his head again. 'Think about it. Don't rush to decide. Don't spite yourself. Just think—'

'Spite myself? Jesus, Luther, did I hear you? Did you say "Spite myself"? Because if you did, I can't see how exactly—'

'OK, OK. Enough. I'm sorry I spoke. Maybe I'll try you at a better time. When you've been sleeping indoors.'

I swung my legs off the sofa and stood up shakily. 'Luther,

hear me. There won't be a better time. Your little girl turned me inside out. Then she came back and did the exact same thing again. Now you're telling me she's on a hat-trick. What d'you expect me to say?'

'Nothing. I don't expect you to say nothing. Just think about it.'

He picked unhappily at the tie around his little bag of bonemeal.

'How d'you know this, anyway?' I couldn't stop myself asking.

'There was a letter. I recognized the writing. I'll look it out for you.'

'Obliged,' I muttered.

'And your keys are in the hall. Where your little friend left them.'

I tried to doze in the bath, but the wrong memories were everywhere. Some were achingly specific. Nights when we didn't sleep. Mornings when we never went to work. Afternoons because it was ages since the morning and even longer until the night. My pulse started to thump as the blue movie spooled through my brain. But it didn't last long. It never did these days. The film began to fray and break up, leaving a few grainy images and finally just a bright white light and the sound of a whirring projector.

It was impossible to hold on to the sex. But the dreams came back stronger every time. We were going to find a place to live. We were going to settle down. We were going to have cute little coffee-coloured kids. We didn't care what people thought. Christ.

I sank lower in the water and stared at the taps.

When I was shaved and dressed I felt better. But not much. I badly wanted just to mope around and listen to all my old records. But I'd done that before and it never worked. So I pulled on my coat and headed for Ramon's.

The weather was getting worse. Something that could well have been sleet was coming down to make things miserable for everyone. The pavements were slippery and the sky was smoggy grey. No one else was out and about. It didn't feel like a big thrill to be alive.

Jeff was behind the bar. 'Afternoon. You look like a man who needs a coffee.'

Michael was round there, too. He managed about one third of a smile and didn't say anything.

'Michael's been clearing the van,' Jeff said. 'Unusual load, by all accounts.'

By Michael's account, presumably. I couldn't believe too many other people were locked into this particular topic of conversation.

'It seemed pretty average to me.' I never could get worked up about furniture.

'I'll take your word for it. But Michael seemed to think one used sheath and a pair of sliced-up panties were something of a novelty.'

He smiled and put a coffee down on the bar. Michael leered through his unfortunate attempt at a beard. It took me by surprise how ambivalent I felt about the previous evening.

'It was dark. The torch wasn't working. They must have been under something.'

'The sofa,' Michael said, suddenly turning on to a sexy topic. 'Which is a bit of a find, actually. Unusual. And not in bad condition.'

I took the news in my stride and looked round the café. Jeff's tax dodge was working today. The place was almost empty.

'How come you're allowed to serve booze all day?'

'New licensing laws,' Jeff said.

'So how did you get a licence?'

Jeff smiled. Michael grinned sycophantically. I sighed and stirred my coffee.

'I hope you have a friend.'

'Several,' Jeff assured me. 'In all the right places.'

I doubted it, but it wasn't my problem.

'So you're happy with the load?'

Jeff took the hint and reached under the counter for a brown envelope. Michael missed it by a mile and started maundering on about the sofa legs, on which the exquisite marquetry characteristic of the period was displayed to such telling effect. I took the envelope and slipped it into my coat.

'I think our boy prefers real legs,' Jeff cut in. 'Not to mention what's between them.'

Michael sulked. He didn't like his aesthetic monologues being curtailed. Especially by sex talk.

'We can't all be male models,' he said nastily.

That was typical. He knew I'd only done it for a few months when I first came out. And it was nothing like the ego trip he implied. I was always the one in the background, filling space and looking adoringly at the number one guy, whose teeth were whiter, whose haircut was better and who looked more trustworthy on a dark night. He was the one who slung the jacket over his shoulder, sipped his lager, stared fearlessly through his shades and splashed on his great smell. I was one of the pack who ached to bond with him.

But at least I wasn't Michael. That was something to hold on to.

I sipped my coffee while Jeff talked shop. It sounded like he'd already found a home – or rather, another dealer – for the sofa with the funny legs. The rest of the stuff was going into Michael's shop. Nothing was so interesting that it had to be driven straight over to Normandy, which was a shame. I enjoyed my away-days at Jeff's expense.

Michael started telling Jeff about a wonderful National Trust house he'd just been to visit. He kept using the word 'revetment', which would have annoyed me even if I'd known what it meant. He deserved to be butted in on.

'So am I off the hook for today?'

'Not quite,' Jeff said, with an alacrity which suggested Michael's precious monologue didn't have a stranglehold on his attention either. 'I've got a small favour to ask. We've got a new washing machine coming this morning. It needs to be installed properly and Stella will only get cross if I mess it up.'

'Sure. No problem.'

The good thing about Jeff was that he never asked favours. Not real ones. He used the word a lot, but if he was asking me to fix his washing machine, then he'd already slipped something extra in the brown envelope. As crooks go, he was dead straight.

'All right, I'm off. Is the key in the usual place?'

'Yeah, but Stella should be there. They couldn't say to the nearest decade when they were going to deliver, so she took the day off. Tell her I'll be back at the usual as long as Colin gets here on time.'

I wasn't looking forward to facing the weather again. But if the alternative was listening to Michael work up an erection over crenellations, I was game for anything. I pushed myself off the bar stool and headed towards the steamed-up shopfront.

Jeff and Stella lived on a small housing estate that called itself an exclusive development. The houses were large and square, with not a revetment or crenellation in sight. But they were comfortable inside. All the garages were double.

Jeff had owned a lock-up shed on a piece of waste ground which the developer needed to make the access road. Jeff paid roughly the same for his house as the developer paid Jeff for his shack.

Stella passed me in her little car just as I was turning into the drive. She gave a cheerful toot on the horn and sprayed gravel over my feet.

I caught up with her when she was unloading the shopping.

'You didn't walk all this way?' she said, handing over a carrier and a cardboard box.

'Empty day. Why not?'

'Because it's a horrible empty day. You'll probably get pleurisy. Come on in and I'll make us some coffee. And I want to hear about your carving.'

I followed her in with the shopping and dumped it on top of the new washing machine, which was standing all wrapped up in the middle of the floor.

'So they delivered early?'

'First thing. I needn't have taken the day off at all. Isn't it always the way?'

I handed over various bits of shopping and watched Stella put them away in her fully-fitted wooden cupboards. There seemed to be enough food around to keep a garrison going through a bitter winter siege. When she opened up the freezer to put the bread in, I saw shelf upon shelf of iced-up animal bits. You could tell Christmas was coming.

We took some coffee through to the lounge. Stella settled in her favourite chair with her feet up on a stool. Bernard the Burmese homed in like a lap-seeking missile. I sat down on the sofa and started talking about my carving.

'I'm working on a girl.'

'You're always working on a girl, Charlie. What's new?'

'No, I mean I'm carving a girl. Only Luther says she looks more like a seal. She's long and sleek and sinewy. Quicksilver. It's going well. And the wood's great. The stuff Jeff picked up in Harrogate a couple of months back. It's lovely to work with.'

Stella stroked her cat. 'You're very loyal to Jeff, aren't you?'

It was a strange question. 'What d'you mean?'

'Well, you're always around to do things for him. You never take any of his stuff like some of the other guys do. And you helped him through a couple of tough times when you could have walked away.'

I shrugged. 'I'd be walking away from the only guy who pays me. Where's the sense in that?'

'So that's all it is? Money?'

I thought about it. 'No, maybe not. I like him. He's a good bloke. You should know – you married him. He always brings me wood from all over the place. There's usually—'

'He buys it.'

'Pardon?'

'The wood. He buys it. All the stuff he says he's picked up from a junk yard or a renovation site or the back of an antiques shop he's clearing out – he buys it. From a place that specializes in wood for furniture makers. It costs him a fortune. He must like you a lot.'

I wasn't sure what to make of that little gem.

'How come you're telling me this?'

Stella swung her feet off the stool and dislodged Bernard, who looked mightily pissed off.

'Sorry. I shouldn't have said anything. Please don't tell Jeff. He'd be furious. I only said it because . . . well, I'm not really sure why I said it. It's just that sometimes I wonder if he's a little bored with me.'

This was definitely not an area of speculation where I felt I belonged. It sounded to me as if Stella was adding two and two together and coming up with something in binary.

'Maybe I should take a look at the washing machine,' I said, hoping she wasn't suddenly going to announce that Jeff had in fact bought it for me.

She stood up. Bernard stared at her sulkily. 'Maybe you should. And while you're doing that, I'll fix us a salad lunch.'

Things were a bit smoother after that. The machine was a German affair, with several hundred programmes and a handbook that promised total control over every aspect of your wash.

It took me about four minutes to connect up the hoses and find the one programme Stella was ever going to use. She handed me a beer when I'd finished. I speculated aloud that soon there'd be a washing machine for people.

'Probably,' Stella agreed. 'But it's a grim thought. It'll do behind your ears every time. Kids'll hate it.'

'Not just kids.'

'You mean you'll always prefer a couple of topless geishas soaping you into a lather?'

'Given the choice, sure. But I was thinking more about the radio.'

It sounded vaguely kinky, as if I wired it up to my genitals.

'Is that all you have for company these days – a radio?'

'More or less. But I'm not complaining. It's less hassle than a cat.'

'What happened to your wild model friend, the one I never got to meet? Topaz? Azure?'

'Opal. She left. Twice. I think she was trying to make a point.'

'But which one?'

A pretty obvious one, I'd have thought, namely that she didn't want to stay. But perhaps this was a typically chauvinist underestimation of the subtlety of female thought.

'Radios are safer than women,' I mused.

Providing you leave the wiring alone.

'Depends on the women, Charlie. You do pick 'em.'

It was true. I was the fool who rushed in. I munched gloomily on another forkful of ham salad.

'Maybe they should take my relationship licence away for a year. God knows how many points it's got on it. Probably enough for a life ban. But a year would sort me out. Then I'd start again with a clean sheet.'

Stella wasn't impressed. 'A year's a long time. And besides, you shouldn't be so defeatist. You make relationships sound like drink-drive pile-ups.'

The analogy clearly struck her as preposterous. I wasn't so sure.

'The endings are exactly like that. I reckon if I can walk away unaided I'm doing OK. Most of the time I have to be stretchered out.'

Stella poured the rest of a beer we were sharing into my glass. 'You talk rubbish, Charlie. I don't know why I listen to it. Except to get my washing machine fixed, I suppose. You should realize relationships aren't pre-packed. They don't come all wrapped up and clearly labelled. Quick-fling relationships, ruby-wedding relationships, car-crash relationships. The idea is to steer them a bit, not just walk away from the wreckage.'

I decided it was about time to make a move, but Stella was warming to her theme.

'It's just wasteful, Charlie. You're using people up. You should be greener and gentler with your human environment. Don't be such an asset-stripper.'

'That's not fair. I didn't finish with Opal. She finished with me. Twice. I didn't make her go. I didn't want—'

'You didn't stop her going. Anyway, that's one girl. One girl who actually stood up to you and said play by the rules or I'm out of here and then stuck to it and left, as opposed to all the others who said the same and then stayed on, most of the time in tears. Think of Kathy. Think of Kim. Think of Sophie. They were tough enough in the beginning. Independent. They had some pride. But they didn't look very tough at the end, Charlie, and they certainly didn't feel it, I can promise you that.'

'They talked to you?'

'Of course they talked to me. Who else could they talk to? It wasn't as if you were actually speaking to them at the time.'

The lunch date was turning out to be a little heavier than I'd anticipated. I was beginning to feel hard done by. It wasn't as if I'd left the transport braces in the washing machine.

'How come you're giving me this lecture?' I said petulantly.

'Because somebody has to. It's a decade overdue. And I think I have the right qualifications.'

'Namely?'

I didn't mean to sound sarcastic, but I couldn't help thinking Stella must have the strangest c.v. She looked at me levelly.

'Between you and me, Charlie . . . I like you. Really I do. But I've never wanted to go to bed with you. In other words, I feel the exact opposite of what most of your girlfriends seem to.'

I put my beer down and listened carefully.

'Not that I can't see the excitement,' Stella added politely. 'But – no offence – I prefer my trade a little smoother. Gideon Charles Lucas is such a superior name. Who'd have guessed you're just a street boy?'

'Just about anyone who gets within a hundred yards of me, from what you're saying.'

Stella smiled. 'Fifty, maybe. But so what? I'm talking about the way you treat women. And because I'm neither recovering from nor fantasizing about your physical attentions, I can nag you until the sun goes down. I care enough to want to see you change. But I don't care so much that I'm afraid to make you angry. It's a useful combination.'

'I notice you waited until I'd fixed your machine before you started in on me.'

'First things first, Charlie. Your spiritual development means a lot to me. But I've got a load of whites that have been waiting three days.'

'So what's my problem?'

'Rules,' Stella said promptly. 'Too many rules. In that home you were in. Then inside. How long were you in for?'

'Four years. Just over.'

'So that makes . . . what? A decade in some kind of institution?'

'It's no big sob story. The home was OK. I see the guy who ran it down the pub sometimes. He buys me pints. And don't forget, Alan and I were fostered out after that.'

'Maybe. But ten years is still a lot of rules.'

'Too much discipline,' I mused, beginning to feel quite sorry for myself.

'Too little. At least, too little of the only kind that matters, which is self-discipline. You've grown up thinking if you don't get caught breaking the rules, you're OK. But rules are technicalities, Charlie. They're not right and wrong. There are no rules about screwing someone one day and ignoring them the next, or screwing someone else, or disappearing on a motorbike for a month and not telling anyone. It's all allowed. It's all legal. It doesn't mean it's right.'

'The motorcycle wasn't mine. There was a rule about that.'

'OK. Good example. The law covered the least important aspect of that little jaunt. Nothing about Sophie thinking you were dead. Or Jeff having to deal with those pushers on his own when he needed back-up. Or Colin trawling every bar you'd ever been in asking who had it in for you.'

'And then consoling Sophie by taking all her clothes off and keeping her in his bed for about a year.'

'So what? Good luck to them. After all, they've got a lot in common. They both know what it's like to be messed around by you. And Colin's all right. He's nicer to Sophie than you ever were. You should realize that.'

'OK, OK. Colin's fine. A real upstanding guy.'

'Exactly. So stop badmouthing him and be a nice boy.'

'Give me a break, Stella. I'm not that bad.'

She leaned over and patted my cheek. 'Of course you're not,' she said soothingly. 'But you could be a lot better.'

It gave me something to think about on the way home. I turned down a lift, even though Stella promised to stay off her new number-one topic. The weather had turned a little brighter. I walked back through the close, counting trees. There were lots. I gave up when I got to a hundred. The place was trying to be the country.

I was glad when I reached the short row of boarded-up and semi-derelict shops that marked the boundary of what I considered home. There was lots more to look at and more reason to stay awake. No wonder green-belt people looked so dopey. No one ever got mugged by a tree.

I chewed over the pasting I'd taken from Stella. Some of it was fair, some of it wasn't. Sophie hated riding pillion on the bike when I had it, so she would never have come down to Spain with me, even if I'd asked. In fact, it was down to her that I'd bought a car in the first place, and what a disaster that was. A heap of rust with an almost religious aversion to starting.

I decided there and then to sell the car in order to buy another bike.

It was a good decision. A positive, hard-thinking, directional approach to the rest of my life. One which neatly skirted the issue of gross personal inadequacy in favour of the less rugged terrain of mechanized transport. I paced the next mile in a happy daze of machine dreams.

Three

I gave Ramon's a miss and came straight back to the garden shed. A few minutes on my knees in front of the paraffin heater produced clouds of fuggy heat and a bitter smell of fuel.

The rain came as I was smoothing away at the seal-girl. I listened to the squalls on the corrugated roof and watched the windows steam up. I tried not to think about the lights. I'd wired them myself the winter before when the days had begun to shorten. I didn't have the right cabling and was too lazy to go out and buy it. The result was an uninsulated, water-absorbent circuit from hell that I was always promising myself I'd renew. In the meantime, flicking the chest-high light switch when it was raining was best done with my feet in rubber-soled trainers – a kung-fu manoeuvre which now came naturally, although Luther pretended to see something strange in it.

The heater was doing its job and then some. Beads of sweat dripped off my forehead on to the wood. I wasn't ready for staining, so I backed off. I'm always surprised at how tired I feel when I've been working. Mostly it's concentration. But there's also walking round and checking the angles, and clamping and planing and shaping. When it's done at sauna temperatures, it becomes a real workout.

I slumped on to the battered sofa and picked up my sculpture book. It was beginning to fall apart at the spine, but it was still the best present I'd ever had. There was always something new. I couldn't believe how most of those statues had been carved. Half of me wanted to rush out and try it myself. The saner half of me knew I'd be wasting my time. Wood was friendly, but stone was another country. One day I'd go there. Then again, one day I'd fix the electrics in the shed.

After half an hour of reading I decided to pack it in for the day. With some effort I managed to douse the paraffin heater without torching the whole shed. I even remembered to put the padlock on the door. I walked slowly down the garden in the dark.

Luther wasn't in, so I couldn't cut through his place. I walked round and let myself in the front door. The house felt cold after the stuffy heat of the shed. I climbed the stairs and began hearing a strange electric squeaking. It was coming from my flat. I tried to work out what it was, but couldn't.

The squeaking stopped when I reached the door. I hesitated. It started again. A tiny, regular, mechanical squeak. A dumb sound, too high-pitched and silly to frighten. I turned the door handle, guessing the lock wasn't on. I was right. When I pushed, the door swung open smoothly.

The girl looked round. In front of her on the table, the battery-powered puppy rocked from side to side. My eyes narrowed in disbelief. The puppy wagged its stubby tail and stared with big, useless eyes at nothing. The girl felt round its neck for the switch. The puppy stopped twitching. Everything went quiet.

'I came back,' the girl said.

'So you did.' I walked into the flat and closed the door behind me. After a day of doing precisely nothing, I suddenly felt tired.

'I hope you're not angry about me copying your key. Only it was great to be here last time. Just to have a shower and be by myself and watch some TV. I cleaned all the bathroom up afterwards. And the kitchen. I thought I'd give you a break and not come back for a while, but . . .'

She tailed off nervously. I couldn't decide if I was angry or not.

'Who's your new friend?'

She beamed. 'Isn't he lovely? All fluffy and soft. I've called him Fred.'

'And what are you called?'

'Julie. Julie Ray.'

She still looked scruffy, but at least the hair hanging over her eyes was clean. And the boots and baggy shirt may well have been trendy. In fact, she probably looked a lot better than I did.

'Well, Julie Ray, if you'll excuse me, I'm going to have a shower myself now. In the new, clean bathroom. So . . .'

'Oh, I've got to go, anyway. But I found your letter. I mean, Luther gave it to me to give to you. But I had to ask.'

She pointed to a white envelope just behind Fred's stubby tail. I recognized the writing. I definitely needed a shower first. And a drink. Maybe two.

'He's got another two letters. But he wouldn't give me them. He said he hadn't read them yet and anyway, they didn't look as interesting. He said he'd hand them over later.'

I smiled. 'Thanks for trying. Maybe next time.'

That sounded pretty much like an invitation, which hadn't been the idea.

'So I can keep my key?'

'You paid for it. It's your key.'

I headed for the shower. She asked one more favour.

'Could I keep Fred here?'

That was a tough one. Squeaking dogs weren't my idea of bachelor décor. There was something about Fred that threatened my self-image.

Julie picked up on my anxiety. 'I'll hide him away some-where,' she promised. 'And I'll make sure he's switched off. It's just that I bought him with my lunch money. And Nan would get really cross. She always goes through everything in my room. She pretends she's tidying. I can't keep anything to myself.'

We both looked at Fred. His little, red tongue stuck out in the gloom, but he stayed politely silent.

'OK. Fred can stay. But you shouldn't have spent your lunch money on him. You should eat. You're too skinny.'

Julie wasn't listening. Anyone would have thought she'd heard it all before.

'That magazine picture in the bedroom. In the frame with the writing on. It's you, isn't it?'

'Yup.' My one and only cover. Lean, mean and unshaven and dressed entirely in black. From my baseball cap to my Doc Martens. Opal framed it. But not before she'd written 'Why so cross? I think you're cute. Opal XXX' diagonally across it in white crayon.

I didn't notice it these days. When I thought about it, it was stupid – a girl who'd been on the covers of half the magazines in the newsagent's, including a few on the top shelf until the money started coming in, and all I had from her was a framed photo of myself. But I'm not a picture person. If it's not real, what's the point?

'So who's Opal?'

'Luther's daughter. She's a model. She got me some work when . . . when I needed some money.'

But I didn't need it that badly. Six months of flashguns going off in my face and I was more than ready for Jeff's van. I would have driven it for free.

'What's she like?'

'She's the sort of girl who can have a name like Opal and make it work, OK? Now I'm going for a shower and you're going home. Once you've hidden Fred. And next time take something out of the fridge to eat.'

Julie left while I was in the shower. I heard her humming to herself as she opened and closed a few cupboard doors, looking for a cosy nook for Fred. She must have found one, because a little later the front door closed and the humming stopped.

I relaxed, but not to the point of singing myself. Luther had threatened to double my rent the first time he heard me sing. He said it sounded like a remand prisoner being beaten up. Which was a shame, because I enjoyed my own arrangements of various soul classics.

I told Luther he was bullying a God-given voice into tortured silence. I reminded him of the ignorant peasants who consigned Mozart to a pauper's grave and were vilified by history. But the man was made of stone.

The front door opened again when I was reaching for the soap. If I hadn't had my head out of the water, I wouldn't have heard it. But I just caught the sound of the catch. It gave me a lot to think about. I waited for the door to close. It didn't. Someone knew what they were doing. Which was more than could be said for me.

I hesitated pathetically, clutching the soap. I couldn't hear anything from the other room, which suggested it wasn't a thief. And that suggested I was in trouble.

I turned the jet on full and fought with the window catch. Flakes of rust peeled away and smeared my hands orange. When the skin broke on one of my knuckles, a line of red dripped into the colour mix. The catch turned eventually, and the rotten sash ground upwards, inch by inch. I was left sweating and shivering, bleeding and staring out into the winter night.

The soil stack held as I swung on to it. One day it wouldn't, because one of the brackets was only half fixed to the wall. There was also the design aspect. Even with the right number of screws, the bracket was meant to hold a four-inch plastic pipe, not a nude tenant on the lam.

I kept my abseiling to a minimum and dropped down on to

the roof of the kitchen extension. The felt was damp and slippery under my feet, but I couldn't complain. It wasn't meant to *be* under my feet. I dreaded to think what a survey would make of Luther's house when I'd finished with it. In the meantime, at least the rain was easing up.

The problem was jumping down. I had a quick prowl round the roof and worked out that I would be better off landing on a flowerbed than the patio. Luther might get a bit narked if I trashed another of his plants, but I'd be able to make it up to him more easily if I didn't have two broken legs. The question now was which plant to jump on.

I guessed wrong. I thought I saw a gap between two bushes, but it turned out to be a rose-bush Luther had cut right back for the winter. My left foot came down on it, with the rest of me close behind. I couldn't believe the pain. I thought I'd been shot. It took me a few seconds of sitting there in the mud to work out what had happened. When I tried to brush the earth off my foot, I found it was stuck there with blood.

I dragged myself up and limped towards the French windows. Nothing was broken, but everything hurt. I felt cold and sick.

The curtains weren't pulled all the way. Luther was sitting down with a big Scotch, talking to some guy with rolls of chin and fat hands folded comfortably over his paunch. He could have been a church elder, but Luther didn't go to church. So he was probably a fence. I started tapping on the window, softly at first, then harder when Luther showed no signs of interrupting his monologue. It wasn't getting any warmer in the garden.

Luther's approach to the French windows was cautious. Over-cautious, if you ask me. He must have known who it was. When he drew the curtains, he winced, which was a bit insulting. I don't think he would have looked anything special himself, stuck outside in his own garden at minus-ten degrees and with nothing on except a skim-layer of mud and blood. Perhaps he was just worried about his carpets.

'Someone's in my room,' I said, scooting past as he pushed open the french window.

Luther hesitated over a formal introduction to his friend, and decided against.

'Not your little girlfriend?'

'No – not my little girlfriend. I mean, she's not my girlfriend, anyway. Come on, Luther. Somebody just busted into my room.'

'So what am I supposed to do?'

'Back me up. I need a knife. Something I can throw.'

'I don't like no knives. Not in my house.'

'Jesus, it's just for show. I've got to have something.'

'How about clothes? They might be better. I could lend—'

'No time. Come on – we've got to move.'

Luther apologized to his guest, who nodded politely and didn't look anywhere near me, then he went to fetch the tiniest knife I'd ever seen, some dolls'-house blade that wouldn't make it through a raindrop. I took it anyway.

The stairs were pretty good about not creaking. I jumped the two that I knew were dodgy and pointed them out to Luther. He frowned and stepped on them anyway. After that, I couldn't think of any reason to wait.

The door was a couple of inches ajar. I kicked it fully open and threw myself into a tuck roll behind the sofa. I caught a glimpse of a white face in the armchair opposite. When I came out of the roll I had my arm back, with the pathetic Barbie knife lined up on target.

I almost let fly. I almost didn't recognize him. It was Tom. What was left of him.

Four

'Fierce knife, Charlie.'

Three words. And by the third he sounded tired.

I sort of smiled. I wanted it to be a joke. I flicked the knife at the armrest under his left hand. It almost broke the fabric, then toppled back on to the floor.

'Could have given me a nasty bruise,' Tom said respectfully.

Luther poked his head carefully round the door. 'Social call?'

'Just passing,' Tom said. 'Thought I'd drop in.'

Luther considered. 'There's a bell. On the front door. It's useful for situations like this.'

'Point taken. Sorry to disturb your evening. But it was quite a show.'

He chuckled. It set my teeth on edge. Tom never used to chuckle. He laughed till the trees shook. Everything about him had caved in.

'Well, I'll leave you two to party,' Luther said. 'Maybe next time you could make some arrangement beforehand. That's if you don't mind losing the surprise element.'

He backed out and closed the door. I hauled myself up on the sofa-back and limped into the bathroom for my dressing gown. I still had a rose-bush-worth of thorns buried in my left foot. The shower was running. When I shut it off, everything went quiet. I took a towel for my hair, to give me something to do with my hands, and walked back into the room.

It was a hard shot to take. One of the hardest. I sat down opposite Tom and watched him play with Luther's ridiculous knife. He let me look. I guess it was easier than telling me.

Four years – that was all.

He used to play rugby on Saturdays. For the pub. He was in the pack. He said it worked off the beer. He said if he ever stopped training, he'd run to fat.

Some joke. He must have been five stones lighter. He wouldn't make the pack in an under-13 team.

I wondered how much time he had.

'D'you want a drink or something?'

He shook his head. 'Milk is about the only thing I can take. It gets boring. I never much liked it in the first place. But you go ahead.'

I didn't want anything. Except maybe an excuse to get up and walk away for a while. I forced myself to stay sitting. But I couldn't think of anything to say. It was crazy. We should have been able to talk for weeks. Now there wasn't even the weather. It was dark outside and nothing was happening.

Tom put the knife down on the arm of his chair. 'Lousy locks on this place. Easiest I've done for a long time. Anyone could walk in.'

I shrugged. 'What's to take? It's not as if I'm rich.'

That brought a smile, at least. I stared at the scar on his cheek. It had faded a little, but so had the rest of his skin, so it stood out just the same. Pale pink on chalk white. Tom saw me looking.

'Not a bad effort. A bit longer than I hoped for, but I can't complain. Though I have to say your acting was dreadful. Much worse than being carved. Dire. I was in agony.'

This was more like Tom, but the script was wrong. I was geared up for a celebration after five years, not a requiem after four.

'How long have you got?'

I hadn't meant to blurt it out. But what other way was there? It wasn't something you casually slipped into the conversation.

Tom looked away. 'I thought maybe we could talk about old times. Have some laughs.'

'Sure we can talk about old times. But you've got to tell me what's going on first. You can't just break in to my place after four years and expect . . .'

Not true. I realized as I said it. He could have walked in any time if he'd been the old Tom. But looking like he did now changed the rules.

'Expect what? What can't I expect?'

'Nothing. I don't know. To start up where we left off, I suppose. I mean, it's not as if things are exactly going to plan.'

'You mean I won't live to spend it?'

I nodded. 'Yeah. That's what I mean.'

I could feel the anger all around him, seeping out uselessly. He used to be a violent man, but never aggressive. When he took people out, he didn't seem to care whether they got up or not. They never did.

Now he was angry all over the place. It wasn't doing him much good.

'You're right. That was the plan. The best-laid one. Better laid even than your women, Charlie. And now look at it. Look at me.'

I did. But it wasn't easy.

'And to answer your question, I don't know how long. There isn't much left of me inside this shell. They keep taking things out. One secondary after another. But I think they've given up now. They can't keep track. I get up a little later every morning. I guess it won't be long.'

I was beginning to shiver. Some of the earth on my shins was drying out and dropping off, taking some scabbed blood with it. My hair, which had been lathered with shampoo when I began my epic dash to safety, was solidifying into a twisted neo-punk disaster. There were goose pimples on my arms. For once, I felt less than impossibly handsome.

'You mind if I take a bath? You can push up the chair to the door or something. Only I'm getting a little cold here.'

Tom waved his arm in a gesture that was too big for him. 'Feel free. I was getting a little embarrassed looking at you. But I figured I wasn't in a strong position to complain.'

I tried to help Tom with the chair, but he wasn't having it.

'I can manage, Charlie. I'm not ill. Dying, but not ill. I've got drugs to take care of everything except the next forty years. I can still push a chair.'

I ran the bath and fixed two glasses of milk. Tom didn't even pretend he was going to drink his.

It really began to hit me in the bath. When I was warm and comfortable and hurting a lot less on the outside. That's when I began to feel it inside.

Tom was behind me in the doorway, out of my line of vision, like some kind of analyst. Only he wasn't very calm. I could tell I was getting on his nerves. I wasn't sure what I'd done. Except not get stomach cancer.

'I want you to do some stuff for me. In a little while. Settle some accounts. I think we can forget about the five-year rule now.'

'Why not take it? Take your share. Now. This evening. You know where it is. I can get it—'

'I know where you say it is.'

I wrenched myself round to face him. Water slopped over the side of the bath. 'What the fuck's that supposed to mean? Why are you turning me over like this? You think I've stolen your money? Is that it? Who the fuck d'you think I am?'

My voice bounced off the tiles, sounding loud and a little hysterical. Which was just about right. That was how I felt.

Tom didn't say anything. For a moment I thought he was

47

going to get up and leave. When I was sure he wasn't, I turned back round and tried to steady my breathing.

'I know who you are, Charlie. I didn't mean that. It's just . . . I don't know . . . hard to accept it's over. There's no more. Just a few final scenes which I keep getting wrong because I'm tired all the time and everything hurts in spite of the drugs, and no one wants to look me in the eye and way down deep I just don't think I'm the dying type. It's not my style and I hate it. It's a mess. It doesn't help anyone. So no, I don't want to go out and buy a Caribbean cruise or a Testarossa or a tart who's prepared to keep her eyes shut and think of the flat she's going to buy with the money. I don't want to sink that low before I go. I want to hold on to something.'

I hadn't thought about it before, but it sounded wrong. To me, the whole point of death was that you didn't get to hold on to anything. I would have taken the tart and the Testarossa and burned.

'Nothing's finished, that's what's hard to take. Everything's in reverse. I always thought after five years we'd build ourselves one hell of a fine life. We got lucky, we took advantage and we were careful. I thought the best times were still to come. Now I'm trying to get used to the idea that the best times have all gone, that they were years ago, so far back I can hardly remember them. Which puts everything else since then on a slope. And here's the low point. Right at the bottom.'

Tom's voice was toneless, with no rhythm. The only way I knew he'd finished was when I waited a while and he still hadn't said anything else.

'What about Maggie? Where is she in all this?'

'She was the best thing that happened to me. The best person. I was lucky. That's one of the things I want you to do for me. You've got to find her and give her some of the money. If anyone deserves it, she does.'

48

'Find her? What d'you mean, find her? You're telling me you've split up?'

'Sharp, partner. You always were sharp.'

'So what happened? She walked out when you got ill?'

It didn't sound like Maggie.

Tom took his time about replying. 'She didn't walk out.'

I hooked my toes round the plug chain and pulled. That committed me to positive action. I hauled myself up and reached for a big red towel.

'Wedding present,' I said inanely. 'About the only one I've still got.'

Tom nodded slowly. 'I'd forgotten about that.'

So had I, almost.

'I'm getting a bad feeling about Maggie. I think you went and did something stupid. Tell me I'm wrong.'

I didn't like having to look at Tom again. He was too small for the chair. And his face was collapsing. Gravity was dragging it down like hyenas killing a zebra.

'It wasn't stupid. It was the best thing.'

'Says who?'

It came out stronger than I'd intended. Tom winced. Christ, he almost cowered. I used to get my head taken off for things like that.

'I told her . . . I said I'd found somebody else. Somebody younger, prettier. That's all.'

He was ten years older than me. He taught me most of what I knew. But sometimes it didn't feel like it.

'I didn't want her to see me like this, Charlie. You can understand that. You knew me. You knew what I was for. And it wasn't for this. Don't kid me – I see the way you look at me now. I remember the way you looked at me then. I'm saying that was the real me and this isn't.'

Some of it made sense. But only some.

'Why did you have to lie? Why did you have to insult her? Why couldn't you just walk out?'

49

'Because she'd have come after me. Like I'd have gone after her. Because it wouldn't have made sense. But this way she hurts for a bit and then hates me, but doesn't come looking. She thinks I'm in some love nest in Barons Court with a girl barely out of school. She has her pride. She won't come near.'

I stopped towelling and pulled on my gown. 'So you'd rather be hated than looked after?'

'I'd rather be hated than pitied. And this way I get to die when I choose. I've got some good whisky. I've got drugs of all sorts. I've even got the right-sized polythene bag. And Frank's ready. He knows I can't take much more.'

'You're staying with Frank?'

'He's a good brother. That's what they're for, isn't it? To be around when you need them.'

'Maybe. I don't know. I nicked Alan's bicycle lights when we were twelve. He's still burning.'

Tom nodded. 'Sensitive guy.'

'Psycho.'

I wasn't having anything good said about my brother in my own house. Or even Luther's, come to that.

Tom nodded again, but he'd lost interest. He pushed his chair back six inches to let me out of the bathroom. The effort showed up the blue veins at his temples. A dull, dead shade of blue against a whiter shade of pale. A feast for the ghouls.

I fetched an apple and settled on the sofa.

'You should go and see Maggie.'

'To save you a Tube journey?'

I took a deep breath. 'I wasn't thinking of that. I can afford the fare these days. I don't jump the barriers.'

I didn't know whether Tom wanted me to lose my temper with him or not. He half answered that.

'You don't get mad like you used to. Anybody needled you, you'd have your thumbs round his windpipe and your knee in his groin before he'd even finished speaking. Have you calmed down? Or are you just not bothering because I'm on my way out?'

'Don't worry. Carry on like you're doing and you won't need the plastic bag and pills. I'll do us both a favour. But yeah, I've calmed down. I count to five now.'

Tom shook his head. 'You lose valuable time.'

I munched steadily through my apple. Tom didn't say any more. When I finished, I ate the core.

'So you want me to give Maggie the money? All at once, or feed it to her?'

'Up to you. Not my problem. Do whatever you have to to stay clean. But I think we're OK. We'd have heard by now. Anyway, it's all in a letter. Lanky's got it.'

'Lanky?'

'It suits me. I want my affairs sorted out by a seedy failure. Nothing suspicious. And there's hardly anything to do except send the letter to you. Even Lanky can send a letter. Now that I've given him a stamp and showed him where the postbox is.'

'So how come you weren't a lawyer?'

It was a little late to ask. But a little later and there wouldn't be anyone to answer.

Tom shrugged. Half shrugged. He moved his shoulders a little way, but it looked as if his bones were hurting.

'Who knows? Much as anything, I owe it to Frank. He used to be a civil servant, way back when. Always talking about the Minister. He and Barbara were having some decorating done and it was the usual story. The guys turned up alternate days, played rock music so loud they could hardly hear the porno chatlines they kept phoning, left the place in a mess every night and kept nipping out to the bookies. He saw a gap in the market. So he formed a company of one, called it something like Brushwork to remind all the middle-class women of the galleries they met their friends in while their husbands were salary-chasing in the City, and had the name printed on a few sets of overalls. He turned up on time with a couple of mates, sometimes me in the early days, stayed till he'd finished, kept the place tidy and had Radio Three on low. When he stopped for coffee, he talked about subtitled French films and the Sistine Chapel. Took him about forty-eight hours to make his first million.'

I could believe it. It sounded a scam.

'Only I was never any good at decorating. And listening to music by dead Germans all day drove me crazy. And I always fall asleep in subtitled films. I worked with him a few times and it was a bitch. So I had to look for my own niche. A traditional lower-class activity that I could muscle in on with proper vowel sounds and a well-organized middle-class approach. Most of my friends were trying to scramble up the social ladder and getting their fingers stamped on. I came down a few rungs and started stamping.'

'I know. I was there. It wasn't pretty.'

'Maybe. But it was necessary. And it was never because of drink. Sometimes because there was someone around I needed to impress. But never when there were cops. Maybe it looked easy, Charlie, but I was thinking all the time. You've got to. There are some real thugs out there. You wouldn't believe. People who've never seen a subtitled movie in their lives.'

'Or listened to Beethoven's Ninth.'

Tom nodded sadly. 'Frank explained to me once what it meant when Beethoven used the human voice for the first time. But what if you don't speak German? How are you supposed to know what he was on about?'

I shrugged. 'Search me. It was something to do with the Berlin Wall, wasn't it?'

Five

There was no sign of Julie when I left the house. Perhaps she'd decided to break the habit of a lifetime and go to school.

I walked to Bernie's Car Emporium. Bernie wasn't there. Steve in the grocer's said he might be at Ramon's. So I walked to Ramon's. Bernie wasn't there. Neither was Jeff. Paul said they'd gone to a car auction and would be back around lunchtime. I stayed for coffee. A few workmen came in and looked around, but there was no one to leer at, so they left.

It was Paul's Christmas vacation from college. His dad knew Jeff. He was filling in at Ramon's to earn some money.

'So what d'you do when you're there?'

I wondered if it had changed. To me, it seemed bizarre. The government paying you to have sex for three years. Stupidly generous. You'd have it anyway. But maybe they figured if they took away all the petty distractions like having to earn enough money to stay alive, you'd have so much in three years that you'd be bored and exhausted and more interested in knuckling down and being a good wage slave for the next forty. Put like that, it wasn't such a dumb idea, after all.

I looked at Paul, checking for signs of sexual exhaustion. He seemed remarkably chipper. But then he was only in his first year.

'Oh . . . you know. Work. Talk. The usual.'

'What do you work at? What do you talk about?'

Paul looked uncomfortable. 'We write essays. We read stuff – you know, criticism – and then we write about it.'

'You write up what you've read?'

This was a key issue for me. I hadn't actually produced a single written word as I streaked like a blazing comet across the academic firmament.

'Yeah. With our own ideas. And then we talk it all over in seminars.'

I stared at him hard, in case he was taking the mickey. It still seemed insane. You read a bunch of books that people have written about other books, you copy out the few bits you can understand, then you talk about the stuff you've copied out of the books other people have written about the bits of books *they* understood and copied out and talked about when they were at college.

'And that's all you do?'

Paul shrugged. 'What else is there to do?'

Well, if he hadn't found out by now, it certainly wasn't my job to tell him. I stared into my coffee and brooded.

'So d'you enjoy it?'

'Sure,' he said doubtfully.

We settled into a strained silence. I wondered if he was playing down the joys of further education because he'd heard about my own modest performance. There had to be more to it than he was letting on.

'How about you?'

The polite question caught me off balance. 'What about me?'

'I mean, what do you do?'

'Same as you. I help Jeff. Only I do it all the time, not just in the holidays.'

Paul nodded, trying rather too hard to look impressed by my career path. He needn't have bothered. It's not one of the things I'm sensitive about.

'So, d'you . . . like . . . protect him?'

I wondered who Paul had been talking to. 'Sometimes. He makes a lot of money. Some people don't like him for that. If they want to do anything about it, they have to not like me first. But mostly I'm just an errand boy.'

Paul nodded again, less confidently. This wasn't the sort of job that turned up in his careers office.

'And what are you going to do when you leave college?'

It wasn't meant to be a mean question, but Paul didn't like it. He was torn between pretending that he, too, aspired to the pinnacle position of odd-job man and part-time thug, and admitting that he was drawn towards occupations that were a little lighter around the collar. He chewed his lip uncertainly.

'It sort of depends,' he said finally. 'Lucy – my girlfriend – wants us to work in Africa. She's very moral. I mean . . . ' He blushed, anxious that I shouldn't mistakenly assume he was being subsidized for nothing. 'I mean she's got a strong social conscience. She doesn't think the rich should just get richer and leave the poor to die.'

I was impressed. Not so much by Lucy's global compassion as by Paul's assumption that they'd still be together after they graduated.

'I used to be interested in City law,' he said, harking back to the golden age, before Lucy made access to her pants conditional on a more reconstructed political outlook. 'Corporate stuff – mergers and takeovers. But now all that seems . . . well, a bit pointless, really.'

But fun. And you get to drive a big shiny car.

'I wanted to be a legal adviser to one of the big raiders. Goldsmith or Hanson – someone like that. That's where the action is. I didn't want to be stuck with conveyancing. But I guess I'm changing. I'm not sure I think like that any more. I suppose that's what university does for you.'

'So ten years from now,' I mused, 'either the most audacious takeover bid in living memory will be on the rocks because you're off in Africa digging wells, or some luckless kid will be

55

dying of thirst because you're revving round the City in a Porsche.'

I tried not to sound too cheerful about it. But there's an undeniable pleasure in loading other people down with responsibility. Serves them right for being white collar. If they want to own the world, let them pay the mortgage.

A man walked in and came up to the bar. He was in his mid-thirties, well-dressed and out of place. He ordered a coffee, then had second thoughts and asked for a Scotch as well. He took them over to a table and opened his paper at the jobs page. After a while, he took out a pen and circled a couple of targets. Then he poured his Scotch into what remained of his coffee and sat there looking glum and unsalaried. Paul watched him thoughtfully.

I told Paul I'd be back later to see Jeff and Bernie and headed off to the gym. Some days – most days – I'm bored by weights. But if I have other things on my mind, the gym can pass the time.

Greg was standing at the door, watching the world go by. He had a new black T-shirt with 'I Don't Kill For Pleasure' in dayglo pink down the front.

'You don't train enough,' he said.

'Hello, Greg.'

This was a pretty standard opening.

'Maybe if I charged you membership like everyone else you'd come more often. Do it properly.'

'Maybe. Who's in today?'

'Nobody. Three new accountants, a couple of nancy-boy models and Brian the Bus. Eight reps each with a toothpick or four with a paperback. It's not a heavy session.'

'I've forgotten my locker-key again. Can I take the master?'

Greg sighed and fished in his tracksuit pocket. 'I'll come in with you. I'm tired of breathing fumes. We'll do a session together. A proper one. To get the blood pumping.'

My heart sank. Greg's sessions were legendary. But it didn't do to show fear. That only encouraged him. I resigned myself to a morning of pain, hospitalization and death.

Greg led the way through to the changing room. The back of his T-shirt said 'I Kill to Eat' in neon green. I started some deep breathing.

'Opal was here,' he said chattily. 'Yesterday, day before. Causing chaos as usual.'

'What sort of chaos?'

'Male chaos, what else? She's taken to wearing this stretchy number that doesn't quite cover everything. The guys go to pieces – dropping bells on each other's feet, falling off the exercise bikes, getting their hard-ons caught in the rowing machines. It's pathetic. And she loves it.'

'I'll bet.'

'But at least it's better than this total silence number I've been getting recently. I hear everyone chatting away while I'm changing. Then when I go in, it's all quiet. It's . . . I don't know . . . it's as if they're all scared of me or something.'

'Extraordinary.'

Greg shot me a look. 'What are you saying?'

I opened my locker and pulled my kit out. 'Well, brother – maybe we can look at this objectively and get a handle on it. Just remind me how tall you are.'

'Six-five.'

'Weight?'

'Two-forty.'

'And would you say you belonged to any . . . ah . . . ethnic minority?'

'Black. Good, strong black. And proud of it.'

'OK. How about distinguishing features?'

'None. OK, I shave my head. But that's because it's cooler in summer.'

'And temperament?'

Greg shrugged. 'I think I put up with a lot. Once in a while I go a bit crazy, but nothing like I used to.'

'And you work out?'

'Two, maybe three hours a day. I'm on site. It's my gym. Why not?'

I tied my laces carefully. 'It's a hell of a puzzle, Greg. I mean, I don't see it at all. You're huge and black and bald and less insanely violent than you used to be and for some reason these guys act nervous when you're around. It just doesn't add up.'

Greg glowered at me. 'Funny man,' he said. 'I hope you're feeling strong.'

Two hours later, I wasn't feeling anything. I was slumped in the corner of the sauna, on the lowest stage. Greg was somewhere above me, hurling buckets of water on the coals.

'If you came more often, it wouldn't hurt so much,' he said reasonably. 'There's nothing basically wrong with you.'

'Uhh?'

'I mean, you could do with more muscle, but you don't give up. You keep going. That's the main thing.'

The man was unreal. I kept going because he kept loading me up with weights when I was lying on my back. It was either take them or go through five years of operations putting my face back together.

'So if you trained twice a week instead of once a fortnight, you'd be up there with Gary and Martin. They've got commitment. They train Monday, Wednesday, Friday. Every week.'

I knew Gary and Martin. And I didn't feel one down.

'They're meatheads, Greg. They've got more tattoos than brain cells.'

'And they've got more muscles than you, so watch out.'

I sighed. 'OK, point taken. I should do more. But it's a busy life.'

Greg ladled some more water on the coals. 'Too many girls,' he said contemptuously, just as the wall of heat broke across my throat. 'Too easy for you. Ever heard of Aids?'

'Yeah.'

'You die from that. It's serious shit. And you don't seem to care.'

'Sure I care. But the only way to make sure you don't get Aids is to live the kind of life which is so boring you wouldn't care if you did. What's the point in giving up something so you can live longer if it's one of the few reasons life's worth living in the first place? Anyway, I'm careful. Most of the time.'

'You'd better be. But I still think you should fool around less. And get a proper job. How long are you going to keep doing Jeff's monkeywork?'

'I thought it was donkeywork.'

'It's monkeywork. And you can't go on doing it for ever. There's no future.'

He clambered down over the wooden slats. The cold air when he opened the door was wonderful. I drew it deep into my scorched lungs and listened to the blood pumping round my head. Then I stood up on shaky legs and walked slowly out of the sauna and over to the plunge pool. I knew it was a bad idea either to feel the water or hesitate. Just pick a gap between the ice floes and jump.

Bernie's Car Emporium was a sprawling yard on both sides of the road. It was littered with dodgy metal in various states of decay. Bernie usually holed up in a big shed and watched daytime television. He left his young assistant, who either rejoiced or despaired in the name Axel, to check all the cars had a wheel in each corner and to halve the mileage.

When I walked into the yard I'd covered a mile from the gym and was feeling every muscle. Intricate networks of pain threaded their way from my toes up to my eyeballs. The only place that didn't hurt was my hair.

Bernie wasn't watching TV. Axel wasn't clocking cars. They were both standing round a very large, very red, very shiny, very ugly and doubtless very expensive Bentley. Neither could quite believe it was there. They couldn't take their eyes off it. I moved into their line of vision to break the spell.

'It's the most I've ever paid for a car,' Bernie breathed reverently. 'When they knocked it down, I just . . . I dunno . . . it was like a dream.'

Axel crouched down to wipe some dust off one of the tyres. 'Fuckin' A,' he said tenderly.

'Genuine mileage,' Bernie said. 'Even more genuine when we've finished with it. Mick says he'll put five on top if I let him have it today, but he's out of his mind. When I find a real punter, I'm looking at ten minimum.'

Bernie and Axel both looked at ten. Their faces came over all dreamy.

'She's so beautiful,' Bernie said, hitching up his trousers. 'I think I'm going to sleep on the back seat tonight.'

'Then you'll be looking at five again,' I warned. 'Maybe three. I think you should leave her alone.'

Bernie smoothed a few hairs down into the sweat on his scalp. 'That's not nice. That's not even funny. What d'you want?'

'Justice.'

They blinked and frowned.

'The heap you sold me a year ago. I want a price on it.'

Axel snorted, which set off a complicated thought train in his mind. He started picking his nose. Bernie pulled himself up a little straighter.

'How many miles have you done?'

'About fifty. It never starts.'

'Fifty miles in a year?'

'Bollocks,' Axel chipped in. I turned to stare at him. He chipped out again.

'It's hard to do sensible mileage in a car that doesn't start. Also, when it does start, it's noisy and slow. And uncomfortable. And ugly. It's just not my idea of a dream machine, so I'm offering it back to you.'

Bernie sponged his palms unhappily. 'No deal, Charlie. I'm sorry. It's a bad time. I've got cars everywhere I can't sell. Maybe in a couple of months.'

He turned back to rest his eyes on his beautiful Bentley. Axel folded his arms and looked at me pityingly. I could see this was going to take some time. I wished I didn't hurt so much from the weights.

'Did you pay for this?'

Bernie looked round reluctantly. 'Of course I paid for it. It was an auction, for Christ's sake. You can't just drive cars away without paying for them.'

Axel sniggered happily.

'I mean, did *you* pay for this?'

Bernie tried his best to look puzzled. 'It's in my yard, isn't it?'

I looked down at my shoes and tried to slow my breathing. Sometimes I'm amazed by my own patience.

'Listen up, Bernie. You don't have this kind of money. Jeff's got to be in for half or more. And if he is, then you're in trouble. Because all I've got to do is ask and Jeff'll pull the rug right out from under your fat little feet. Which means no hanging around for the right punter. Which means no more looking at ten. So be nice to me, Bernie. I can't make it any plainer than that.'

He shuffled from foot to foot and put on his bravest sneer. 'Since when does Jeff take orders from his shoeshine boy?'

'Since never. But he owes me.'

'Tell me about it.'

'I don't need to. Think of Kevin – when his head went through the window during our little scrap. Only he kept saying nasty things about Jeff, so it just happened that when his head got jerked back through the window a shaft of glass went right through his cheek. They never found the half of his tongue he coughed up, so he can't even chant in the stands, and that was his thing.'

I took the car keys out of my pocket. Bernie sighed. He was sensible enough not to be taking any of it personally. But Axel was that little bit too young.

'If you weren't such a stupid cun—'

The keys caught him in the left eye. I was aiming for his nose, so it wasn't a bad shot. His head jerked backwards and his hand flew up. He turned away in a crouch, covering his face and saying fuck over and over.

'The car's at the end of my street. You can leave the money with Jeff or bring it to me direct. I don't care. But I want it soon.' I turned and started walking out of the yard. 'And don't forget your jump leads.'

The afternoon was trying hard not to be as dull as the morning. The odd ray of light filtered down through the clouds. You could almost believe there was a sun up there somewhere.

Luther was digging around in the front flowerbed, planning ahead for spring. He had the dreamy, faraway look that Bernie and Axel only got when they looked at ten.

'You're a pure man, Luther. You're on a higher plane.'

He looked up suspiciously. 'What you doing, Charlie?'

I wasn't sure if he was asking how I was spending my time or what drugs I was on. I gave it to him straight. 'I've sold my car.'

He shook his head and dug on. 'I thought you'd grown up. I thought you'd seen the light.'

'What light?'

'The light that says you're too old to be a wild boy now. Minding out for that guy with the bar, getting into trouble, biking round annoying everybody. You should settle down.'

'I have plans, Luther.'

'You should find someone special.'

Luther was the right guy to have on your side. He never gave up.

'You wouldn't happen to have anyone in mind?'

'No one,' Luther lied firmly. 'Fact is, any girl worth settling down with is going to want more than you're offering. You're going backwards. At least you had a car. Now I'll bet you want a bike again. And what sort of girl wants to be freezing and scared on the back of a motorcycle, with her hair all messed up under a crash helmet, when she could be warm and comfortable and listening to music in a car? It doesn't make sense.'

'I'm not thinking about passengers right now, Luther. There's things I've got to do. And maybe I won't get another bike. Maybe I'll take taxis.'

Luther hmphed and carried on forking. I went through to the shed to smooth some wood.

Helen phoned later that night. She'd left it six months.

'Got company?'

'Nope.'

'Mind if I come round for a drink?'

That was a harder one.

'Maybe. It's been a while.'

'That's why I want to come round.'

She turned up half an hour later. I was reading about Tyburn.

'They hanged a man for stealing two woolly hats,' I said, working hard on my class fury. 'Jeremy Bentham testified against a servant who stole two damaged silver spoons and sent him to swing. And he was meant to be one of the good guys.'

Helen took off her coat and slung it over a chair.

'How come you never read those books when you were meant to?'

'Where's Matthew? Where's Malcolm? And how come you haven't been round for six months?' If she wasn't answering my question, I wasn't answering hers. I fixed us two beers.

She sat down in the battered armchair. I took the sofa opposite. We watched each other carefully.

'With my parents. Geneva. And because I couldn't.'

'Why?'

'Why d'you think? I love my son. I love my husband. I didn't want to start loving my lover. It was a mess. We'd been there before.'

'So how come you didn't say anything? How come you didn't even ring?'

'I ring before I come round, not before I don't come round. I wasn't coming round, so I didn't ring. It's simple.'

It didn't sound simple to me. 'So why are you here now?'

There was a soft tap on the door. Helen looked round.

'I thought you weren't expecting company.'

I shrugged and watched the door. I had a hunch who it was. I gave myself ten out of ten when Julie Ray came in.

She stopped when she saw Helen. 'Oh. Sorry. I didn't know . . . ' She looked at me. 'They're asleep. I can't play any tapes. I thought I'd come round for an hour. I thought you'd be out. I guess I'll go back now.'

'You can stay. We're just talking. Get some Coke from the fridge.'

She hesitated, then closed the door and walked through to the kitchen. I head her murmuring a loving greeting to Fred and worked out he was hidden in the pan cupboard. I had to remember that. It would be embarrassing to boil him with the broccoli.

Helen was looking at me like she had a couple of questions. Which was fine. She could ask them or not. As far as I was concerned, Julie had done me a favour coming round. It stopped me asking my own questions about why Helen kept walking in and out of my life. More to the point, it stopped me hearing the answers.

Julie came back in with her Coke and sat down next to me on the sofa. I introduced her to Helen. The two women in my life. A teenage runaway and a doubly ex-lover. It didn't exactly reek of emotional commitment.

The three of us sat in silence. I wondered about putting a tape on, but decided not to. That just left more sitting.

'Charlie lets me use his flat,' Julie blurted out. 'Sometimes. When he's out. I clean things for him. I did the kitchen last time.'

Helen smiled at us both. Perhaps she was being friendly. Perhaps she was just relieved to hear the quid pro quo involved Jif and not baby oil.

Julie sipped her Coke. 'So how do you two know each other?'

'We met at university,' Helen said.

Julie looked at me curiously. 'You went to university?'

'Not for long.'

'Long enough.' Helen was beginning to enjoy this. 'He was a bad boy on a quota system. He didn't have the right exams, but the council got behind him because he read a bit and hadn't had the breaks. They did a deal. I still don't know what it was. What was the deal, Charlie?'

I shook my head. 'Nobody told me.'

'Which means he probably still owes them money from when he skipped off.'

That was certainly true, but it didn't bother me. What did was the idea that I'd wrecked the scheme for the people coming after me. I even wrote a letter saying I was sorry. But I never posted it. I was abroad somewhere, and the postmark looked insincere.

The sad thing was, they didn't mind. I only found that out years later. Two and a bit terms was one and a bit more than they thought I'd last. They called it a success. Who knows, maybe it was. At least when I skipped class, I went east and kept going. To all the places I'd heard about from people who'd taken a year off. If I hadn't seen those people, I would have headed back to Soho to play the fruit machines.

'. . . like, his girlfriend?'

I came back in to hear Julie asking more questions, Helen looking amused.

'I was one of them. We had a few weeks together. A long time ago.'

'So you're not his girlfriend now?'

Helen shook her head. 'I'm married now. I've got a little boy called Matthew.'

Which half answered the question and half didn't. I thought about Malcolm. People who are so high-powered they have to go abroad to do whatever they do get on my nerves. If they're so brilliant, why do airport bookstalls just stock blockbusters and porn?

Matthew sounded OK, though. At least he wasn't going to nursery in Strasbourg.

'I don't have a boyfriend,' Julie said. 'Terry in my class keeps sending me notes. He says scummy things. I'm not going out with him.'

'Good,' Helen said. 'You can do better.'

Well, maybe. She still looked a mess to me. Grubby sweatshirt, baggy trousers and hair like she'd just come in out of the rain. I wondered if Terry could afford eye tests.

'He's always writing on his hand. Stupid things. "We Are Millwall And We Don't Care." Stuff like that.'

This was Julie on Terry, not Helen on Malcolm.

'Boys are a problem,' Helen agreed. 'I should just talk to the ones you like and ignore the rest. Terry's got his brain full of hormones at the moment. Don't expect him to make sense.'

I was a little uneasy about sitting in on the consciousness raising. Julie wasn't sure about it, either.

'Some boys are OK. I have double physics on a Tuesday. I usually go in for that. I do experiments with a guy called Toby. He writes it up better than I do and he always lends me his book. He's all right. But he's got spots.'

Christ. Who'd be young again? You take people half-way between kids and adults, who don't know who the hell they are because they haven't actually done anything yet, who feel bored all the time because everything they used to enjoy is uncool and they're too scared and mixed-up to think of anything better, who spend most of the time mesmerized by all the sex they're not getting and by the moronic posturing of no-brain pop stars, and just in case one or two manage to come through unscathed, you trowel on a generous layer of pus all over their faces and watch them try to cope.

' . . . still come round?'

By the looks of it, I'd missed a good question. Julie was looking carefully at both of us. Helen wasn't sure what to say.

'We're friends,' she began hesitantly, glancing over at me. 'I like coming round here. Like you do.'

Whoa. Wait a second. The last time Helen was here, I watched the sun go down over her bare shoulder. She was on top of me, moving slow, then faster, then slow again. I had one hand cupping one of her breasts, the other down low. And she had tears in her eyes. It wasn't the same thing. It wasn't the same thing at all. I wondered which of us she thought she was fooling.

I stood up to clear my head. 'I'm going to make some coffee.'

Six

I woke up early, which was probably a mistake because it raised the problem of what to do next. Nothing sprang to mind.

I had a shave and a piece of toast and then started reading a fat book about the My Lai massacre. It made me feel a bit better. I hadn't accomplished much in my life, but at least I hadn't tossed babies into irrigation ditches and riddled them with machine-gun bullets.

There was a downside. Letters to the White House went one hundred to one in Lieutenant Calley's favour. That made me feel worse. Maybe we really don't like children in the West.

I couldn't face going into the shed and messing with wood, and the only alternative was Ramon's. I got together an outfit that leaned rather heavily on denim and set off.

Luther was fussing over his roses. The police had reported an escaped blackfly in the area and he was taking no chances. Liquid bug killer glistened on the leaves. That tipped me off about the day being warmer than I thought. I squinted suspiciously up into the sky. Yup. It was definitely the sun.

The denim was a big mistake. But it was too late to change.

'Racy shorts, Luther.' The Jamaican flag, long on each leg.

'Feeding my tan, whitey. Y'ever heard of summer?'

Well, rumours.

'Am I behind with the rent yet?'

'Nope. You been good. Gave me a stack a few weeks ago. I'm still counting it.'

The morning was looking up. I vaulted the gate with weight-trained muscles and turned my jean-jacket collar up against the fierce Stoke Newington heat. Luther was impressed.

'You should have saved that for Opal. She's coming round later. You know she ditched that lawyer guy. Great clothes and family money, but he was a big snooze.'

'I don't want to hear it, Luther,' I said, stopping and listening hard.

'Well, she did. Before she wrote you. Way back. And you should have replied. Don't think I didn't notice.'

'I never thought that, Luther. Believe me. But you shouldn't take it personally.'

Luther lowered his spray gun in disbelief. 'Somebody has to. You can't just leave letters unanswered. And if you don't do it, that means I have to. If that isn't taking it personally, I don't know what is.'

Well, quite. That's just what I was complaining about. I couldn't help wondering why so many of my conversations with Luther came out upside down.

'You should be grateful. I'm like a secretary to you.'

'I thought secretaries wrote what their bosses told them. Since when have they just lobbed out letters when they felt like it?'

'Since now, Charlie. Listen up. I'm being proactive. That's what they call it these days. I know. Opal told me all about it.'

'Uh-huh. So what are you meddling in at the moment?'

Luther shook his head slowly. 'That's a hurtful thing to say, Charlie. I'm fighting as hard as I know how for you and you don't give me no credit. I got a running battle with the electricity over a disputed meter reading. I can't believe you used that much. The Social Security want money they say they overpaid back when you were working as a model. I told 'em three times to butt out. And there's a guy who says you crashed into his car and won't pay the insurance. I can't believe that. Your car never starts. I told him he's crazy and he's seeing things and to leave you alone.'

I'd forgotten about the guy whose car I hammered. And I was grateful to Luther for taking him on. I had a feeling there was a problem with the insurance. Or at least there might have been, if I'd had any.

'You're good to me, Luther. I'm sorry. I don't mean any harm. I was just wondering about the personal stuff, that's all. Like whether you said anything to Opal.'

'What is this? She's my daughter. Of course I say things to her. What's wrong with that?'

This was bluster and we both knew it. Luther started spraying furiously and not looking at me. I waited for his conscience to catch up with him. It didn't take long. He was a good man.

'OK, I may have said something. Just in passing.'

I picked a dead leaf off a trailing ivy and waited some more.

'What is this, some kind of inquisition? Stop staring at me like that. All I said was a couple of things. That's all.'

'What things?'

Luther stopped spraying. But he didn't look at me.

'I told her you still loved her and were thinking about it. And if that ain't the truth, then I'm not standing here and these roses haven't got blackfly – all right? Hey! Where you going?'

I crossed the road, past the house with the For Sale board, walking fast. Hoping I could stay angry at least until I turned the corner.

Jeff was behind the bar, talking on the phone. Two young girls were sitting over coffee and a magazine at one of the tables. A telephone engineer bunking off for a quick pint watched them as they giggled and whispered. His eyes were glazed. I dreaded to think what positions he was putting them in.

'Another week I can run to. But next Thursday I need the money. Let's wrap this up, Bernie.'

Jeff flicked his eyes my way, but didn't smile a cheery hello. He listened to Bernie on the other end.

'Yeah, right here. But don't worry, I'm not sending him over. We've settled that, remember. So don't try and jerk me around any more.'

He hung up without saying goodbye. Something told me the summer sunshine had yet to work its way into his life.

'Why d'you go in with Bernie? I could have told you he's trouble.'

'Could you, now? Well, next time I'm up for a deal, of course I'll fax it through for approval. Just remind me where you did your MBA. Harvard, was it? Or Fontainebleau?'

The attack came out of nowhere. I struggled to hit back.

'Bernie's a slimeball. You don't have to know much to know that. And now he won't sell the car quick enough and you're getting all pissed off and you're taking it out on me. Brilliant. Thanks, Jeff.'

I pushed myself off the counter stool thinking the sooner I was out of there the better.

'Brilliant and wrong. Again. Sit down, you might learn something.'

I stayed standing. But I didn't walk out.

'Yeah, I'm in with Bernie for half his motor. It was a quiet week and an easy two-and-a-half. And yeah, Bernie's a greasy sonofabitch who wants to hold on for more. But that's not why I'm pissed off. I'm pissed off because I should be putting the screws on Bernie and instead he's putting the screws on me because you went and half-blinded his little friend.'

'I did what?'

71

Jeff looked at me wearily. 'You threw some keys at him. They went in his eye. Some flake of metal came off. I don't know. He was at Moorfields. Seems he's only ever going to have half vision in that eye. Now d'you remember?'

I remembered. Christ, what a loser. Most people you throw keys at, they get a little red mark on their cheek for about thirty seconds – they don't go round losing half an eye. That's why I didn't feel sorry about Axel. Anyone who's that much of a victim is going to get it in the neck sooner or later. If they don't get it in the eye first.

'They sold me a lemon. They wouldn't take it back. What was I supposed to do?'

Jeff sighed, but couldn't be bothered to run through the list of alternatives to blinding Bernie's sidekick. He reached under the counter and pulled out a battered envelope.

'Bernie dropped this round. It's what you paid for the lemon. Minus a hundred which I took out and told him to give to Axel. As an apology from you. If he leaves it at that, we're well ahead. So let's hope.'

I took the envelope and folded it into my jeans. I couldn't remember how much I'd paid for the heap. But it was nice to have the cash back. Even minus the hundred. I wasn't too happy with Jeff for that. It was tempting to go after Axel and get it off him. Especially now he couldn't see me coming.

'Anything you want doing today?'

'Yeah. I want you to go to an auction this evening. Check what happens to a couple of lots. I've marked them in the catalogue. Try and see who's bidding.'

The catalogue was by the phone. Jeff handed it over.

'It's an upmarket bash. I think a suit might be appropriate.'

I walked out into the sun. Typical. The best day of the year and I was going to be trussed up in a suit. But not yet. I still had a good few hours.

I patted the envelope in my pocket. That was the good part of the day.

I checked my watch. The auction wasn't until six. I could take a cab there on Jeff. Say an hour to clean up and get into some decent clothes. That still left plenty of time to play. Things were looking good.

I still minded about the missing hundred. And the bollocking. That's the trouble with other people's bad luck – it rubs off. They never keep it to themselves. All in all, I was getting pretty irritated with Axel for losing half his eye.

Anton rented two lock-up garages and the back half of a semi-derelict shop. The bikes he worked on were old and battered. And mostly small. But they kept him in leather trousers.

'Lost another customer at the weekend,' he said cheerfully, pouring scaly water over two mouldy-looking teabags. 'Riding a Vision moped at about four miles an hour, being overtaken by a cyclist, wearing a fluorescent safety jacket and probably giving hand signals because he never trusted his indicators. Car and a van went head on and the van toppled right on to him. Splat.'

He stirred some milk into the mugs. 'What is it they say about statistics?' Neither of us knew. 'Well, whatever it is, it's true. Load of crap.'

Anton had turbocharged his own ZZR-1100. He was rarely seen travelling at less than double the legal speed limit, never used either indicators or hand signals, and always wore black so he couldn't be seen at night. His only accident had been at precisely nought miles per hour, when the centre stand of a bike he was thinking of buying collapsed and it fell against him. He'd had a nasty bruise on his thigh for three days.

One day, Anton's number would come up. And when it did, it would be a very high one.

'Thought you had a car now,' he said, sipping his scalding tea and investing the word 'car' with definite herpes overtones.

73

'I did. But it didn't go. So I got rid of it.'

I hung my head in shame, hoping to be welcomed back into the fold. Forgive me, Father, for I have sinned.

'So you still got all the gear?'

I said I had. Several cows' worth of leather, folded in the bottom of the wardrobe. When I put it there, I knew I'd finally grown up and said goodbye to adolescence. I hung on to it in case someone my size started going through the same phase. I didn't anticipate my own regression. Just hoped for it.

'So what are you after?'

Anton looked at me challengingly. This was a question to sort the men from the boys. I squared my shoulders.

'Oh, you know – something throbbing and butch. Something that oozes machismo. I thought maybe a pizza-delivery moped. If I could get the suit that goes with it.'

Anton shook his head. 'You've been off the road too long. Some of those buzzers are quite nippy. Why not just get the suit for the moment. And maybe an in-line rollerskate. Just the one. Then you can sort of scoot along and get the feel of things.'

It made sense, but it was still a bit scary.

'You're pushing me too fast. How about if I just run around a bit in the garden with a helmet? Get used to speed again.'

He shrugged. 'Whatever.'

There was a sharp rap on the rickety door and a middle-aged guy in an open-face helmet peered into the gloom.

'Brought the Cub,' he said to Anton. 'Six-month service. Seems to be going fine.'

Anton helped him bring the bike into the crowded workshop. The guy took off his helmet and smoothed a couple of strands of hair over from one ear to the other. It was a slick and practised movement. And all the more pathetic for that.

'I'll leave the helmet here, if that's all right? And come back for the bike tomorrow afternoon.'

Anton took the helmet and said tomorrow afternoon would be fine. The man smiled quickly and backed out of the workshop.

'You scared him,' Anton said accusingly when he'd gone. 'He likes to rap, does Mr Richards. All about Gold Wings and Harleys and big, fat bikes that he'll never own. God knows who he thought you were.'

'Probably the receiver.'

Anton went over to a card index and fiddled around. 'You don't look like a receiver. Or rather, you don't look like the legal type of receiver.'

He plucked out a card and went over to the Cub. Peering at the odometer, he let out a low whistle of admiration.

'He's been racking 'em up this time. One hundred and twenty miles in just six months. He must have done the west coast of Scotland.'

Anton picked up a big padlock and headed for the back door. 'Come on. Let's do the rounds, see what's out there.'

'I haven't got a lid.'

He thrust Mr Richards' open-face into my hands. 'Pristine condition. Probably never had the sweat of fear darkening its lining. About time it was baptized.'

It was an afternoon in the old style. We spent it buzzing around Anton's dealer friends, drinking tea and talking endlessly about torque, wet-clutch transmission and mono-shock suspension. Anton's friends were as cheerful a bunch of monomaniacs as you could ever hope to meet. None of them had any interest in selling me a bike. The ones they had in weren't fast enough, or didn't corner properly, or would be OK with new Phantom tyres and maybe a 38 sprocket instead of a 40 for smoother touring.

'OK for disc jockeys and pimps,' Des said disgustedly of his bargain of the week. 'But if you're into serious riding, forget it. This one's a straight-line blaster. You want to corner, you've got to drop down to thirty.'

After a couple of short journeys with Anton, the idea of gentle cornering had a powerful allure. Mr Richards' helmet had been baptized all right. By total immersion. The fabric was already beginning to rot.

I began to wonder whether my expedition had been misconceived. Not only the staying alive bit, but the buying a bike bit. Tagging round with Anton gave the wrong impression. I wanted a bike to get me around. I didn't want to worship it, or customize it, or spend half my time riding it on just one wheel.

For Anton's friends, nothing was good enough. We ended up back with Brian, the first guy we'd tried, because he had a fridge in his office and Anton was ready for a beer.

'You're still on the one bike,' Brian observed acutely as we pulled up.

Anton killed the engine. 'It's all crap out there. Nothing doing. Everything's for the oldies these days. Retro mania at twenty miles an hour. There's nothing scary around.'

Brian grunted and led the way up some stairs to his office. He could spot an acute beer craving when it pulled up on his forecourt. Anton settled down nearest the window, where he could keep an eye on his rocketship; make sure enough people were stopping to admire it.

'I blame the government,' Brian said firmly, settling down in his leather swivel chair and resting his ice-cold can on his stomach. 'All this safety stuff. Training. Who the hell's going to go training unless they're over fifty? I tell you, I remember the good times when we were losing one seventeen-year-old a week. And they never got far, so you had some good low-mileage bikes to sell on. Now it's tragic. Everyone just bikes down to the post office to get their pension. And they live for ever. No turnover. Something's got to change.'

I butted in at this point, not to offer my own thoughts about the crisis in modern motorcycling, but to observe that a pick-up truck had drawn up on the forecourt, narrowly missing Anton's bike. He may have been by the window, but he wasn't concentrating.

'Oh, yeah,' Brian said. 'I forgot about that.'

He lumbered to his feet and set off downstairs. Anton and I followed.

'This guy, right,' Brian said over his shoulder, 'he decides to go to Africa. So he buys an Africa Twin. Only he's about two foot tall, so his feet don't touch the ground. He wobbles off down to Portsmouth and manages to fall off the ramp going up to the ferry. The bike falls back on him, snaps both his tiny legs and bounces into the water. They fished it out with a freight crane and now he wants to sell it.'

The story seemed to cheer Brian up. He waddled out of his shop humming loudly. The guy in the pick-up was slipping knots on the tarpaulin. He pulled it back to reveal the amazing Submarine Twin.

'What's the damage?' I asked Brian.

He shrugged.

'God knows. Strong bike, but the salt's probably eating away from the inside. Hope I can sell it before it comes through.'

'How much?'

Brian looked at me with interest. 'You serious?'

I took the envelope out of my jean-jacket pocket and counted out the notes. 'That's all I've got.'

The delivery guy was making a big deal of hauling the bike upright in the back of the pick-up. Anton went to help. Together, they managed to balance it on a plank and roll it precariously down to the ground. It was the size of a small car.

Brian rubbed his chin thoughtfully. 'If it's sound, you're getting a steal. If it's not, you're getting ripped off. You want to take a chance, it's up to you.'

I handed him the money. He tucked it in the waistband of his trousers, which was asking a lot of some already over-stretched fabric.

'Come back tomorrow. I'll make sure it starts, at least. After that, you're on your own. No guarantees.'

Anton moved over to his own machine and started her up. Every window for several blocks began to shake. I put on my own helmet.

'Weird choice,' Anton said, as I climbed on behind him. 'What d'you want one of them for?'

'I'm going to convert it to run on seaweed.'

Seven

The jewellery went under the hammer first. Lots and lots of big old rocks. Judging by the numbers, there wasn't much zircon around.

One guy was doing most of the buying, and he didn't mind who knew it. His catalogue flicked up and down busily just in front of me. He lost out on a rock big enough to start a respectable avalanche to a guy standing at the side with a cellular phone wedged between his shoulder and his ear.

It was a mid-range affair. Not a downmarket one, where the punters are sitting on most of the lots. And not a big dead artist one, where people applaud any maniac crazy enough to spend the GNP of a small African country on some fast-disintegrating pigment.

I checked in the catalogue for the lots Jeff wanted me to keep an eye on. They were all furniture. Louis This, Louis That. Stuff which hadn't been trees for hundreds of years. I couldn't see the attraction.

Jeff explained it to me once. He said I just didn't under-stand the complexities of being rich. Or rather the lack of them: 'Everyone needs to feel they're achieving something. For most people, it's staying alive. And housed. And solvent. If you're rich, you're not so lucky. Life's easy. So you've got to make it harder. You've got to stay alive in the right style, in the right house, with the right furniture, doing the right things. You create lots of meaningless rules and then stick to them as if your life depended on it. It's a grown-up version of not stepping on the cracks. You'd be surprised how many jobs depend on it. Mine and yours, for a start.'

I brooded on these words of wisdom as the lots came and went. Occasionally I marked down a price to keep myself awake. Sometimes the rap of the gavel brought me round.

Jeff talked about the rich as if they were other people. I thought about that for a while and decided he was right. Jeff wasn't rich. Not in that sense. He just had a lot of money.

Lot 59 was the first one Jeff had marked down for me to keep an eye on. It was a small sofa, more like a double chair, covered in precious pink fabric and with a curvy back. It looked like nothing you'd want to eat a TV dinner off.

All of a sudden, it became harder to spot the bidders. The auctioneer kept saying the bid was with him at seven and a half and a whole lot of Vodafones came out of the woodwork. From what I could see, the higher the bid, the smaller the movement required to make it. For the cheap stuff, you raised your catalogue. For the medium stuff, you nodded your head. For the pricey lots, you twitched an eyebrow. For the star lots, the guy with the gavel was expected to notice a modest stirring in the front of your trousers.

Jeff had told me to remember who was bidding for what. Seeing as I didn't know anybody, this was hard. I dutifully jotted down word portraits of the prime movers, which brought some strange looks from the guy next to me, who was obviously trying to work out why novelists go to auctions when they don't make any money.

The four lots Jeff had marked generated the most interest. Two of them went to the same buyer – a guy in the corner with a phone who kept fingering his tie. The third lot, a round table which pivoted in various complicated and unnecessary ways, went to a fluttery, overdressed woman with huge bauble earrings. She seemed to be bidding against the auctioneer most of the time ('Nine and a half with me, may I say ten?') so he was probably just winding her up. When he got bored with his little game and finally let her have it, she looked round with a rather hysterical smile for approval, but everyone else had lost interest and wasn't impressed. So that was a dozen grand wasted, plus taxi fare.

The fourth lot was a puzzle. Eight dining chairs, including two carvers, all looking as rigid and uncomfortable as hell, but whittled out of some primeval forest by a Piltdown chippie. The bidding was as brisk as it was invisible. I looked round everywhere – eyebrows, catalogues and trouser fronts. The twitches were random, and suggested moderate psychological disorders rather than serious financial intent. The more I looked, the crazier it seemed. And watching the chief rapper didn't help. From the line of his eyes, the bidding was a fierce three-way scrap between the doorjamb at the back of the room, a picture of two semi-obese and disastrously underendowed cherubs on the right-hand wall, and an empty chair on the end of the front row. In the end I think the cherubs sneaked it, but I couldn't be sure.

It was a disappointing end to the evening. I closed my notebook and stood up with everyone else. The problem was, they all knew each other and I didn't. I couldn't tell them which school I had my son down for or where my holding company was registered. And I certainly couldn't share their enthusiasm for dead wood chiselled around in fussy ways.

A couple of house flunkeys came out of a side door, carrying trays of drinks. Flutes of champagne to go with the flutey voices. If they'd brought them before the auction began, the bidding might have been livelier. But perhaps that would have looked cheap.

Four guys in spotless overalls and gloves were carrying the chairs out, trying not to drop them. The auctioneer had come down from his lectern to congratulate a guy with no hair on having so much money and to enquire challengingly what it was like being both so rich and so important.

I picked a glass of champagne from a passing tray and wandered over to the no-willy cherubs. When it became clear that nobody was going to invite me down after Ascot, I finished my drink and placed it carefully on the cabinet under the painting, where I hoped it would make a neat ring. Then I loosened my tie and walked out.

It wasn't late and it wasn't cold, so I started walking. When a bus came along, I caught that for a couple of miles, then did some more walking. I wasn't sure how soon Jeff wanted to know about the bidding, but no other social engagements were pressing.

The ambush happened half-way up the drive. Bernard the Burmese scooted out from under a laurel and tried to walk along between my feet. I hopped and stumbled towards the front door, saying fuck even more than Axel had when I'd thrown my keys into his face. Bernard ignored me. When I rang the bell, he hid behind a milk bottle, listening to the countdown of feet approaching the door. It was Stella who answered. Bernard shot forward like a Santa Pod dragster and was upstairs and fast asleep on the spare-room bed before I'd even said hello.

Stella was wearing little round glasses. 'We're watching television. I hope you like otters.'

She led the way through into the lounge. Jeff was engrossed. 'It's criminal what they're doing to the river banks,' he said, without turning away from the screen.

I made my way to an armchair and tried to work it out. Normally if Jeff said something was criminal, it meant he was seriously impressed and wanted a slice of the action. But this time he sounded cross. I looked at the screen. The otters were splashing around with twigs in their mouths personalizing the opening to their river-bank home so it didn't look like a council house. I tried to see it as a criminal undertaking, but couldn't.

'They're otters, Jeff. They're allowed to do that kind of stuff.'

Jeff looked up impatiently. 'I'm talking about people. In boats. They're wrecking the river banks. Eroding them. It's a disaster.'

I did my best to look concerned. Stella offered me a coffee, which I accepted. A couple of minutes later, sensing I wasn't going to get much change out of Jeff for a while, I followed her out to the kitchen.

'He gets very engrossed,' she said, filling the kettle. 'And he worries at night. You'd be surprised.'

'About otters?'

'And rainforests. And water tables. And population.'

I thought about it. 'So that's why he's planted those silver birch trees and bought a birdbath and not had any kids?'

Stella shot me a look. 'Not exactly.' Maybe I'd hit a nerve. Well, I could live with that. She'd pummelled most of mine to pulp the last time we'd met.

'Have you forgiven me yet?'

So we were both thinking of the same thing.

'For liking your trade a little smoother? No, I can never forgive you for that. I'll just have to pine.'

'Yuck. Is that what happens to you when you put on a suit? You turn into a smarmball?'

I asked about the washing machine. Stella said it had delivered everything it said it would, and that she now had total control over every aspect of her life. 'Quite a machine, Charlie. Maybe you should consider one. Which reminds me,' she added, pouring the coffee, 'what do you know about burglar alarms?'

I looked at her hard, fearing a joke at my expense.

'I mean, fitting them. I ran into a friend the other day – a girl I shared a flat with before I met Jeff. She's just moved and the crime prevention officer's put the fear of God into her. She wants locks and alarms and everything. I said I knew

83

someone who might be able to fit them and wouldn't give out the combination to all his friends.' She handed me my coffee and walked over to the memo pad by the phone. 'She's called Maria. And I have to warn you, she likes her trade even smoother than I do. But she does know all about being given a hard time.'

She passed over Maria's number, which I folded and put in my suit pocket. There were real advantages to being single, I decided. You can walk round with women's phone numbers in your pocket and not worry that genuinely innocent explanations about locks and burglar alarms will come out pathetically lame and drenched in guilt.

I took my coffee back into the lounge. Stella followed and tucked herself into an armchair. Credits were rolling on *State of Nature* and a voiceover was tempting viewers with an otter fact-sheet. I think Jeff would have noted down the address if I hadn't been there. As it was, he had to make do with next week's trailer, which promised progress reports on melting ice floes and a weird-looking jungle snuffler with a long snout.

Jeff hit the red button on the handset and the picture died. He settled back into his chair and picked up a glass of brandy the size of a small dolphinarium. 'Nice suit. Did you have a good evening?'

I sipped my coffee and tried not to covet Jeff's brandy. Not that I really like brandy. It just looked luxurious.

'Sure. My kind of people. I got a few invitations to go shooting at the weekend.'

Jeff nodded. 'Just don't disgrace yourself. Throwing knives at the birds isn't an acceptable alternative. And nor is buying a piece from Terry and carrying it in a shoulder holster. You use a proper gun that hasn't been sawn off or you stay indoors screwing the wife. Those are the rules.'

I was grateful to Jeff for this piece of etiquette. I could never find my *Debrett's* when I needed it.

It didn't take long to tell him about the auction. He was really only interested in the last lot, and didn't seem disappointed that I hadn't spotted a single bidder. In fact, he was so pleased he gave me one of his brandies.

'Figures,' he said, decanting most of the bottle until it almost covered the bottom of the glass. 'Those chairs were wasted on that cheapskate crowd.'

'So who was doing the bidding?'

'I was.'

Half a swimming pool of brandy went straight up my nose, doing more damage than a decade of cocaine sniffing would have done. I tried not to choke. That would have showed a lack of breeding. Tears welled up in my eyes.

'He was on the phone,' Stella said, when she realized I was in no state to ask any questions. 'I expect the auctioneer had an earpiece.'

It still seemed something of a betrayal.

'Why didn't you tell me?'

Jeff was firm. 'Because you wouldn't have been concentrating. I wanted to know who else was out there bidding. You can't be too careful.'

Jeff sat back, looking happy and smug. I sniffed experimentally, to see if my sinuses still hurt. They did, but not as much.

'I could have bid for you.'

That wiped all trace of smugness from Jeff's face. He had to battle desperately for his composure as several doomsday scenarios crowded into his mind.

'I think not,' he managed to say eventually, as beads of sweat stood out on his brow.

'Suit yourself.' I felt insulted. Obviously I wasn't taken seriously. But at least the pressure was off. I could ask for a can of Coke to slosh into my brandy without kidding myself I had a reputation to keep.

Jeff looked suitably heartbroken as I diluted his priceless

booze with one of Stella's diet specials. He had to start talking about money to cheer himself up.

'The chairs are going to a Trust house. Only they haven't finished raising the cash yet. I knew they'd try it on at the auction, but they were never in with a shout. Now, when they've raked in all the appeal money, they'll have to come to me. It's perfect. A guaranteed sale. With a soupçon on top for me.'

'Hey!'

The spirited shout came from Stella. Jeff realized his mistake.

'Sorry. For us, I meant. Stella was the third bidder.'

Unreal. 'So what's the big idea of bidding against each other?'

'Just to get the price up a bit,' Jeff said airily. 'I told the Trust I'd be putting a fixed percentage on the chairs when I passed them on. I wanted to get some action going. And Stella was home early. She used the other line. Bid on Colin's account.'

'So who won in the end?'

Stella glanced at Jeff. 'He did. I let him – he'd only have sulked.'

'I do not sulk,' Jeff said. 'It's not in my nature. When have you ever known me sulk?'

'How about two weekends ago at Mike's when that Australian architect was chatting me up? You were sulking then. You went all quiet.'

'I was not sulking,' Jeff insisted sulkily. 'I was merely observing the scene with quiet detachment.'

I toughed out the phoney squabble by fixing a middle-distance smile and looking around at the furniture. It was the shock of the new all right. Shock of the shiny, too. Not grotesque plated Arab-shiny, more French polished wood-shiny. If I looked hard, I could see bits of my reflection in two occasional tables, an outsize lamp base and the front of the drinks cabinet, which was kind of cheating because it was partly glazed. Jeff had a lot of his furniture made for him. Obviously he liked to know a bit of elbow-grease had gone into the job.

The phone bleeped discreetly over by the window. Jeff cut into whatever elaborate compliment he was paying himself at the architect's expense and said it was bound to be Ben, so he'd take it upstairs. Stella didn't say anything and neither did I, because I'd drifted out of the conversation and wasn't sure of the way back.

I watched Jeff lope rangily out into the hall and heard him jump the stairs four at a time. Stella sighed and put her feet up on a footstool. She looked around absentmindedly for Bernard, but for once his lapscope was turned off.

Eight

Luther's floor-to-ceiling curtains were inches thick and dog-mess brown. No one in *Hello* magazine had anything like them. I think they were also lined with lead. One end of the rail was going to give out any second. But they didn't take any shit from sunshine. For a tenant who kept irregular hours, those curtains were precious.

What they needed to complement them was a neat radio-alarm clock with glowing green numbers telling you it was time for *Woman's Hour* even though the room still looked like a midnight tomb. What I had was a cheap watch somewhere on the floor under a pile of clothes. Usually it turned up in one of the legs of my jeans, which was strange, given that it was definitely my wrist that I wore it round. This time, it had rolled free towards my socks. I stretched out a hand for it, and missed.

It was while I was lying flat out on the bed that I noticed a strong smell of coffee coming from downstairs. My stomach growled and I closed my eyes helplessly. A gentle wave of self-pity washed soothingly over me as I contemplated the dismal downside of the bachelor state – emotional emptiness, sexual frustration, a feeling of being incomplete. And no one to bring you coffee in bed in the morning. I sighed pathetic-ally and tried not very hard not to drool on my pillow. That was the upside of the bachelor state – it didn't matter if you drooled on your pillow. To make things worse, Luther was treating himself to a cooked breakfast. If I lay still, I could hear the hiss of a frying pan. This was a bad way to wake up.

I pushed my face down into the pillow and started thinking about where I'd gone wrong. It was an avenue of exploration both wide and endless. Fortunately, I was running short of oxygen by the time I reached my primary-school reminiscences, so I had to come up for air just after the GBH incident, where I set fire to a girl's hair to make her notice me and so we could have a laugh about it afterwards. As witty introductions went, it was a devastating success. She never took her eyes off me for the next two years we shared at school. By which time I'd long ago lost interest in her – who wants to hang around with a girl whose raven tresses have been scorched into piebald five o'clock shadow? – and social services had developed an abiding fascination with me.

I turned on to my back and tried to call up the face of Mr Hatchard, the headmaster, who eschewed corporal punishment in favour of searching questions about whether I wanted to grow up to be a gentleman. It wasn't something I'd given a lot of thought to, but I said yes, which was clearly the right answer, because it allowed Mr Hatchard to leap in with his decisive thrust along the lines of a gentleman makes it a point of honour never to bonfire a lady's hair. Social services were more direct and less King Arthur about the whole thing and said one more stunt like that would land me in approved school.

My mood lifted. Over the years, I'd built up a collection of last chances unmatched outside the death rows of America. But my first one was still special. What I couldn't work out, though, was why the smell of bacon and scrambled eggs was so strong in my bedroom, when Luther's kitchen was over the other side of the house. And why the sound of frying was so loud. It was almost as if—

'Are you awake yet?'

The voice reached me just as my one-byte brain had powered up. I ran a quick check on all the bits of me that had to stay tucked under the duvet and said: 'Come in.'

Julie's head came cautiously round the door. 'I thought there might be someone else. I've made enough for two.' Her eyes scanned the room, in case my overnight friend had crawled under the bed in an agony of regret and mortification. 'I bought eggs at the shop on the corner. They sell them in ones. And I found some bacon in the fridge. D'you want to eat now?'

I nodded, and the head disappeared. That left me a couple of minutes in which to stare at two concentric brown rings on the ceiling and contemplate the ruins of my privacy. It was clear I was faced with a quite outrageous and completely unjustified invasion of my personal space. Words would have to be said. And I would definitely have to find out what parameters were, so I could lay some down.

Julie came back in with two cooked breakfasts and two mugs of coffee, on a tin tray which I didn't even realize I had. She put it down on the end of the bed, carefully avoiding my feet, and went over to draw the curtains.

'Yours is the bigger one. I only had enough money for three eggs, and I'm not really hungry.'

I leaned forward gratefully, scooping up the plate and cutlery with one hand and the mug of coffee with the other. Julie fought hard with the curtains and managed to push them back a few inches.

'You shouldn't have spent your own money.'

She came back over and settled on the bed, ignoring that remark. I pressed on.

'There's some spare money in one of the cupboards. The left-hand one. Under a plate.'

'It's the middle one,' she said matter-of-factly. 'I found it when I was looking for a place for Fred. A couple of twenties have slipped down the side.'

'Did you take them?'

Her knife and fork crashed down on the china plate. 'Fuck off. I've told you before. I'm not a thief. Why do people always think I'm going to steal from them?'

The vehemence caught me off guard. So did the tears she was blinking back. I chewed thoughtfully on my fried bread. 'Calm down. Who said anything about stealing? All I meant was if you're buying eggs for me, or anything else, like all those bottles of cleaning stuff I keep seeing around the place, then you shouldn't be paying for it yourself. It's nothing to do with stealing. You're shopping for me, so you use my money. OK?'

I took a sip of coffee. Julie had turned away. Her hair hung down, shielding her face. She sniffed and said, 'OK.'

I carried on eating my breakfast. After a while, she brushed her eyes roughly on her sleeve and turned back to her small plate of eggs. She wouldn't look up at me, though. This was turning into more of a working breakfast than I'd bargained for.

'And what would you have done if someone else had been here?'

She glanced at me then, quickly and suspiciously. 'What d'you mean, what would I have done?'

'There's enough food for two people here, not three.'

She shrugged and wrapped her hands round her coffee mug, lacing her fingers. 'Like I said, I'm not really hungry.'

'But—'

'And don't start on at me about eating properly, because I get enough of that from my nan.'

We sat through another tense stand-off. I looked out of the window – or at least out of the gap between the curtains – and tried to gauge what sort of day it was outside. The visual clues were muted and mixed. Patches of grey, patches of vague blue. Nothing meteorologically conclusive.

'They're trying to get me to go back to school,' she said suddenly.

So that was what this was all about. I nodded, but didn't say anything. She gave me another combative look. 'I bet you think they're right, as well.'

It was my turn to shrug. 'Sure. But that doesn't make it any easier.'

She'd given up on her breakfast by now and was twisting a knot of hair round one index finger.

'Why?' she said.

'Why should you go back?'

She nodded, tensely. The feeling was mutual. I'd lined myself up to deliver a homily on the value of education, but it wasn't exactly tripping off my tongue.

'Um . . . well.'

The sneer I could see out of the corner of my eye was vintage Elvis. I held steady and tried to explain why at least a hint of educational achievement – even a hint of educational attendance – was desirable, unless you wanted to end up in the gutter, or as Prime Minister.

'It's the deal,' I said hesitantly. 'You either have a shit, boring time in your teens and get to cruise through the rest of your life, or you go wild and show them all when you're young and spend the next sixty years grovelling. And like the lady says, it's better to die on your feet than live on your knees.'

'What lady?'

'La Pasionaria. Dolores somebody-or-other. She was Spanish.'

'So why was she mouthing off about schools?'

'She wasn't. Not exactly. It was more to do with the Civil War. But it sort of fits.'

Julie Ray thought about it. 'No it doesn't. She's saying fight. You're saying choose between living on your knees when you're young, or for the rest of your life. It's not the same at all.'

Indeed it wasn't. Even I could see that. But would La

Pasionaria have cut it with a slogan exhorting her followers to live on their knees for as short a time as possible?

'Ibarruri,' I muttered irrelevantly, remembering Dolores' surname.

'And what about you?' Julie said, sidestepping this show of learning and going for the kill.

I took a long sip of coffee. 'I got it wrong. I stayed on long enough to get bored and angry, then flunked it. Worst of both worlds. Teens were a war zone, now I'm scavenging for scraps. I don't recommend it.'

End of lecture. Another don't-do-as-I-do whine. Christ – no wonder the young get sick of us. I risked a quick glance at Julie, who was just managing to keep her breakfast down. But she didn't look impressed. I guess she just hated school and that was it. Or maybe she adored Franco.

'What are you going to do?'

The question was from her, not me. I'd given up on questions. I didn't feel I had the right to ask any more.

'Today, or for the rest of my life?'

'Both,' she said.

I frowned. 'I'm going to have a shower and a shave. Then I'm going to visit someone called Maria in the Caledonian Road. Then if I've got time I'm going to pick up a motor-cycle.'

She tugged on her hair. 'Who's Maria?'

'No one you know.' It came out sharper than I meant it. 'No one I know, come to that. A friend of the guy I work for. She's got some problem with security.'

I wondered about having some cards printed up, with 'Security Consultant' on them. It sounded good. Much better than 'Thief'.

'So what about the rest of your life?'

For a morose teenager, Julie Ray certainly had a chatty streak. Maybe it was not going to school. That's usually enough to cheer anyone up.

'It can only get better,' I said, thinking with a surge of warmth about the Africa Twin. Maybe that's what caused the sudden, massive loss of concentration. A dumb, happy, stupid feeling. 'You know, I'm pretty rich.'

She looked at me. I looked at her. Neither of us could quite believe what I'd said. I stayed very still and listened to my own breathing. Any second, I expected to feel as if I'd stepped into a lift on the twenty-eighth floor and the cable had just snapped. But I didn't. The seconds dripped by like time on a Dali clock.

After a while, Julie Ray asked, 'How come?' Her voice sounded quiet and sad, but I couldn't work out why.

'I stole some money. A lot of money. With a friend called Tom. We're waiting five years before we touch it. Only now he's dying.' I picked at a loose thread on the sheet with my fingernail. 'So he doesn't want any of it. And it was all his idea in the first place.'

Julie heard me out, then slipped off the bed. She picked up her mug and plate, but didn't look at me.

'I'm going to talk to Fred,' she said.

I gave Julie a few minutes, then pulled on my dressing gown and padded through to the bathroom, carrying my denim for the day. I didn't see her on the way, though I heard Fred's dumb squeaking from the kitchen, and some murmured endearments from her.

The taps shone. With some careful angling of my head, I could have shaved in the reflection. And there was no mush under the bar of soap, nor any toothpaste spatters on the mirror. The overall impression was alarmingly unsqualid.

I took my time in the shower, but held off from singing. I figured I had the edge on Fred, but it might be a humiliatingly close call. And I wanted to think about what I'd just done. But I couldn't. My brain was playing hard to get. It slipped and skittered like a dog on marble and I couldn't do a thing with it. In the end I gave up and thought about football, which I never do, then about whether there was any point having an earring when my hair was this long.

Yes, I decided twenty minutes later, scything stubble off my face with a razor that had seen sharper days. First, because there was always the possibility – perennially unattractive but eventually inevitable – of a haircut. Second, because an earring under long hair is like a coat with a mink lining – the sophistication is there to be glimpsed, not flaunted for the vulgar throng to see. And third, because if I took it out after however many years, my head would be crucially destabilized and I'd be walking around with my eyes on a diagonal like a spaniel hoping for a chocolate drop. And even though my disco-prowling days were long gone, this still wasn't an image handicap I could comfortably deal with.

This lengthy and pointless internal debate carried me through my beauty routine of lather, talc, gel and spray, and out into the front room, where Julie managed to scramble to her feet just as I came through the door.

'I was just going,' she said, having clearly waited half an hour to make this announcement. She took a couple more unconvincing paces. 'I filtered some more coffee. It's still hot.'

I nodded and smiled. 'Well—'

'About what you said . . . '

I nodded again, slowly, but the smile faded fast. I perched on the arm of the sofa and waited.

'It's just . . . I wondered . . . you know, how many people know. About you and Tom. The money.'

She was looking down at a patch of carpet, faded over the years by what little sunlight the curtains had allowed through. It was looking even more faded now, probably because all the dirt had been vacuumed off it.

I took a deep breath. 'Only you.'

95

I braced myself for a question beginning with 'why' – and ending with it. What more was there to ask? – but it didn't come. 'Oh,' was all she said.

I settled uncomfortably on one of the tall stools in the kitchen, drank most of the coffee and munched through an apple. The cooked breakfast had given me an appetite. I stared at the vinyl floor which, like the carpet, seemed several shades lighter. It was pulling back from brown and heading towards green. A couple more Flash attacks from Julie and we'd be in the yellow spectrum. Or down to bare floorboards.

I sighed and wondered how I'd managed to land myself with a teenage cleaning lady on the run from double maths. It was embarrassing enough having her around. But not paying her anything and then unloading all my soul secrets showed . . . well, I didn't like to think what it showed.

I remembered Tom lecturing me about the Italian guy who pulled the Knightsbridge safe-deposit raid. How he would have made it clean away to Colombia if he hadn't decided to hang on one more week while the export licence for his Ferrari came through.

'A lifetime of more money than you could possibly spend traded for life inside plus a week driving a shiny car. Now that's what I call depreciation.' Tom shook his head, but I could tell he was impressed – who wouldn't be? – by the sheer scale of the misjudgement. Impressed and also nervous.

'Promise me you won't do something like that, Charlie,' he said. 'Don't go all working class on me. We're talking delayed gratification with a vengeance here. Because if we get this one wrong, believe me, the best we can hope for is that the cops find us first.'

I promised. And now I couldn't remember if I'd had my fingers crossed.

I stared gloomily into my mug of coffee, then dropped the apple core into it and headed for the door. It was a while since I'd had an attack of nerves. They'd come more often in the early days. After a while, I worked out the best way of dealing with them was to keep moving.

A burst of determined energy took me down the stairs and out into the world, where I quickly found it was breezier than I'd thought and I really needed a jacket. But going back would have blown the momentum, and there was something to be said for the fresh feeling of goosebumps under a summer shirt. I picked up the pace and crossed the road.

A couple of turnings on, the unmistakable sound of ragga at two hundred decibels screamed up behind me, melting down my eardrums and kicking me rhythmically in the chest. I took a couple of steps back from the edge of the pavement and put my fingers in my ears. It wasn't a street-smart pose, but I'd been caught this way before and didn't want another four-day migraine complicated by heart murmurs and acute depression.

The black Mini came thumping up the road, exploding blossom off the trees and whipping up a vicious dust storm. I closed my eyes too late. Particles of grit bounced around my retinas like breadcrumbs in a Moulinex. The tears began to flow.

The Mini cruised to a halt beside me. I didn't see or hear it stop, but I knew it had because I suddenly lost the ability to breathe. My chest imploded and my lungs collapsed. I waited to die. With one last supreme effort, I blinked one eye open for a last look at the world I was leaving. Veins in my eyeball crackled and popped.

Through a cataract of blood and filth, I saw Greg's head looming out of the passenger window. It was quite a trick, given that he was driving, but if you're six-five in a Noddy car, you can pull it off. Greg looked up and grinned, and a huge wave of silence broke over me. My chest began to reinflate and blood surged boldly back into crucial organs. I took a risk and opened my other eye. Trees in my line of vision were swaying gently, the sandstorm was settling and cats all along the street were peering cautiously out of catflaps. Woodland creatures thirty miles away were starting to rebuild their collapsed sets, shattered nests and pulverized burrows.

'Lift?' Greg said.

'Where to?'

'Anywhere. I've got the afternoon off.'

I climbed in and told Greg I was heading for the Caledonian Road.

'You're losing it,' he said succinctly. 'You used to be able to jive in loud clubs. What happened?'

I thought about it. 'I guess—'

'I'll tell you what happened. You quit going to my gym. Now you look like a heap of flab if you don't have your corset pulled tight, so you steer clear of clubs where it's going to be obvious you've got no muscle tone, and now you can't deal with funky music. Face it – life's over for you.'

I brooded on this predictably savage attack and was pleased to track down a logical flaw.

'When I go to clubs, I keep my clothes on.'

Greg shrugged his huge shoulders. 'Ain't you old.'

His ridiculous car bounced from pothole to pothole, along cycle tracks, in between juggernaut wheels and up on the pavement with despatch riders. I had no idea where we were. I tried to work out which part of London had grey walls along the side of every street, before realizing I was looking at the kerb.

'This car's insane,' I grumbled ungratefully. 'You're bent double. You don't even begin to fit. What came over you?'

'I bought it for the sound system,' he growled. 'They don't come any better. The guy who put it in mixed for the Stones at Wembley – he knows what he's doing.'

Namely, putting the whole amplification system from the 'Nineteenth Nervous Breakdown' comeback tour into the boot and doors of a Mini. Doubtless he knew what he was doing. Perhaps a more apposite question was why.

I thought about asking it, but Greg was clearly getting riled. He tried to pin me to the back of my seat by accelerating hard away from the lights, but ran out of gears at about 15 m.p.h. and was cut up by a mobile hot-dog stand. He thumped the steering wheel in frustration.

'This thing's no fun to drive without noise.'

'What . . . ah . . . ?' I had to think fast, because one thing I couldn't face was listening to Snoop Doggy Dog's humanist vision at Wembley volume from inside a mobile speaker. 'What's up with the gym?'

Greg was distracted, in the way a dental patient is distracted when the drill goes into the root canal before the anaesthetic has started to work.

'Two grand's worth of glass and plaster is what. The mirror that goes right down the side – that came loose and brought the wall down with it. Place looked like Beirut on a bad day.'

I nodded sympathetically, which is harder than you'd imagine when your head is wedged against a car roof. But it was easier for me than for Greg. The only way he could try a stunt like that was by winding back the sunroof.

'You can claim for it, can't you?'

It was a crafty question to test my sunroof theory, but Greg was equal to it.

'I'm not insured against sexual terrorism,' he said, keeping his chin rigidly horizontal and choking with indignation as a woman on one of those adult tricycles with her weekly shopping in the basket pulled out to overtake us.

'Sounds interesting.' It sounded like someone I knew as well.

'Your friend,' Greg said, right on cue. 'Man, I don't know whether she's better off with or without you. When you were together, you were always screaming at each other and walking out. Either that or almost screwing in public. But now . . . well, now she's just out of control. I don't know what to do with her.'

There's nothing like an outside perspective on the most important relationship of your life. I winced as my rose-tinted spectacles were clubbed off my face and ground into the dirt.

'So why did she smash up your gym?' Perhaps it was because Greg had referred scathingly to one of her previous relationships. A particularly important one. It was a comforting thought.

'She didn't,' Greg said. 'Not exactly.'

I caught my breath as a football bounced into the road ten yards ahead of us and a gang of kids began to shriek. Then I remembered whose car I was riding in and relaxed. Sure enough, a pale boy with a savage ginger crop darted out with no warning from behind a parked van, scooted across the road, retrieved his ball, reached into his pocket, unwrapped a stick of gum, popped it into his mouth and skipped back across in front of us as we closed relentlessly to within eight yards of him.

'So what happened?' I said, as Ginger languidly rejoined his mates, not even bothering to pretend he'd had a close shave.

Greg stared glumly through the windscreen. 'Well, I said to her last time, when she turned up in all that skimpy stuff – you know, told her it was distracting the guys, they weren't getting any serious lifting done – I said could she maybe wear something that wasn't little or sexy. She laughs, says sure thing, and turns up yesterday with a duffel bag over her shoulder saying the least sexy clothes she could think of were what her dad wears this time of year in the garden, so she's gone and borrowed them.'

I tried to remember what Luther wore to garden in during the summer. Nothing that got me uncontrollably inflamed, but I still picked up the danger signals. Greg treated himself to a long sigh.

'White shorts, with grass stains,' he said. 'About twelve sizes too big, so she has all sorts of trouble keeping them up. And a string vest. Nothing else.'

Now that he mentioned the outfit, I could see Luther in it, pottering round and polishing his roses. But it was hard to keep my mind focused. I'd never asked Opal to dress up in her dad's gardening gear, even when we were way out of it on whatever Royale had been dealing. It was tempting to start imagining what I'd missed.

'So what happened with the mirror?'

'I was out front, so I didn't see it. And it was murder getting a straight story. None of the guys would admit anything. I had to have words with a couple of them.'

He paused to brood on the one satisfying aspect of the whole sorry business.

'It was love-bombing. I just hugged 'em and hugged 'em and squeezed 'em tight until they told me everything. And now they don't mind about the gym being closed, because it'll take a while for their ribs to mend. But still – it was a bad deal. Opal was doing warm-up stretches. Far as I can make out, the first guy who copped an eyeful was on the running belt. He couldn't believe his luck, tripped over his feet, went face-down on the machine and bounced off backwards into Martin, who's holding two bells over his head. He manages to hold on to one of them as the face-bouncer goes feet-first into his kneecaps, but he lets go of the other and drops it on to the groin of the bloke doing sit-ups next to him, who screams so loud as his bollocks are mashed to paste that his friend on the exercise bike twists round in panic, loses his balance and tips sideways on to the next bike, which tips on to the next, so you've got four bikes and the guys on them going over like dominoes, and the fourth one, the guy on the end of the line, reaches out to grab something to keep his balance and puts his fist through the glass of the emergency fire door release. So that's the first thing I hear – guys screaming, crunching metal like a motorway pile-up and the fire alarm wailing. I figure the boiler's exploded or something, so I grab a couple of fire extinguishers and leg it through to the weights room, where everyone's lying around moaning except the guy who went flat out on the running belt, who's picking himself up to see whether his nose is broken. I ain't got time to ask questions, so I just heave one of the fire extinguishers in his direction, but instead of catching it, the useless fucker ducks and it skims over his head and smashes into the mirror, which explodes into a million pieces, and the plaster on the wall behind just gives up and caves in, bringing the whole wall down like the slow motion stuff you see of tower blocks being blown up. So I'm stood there in a zero-visibility dust storm, wondering where the fire is, and everyone else is yelling about how they've got needles of glass in their eyes or tomato ketchup where their balls used to be, and the fire alarm's still going and then right in the middle of it all Opal straightens up from the side bend that caused all the trouble because it left most of her outside Luther's vest and says: 'You know, this place has really changed. It used to be a nice, quiet gym.'

Nine

The bookies was one of a row of shops that had been grafted on to the front of some reasonable Edwardian houses. I was pretty impressed with myself for making this observation – if Michael had been there, I could have casually let it drop and he'd have seen me in a new light. On the other hand, there was some risk involved. I wasn't entirely sure the houses were Edwardian. I just guessed they were because they looked sort of Victorian, but less pretty.

Whatever their age and architectural merit, grafting bookies, launderettes and newsagents on the front hadn't done them any favours. What it had done was create generous first-floor roof terraces, and if traffic-watching was your thing, these were a definite plus. The door to the flat was to the left of the shop front, but the entryphone had two wires hanging loose and looked more lethal than useful. I took a step back, thought about shouting up, but the flat was set well back and I didn't want to be pegged as one of those nutters who stand in the street yelling their heads off. So I had a lazy look around, took a petrol station points card out of my back pocket – yobs who use Amex for this kind of stunt are showing off – and slipped the Yale. On reflection, I needn't have bothered with the look around. Probably more people in the area used plastic than door keys. As I peered around the dim hallway for a light, I felt relaxed and at home. This was my kind of place.

I found the time-delay light switch eventually, fixed bizarrely a couple of feet above ground level on a dirty mustard wall. I pushed it with my knee and nothing happened, so that was wasted effort. But my eyes were adapting surprisingly well to the gloom. My pupils hadn't been this large legally for some time. I noticed the empty bulb socket in the ceiling light fitting – bingo – and the door off to the right which must have led into the shop. The other door, straight ahead, had a hole the size of a boot kicked out of it, again at about knee height. Evidently, I'd walked into the lair of a severely pissed off dwarf. I walked up to the damaged door, tripping slightly on folds of threadbare chocolate carpet. There was no bell, nor even any loose wires. I knocked carefully, unsure how much more punishment the door could take, and stood listening to the muffled commentary coming from the television sets in the bookies.

'Hello?' Maria said from behind the door. I hadn't heard her come downstairs. Either she was light on her feet or the carpet on the other side of the door was a cut above.

'Charlie Lucas. We talked on the phone.'

She opened the door – a pale, slight woman with straight nondescript hair to her shoulders, small round glasses, smoking a thin cigar. 'Come on up,' she said, but didn't smile.

I followed her up two steep flights of stairs – always a test of gentlemanly deportment. Where do you look? Or rather, how do you make out that you're not looking where you obviously are looking. If there are no interesting posters and the cornice on the ceiling is plain and dull, you're never going to convince. Also, if you stare too hard at the ceiling, you run the risk of losing your footing and tumbling back down the stairs, which can be dangerous and is definitely uncool. All in all, I'd decided a while ago, the game's not worth the candle. So I watched Maria's bum, which was small like the rest of her and sheathed in black leggings, and breathed in the cigar smoke as I climbed the stairs. What the doctors might call moderate exercise.

At the top of the stairs, she went left into a small square kitchen. 'Go on through. I'll make some coffee.'

There wasn't much furniture in the main room – a low, futon-type sofa with its uncomfortable-looking folded-over mattress, and a couple of old cane and wicker chairs which didn't look odds-on to take my weight. In the corner was a trestle table being used as a desk. A few handwritten sheets of A4 were strewn over it, while on the back left corner was a neat pile of printed-out manuscript. The handwriting on the loose sheets looked like seismographic tracing superimposed on a headline-and-underlying inflation chart. The top sheet of the manuscript was more legible – we were talking bubble-jet, maybe even laser printer – but that was where the problems started. I couldn't understand a word. I made several brave attempts at the same paragraph before deciding I was never going to make it and cutting my losses. There were two windows looking on to the diseased asphalt of the bookies' roof. I stood and watched a few puddles of rain which had collected in various hollows and dips, but they weren't drying fast enough to make it a spectator sport.

I still wasn't keen on any of the available seating, so I walked over to the only picture on the wall – a photograph in a clip-frame, hung much too high on a nail that had obviously been there already. It showed a slim, fussily dressed blonde girl, squinting into the sun and clutching the top half of a weary, vertically stretched Siamese. It was hard to guess the age of the girl, because her face was overexposed in the glare of the sun. Judging by the comparative size of the cat, she was about thirteen. Either that or she was much older and it was a leopard.

As photographs went, it was comprehensively inept. As a wall decoration, it was a puzzling, forehead-level disaster. I was still transfixed by it when Maria came in with a couple of coffees and a tiny, uninteresting-looking cake.

'I'm sorry I'm late,' I said, embarrassed to be caught

peering at the photo and keen to apologize for something. 'Someone gave me a lift.'

It didn't sound quite right. Maria frowned as she handed me my coffee. I considered explaining about Greg's car, but it wasn't the sort of thing women are interested in.

'And I'm sorry I was unfriendly. I'm a bit touchy about my smoking breaks. I use them as my thinking time, so I'm never happy to be interrupted. I know it's not very fair.'

I nodded understandingly, which was easy as I hadn't even realized what an irritant my presence was, and asked how many smoking breaks she took, with a view to being well out of the way when the next one came round.

'Three,' she said, settling lightly on a cane chair. 'Morning, afternoon, evening. Fifteen minutes each. It's my strategy for keeping sane. Some days it works better than others.'

The last comment came with a fractional smile, which was gone in the blink of an eye. Like most of us, Maria looked better when she was smiling. I was pleased I hadn't been blinking.

Reconciled to a brace of slipped discs and a year or two of osteopathy, I lowered myself on to the sofa.

'Would you like some cake?'

Christ, no, I'm taking enough punishment, was the answer that leapt to mind, and which I managed to suppress in favour of a rather more muted, 'No, thanks.' Maria looked dubiously at the cake, which she'd put on the floor at her feet.

'I don't blame you. I'm not sure what came over me. I don't think I realized what sort of . . . when Stella said . . . I mean, when she described . . . ' Maria wisely gave up stumbling through this particular minefield and came clean. 'I sort of imagined workman's cleavage and overalls and . . . well, cake, I suppose. You know – with tea.'

I nodded. Cake and tea and workman's cleavage. Stella had been on form.

'Oh, well, I suppose I can put it out on the roof for the birds. I wish it wasn't only pigeons.'

Personally, I didn't much care what ate the cake as long as it wasn't me.

'That photo of you . . . when you were younger . . . '

The sentence went up in my face like a letter-bomb. I'd been lulled by lack of back trouble into conversational expansiveness and was paying the price. For a start, it's never a great idea to point out to a woman how much older she looks than her photographs, even if in the photos she's wearing a hospital tag round her wrist and you're talking to her at her Golden Wedding party. And there wasn't anything I wanted to know about the picture except why on earth it was there, which wasn't a question vying for promotion into the Premiership of tact.

I noticed Maria drawing quietly on her cigar and watching me. Her eyes flicked with disdain towards the photograph. Or perhaps, I thought glumly, they were registering disdain before they flicked anywhere.

'The cat . . . ' I said, and very quickly wished I hadn't. I'd brought off a subtle shift in the line of enquiry, but at terrible cost. What could I possibly ask about the top half of a Siamese cat?

'Um . . . what was its name?'

I could see Maria's eyes narrowing behind her little round glasses. She took her time about answering.

'Lucky,' she said eventually.

I nodded. Lucky the cat. How sweet.

'My parents brought the photograph when they helped me move in,' Maria said, to put me out of my misery. 'Dad wanted to put it up. God knows why.'

I didn't want to appear to be getting above myself, but I thought I had a fair idea. I looked again at the picture, this time checking out the background – a wide garden, with early autumn trees, and the corner of what was either a conservatory or a very upmarket greenhouse.

'It's not the Caledonian Road,' I said, and left it at that. I'd already told Maria she was ageing fast. Now I was pointing out how far down the world she'd come.

'True,' Maria said mildly, and also left it at that. Maybe she was offended, but she didn't look it. She just seemed tired. And anyway, I had a point. No father's going to enjoy moving his daughter into an area where he has to keep running to the window to check no one's stripped off his hubcaps. He's going to start wondering what other liberties are going to be taken with his little girl, and by what sort of men. Nostalgia for the days when she was safe at home and loved her cat most of all seemed a natural reaction.

'So how d'you know Stella?' she asked, just as I was beginning to feel unbearably wise and toying with the idea of growing a beard.

'Through Jeff,' I said. 'I do most of my work for him.'

Most of my work. As if I had a few peripheral but nonetheless promising business ventures of my own, which I liked to run in parallel for my own self-fulfilment as much as for the money.

'How about you? How do you know her?'

'We were best friends at school,' Maria said, and then added pointedly, 'a long time back.' I wasn't sure whether to smile or not. 'And we came through the two toughest tests a friendship can take. She got a pony and I didn't, and then we fell for the same guy.'

Maria drew with quiet satisfaction on her cigarillo as she contemplated the awesome potential of female solidarity.

'So how did you cope?' It seemed only polite to ask.

'She let me ride her pony,' Maria said simply. 'And a few years later, I suppose I returned the compliment with Robert, seeing as he came on to me first. All in all, we handled it pretty well.'

I felt a touch uneasy about the arrangement. 'Did you keep Robert stabled up with the horse?'

Maria smiled, briefly. 'Not quite. We just decided as it was first time around for both of us, we might as well go with the same guy and then the comparison would be more valid. Besides, he was the only remotely sexy sixth former, as far as we could see. And he wasn't complaining. He thought he was two-timing us, which went down a bomb with his laddy mates.'

'So what happened in the end?' I wasn't feeling any less uneasy.

'We ditched him,' Maria said brusquely. 'Neither of us was that impressed in the end. I remember going out for a drink, all three of us. It was summer, we were sitting outside. I think his teenage head was boiling with three-in-a-bed fantasies for the end of the evening. He seemed to be sweating more than usual. We were nice to him for a while, then we got bored and told him he was a cheating bastard, dumber than he had any right to be and a fourth-rate lay.' The half-smile of satisfaction made a fleeting return. 'He actually started dabbing at his forehead with a handkerchief. I didn't think anyone under sixty still carried handkerchiefs. I suppose it must have been his dad's.'

I sipped thoughtfully at the last of my coffee. 'Sisterhood is powerful,' I murmured, through the acrid dregs.

Maria shrugged. 'Rarely. But we have our moments.'

We both laughed – with satisfaction in her case, and in mine with slightly hysterical relief that I hadn't come across Stella and Maria when I was seventeen.

'Anyway, Robert didn't do too badly. He presents some daytime TV quiz show now. Women swoon and send in their knickers. Who am I to say it's a waste of good underwear?'

'And you've kept in touch with Stella ever since?'

'Off and on,' she said. 'We've had a few men problems since the glory days of co-operation over Robert. Jeff and I never made much of an impression on each other and I don't think Stella thought much of James. So we had to accept our double-dating days were over.'

'So what's your problem with Jeff?'

She looked at me levelly. 'Jeff thinks I'm an overeducated, stuck-up little bitch,' she said, with little apparent concern.

Somehow we seemed to have wandered off the subject of Lucky the cat.

'Which presumably means he put the moves on you, but you weren't interested.'

I was impressed by my own intuition, if a little concerned that I seemed to be toadying to the feminist line. I didn't want Maria to think I was a creep.

'He did. And I wasn't. But to be fair, he thought I was an overeducated, stuck-up little bitch well before he tried anything on. Or tried to get anything of mine off. So I can't pretend his opinion of me was the product of rejection. But it does leave the problem of why he wanted to sleep with a woman he had something approaching contempt for.' She raised a lazy eyebrow. 'Perhaps it's a male thing. I don't know – you're a man. You tell me.'

It was beginning to look like whatever was in the envelope after this trip wasn't going to cover the half of it. Stella hadn't warned me I'd have to explain her husband's sex drive to her best friend, whom he'd once unsuccessfully groped. And the question was both easy and hard. Sure, if you're hot for a girl and she's got all these letters after her name that make you feel small, then you're going to imagine her lying underneath you on a rug, with her clothes torn off, gasping and sinking her teeth into your shoulder, while with every surging stroke, you're thinking, What good are your A grades now? This is life, baby, and you're learning it from me. Simple. But if you feel like explaining it in mixed company, be my guest.

'I guess . . . ah . . . ' I tried a few sentences in my head, but this was rough ground. 'Isn't it true that women prefer at least to like the men they sleep with? Whereas men . . . ' I was pleased with myself for saying 'men' rather than 'Jeff'. It was more academically detached, and less hopelessly disloyal. 'Men are more . . . um . . . well, there's this power thing. And they're more likely to be turned on by women who look good.'

Something like that. It was a while since I'd read *Cosmo*, but I was pretty sure I still had the gist. Maria was looking coolly at me. It was probably a while since she'd read *Cosmo*, too. I wondered what Derrida had to say about screwing women until they begged for mercy. Nothing very exciting was my best guess, and that would take some doing.

The conversation seemed to have come seriously unstuck. Maria glanced at her watch, which was uncalled for. As a couple, we seemed to be losing track of who was doing whom the favours.

'Stella said something about you wanting a burglar alarm,' I said firmly, relieved to have got through an entire sentence with no reference to sex.

'In a flat like this?' Maria looked incredulous. 'You must be joking. A few locks might be nice. And maybe something to cover the hole in the front door. But look around you – it's not exactly an infra-red scene, is it?'

Just what I'd been thinking, but had been too polite to say. My manners were trickling back.

'Not that I'm complaining. It's a free flat for me and Louis – and Jeff needn't have gone the extra mile, especially for me. I guess it's a favour to Stella, so presumably he's had better luck with someone else than he had with me and is feeling guilty. Isn't that how marriages work?'

I shrugged. 'I wasn't married long enough to tell.'

And I'd never owned any real estate, however crummy, that I could let rent-free to the friend of my wife's who hated me most. Anyway, I thought her bloke was called James, not Louis.

'How come you hate Jeff so much?'

'I don't,' Maria said.

I waited for her to expand on her answer, until the silence grew embarrassing.

'So what do you think of him?' I liked to think loyalty to my employer was the motivation behind my persistence. More realistically, I was just surprised to find myself in a dialogue with someone whose manners I considered worse than my own. Maria looked as if she wanted to bring her evening cigarillo forward a few hours.

'I think he's an undereducated wide-boy on the make. But then I would, wouldn't I? I realize he's your gaffer and I realize this is his flat.' She paused, shrugged. 'But I'd be a hypocrite if I pretended I liked him or had much respect for him.'

If Maria was this tough on people who helped her out, I wondered how many people who crossed her came out alive.

'Thanks for the coffee. I'll leave you to . . . ah . . . ' I wasn't sure what I was leaving her to. Watch *Home and Away*? Do sit-ups?

'George,' she said, adding another name to her list of mystery males. James and Louis obviously had the afternoon off. Perhaps they couldn't take the pace. I wondered what she did to them that was so special.

'Perec,' she said. 'Georges Perec. My thesis. I'm writing it up, and it's heavy going.'

So that was what the manuscript pages were about.

'Interesting guy,' I observed chattily.

'You think so?' Maria asked rhetorically, turning towards the door.

'I do. I don't know about you, but I've always seen him as a sort of severe realist with an almost Flaubertian classicism of style and a compulsive disdain for consumerism.'

Maria's eyes widened very fast in surprise, then narrowed even more rapidly in suspicion. It was an impressive burst of muscular activity behind those little gold glasses.

'But when you look at his later work, he comes across as a post-modern fabulist – if you like, a Balzac with ambitions to be a Borges.'

There was an awed pause after this conversational gem. Maria gave it her full consideration, then treated me to her only genuine smile of the afternoon. 'Nice try – but it's the other way round. A Borges with ambitions to be a Balzac. At least,' she added politely, 'that's the line I set out in my introduction. If you really do see it the other way, I'd be interested—'

I waved a dismissive hand. 'Sorry. Never heard of the guy. I just read the top page.' And remembered it pretty impressively, I thought. Transposing a couple of B-names is easily done when you've no idea what you're talking about.

'You haven't missed much,' Maria said, with a weary academic overfamiliarity. 'He was a depressive stay-at-home who once wrote an entire novel without the letter "e".'

I nodded. It was much as I'd expected. Another French intellectual whose brains had gone to his head. But the 'e' angle was a new one on me. The cover must have been a bit weird. Gorgs Prc, presumably.

'I'll get some locks and wood and stuff,' I said, grinding down through my mental gearbox from intellectual to artisan, 'and give you a call.'

'Sure,' Maria said. 'Thanks.' As I reached the top of the stairs, she cleared her throat nervously. 'About how much d'you think it will cost?'

'No problem,' I called back breezily. 'The wide-boy's paying.'

Even the diesel-soaked air of the Caledonian Road was a relief after the stuffiness of the flat. I hadn't realized how fuggy it had been when I was in there. Thinking back, Maria was just the kind of skinny type who felt the cold. Or maybe, with all those men she mentioned, life was one long massage session and I'd been lucky to catch her in one of her rare hours alone and with her clothes on. Lucky or unlucky, I mused briefly, before deciding I'd been right first time. I couldn't believe there was much to see – and anyway, with James and Louis prancing about with petri dishes of aromatic oil, it would be hard to concentrate.

It was a vivid picture of Cally Road life that I'd conjured up, with definite King's Cross overtones. I let a couple of buses go by, enjoying the walk past shops selling shabby second-hand furniture and even worse new stuff, garages fitting exhausts that wouldn't quite fit and re-treads that wouldn't grip, and open-all-hours mini-marts with tiny displays of rotting fruit and groaning shelves of alcohol. In one of these I managed to find an apple that I reckoned was at least this year's crop, albeit from the first harvest. The guy behind the till, used to ringing up crate after crate of Special Brew with a few tubes of glue thrown in, looked at me suspiciously. His left hand dropped to the under-counter alarm and didn't creep back again until I was safely out on the pavement.

I checked my watch and found there was still time to collect the Africa Twin if I started catching a couple of the buses that were cruising past with surprising frequency. But the mood wasn't right. I wanted a bright and breezy new-day-dawning feeling when I picked up the bike, not a late-afternoon, urban-greyness feeling. If it was going to be the first day of the rest of my life, I should at least make an effort to start it before everyone else made it home from work.

I paused briefly outside a locksmith's and peered through the window at various catches and bolts. It was going to feel strange fitting the things instead of levering them out of splintered wood. From what I could see through the dirty glass, nothing much was new on the sash-lock front. I thought about slipping in to buy a few, but I didn't have much money on me and I had a hunch they were going to be pricey. It made me wish I'd saved some of the ones I'd jemmied out.

I gave up on window shopping when I reached the next bus stop, where a hopeless bundle of rags slumped on a tiny red seat looked me up and down and decided I wasn't even worth touching for money. It made me wonder, not for the first time, if I should wear my hair shorter. Or shave closer. Or dye my eyes blue.

When the bus came I swung myself upstairs on to the top deck and was pleased to find the front seats on both sides free. Some kids in school uniform were slouched about half-way down, which was a puzzle. In my day, if you were young and eager, you sat forward and stared down from the front seats. If you were mature and world-weary, you sprawled over the single seat at the back. Presumably, teenagers nowadays had reached a new plane of sophistication and were so blasé, they didn't care where they sat.

Big mistake, I thought gratefully, making my way to the front of the bus and pitching on to the left-hand seats when it lurched out into the traffic. I straightened up, braced for the inevitable sniggers from the kids. But they didn't come. The youth of today was either almost impossibly adult or completely out of it on glue. I leaned my head on the side window and watched the scurrying going on below.

A thud of boots and the scrape of scuffed bags on the stairs brought a couple of lads up on to the top deck. I watched carefully, sitting sideways on my front seat with my feet up, daring them to approach. It was the sort of challenge I could never resist when I was fourteen, but these guys didn't even blink. Bearing out my theory of the nihilism of modern youth, they slumped on to the first empty double seat they saw, with no apparent concern for its positional status.

'Fucking high definition monitor,' the guy on the left said, in the tones of aggressive contempt which even I knew denoted extreme admiration – at least some things stayed the same. 'Screen double the size of the one I've got. All the Streetfighters, Kombat, as well as Sonic and Mario and all the early stuff. He's given away more than I ever had. And he can tap into that network where they send down pictures of girls and you can take their clothes off. And what do I get? Fucking quality time!'

'Quality what?' This was one game his mate had never heard of.

'Quality time. My folks say parents who both work feel guilty and buy their kids all this stuff instead of loving them. Hippy shit. That's why they both work part-time, so they've got fuck all money and one of them's always in when I get home. Drives me insane. They're always under my feet, asking questions, not giving me any peace. And then my birthday comes round and I get a book token. Christ.' He bunched a fist and thumped it down on the metal top-rail of the seat in front. 'Fucking quality time.'

His mate shuddered. 'Gross,' he said.

A bus journey on the crumbling remains of the capital's public transport network had done wonders for my mood, though I wasn't sure why. Maybe it was the perspective that being five yards off the ground brings. Maybe hanging out with the juveniles and no-hopers who rely on the system made me feel like an overachiever. Or maybe it was the sheer speed and efficiency of the whole system when contrasted with Greg's Mini. Whatever it was, I felt clear-headed and fit as I took the stairs two at a time, three on corners, up to my flat.

Visibility was down to a couple of feet inside my front door. Clouds of water vapour billowed around the living room, pushed this way and that by competing draughts from the opaque and dripping windows. The sofa back, when I reached for it to guide myself in the direction of the kitchen, felt like a dishcloth.

'I'm in the bath,' Julie Ray called out, unnecessarily.

'Yeah.' I used the remnants of my cataracted vision to stumble over to the nearest window and push it up. The cold air was sweet. 'D'you want a coffee?' I tried to remember if I still had my swimming goggles in a drawer somewhere.

'When I come out,' Julie Ray said, sensibly. I hadn't thought it through.

'OK.' I was reluctant to head for the kettle right away. The idea of switching on anything electrical in the current humidity was scary. I might as well be in the shed. So I headed for the fridge and, being careful not to touch any part of the metal handle, pulled out a small bottle of French beer. Just right for when you like the idea of a beer, but can't face the real stuff. I wrenched off the top and stood there, tipping it up from time to time, watching the steam clear slowly from the room.

Thinking about electrics made me want to take my small beer out to the shed and do some carving. I had a new piece of yew to work on, and plans for a totem pole with lots of faces. I needed practice on faces. The last time I'd tried, working from a perfume advertisement torn from a magazine, the ethereally beautiful model had turned out looking more like a gargoyle. Not for nothing was the last major piece I'd finished the seal-girl. You don't get many features on a seal.

But I'd promised Julie Ray a coffee, so I couldn't walk out. It seemed like I'd have to stand around drinking pretend-beer for a while, feeling as trapped as an assembly-line worker with three kids, negative equity, an agoraphobic wife and Christmas coming.

I heard the plug being pulled and some heavy splashes as Julie Ray pulled herself up and out. I hoped she hadn't disturbed the boats. When you're three quarters of the way through the battle of Jutland, formation is the key. In the meantime it was getting chilly in the room with one of the windows fully open. I reassessed the visibility–warmth trade-off, crossed to the window and pulled the sash down, and then did some more standing around with beer.

When Julie Ray ambled out of the bathroom she was wrapped from neck to ankle in a white towel the size and thickness of a double duvet and slowly combing her wet hair.

'I thought you were going to make coffee.'

'Give me a chance. I couldn't even see the kitchen until a couple of minutes ago. And where did that towel come from?'

'Heal's. I used some of the money that was in the drawer. Your towels were all thin and hard. I bought a blue one for you and a white one for . . . ' She looked at me hesitantly. 'For your guests.'

She pulled the brush a few more times through her hair, keeping her eyes on me.

'You went all the way to Heal's for a couple of towels?'

'Sure. Why not? It's only a couple of lifts either way.'

'What d'you mean, lifts? You're saying you hitched to the West End and back? Are you crazy? What happens if you meet . . . someone. You could be—'

I stopped in my tracks. How much d'you tell teenagers, and how early? It wasn't the sort of problem I'd lost much sleep over in the past. Julie Ray was treating me to her weariest generation-gap look.

'Relax. People are nicer than you think. Only one guy's ever tried it on and that was my fault for flagging him down around King's Cross. I'll never do that again.'

'What happened?' I wasn't sure if I really wanted to know, pretty sure I oughtn't to want to know, but the question was out before my moral sensibilities had engaged.

'Nothing,' she shrugged. 'He stopped the car in some goods yard and said I had to earn my lift. Then he took his thing out. I told him I knew a special trick and he'd have to take his tie off. When he gave it to me, I made a noose around his bits and pretended to start playing. He thought it was great. Then I tied the other end in the hardest knot I knew to the steering wheel, grabbed his keys and ran.'

It wasn't my idea of nothing – and it probably wasn't the guy's either, unless he was sanguine beyond belief.

'I'm good at knots,' Julie Ray added with satisfaction. 'My grandad was a sailor in the war and taught me lots of different ones.' I nodded. A useful lesson well learned. 'And it'll be a while before that guy asks for a trick from a hitchhiker again.'

Here I was sure she was underselling herself. I couldn't see the would-be punter ever giving anyone a lift again. His kids were going to have to walk to school. Slowing down below thirty within a hundred yards of a pedestrian would probably bring him out in a cold sweat. And when his wife asked why he never wore that tie her mother had given him for Christmas, he was going to have to think fast.

'By the way,' she said, 'you've got a letter. With "personal" all over it, which must have scared Luther off. I brought it up.'

She turned and headed back towards the bathroom. 'It's on the side in the kitchen. I'm going to get dressed now. Can I have three sugars in my coffee?'

Ten

Well, Charlie, it's over.

Tom's handwriting was ridiculously bad – tall, spiky, going uphill to the right. As a medium of communication it wasn't much better than a jammed radio signal. I made it through the four words eventually, feeling pretty much as I'd expected to feel. It was time for a break.

I went over to the kettle and stood next to it for a while. Eventually I turned it on. When it finally boiled, the steam poured up into my face, scalding my eyes, bringing tears. I stayed as I was, looking down into the spout, until it switched itself off and the steam petered out into the cold kitchen air. I made Julie Ray's coffee, remembering the sugar, and then began hunting through cupboards for an old bottle of supermarket-blended whisky which I knew was round somewhere, because I was hardly likely to have drunk it.

The whisky turned up in the eye-level cupboard next to the boiler, under the internal shelf which had collapsed diagonally under the weight of three rubber gloves. I found a glass from a slightly more salubrious cupboard and poured out a double, wondering morosely what I could add to it to make it drinkable. A quart and a half of Fanta might almost have done the trick, but I wasn't that thirsty. So I thumbed a couple of ice cubes out of a grubby plastic tray into the Scotch and took it back into the sitting room with the coffee.

I sat down, facing the letter and the whisky. I stared at both for a while, then picked up the letter.

And there's not much more to say, really, is there?

Which is just as well. I can't get the hang of morphine at all. I'm out of my head most of the time, and asleep the rest. Sometimes I just give up on it and go down to the pub and drink through the afternoon. Frank fetches me. I've even made some friends. They give me racing tips, which is sweet. What would I need a big win for now? But I still place the bets.

I'm glad I saw you again. I think it was just in time. And I hope you enjoy the money. I don't mind about it now. It's funny how much I don't mind. Please give my half to Maggie. You can explain or not, I don't care. And I'd like something to go to a girl I met a couple of months back. She's called Solange and she's worth it. Look for her in a club called Easy E's.

But if it isn't safe, forget it. It's no big deal, although I don't expect you to see it that way until you find yourself where I am now. Not for a long time, I hope.

You won't be coming to the funeral. There's no point. I won't be there, and you never know who else might be. And Frank's been told not to have anything to do with the ashes. So you'll just have to make the effort and remember me, without props, as a friend who cared for you and wishes you well.

I didn't taste the cheap whisky as it went down. That was the only good thing about the evening. But the Scotch wasn't strong enough. Or there was too much ice. Or it wasn't the answer in the first place.

Julie Ray came out of the bathroom in a tracksuit, carrying her clothes in a neat pile in front of her. Her pants and bra must have been folded up and tucked away discreetly, because I couldn't see them. Then again, what the hell was I doing looking?

She sat down in the chair opposite – the chair Tom had sat in the night he came round – and put her clothes carefully down by her feet. Then she reached forward for her coffee.

'Thanks for this. I love having a coffee when I come out of the bath. It's luxury.'

I smiled. It's touching how little some people expect from life. And perhaps depressing how little most people get. Not necessarily the same people, either, which is where the problems start.

'And I've got another favour to ask.'

Well, well. So much for philosophizing on the wantlessness of the poor.

'Ask away.'

'I was wondering . . . as it's late, and cold out, and my hair's wet – could I stay over tonight? On the sofa,' she added quickly, and blushed.

It didn't take long to decide I couldn't care less where she spent the night. But I made a real effort to focus on the question in an adult way.

'What about your nan and grandad?'

'They think I'm at Natalie's. I told them I was going there. And I still can if you don't want me to stay.'

I wondered if I was supposed to know who Natalie was. Maybe she'd figured in a lengthy teen saga that I hadn't been fully tuned into.

'But Natalie's got Darren round,' Julie went on, taking my hesitation for resistance. 'He's always there. Her mum lets him stay late. They can do anything. Even sometimes . . . well, anyway, I'd just be in the way, that's all.'

I gave up trying to remember who Natalie was and decided that all my adult focusing had taken me right back to where I started – she could sleep where she liked, it was nothing to me.

'Sure. Stay over. Take the bed if you like – I won't be using it.'

'How come?' It came out quickly. She started to blush again. 'I mean, are you sure I can stay?'

I nodded. She said thanks and then looked at me again, realizing she'd been on the wrong track. 'So what will you be doing?' she said, confident it wouldn't be the same as Darren and Natalie.

I didn't have a clear itinerary in my head. But it wasn't hard to guess at one. 'First, I'm going to drink some more of this whisky. Then I'm going to drink a lot more of this whisky. That should get me through the early part of the night. Then I'm going to go for a long walk in the hope that some punk tries it on, because beating the hell out of someone would feel just fine, and if he beats the hell out of me, I'll be too drunk to care. Chances are, neither will happen. So I'll just come back, climb all the stairs for the thousandth time, make myself a coffee and play some blues into the dawn. Low, so you won't hear it. That's what I'll be doing.'

About half-way through this little speech, Julie Ray noticed the single sheet of letter paper on the arm of the sofa. By the end of it, she'd more or less worked out what it said. I could see it in her face.

We watched each other for a while. I guess she was working out if there was anything she could say to make it better, and deciding there wasn't. That set me wondering why so many kids who weren't half as smart as her were going to do so much better in life.

After a while, she stood up and went into the kitchen. I heard her opening a cupboard and moving something – a glass dish or a baking tray, something that scraped and grated. She closed the cupboard more quietly and came back holding Fred. She had the sense not to switch him on, so there was no squeaking. She just sat down again, with her feet curled under her and Fred on her lap.

I felt the tears start to roll and tried to hold them back.

They came anyway. Julie Ray looked down and stroked Fred's head with one finger. I blinked hard and looked up at the ceiling, thought hard about whether it was a dirty cream colour or a really filthy white, decided I didn't care and that it was pathetic to pretend I did – even more pathetic than crying in front of a juvenile. I looked down, tried to control my breathing, make it steady, took deeper and deeper breaths and held them until I felt dizzy and waited for my eyes to clear. I couldn't wipe them because that would have been an admission that I was crying. But nothing worked. I still couldn't see much more than if I'd been swimming under-water.

I was scared that at any second, moved beyond endurance by the crack-up in front of her, Julie Ray would offer me Fred to cuddle. And worse, that I'd take him, because the thought of a battery-powered furball on my lap wasn't nearly as ridiculous as it should have been. I stood up and walked over to the window. The breeze was getting up. Lit from the side by Luther's patio light, the tree nearest the house was casting wavy shadows on the lawn. The branches were all out of synch, like a primary-school chorus line. Half-way down the garden, the silhouettes merged to black. I turned away from the window, saw the beat-box on the shelf, thought about putting in a cassette, but couldn't decide which one. I stared at it for a long time.

'Tom said once . . . ' My throat was clogged. I swallowed and started again. 'He said he was in a pub once and two guys at the bar were talking, and one said in this angry voice: "I mean, look what they've done to the blues." Tom thought it was funny – the perfect blues lament in itself. Like that joke about nostalgia isn't what it used to be.' I looked over at Julie Ray. She'd stopped stroking Fred, but was still holding him tight. 'Tom loved the blues. And he was just about to go over and say yeah, right on, there's never been anyone since Lady Day, when the guy who was speaking shakes his head, takes a long pull at his beer and says: "It's crazy. You're never going to play two–four–four and not let in goals.'"

The night went pretty much to plan, except that I'd forgotten how much I don't like whisky, so I gave up drinking and went out well before I was as drunk as I wanted to be. I told Julie Ray I wouldn't be back, or if I was I wouldn't be sleeping, but she wouldn't take the bed. I left her curled up on the sofa under an old blanket I'd taken from a long-haul flight at the end – the premature end – of my student days. Fred sat loyally on the floor, looking up at her.

She had her eyes closed when I left, but I don't think she was asleep. I closed the door quietly and padded down the stairs, remembering half-way that I'd come out without a jacket. I carried on. If you're going for a big knock-back-the-Scotch-and-head-out-into-the-night gesture, you don't make a fuss about keeping your chest warm.

All the same it was bloody cold the minute I was out the front door. I looked round and began to shiver, wishing I'd given the whisky more of a chance, or maybe skipped to stage three and curled up opposite Julie Ray with an all-night radio station on low. The more I thought about the warm flat I'd just left, the more I shivered. So I took a deep breath and started to run down the path: three quick strides and then a jump over the low front wall to the right of the gate. I was away, and the new plan was to keep running until I didn't feel cold any more. But it was too long since I'd run any distance and my lungs began to burn long before the rest of me warmed up. I pushed on anyway, because there was no plan B, and was pleased that after a while my lungs began to hurt a little less and the rest of me didn't feel cold any more. Then I began to relax. Out of habit, I kept to the darker side of the roads, drawn towards stretches where the streetlights were out, and away from shops whose safety lights stayed on the whole night. There weren't many of them. Most owners had worked out long ago it was worth paying the extra for shutters.

It was strange to be out in the night again, and that seemed funny when I thought about it – respectability was encroaching into my life like bindweed into an untended garden. I couldn't decide if it was any more welcome.

'You know,' Tom said softly, the evening he came round, 'I still think I made the right choice. I think crime is well underrated as a career. Even now, when it hasn't worked out for me, I think that. I really hate it when people assume only stupid and deprived people turn to crime.' He sighed and looked down at the glass of milk he was holding, but was never going to drink. 'And this latest thing – tough on crime and tough on the causes of crime. I mean . . . ' He shook his head in disbelief. 'What utter bollocks. You've only got to look at a police press conference to realize all they're capable of being tough on is the English language. Everyone knows the only danger to criminals comes from other criminals grassing them up. And as for the causes of crime . . . ' The sentence tailed off. I thought he'd finished, but he was just pausing for breath. 'Any crime worth the name is caused by people who don't want to work nine to five for peanuts, who don't want to be bullied by nonentities, who don't want the humour ground out of their lives, who don't want to be shackled to a shit-boring job for decades because they have to support a wife who wants a fitted kitchen and whiny kids who want new bicycles and maybe even a reasonable education and who do want to make enough money in a reasonably short space of time so they can fuck off somewhere decent where it doesn't rain all the time while they're still young enough to enjoy it.'

His voice had risen slightly during this litany. Then he closed his eyes and seemed to shrink back into his chair, as if he wanted to go to sleep. I couldn't look at him without a shudder. His skin was such a sick colour.

'My father was in Italy,' he said suddenly, only opening his eyes at the end of the sentence. His voice was quiet again. 'At the end of the war. Landed at Anzio, fought right the way up, the whole campaign, while his friends were shot up and blown apart around him. He was nineteen. And he never mentioned it, except once, when my mother went to stay with her sister after an operation. He started talking over dinner and he just kept going. And when he got to Monte Cassino, he started crying. Frank and I, we just sat there while our food went cold. It must have been two hours. Afterwards, we went and looked up all the names in a history book. Frank drew a map with lots of arrows. Dad never mentioned it again, and we never asked. But I can remember chunks of it word for word. And I kept thinking, when you've gone so near the edge and looked over, it must stay with you for ever, underpinning everything, putting it in perspective. I kept asking myself, where are you going to find that intensity these days and stay within the law?'

A cat chewing something disgusting in the gutter looked up and tensed as I pounded towards it, but judged correctly that I was in my own world and stayed put as I ran past. I eased up near the end of the road, where there was a complicated, well-lit and deserted junction. The traffic lights flicked robotically through their phases, looking both sinister and silly with no cars to control. I chose to veer right, after vaulting the railings on the central reservation in a way I'd never have tried if the street was packed with shoppers in case a trailing ankle flipped me into humiliation and the fracture clinic. But running through the night was OK – certainly something I'd try again in a couple of years – and by now I had a fair idea where I was going, though I wasn't ready to admit it or to work out what I was going to do when I got there.

A couple of hundred yards on, the stitch that most people associate with running cross-country at school, but which always reminds me of one particular time when I had to scramble over the fences of a whole street's worth of back gardens while overweight coppers desperately hammered on front doors and charged through French windows on to lawns I'd just left, started twisting into my left side. Back then I'd kept going, for obvious reasons, while the muscles in my chest tore like Velcro and astounded bookies halved the odds on me winning the Grand National with a horse on my back. This time, with no Patek Philippe watch and a clutch of stone-clogged rings in my pockets, I was happy to slow down and pay my dues at the pain barrier rather than crash through. I'd got what I wanted from the exercise – some heat and a bit of momentum – and at something like twenty to four in the morning, according to a clock above a jeweller's on an intersection, I wasn't in danger of being late for any meetings.

The cold set in surprisingly quickly once I'd slowed down to a walk – there was no one around to throw a blanket over my back and lead me to the winner's enclosure. I dug my hands into uncomfortable, hard-edged jeans pockets and thought about running again. But not for long. I kept going until I couldn't get any colder by stopping and then sat down on a brand new and unvandalized pavement bench facing a deceptively sharp corner where fresh road markings merged two lanes into one and a half plus a filter. It looked like a particularly inventive accident black spot to me. I could only admire the council's initiative in tackling two scourges of modern life: too many cars on the road and too many old people with nothing to do but watch traffic. Even around dawn, the few lonely vehicles which came round the bend – mostly vans – started veering around wildly as one lane disappeared from under their wheels and a bunch of arrows started pointing every which way, one of them straight at a no-entry sign. The more I studied it, the more it looked like the work of a sacked subcontractor with time on his hands and a sense of humour.

I was reluctant to move on, but a fine drizzle was just starting and I felt it would be too pathetic just to sit there and let the water slowly soak into my clothes. I remembered telling Tom something I'd read about Oscar Wilde sitting outside a closing café in Paris in the pouring rain (the waiter had piled up the rest of the chairs and wound back the awning) because he couldn't pay for the drinks he'd ordered to avoid going back to his squalid lodgings. I couldn't understand how someone that famous could be that poor.

Tom nodded thoughtfully. 'Frederic Boutet told that story. In 1899.'

Most of what I knew, Tom knew first. But he was always encouraging. 'Read and learn, Charlie,' he'd say. 'I want you to be a credit to our profession.'

Nervous that I was about to be handed a reading list with heavy initial emphasis on Plato, I pointed out that Wilde's reading and learning hadn't been enough to save him from a wretched end. Tom just shrugged. 'It happens to the best, it happens to the rest.'

I was always going to be one of the rest, but I wasn't going to sit in the rain. I started walking through what looked very much like a grey dawn towards a neon-lit filling station. I crossed the forecourt to the security grille and managed to buy a pint of yesterday's milk, which the attendant wasn't supposed to sell me for some reason he was incapable of explaining, and which got wedged in the scooped-out credit-card hatch when he finally decided it was slightly less than his job was worth, after all. But with a bit of co-ordinated tugging, I got the milk and he got the silver and no one lost their temper.

I found another bench a few hundred yards on and watched the picturesque Holloway Road slowly coming to life. First the contracted-out street sweepers, who obviously had an intriguing brief from the council to collect exactly one third of the rubbish, as long as it was stationary in bins and not awkwardly blowing about. Then the red-route runners, mostly trucks, cheerfully ignoring the grey speed cameras and treating the traffic lights as advisory only; the newsagents with their piles of papers brought in from the pavement and harsh striplights to wake themselves up; then a few early commuters, their jackets on hangers in the back of their cars, who either had to be in Birmingham by mid-morning or the City by the time some esoteric foreign futures market opened (the cars heading south were noticeably classier than those heading north. I daresay the jackets were, too, but they looked disappointingly similar); and finally a girl in a suede jacket over last night's little black number who hurried round a corner and then stood self-consciously at the bus stop, shifting from foot to foot in her evening shoes either with cold or embarrassment and looking around constantly for a taxi. She had dark, curly hair, large brown eyes and no make-up and was the sexiest sight I'd seen in a long while. Which was partly down to her and the fact that the little black number only just came down below the suede jacket, but mainly because here she was, at a bus stop in the very early morning, in last night's clothes, having stayed over somewhere certainly against her expectations, probably against her better judgement. I drank my milk from a surprisingly successful tear in the carton and imagined the other half of the picture – the guy still stretched out in a warm bed, pushing the snooze button on the alarm to give himself another ten minutes to remember some of the highlights of the previous few hours – while the girl made one last attempt to read the partly defaced bus timetable, gave up, looked round again for a cab and then started walking towards Highbury and the hot bath she was longing for. I was sorry she was going and wondered if I'd been in at the start of a romantic courtship which in time would lead to marriage, two boys and then a spoilt daughter and a move to Hertfordshire. It was a long shot. She'd left too early, in too much of a hurry, without ringing for a cab – and he hadn't driven her. It looked to me like she was already regretting the gymnastics she'd been put through during the night, and he was probably lying there not quite believing his luck. I finished my milk and tossed the carton into a newly emptied metal bin. It brought it all back. The feeling that some days – and nights – you just can't lose, everything rolls right, you end up with much more than you deserve and she ends up with a lot less clothes on and a sharp reminder how hard it is to find a cruising cab in the early morning. Sometimes it's good to be reminded, in the teeth of all these whole-some let's-be-open-and-work-through-it-together videos, that there's still a lot to be said for sex played as a zero-sum game.

Once the girl had gone, a lot of interest went out of the Holloway Road. I watched some more traffic go by, and a few more people, but they were a pretty down-market crowd and I couldn't believe they'd been up to anything the previous night. And if they had, I certainly didn't want to imagine it. So I moved on quickly, happier now that I had a stomach lined with milk and the sun was . . . well, not coming up exactly – you couldn't see it, or anything Mediterranean like that – but it must have been out there somewhere, because it wasn't dark any more. I'd covered a fair few miles, perhaps not with the relentless pounding rhythm of the toned triath-lete, but with a stop–go persistence that pleased me. It was too long since I'd stayed up and active through the night. If the slide had gone on much further, I'd have been sitting the first of my accountancy exams and buying a TV licence.

The last half-mile was uphill and slow going. I didn't want to admit there was no one else I knew here except my twin brother, and no reason for being here except to visit him. I could run through a whole month's course of Valium and still be wired when I met Alan, and there's not many people who can do that to me. Two, in fact, and with Opal it's for a slightly different reason.

I once tried to work out when I stopped hating Alan and started to be scared of him. Being hit harder, pound for pound, than I've ever been before or since definitely came into it. We must have been thirteen or fourteen. I can still see Alan sitting on the floor, taking apart the handset of a remote-control car that was definitely mine, but which I'd long ago half-broken and lost interest in. He was always messing with things, trying to fix them. This time, I told him to lay off my toys. All of them. For ever. He shrugged and tossed the handset at my feet, where it exploded into a tangle of unsoldered wiring, tiny screws and cheap circuit board. I swore at him and told him to fix it – right now. He asked how he was supposed to fix it if he couldn't touch any of my stuff ever again. Up to this point, I was feeling good. This had been coming for a while and I was ready. I was taller, heavier and with a longer reach, which I knew from watching fights on television was important. I could see myself landing the haymaker to the chin which would put the lights out. And if he got up, I'd dive at him and we'd be rolling over and over, western-style, kicking and punching, if not in the mud and the blood and the beer, then at least in the mess of broken toys, footballs and motorcycle magazines. No two ways about it, I was up for this one.

The action, when it came after the statutory insults and impossible-to-meet conditions for peace in our time, lasted around three seconds. I led with my famous atomic right, along an arc that took in most of the known universe. Alan tipped his head back a couple of inches, then stepped in and slammed his left fist just under my ribcage. I wondered what the hell he was doing and while I was staring at him, wide-eyed, our faces a few inches apart, he did it again – same hand, same side, same strength. Then he stepped back a pace and I made the mistake of trying to breathe and collapsed straight down like a dynamited building. I can remember the fear. I thought he'd killed me. There was no way I could imagine ever being able to breathe again. He turned away without a word and walked towards the door, leaving me mouthing desperate, pathetic and utterly silent pleas for help. He looked back briefly – a look of such rock-hard, terminal contempt that I gave up all thoughts of begging and just rolled my face down into the ugly patterned carpet and waited to die.

Well, you live and learn, and by the time I'd managed to get my knees under me, with my face still pressed into the carpet, drawing millimetric breaths through the pulped remains of my internal organs, I'd learned a lot about hooks to the body. And I can't pretend the lesson hasn't come in useful since. But thirteen is still pretty early for the definitive power struggle of kinship to be so comprehensively settled. And it really was. There was no way back. I don't think Alan ever hit me again. He didn't need to.

I'd started chewing on a nail as I walked up the hill. The block looked just the same from a distance. A rectangular slab which stood on bizarre, green stilt-pillars, with no ground floor and no conceivable reason why, given that it was comfortably above sea level and not in Bangladesh. Maybe the council had planned to put garages in, but had run out of poll tax. Maybe it was so children could tear around the acres of asphalt, kicking and throwing balls with impunity as long as they didn't try any lobs. The lace curtains in the windows were spectacularly pointless, given that the only opposite neighbour was a low-rise filling station whose cashier – even if consumed with a voyeuristic lust to know what the residents were watching on television – had his line of vision totally blocked by a massive green canopy.

As I approached and made for the gate, I realized a few things had changed. First of all, there was a gate to make for: a huge double-width, wrought-iron number, fixed open with a hook to the waist-high wall that went right round the block. That was new, too – it had replaced a fence. And the asphalt had been re-laid. I couldn't see any of the ankle-turning, axle-shuddering potholes. And there was no graffiti. That was a stunner. I looked round in disbelief. A quarter of a mile of new wall and not a single soccer team's acronym or a tag sign. I took another look at the block as I went through the gate. A lot of the paint looked new-ish. Unpleasant as ever – the green of the stilts was obviously going to be there until the Jurassic plates heaved along the King's Cross faultline and took everything down once and for all – but neither peeling nor flaking. There was no paint, old or new, on the windows, which were PVC-framed, but I couldn't remember if they'd always been like that. There was no litter. The overall impression was of a lot of work having gone into something that wasn't worth half of it. Which was easy for me to say, because I didn't live there. Why Alan did, God knows.

There were a few cars scattered over the site, several of them either being dismantled for parts or put together in stages from other cannibalized carcasses. Of the unviolated examples, a neat row of half a dozen stood out: shiny Fords gathered protectively round a silver Porsche whose number plate – 131 GAL – had been illegally calligraphized to read BIG AL. Just in case anyone doubted who the main man was around here.

I walked towards Big Al's car, which looked as if it had recently been valeted off its chassis, with the wheel treads vacuumed and the inside of the exhausts polished. Probably it had just been for its regular seven-hundred-yard service. I circled it once and then cupped one of my hands into a visor to peer through a side window. It was the usual story. Lots of padded pale hide with dark edging, penis-sized gear knob (presumably to create a pseudo-masturbatory environment, rather than a rampantly gay one) and a few tapes. I squinted harder to pick out the groups big brother was listening to these days, pressing my nose to the glass and leaning forward

– just about the worst position to suddenly hear the click of an Escort door opening and feel a sharp rush of air as it swings towards you.

I took most of the door's weight on the funny bone, just about the least amusing place you can stop a door, and lurched sideways. The guy leapt out, dodged the door as it came back at him, grabbed me by the shoulder with one hand, used the other to twist my battered arm most of the way up my back until I was virtually tickling my own neck and hissed: 'Don't even think about it, fuckface.'

I relaxed as much as I could. He seemed disappointed at the walkover and slammed my head down on the bonnet in a fit of pique.

'Know what happened to the last guy who tried to take this, dickhead?' I wasn't sure whether I was meant to answer or not. I stayed silent, waiting for my head to clear, gazing at the blurred reflection of a quarter of my face and my shirt collar in the bonnet. My arm was beginning to hurt. 'We drove him home.'

This not-too-frightening punchline was delivered with a hammy chuckle and a further wrench to my tendons. I waited for the explanation and wasn't, as they say, disappointed. 'We tied his wrists to the back bumper of my car and off we went. Both shoulders came out on the first corner and then he knocked himself into next week by not keeping his head up over the speed bumps, stupid bastard. And he's never been back to say sorry.'

This Bond-villain routine was beginning to get on my nerves. I hoped he didn't have a favourite back-catalogue of stories involving trap doors and sharks. I tried to get my breathing deeper and more even, feeling a twinge in my lower back where something was digging in. Presumably a spanner or wrench in his pocket, unless he'd taken an instant shine to me, which on the surface seemed unlikely, although people do have very different ways of showing affection. I was relieved when he pulled me back upright and started marching me towards the main gates.

'This is where we say goodbye, bum-wipe,' he said, clearly bored with his non-playmate. 'But it's a once-off. I see you around here again and I'll hurt you. Badly. So believe me – and tell your friends.'

He gave me a sharp shove with both hands and simultaneously hooked a foot round my ankles. I managed to turn away from the shoulder he'd messed up as I went down, taking most of my weight on my other forearm, which twisted awkwardly under me. Something about the last few hours was really making me feel my age.

'Get this straight,' he said, just when I thought I'd heard the last of his *Sweeney* audition-speech. 'I don't mind you coming back. I'm paid to deal with losers like you. You're the one who'll mind coming back. You really will.'

I took a good look at him for the first time, wondering whether he really thought I was so stupid he had to say everything three times, or whether he just loved saying it. His peroxide hair was slicked back and his cheekbones were disturbingly untainted by beard despite his night on guard in the car. He was wearing the obligatory white T-shirt under some expensive-looking but scuffed black leather. I was glad to see who I was dealing with, but it was a mistake to hang around in the dirt. He took a couple of steps forward. I saw the boot go back and managed to tense most of my muscles before it came thudding into my chest.

'I said fuck off – now,' he said, as I groaned and rolled away on to my stomach. I'd managed to get to my knees when I saw him coming in again.

'Wait,' I gasped, overplaying it a bit because the boot had come in too high and hadn't done any significant damage. 'I'm Alan Lucas's brother. I came to see him.'

'Brother?' The voice wavered between disbelief and anxiety. 'He's never said anything about a brother.'

I pulled myself on to my knees and coughed a couple of times. 'His twin. Gideon. Go ahead and ask him if you like.'

'Gideon?' The name swung it. A story this bizarre had to be true. True, but weird. 'You don't look like Alan,' he said defensively. 'And it's a fucking stupid time to come calling. Why didn't you say who you were?'

If you'd been less keen on beating me up and torturing me with B-movie dialogue, I might have had the chance, I thought tetchily, as I straightened up, cleared my throat and spat noisily on to the asphalt. He stepped back in distaste. I ran a quick check on the muscles and bones that had taken the brunt of our little encounter and came away cheered. A lot of small pains, no big ones. I started walking back towards the cars, slowly, watching my feet. My escort followed at a discreet and suspicious distance, which was no good to anyone.

When we were almost back level with the Porsche and my lungs had reinflated with fresh air – or as fresh as it came round these parts – I paused and leaned forward with my hands on my knees.

'Bats dance sad lines,' I muttered nonsensically at my feet.

'What?' he said, coming up behind and leaning forward to catch what I'd said. The non-damaged elbow I sent back and up caught him right on the bridge of his nose. His eyes skidded everywhere before his hands flew up to cover his face. He staggered a bit, but stayed blindly on his feet, which was perfect. I stepped back, balanced myself and sent my right boot through most of his left kneecap. The IRA use bullets, apparently, but you can do a lot with timing and the proper footwear. He pitched forward and down, but I grabbed him by the collar before he could crumple, turned him round while the adrenalin was still pumping and drove his head, with a fistful of hair in my right hand, through the nearside window of the Porsche, which exploded gratifyingly into life with the alarm shrieking and the hazards flashing gaudily in the grey dawn.

Sunny boy was down on his knees – one of them, anyway – with his head in the car, not moving much. But his body felt too tense for him to be out cold. Presumably he was being sensible and having a think. I shoved him a bit further in, so the top of his chest rather than his neck was resting on the broken glass of the window. Over the years, I've become a bit of a specialist in heads through glass – force of circumstance, I reckon, though Tom claimed to see something more in it – and I know you can get in a lot of trouble if you don't stick to the rules. Kevin was a case in point. It was true what I'd told Bernie, that he'd left most of his tongue behind. But that was because I'd helped him back through a window that was already broken, and you have to really dislike someone to do that.

I walked briskly away from the screaming car, noticing a few more lights coming on in the flats and some shadowy faces peering out from behind curtains. The surge of energy was seeping away like water into desert sand and I was feeling more and more like someone who's walked all through the night and then been beaten up. And I was suddenly cold. It was a relief to make it to the black door that looked as if it led to a dustbin cupboard but was in fact the main entrance to all the flats. Inside, the asphalt gave way to stone, which if anything made me feel colder, and the walls had abandoned the insipid green of the pillars in favour of arctic blue. I could smell bleach. The whole place felt like the big, crumbling primary school Alan and I had both been sent to. Which can't have been the attraction for him, because he'd hated it and managed to get himself expelled while I was still keeping my options open, largely because I enjoyed playing in goal for the under-11s.

There were two lifts this end of the block, neither with an 'out of order' sign and both looking infinitely preferable to the stone steps and metal banisters. I pushed the up button and one of the lifts opened immediately. That was the good news. The bad was that inside, the top half of the lift was mirrored, and the glass wasn't tinted or broken. I took a quick look and winced. I'd always wanted to be chauffeured over to Alan's in my Bentley, straight from a short restorative stay at Champney's. Instead, I looked as if I'd been dragged backwards all the way from the lions' enclosure at London Zoo by one of the more fastidious members of the pride who objected to me cluttering up an area already mane-deep in schizophrenic care-in-the-community patients.

I pushed eight and the lift ground slowly into action. It felt like a couple of guys in the next shaft were having to pull like hell on the counterweight. The lights flashed slowly on and off, like a counting aid for retards, as the tin box bucked and shuddered. Normally I'm OK in lifts – certainly a lot happier than when I'm hauling myself up the stairs – but this one was beginning to spook me. I tugged gently and rhythmically at my earring, wondering if Alan had rewired the whole shooting match just to unnerve his visitors. It was his sort of humour. I'd done pretty well at not thinking too much about him over the past quarter of an hour, what with one thing and another, but time was running out. I let go of my earring and unwisely tried to square my shoulders, jerking taut the trapped nerves in my left one and exploding a cluster bomb of pain in my head. As the lift doors opened straight into Alan's flat, I had tears in my eyes for what seemed the twentieth time that day.

Eleven

'Well, well – little brother.'

By something like two hours, but it was enough for Alan. I stepped out of the lift and the doors closed behind me. Alan aimed some sort of handset over my shoulder.

'Kids,' he explained, 'come up here as a dare.'

And now, presumably, the doors on floor eight were resealed against unwelcome visitors. Or at least unrecognized ones. I didn't want to make extravagant assumptions.

'How did you know it was me?' I hadn't noticed any closed-circuit cameras. Perhaps they were behind the mirror in the lift.

'I saw you from the balcony,' Alan said. 'I thought I'd stroll out to see who was using my car as a doorbell. And Sean as a doorknocker. I hope you weren't too hard on him.'

I didn't want to be drawn down that particular avenue, so I took a slow look around. The flat was huge and open-plan: two or three flats knocked into one, plus the hallway, which the lift opened into. It was like a warehouse conversion, except with low ceilings, no river views, no warm colours, no interesting ethnic wallhangings, no trendy gallery or spiral staircase, nothing, in fact, to indicate any normal human being took the slightest pleasure in living there. The floor was linotiled in black. The kitchen area at the end of the room was spartan to a degree that would have had even a Spartan begging for something split-level. The two sofas and one upright chair becalmed in the middle of the oceanic floor-space looked skip-salvaged. The three doors leading off to the bathroom and two bedrooms were made from the world's thinnest plywood, about the strength of a cereal packet but without the interesting text or tempting offers.

The only two signs of wealth – or even of subsistence – were a computer, with some colourful graphics spooling away incessantly across the screen, and a sound system that was so upmarket it didn't have its name on any of the components. The speakers were on stands and looked as if they'd been carefully positioned to serve the longer of the decaying twin sofas.

I suppose there was a third sign of wealth – the dressing gown Alan was wearing. A rich blue, with golden dragons capering about foolishly in a jungle setting. It looked exquisitely detailed and not very warm.

'Since when have you been able to drive?' I said. There were no L-plates on the Porsche.

'Since never. It's a toy for the boys.'

Ah, yes. Alan and his boys. As motley a collection of pretties and toughs as you're ever likely to run up against. I used to think he slept with them – the pretties, anyway – but then I changed my mind. He wasn't one to rack up debts.

'Nice present,' I said, as neutrally as I could.

Alan shrugged. 'It's useful to get lifts everywhere. There's always someone around who wants to drive it. I can't see the attraction myself, but you can bet someone's on the phone right now to his mate who runs a windscreen replacement call-out, and someone else is desperately hauling Sean off the seats and pouring on gallons of upholstery cleaner. They'll be devastated if there are any stains.'

I still wasn't keen to engage in Sean-talk. 'And how long have you been calling yourself Big Al?'

He smiled and moved away towards what passed for the open-plan kitchen. 'I'm going to have some hot chocolate.

Steve will be bringing croissants, but we're a bit early for him. D'you want a cup?'

I nodded and watched him pour two mugfuls of milk into a tin pan, which he put on the front ring of a dilapidated electric cooker. The knob for the ring had gone, but there was a pair of pliers on top of the grill which he reached for automatically to turn the spindle.

'I can't say it's really me,' he said. 'The boys made it up as a present.'

'What d'you mean, "made it up"?'

Alan yawned and pulled a tin of drinking chocolate out of a wall cupboard with no door. 'What's the fine for having an incorrectly registered car?' he asked rhetorically, before remembering who he was talking to and leaving a polite pause just in case I'd been done for it recently. 'Whatever it is, it'll be a lot less than buying one of those stupid plates and keeping it on a moped or whatever you have to do while the transfer goes through.'

I'd tracked over towards the kitchen, keeping the distance between us constant so I didn't have to shout. Nothing much seemed to be happening on the hot chocolate front, pliers notwithstanding, and I'd developed my opening conversational gambit just about as far as it would go, so there wasn't much to do except stand and watch. Alan still struck me as basically a neater version of myself. Slightly shorter, smoother featured, better haircut, no earring, good clothes. Everything under control. Brighter and better mannered, of course, but there wasn't much there in the way of raw excitement, I always felt. Also, he was a supercilious son-ofabitch.

'I should go and sit down,' he said, clearly feeling crowded now that I'd closed to within ten feet of him. 'This cooker's slow – you won't be getting your drink for a while. Put some music on if you like.'

Agh. Christ. What an invitation. 'I'd rather go down and

reglaze your car window. Last time, you treated me to an hour of Slaughter and the Dogs, plus the same again from some unbelievably crap group with an equally stupid name. Rocket Up Your Arse, or something.'

Alan pursed his lips. 'Rocket from the Tombs,' he said humourlessly. 'But you can relax. My campaigning days are over. The reel-to-reel's gone. Most of the CDs are no more radical than John Coltrane.'

I hadn't noticed the tape machine was missing. It was a good sign. 'So you've finally given up on all that stuff?'

Alan shook his head disbelievingly. 'You can never give up on all that stuff,' he said mystically. 'And if it gives up on you, your soul's on ice. But the collection was getting out of control, and while it was around here there was always the risk something would get damaged. So I moved all the tapes to an air-conditioned vault in one of the banks I work for. Payment in kind. It's all stacked up with the foreign currency and the bonds. I love going to see it. The best collection of bootleg punk there'll ever be, remastered and perfect, just waiting there like a timebomb in the heart of the City. Isn't that brilliant?'

The symbolism was lost on me. A bunch of tapes that no one would ever listen to and a pile of money that no one would ever spend. But as long as the tapes weren't anywhere near me, I wasn't complaining. I walked over to the sound system and took my time about picking a CD from an untidy pile on the floor. In the end I went for Handel's *Sinfonia*, hoping to God it wasn't the name of yet another bunch of punk losers who justifiably never made it. The system itself was the next problem. Nothing as crude as a button or lettering – just a few touch sensors, discernible only because they were a slightly darker shade of jet black, sprinkled at random over numerous black boxes. I touched everything I could, in true teenage style, and figured it out eventually, but a blind man could have learned braille faster.

When the sound came on, though, even I could tell it was er, full. Round. Whatever. And I was pleased with my choice – no nasty surprises. Back in the tape days, I'd once picked out something called Flowers of Romance, thinking it was some godawful K-Tel love compilation but desperate for something that didn't have shrieking and gobbing all over it, only to learn the hard way – the very hard way – that the Flowers of Romance were Sid Vicious and his mates before he defected to the Pistols, carved up Nancy Spungen and overdosed on heroin thoughtfully provided by his mother.

'D'you actually like punk – the music?' I settled down on one of the ratbag sofas, which was surprisingly comfortable, and wondered why I'd never asked before. Probably because it was almost unheard of for Alan and I to spend so many consecutive minutes in each other's company without scrapping.

'I don't listen to the music,' Alan said. 'I listen to the sound of a society being beaten up. That's the real pleasure.'

Maybe I'd changed, I decided. When Alan used to say things like that, I used to call him a pretentious wanker and walk off. Now I liked to think I'd evolved a more sophisticated style of argument.

'You're a pretentious wanker,' I said, staying exactly where I was. 'Punk achieved nothing and you know it.'

Alan looked up from the non-boiling milk, clearly amazed by my new-found cogency. 'Then why this desperate revisionism? Why is it constantly being rammed down our throats that the eighties were these appalling years of greed, when it's obvious to anyone with a brain that every decade since the dawn of humanity has been a decade of greed and the only difference with the eighties was that the wrong people were being greedy? And lucky. Don't forget, Charlie, I was there. I saw it from the inside. I saw broking houses who only ever took from Oxbridge advertising for traders in the *Sun* and getting boys who were so wide they could scarcely squeeze through the door. Their manners were atrocious and they never got invited down to the country at the weekend, but boy, could they deal. And then came the good part. Instead of setting up trust funds for their kids' education, or buying a couple of dozen more acres for the estate from the farmer next door who was going under, they spent it. Unbelievable. They roared around in Porsches, they rammed twenties down waitresses' cleavages, they bought their mums ridiculous and unsuitable furs. They spread it around, had a blast, kept others employed. Keynes said in the long run we're all dead, and these guys believed it. No wonder the tightwads are panicking to get the lid back on, but it's not going to happen. The eighties blew it all apart, and it was punk in the late seventies that lit the fuse. And we knew it then, Charlie, we really did. That was the beauty. From the day they rigged the charts to make Rod Stewart number one for the Queen's jubilee rather than the Pistols' 'God Save The Queen', we knew we had 'em. They were history. All we're waiting for now is the funeral.'

The last word thudded heavily into my brain, wiping out the sense of the preceding speech, which I'd heard plenty of times anyway, and reminding me why I was there.

'I've come for the money,' I said, shifting the gear of the conversation smoothly from fifth to reverse.

Alan's face hardened when he realized I wasn't up for a rap with him on the state of the nation. 'So I figured,' he said flatly.

The second of the three doors off the main room opened and a tall, sleepy guy in a blue tracksuit ambled out, yawning. He looked at me with vague curiosity. I looked back with astonishment. I don't know why – he just wasn't what I was expecting.

'Put the kettle on, would you, Al?' he said in a strong Australian accent, then came over and slumped on the other sofa. 'I'm Bruce, believe it or not. Have you come to fix the

145

car window? Sounded like a bloody riot out there this morning.'

'Yeah,' I said, referring to the riot. Over by the counter, Alan moved decisively to avoid electric overload by taking the milk pan off the ring and replacing it with a World War II Desert Rats canteen kettle. He took his time about making the two mugs of chocolate, stirring until I felt dizzy.

'This is Gideon,' he said eventually, tossing the teaspoon into a freestanding sink on metal legs. 'My twin. Who caused the riot in the first place by throwing Sean into the Porsche.'

'No kidding?' Bruce said, showing some surprise of his own. 'You never mentioned a brother. Certainly not Gideon the twin.' A thought struck him. 'Hey, you're not called Aloysius, or something, are you? You haven't just adopted Al as a demotic housing-association pseudonym?'

Alan almost smiled as he brought over my hot chocolate. 'One of only two things I've ever been grateful to him for. That I was just Alan and he was Gideon Charles.' He handed over the mug and then headed back towards the cooker, carefully avoiding the problem of which of us to sit next to.

'You know,' Bruce said, 'I think I'd be tempted to try to trace my mother just to ask her what her policy was on names.'

There was a limit to what even Bruce could get away with. Alan stood with his back to us, staring at the kettle. I sipped edgily at my hot chocolate, which was almost warm.

'We figured she's probably not much older than we are,' I said, when the silence grew uncomfortable. 'Though we couldn't decide what drugs she was on. Most people call me Charlie, by the way.'

'Smart move,' Bruce said, watching Alan, trying to calculate the damage. 'So what happened between you and Sean, if you don't mind me asking?'

I tried to think of a reply out of Sean's little book of James Bond dialogue, but gave up and just said: 'Oh, you know . . . the usual.'

Bruce seemed to find this funny. 'Not that usual, mate. It's some time since I've been up at this hour.' He'd obviously decided to let Alan sulk for a while, so turned his attention on me. 'What's with you guys, anyway? How come you never see each other?'

His style was direct and uncomplicatedly amiable. And he looked like someone I'd once been in a shirt advertisement with. But he didn't have the preening narcissism that had caused shirt-man and me a few problems during the shoot.

I glanced over at Alan, who was having nothing to do with any line of conversation that eschewed modern social history in favour of rather more personal reminiscence. 'Well, I guess we never liked each other much.'

Which was true. We were never the twins who huddled together talking a made-up language of our own and not mixing. And the more the social workers fell over themselves to write reports stressing how vital it was that we be fostered together, the less we liked each other. After a while, it became something between a habit and a pose. The twins at war. We both traded off it to some effect.

'And isn't that one of the good things about growing up – you can see a lot less of people you really don't want to see at all?'

It came out harder than I'd meant, but it was interesting to see Bruce's distaste for the idea of anyone not wanting to see Alan. 'So why are you here now?' he said, with no warmth at all. And that wasn't an easy question to field. I could have done with a couple of clarifiers – what's the deal between you two and how much do you know would both have been useful at this point – before I could commit to a full answer with any confidence. So I sipped my drink, which was pumping some welcome sugar back into the system after my night on the move, and ran through a few replies in my head.

'He's come for the money,' Alan said, when I'd just decided

to say I was at a rave round the corner and it was a spur of the moment thing.

'What money?' Bruce said.

'The money I gave you four years ago,' Alan said, bringing a slight frown to Bruce's face and almost making me throw up. 'The error account.'

'The error account?' Bruce was still some way off the pace, but catching up. I hadn't even reached the stadium. 'You never told me that was your brother's money.'

'How could I? I never told you I had a brother.'

This tidy piece of logic left two out of the three of us less than happy. For Bruce, the issue was personal – how much is it legitimate to keep back in a relationship. For me, it was more practical – where the fuck was my money?

'Where the fu—?' I managed to say, before there was a loud ping and the light above the lift flashed red. Alan sighed and reached into his dressing-gown pocket for the remote control. It didn't work first time, so he had to take a couple of steps away from the cooker and towards the lift, abandoning the kettle at one of the many non-crucial points of its boiling cycle.

The guy who came through the doors was wearing grey and white leathers and motorcycle boots, had carefully-highlighted auburn hair to his shoulders, and as much spare flesh on him as a bulimic whippet. There was a hint of eyeliner, the same grey as the leathers, under baby blue eyes.

'Croissant time,' he said cheerfully, tossing a white paper bag over Bruce's sofa to Alan. He shot me a quick look, obviously deciding both that I was responsible for the bizarre music and that it would take more than eyeliner to turn me into a prospect. 'Thirteen minutes – fastest yet. Amazing what new tyres can do.'

I was all for joining in a bike conversation, but I couldn't shake off the panic enough to say anything that made sense.

'So thanks for those,' Steve concluded politely, drawing a

cursory nod from Alan. 'And Mum says your plumber fixed both radiators and even serviced the boiler. She'd come up and tell you about it herself, only her knee's bad.'

'Well, who wants a croissant?' Alan said, keen to move the conversation on from the topic of his own largesse.

Steve looked uncertainly around and did some simple and dispiriting arithmetic. 'Ah, I've got to go. Pick-up at Heathrow,' he said sadly.

'OK,' Alan said, bending down to pick up three plates from a pile on the floor to the left of the sink. He put one huge croissant on each and brought two over to Bruce and me. Steve averted his eyes. I consoled myself with the thought that I was doing him a favour. All those calories.

'By the way, Rob thinks he might have tracked down another tape for you,' Steve said, backing towards the lift. 'He ran into this Yank at the Fridge who used to be a floor manager at CBGBs. Or the Bowery. I can't remember – one of the two. Anyway, he was bootlegging Richard Hell and the Voidoids the night the cops launched a drugs raid. The punters thought it was part of the act and started pogoing around and gobbing at New York's finest. The band kept playing. Apparently it's worth a listen.'

Alan allowed himself a faint smile of anticipation. 'How much does he want for it?'

Steve shrugged as he reached the lift and pressed the down button. 'Dunno. He's heard of you unfortunately, so that'll push the price up. I suppose you could always send Sean over to lean.'

Alan and Bruce exchanged glances. I munched through my croissant and kept my head down.

'No, that's OK,' Alan said. 'If it's a good tape, I'll pay. Tell Rob he can go ahead and negotiate. Usual terms. And tell the mastermixers there may be something on the way.'

The lift pinged, the light above it flashed and this time the doors opened without Alan having to wave his magic wand.

'Later,' Steve said, stepping in with a last backward glance at me. Perhaps he was torturing himself with regret that we hadn't been introduced. But I expect he was just hungry.

Bruce gave a lazy wave. Alan had turned his back and was heading back to resume his kettle vigil. I had my mouth full of croissant. It wasn't perhaps the send-off Steve deserved. When the lift doors had closed, Bruce looked over at Alan and smiled. 'Happy, now?'

It was a strange question for Alan, and an alarming one for me. I'd never known Alan happy. Nor had I ever met anyone who cared whether he was or not. And I'd certainly never met anyone who could make him happy. Or even wanted to try. The possibility that I'd strayed into a tableau of domestic harmony played havoc with my composure. I started stroking my earring.

'About what?' Alan said tetchily, raising my hopes again.

Bruce wasn't in the least perturbed. 'Richard Yell and the Haemorrhoids, of course. Live at The Granary or BCCIs. Mmm, can't wait to hear that one, Al. Matter of fact, I was probably there. I never liked to miss one of Dick's gigs when I was making the SoHo scene.'

The muscles of mine that weren't already stiff from damage tensed convulsively. I waited for Alan to whirl round, hurl the kettle of boiling water into Bruce's face, vault the rickety formica-topped unit, take two huge strides over to the sofa, grab him by the throat and hiss into his face that if he ever felt the urge to be funny again, he should remember the pain now and think twice. But I'd overlooked a crucial detail. Bruce wasn't Alan's twin. So Alan just smiled. Properly. Using almost all the muscles normal people use when they smile.

'Voidoids,' he said. 'Richard Hell and the Voidoids. Go ahead and mock, but history's on my side.'

He took the kettle off the ring and busied around making Bruce an instant coffee. 'And to answer your question, no, I'm not thrilled at the prospect of paying over the odds for an import, however amusing. I prefer the homegrown stuff. We did start this gig, after all.'

'It could have gone the other way,' I chipped in knowledgeably. 'Charles Manson auditioned for The Monkees.'

Alan took the news in his stride. 'What might have been,' he mused softly.

What indeed. The Beatles were great because of the friction between Lennon and McCartney. The Stones still have Jagger and Richards in and out of love. Manson and the Monkees would surely have pushed creative tension into the next galaxy. Dante goes Eurovision.

'Are you going in today?' Alan said, bringing Bruce's coffee over and settling safely in the single chair. He hadn't touched his croissant.

Bruce shook his head. 'Working from home. Restructuring. Arbitrage department's a joke. It's easier to stay away from it, so you don't have the useless fuckers you're going to sack peering over your shoulder and seeing themselves described as useless fuckers who are going to be sacked. Nor do you get the ones who can actually count beyond their fingers and toes hovering around asking complicated questions to which they already know the answers just to get across the message that they know what they're talking about. But most of all, you don't get an unutterable wanker like Henry, who's the nominal head of section even though the only numbers he knows have Ms and Cs and Vs in them and relate to the number of phalanxes Scipio Alexander was able to deploy at Thermopylae – you don't have him dripping round uselessly asking if you've seen *The Glory of Venice* at the Royal Academy.'

'Hmmm,' Alan said, having got slightly more than he bargained for in answer to a simple question. He probably just wanted to know how many slices of pizza to take out of the freezer for lunch.

'And you know who's to blame?' Bruce thundered on like a

runaway train. 'Those cretins in personnel, looking for rounded personalities. I must have sent 'em a dozen memos explaining that all we're interested in is motivation and ability. I've even told them exactly how to recruit. Call the applicants in at six on a Sunday morning, make them write eighty lines of program before you give them a coffee and then make them play three hours of poker with their own money. Then as they're walking out the door, ask them if they've been to a play, art gallery or concert in the last three weeks and if anyone even mentions the Priestley revival or the re-hung Tate, you've saved yourself the bother of even looking at their program. It's so easy. But instead, personnel invite them in on a Friday afternoon, with the chairman sitting in, of course, because he likes an easy end to the week, and they completely waste two hours asking them what they think their greatest achievement has been so far and how exactly their VSO experience welding septic tanks in Kenya has helped them towards a more compassionate world view. Then they hire them. Then they remember they're a finance house, not a merchant bank, after all, and get me to fire them. And so it goes on . . . '

So Bruce went on, whether to Alan or to me, I wasn't sure. I was getting the drift, but it wasn't my world. The poker I could maybe cope with, maybe even enjoy, depending on whether it was draw or stud. But somewhere in my flat I did have the *Just One Cornetto Guide to Venice*, which had come free with five gallons of petrol in those fleeting days when my car still worked. And my maths wasn't really there. I'd feel embarrassed being the only arbitrageur still using Venn diagrams.

'So, are you two in the same line of work?' I was pleased with my question, which was both intelligible and concise. And more controlled than the one I really wanted to ask, namely: Where the fuck's my money?

'Sort of,' Bruce said.

'Not really,' Alan said.

'Well, OK. I write the programs, when I'm not being asked to sack people because blunt Aussies do it so much better. Alan keeps them clean.' Bruce was a born conciliator. 'I like to think I'm doing all the exciting attacking stuff and Al's keeping it tight at the back. What d'you reckon?'

The question was directed with a smile to Alan, who never even came close to answering it. He was watching me coldly.

'Why now?' he said. 'A year early.'

'Change of plan,' I said, lying out of habit. But it seemed more than usually pointless. 'He died,' I said, and shrugged when I couldn't think of anything else to add.

'Who did?' Bruce said.

Alan was taken aback for once. 'Charlie's . . . co-investor,' he said finally.

'Oh,' Bruce said, and the three of us sat in silence for a while.

'So I've decided to take the money now,' I prompted, when neither of them had actually started stuffing fivers into my hand.

Alan looked over at Bruce, who nodded. 'OK,' Alan said. 'We can arrange a transfer. Just give us an account number and a couple of days.'

'Cash,' I said.

There was another pause, less reverent because it had nothing to do with the dead. Alan cleared his throat.

'Look . . . um . . . Charlie,' he said, and then had to take another run at it. 'Look – the money you gave us. It's like this . . . we're not giving you the same amount back.'

Right on cue, a huge cloud rolled over the pale morning sun, blocking out most of what little light made it through the grubby and undersized windows. The near-empty room felt ice-cold.

'What are you talking about?' I said softly, in shock, trying not to choke on the words. I don't know how it came out, because I couldn't hear above the thumping of blood in my temples. Probably not very well. Less Vincent Price, more Barbie doll on Prozac. I felt dog-tired. And I kept thinking about hot baths.

Alan shifted in his chair. 'Maybe Bruce should answer tha—'

'No!' I found the volume from somewhere, but not the control. 'This isn't a fucking press conference, Alan – you can't just say, Ah, yes, good question, if I may I'll bring in our head of arbitrage on that one. He's got nothing to do with it. I gave you a small fortune that belonged to me and Tom and now I want it back – and I haven't walked all night across London and been beaten up by one of your pretty-boy thugs just to be told I'm not going to get back what I gave you. So why don't you just tell me what the fuck you've done with it.'

I shuddered to a halt like a squeaking clockwork toy. The finger I'd been jabbing at Alan ended up in midair, trembling slightly. For a sickening moment I thought I was going to cry. Alan tented his fingers and watched me over the top of them. He waited until he was sure I'd finished and then said, very quietly: 'Quadrupled it.' Which, as one-liners go, was not bad at all, and certainly better than anything I'll ever deliver in my lifetime.

I brought my jabbing finger down to a controlled landing on my lap and waited for the strange pricking behind my eyes to go away. 'You're saying . . . you gave my money to your boyfriend so he could gamble it? Is that it?'

It was Bruce's turn to look uneasy. 'Yes and no,' he said helpfully. 'I didn't know it was your money.' He shot Alan a look which suggested they would have plenty of things to discuss after I'd gone.

'He told me five years,' Alan said calmly. 'I would have told you before then.' His tone made it clear that after I'd gone, he'd have better things to do than yak on about families. Through my own confusion, I felt a stab of sympathy for Bruce. Living with a control freak must send you right into orbit.

'Bruce shadow traded alongside a currency guy at work,' Alan explained briskly to me. 'Someone with a good reputation. Not that you needed more than twenty per cent vision in one eye to see the ERM shambles coming. Anyway, he made a lot of money for you and deserves some credit. I took a cut because we need new lifts in this block, and the playcentre roof is falling in. That leaves you with about four times what you gave me. If you leave it in another year, like you said you would, we can make you more.'

The questions were stacking up like baked beans in a supermarket, but I didn't have the energy to order them. So I just went for the last one that registered. 'What's all this about buying lifts with your own money? What are you talking about? Where's the council in all this?'

Alan was losing interest in the conversation fast, and not even the novelty of carrying it on with his brother could keep him from flagging. He stared vaguely at a patch of shot plaster somewhere over my right shoulder. 'The council's broke,' he snapped. 'What d'you expect them to say? They send an inspector round every couple of years to check the work's been done to at least twice the standard of their own teams, and then they go away and leave us alone. But it's not the ego trip you think. Most of the residents hate me. They think I deal drugs. It's the only way people round here can imagine anyone making any money. They've even drawn up a peitition and sent it to the housing department saying I should be evicted.'

This seemed to be balanced so finely on the outer edge of weird that I couldn't think of any comment to make. Except maybe something along the lines of why not shaft the fuckers then, which seemed basic common sense to me, but which doubtless missed the point of some complicated and masochistic salvation routine that he had going. Besides, I reckoned I had one more question before Alan gave up on the whole conversation and walked out. So this one I chose carefully.

'What would have happened if you'd lost the money?'

Alan abandoned his contemplation of the flaking plaster and sighed. 'Charlie,' he said, looking straight at me, or rather through me – and then he hesitated, as he had done a few times already, which was strange because if there was anyone who just said what he had to say and then shut up, it was Alan. He tried again. 'Whatever you did to get the money, I hope it makes you happy. Really. Looking at you, you need a break. And I'm sorry your friend died. But you've got to understand, it was no big deal for us. Most of the traders we know . . . well, if they got what you gave me as their annual bonus, they'd be faxing out their c.v.s the same afternoon. I know it's a lot of money – don't get me wrong. But not to everyone.' He was watching me closely now, to check the damage he was doing. What was eerie was that he was actually trying to avoid it. 'You were always going to get your money back, Charlie,' he said softly. 'We just wanted to help. So why not let us set up an account for you?'

I took stock of the damage to my ego, which was perhaps more containable than they both feared. Bruce was staring down at the faded lino with the intensity of a man who'd give at least half his annual salary, including bonus, not to be in the room. Handel's *Sinfonia* was still churning away. After the initial relief that it wasn't in fact Siouxie's first band, I hadn't listened to a single bar. Alan was studying the nails of his well-manicured hands.

I cleared my throat and they both looked up, which was unnerving. 'It's OK, Alan. I know it's a different world. I'm just happier in mine, all right? Where money comes in envelopes and bags. So whatever you've got for me, I want it in cash.'

This short speech left me nervous and out of breath. No one else said anything for a while. Alan and Bruce exchanged glances. Bruce gave the briefest of nods. Alan turned back towards me. 'Give us a week.'

That was my exit line. Alan stood up. The audience was over. But something hadn't been said. Not the easiest something, either.

'Um . . . ' I began, but quickly lost heart when I saw the expressions on their faces. They obviously thought I was going to start specifying currencies and serial numbers. I ploughed on bravely. 'Yeah, well, thanks.'

Alan was already half-way to his bedroom. He didn't bother to turn round, so I couldn't see if there was even a trace of a smile when he shrugged and said: 'One good turn . . . '

Twelve

The good turn I did Alan – the second of the two things he'd been grateful to me for over thirty-odd years, and the first wasn't exactly down to me – was an enjoyably strange experience. I could even have learned from it, if I'd understood what he was talking about.

I was drinking in the Pig in Hiding with Tom, who was obviously tiring of my conversation and had decided to start a fight by saying indefensible things at ninety decibels and making lots of eye contact.

'Useless sods,' he boomed, scouring the bar for any takers. 'It was one of their own managers – their own managers – who said "Football isn't a matter of life and death, it's more important than that." And God, didn't they laugh at his wit and quote it bloody endlessly on *Match of the Day* and *Question of Sport* and all that crap and then Hillsborough comes along, right on cue, to prove his point and what happens? They go all weepy, fall apart, stop buying their favourite paper just because it mentions pissing on corpses and start this ridiculous game of strewing flowers everywhere to make themselves feel better. And Shanks doesn't get a mention any more. The only joke he made in his life and no one thinks it's funny now, just because the Man Upstairs took him at his word.'

By this stage, I was looking around nervously, convinced that Tom's robust contempt for working-class culture might have strayed – OK, stampeded – across the line. If the scousers felt strongly enough about this to forgo their daily ration of newsprint tit, I couldn't see they'd think twice about taking a swing at us. And I wasn't in the mood.

'Someone's watching you,' Tom said, in a lower voice, looking over my shoulder. 'First, I thought it was me he fancied, but I'm beginning to lose heart. Been there half an hour easy. One drink.'

I had a think about who it could be, but didn't turn round.

'Dark hair, dark eyes, dark clothes,' Tom said helpfully. 'Pale skin. Almost pretty. You been swinging both ways recently, Charlie?'

Tom could be hard work when he was feeling boisterous. 'Too drunk to remember,' I muttered, concentrating on my beer.

'Well, think fast, because he's coming over. This could be interesting.'

I hoped he wasn't a militantly gay Liverpool supporter who'd lost his boyfriend in the crush. It made me uneasy, still having my back to him. I turned round just in time to see it was Alan walking over, nursing a powerful shot of Britvic 55.

'Who are you?' Tom said rudely.

Alan ignored him. 'I want to talk,' he murmured to me, before taking a final pull of fizz and putting his glass carefully down on one of the bar towels. 'Outside.'

It was an arresting overture. Alan never wanted to talk, full stop. And he especially never wanted to talk to me. 'All right,' I said. 'When I've finish—'

'Now.' He turned on his heels and walked out of the pub.

Tom watched him go, open-mouthed. 'Christ,' he said. 'His manners are worse than mine.'

I finished my own drink and dumped it on the bar. 'Sometimes,' I said, though overall I reckoned there wasn't much in it. 'I'll catch you later.'

Tom reacted badly to being left. 'What's that little creep

got that I haven't?' he whined loudly. Heads began to turn. 'Don't do this to me, Charlie.'

'Shut up,' I hissed. 'He's family.'

And with that bizarre turn of phrase (what family? Who was I kidding?) I followed Alan out into the street.

It was dark and raining, neither of which it had been when Tom and I went in. I turned up the collar of my rugby shirt – a gesture of more psychological than practical value – and dug my hands into my jeans pockets. I couldn't see Alan, so I just started walking, and sure enough, ten yards down the road, he stepped out of a doorway in front of me.

'You doing anything on Thursday?'

This was par for the course. No messing around with how have you been, what's new, I hear you got married, she pregnant or something? Over the years, I'd got used to it. And I could see the logic. If you don't care, why pretend?

'Thursday . . . ' I said thoughtfully.

'Day after tomorrow,' Alan said, clearly thinking my drug problem was way out of hand. 'Only I want to ask a favour. There's this guy I want to see, in a bank, only he won't take my calls and won't answer letters. I want to explain some stuff to him and I don't know how he'll react. It would be useful to have you along.'

We walked under a railway bridge. The clack of Alan's shoes on the wet pavement echoed sharply off the girders above us. 'You'd need to wear a suit,' he said. 'And get a haircut. And the earring would have to come out.' He sounded almost apologetic.

'Why won't this guy talk to you?'

Alan shrugged. 'No idea. His face looked tanned, but I couldn't tell if it was streetlighting or sunbed. 'Maybe he doesn't understand what I'm talking about. Maybe he understands but doesn't reckon to talk to people who haven't been through Eton and the Guards. Maybe we can find out.'

Eton and the Guards – a good name for a punk band, I thought, but decided not to share it with Alan.

'Why me?' I said, shivering because the rain was coming down harder. I turned left, heading for the high street and the bus stops, and Alan sighed and followed, obviously flagging after our lengthy conversation. I made a silent resolution: if he bothers to answer, I'll do it.

'I didn't want to ask a friend,' he said. 'In case it went wrong. They might say yes when they didn't want to do it and then lose their nerve. Turn out a mess. I don't need someone I like. I need someone I can trust.' He even sounded serious. Obviously the distinction was a big deal to him. 'And the way I see it . . . well, if you don't want to do it, you won't do it. But if you do, then I can trust you. Because if I can't trust my twin brother, I might as well pack up and go home.'

I was glad we hadn't reached the high street, and the side road was badly lit. I must have looked gormless as hell with my jaw hanging down and my eyes staring wide. But it was a stunner. I ran a quick mental check and decided that on a list of people I trusted, Alan came about thirty-fourth. On a list of people I'd ask favours from, fifty-ninth. The idea that, despite a lifetime of mutual antipathy, we were still irrevocably, mystically bound by our essential twinship was the wackiest theory this side of a UFO convention. I couldn't wait to tell Laura.

I turned left again into the high street, trying to rearrange my face into an appropriately grave expression before the permanent glare of the building society facias blew the whistle on my amazement. Alan was looking the other way, trying to spot a cab, which gave me a couple more valuable seconds.

'OK,' I said, as he curled two fingers into his mouth and produced a whistle that shook the reinforced glass of the shopfronts and sent crisp packets eddying down the pavements.

A few yards on, the cab drew level and pulled up to the kerb. Alan opened the door. 'Drop you?' he asked politely, slamming it quickly behind him.

'Pick me up Thursday,' I said, as the cab pulled away. I wasn't sure whether Alan had heard, but repeating it would have sounded too plaintive. Plus I'd have had to skip alongside the taxi as it gathered speed down the road, which is nobody's idea of cool. So I entrusted the message to Gemini telepathy and carried on with the business of walking up the high street in the rain.

Laura and I were living on the ground floor of the sort of block Alan still lives in. The lifts didn't work half the time, and that was a disaster, because you were constantly running into old dears with shopping who lived on the fourth floor, and if you didn't want to feel like a complete reptile you had to schlep up four flights and then all the way down again, whereas at least if you lived up there yourself you were heading in that direction anyway. The good thing about living on the ground floor was that I could leave my bike right outside and run a chain in through the window, if necessary attached to my wrist, which was just about the only way I found to make sure the bike was still there in the morning. The drawback was that the window had to stay open right through the winter, but as the heating never worked properly anyway, I couldn't believe it made that much difference. Laura didn't like it, though. Nor did she like the fact that she shared a name with the teen queen three flats along, who either slept around or more probably didn't, thereby inflaming the libidos of the block's mini-yobs, who were prompted to aerosol their torrid fantasies all over the available wall space. The contribution to the left of our front door – LAURA TAKES IT UP THE BUM – though both mild and succinct by comparison with their other excrescences, wasn't something she enjoyed coming home to at night. And she hated her aunt visiting.

That Thursday, I lay on our bed after she'd gone to work, vaguely annoyed with myself because I'd phoned in sick to the dairy after promising her I'd take a day's leave. The draught through the open window was chilling my newly exposed ears. Laura had loved the haircut, had run her hands through it a lot and whispered all sorts of promises which would have bent the graffiti artists right out of shape. She'd even delivered on a couple of them the night before, which had been great at the time, but left behind a feeling of unease. I wasn't ready for respectability yet.

I showered and spent longer than usual brushing my teeth, as I imagined bankers did. I also shaved more carefully. Taking the earring out left a tiny patch of pale skin on the lobe and a big emotional void. I felt naked and alone and kept having to stroke the ear to reassure myself it wasn't just a precious metal cross that held the disparate parts of my psyche together. I wrapped the earring carefully in a tissue and put it in a suit pocket, so I could slip it back in as soon as we cleared the building.

Alan arrived as I was tugging at my tie, trying to get the knot right. At least, I presumed it was him. A taxi drew up alongside my bike and the cabbie leaned on the horn. I started again with my tie, making fractional length adjustments to achieve the perfect drop. I was beginning to wonder how bankers ever made it to the office before lunchtime.

As a final touch, I dabbed on some aftershave. Then I picked up my keys, reluctantly unshackled the bike chain from the radiator so I could close the window, and, as usual, didn't bother to mortise-lock the front door: with any luck they'd burst in and ransack the flat, but leave the bike alone.

Alan actually opened the taxi door when he saw me coming. 'Nice suit,' he said, as I climbed in. 'You get married in that?'

I nodded, and that was our conversation over for the journey. Alan had an attaché case standing on the floor between his knees and kept flicking the handle from side to side and staring expressionlessly out of the window. I spent a lot of time watching the orange digits of the meter and listening for the remorseless little clicks, which weren't there any more and showed how long it was since I'd last taken a cab. The climbing total was pretty impressive. People I knew had bought cars for less – though not, admittedly, with MOTs. The cabbie had his partition closed, but I could hear his radio faintly as we surged and checked through the traffic. I was waiting for Alan to fill me in on the background, and beginning to realize he wasn't going to. Maybe, in the true spirit of punk, he'd decided that over-rehearsal would kill the power of our performance. I tugged gently at my naked earlobe, wondering what I'd let myself in for.

By the time we drew up outside a large, rectangular slab of building, with columns flanking two enormous revolving glass doors, the taxi's diesel rumble and cocooning shell had come to symbolize a world of sleepy safety and I was in no hurry to get out. I followed Alan reluctantly into the chill morning, and was taken aback when the cab pulled away sharply as soon as I closed the door.

'What's with him?' I said bemusedly.

'Account,' Alan said, squaring his shoulders and pulling his cuffs down half an inch under his jacket sleeves. Not wanting to let the side down, I did the same.

'Ready?' Alan said as he picked up his case.

For what, I wanted to know, but Alan was already half-way up the deep stone steps that led to the glass doors. I didn't catch up until we were both inside and he'd almost reached the reception desk, which was angled at forty-five degrees in the centre of a vast marble-floored hall. Above us was a chandelier the size of a space shuttle, which had to be mainly for show because the rest of the planetarium-sized ceiling was pocked with recessed halogen spots. I tried to see how the chandelier was fixed. If the contractors had botched it, the world's biggest cluster bomb was just waiting to fall.

After a while, I decided that gawking at ceilings was probably non-U in the corporate finance world, so I tilted my head back down and tucked in behind Alan.

'Here to see John Harris, head of technical services,' Alan said to an old guy in uniform behind the great slab of desk. 'We're from Spinker Bull, solicitors.'

The uniform buttons reflected the halogen beams with a ferocity that caught me off guard. I blinked and looked away. It was no surprise there weren't any plants around. Presumably someone forgot to mist them one day, the security guy fell asleep, the reflected light sparked the tinder-dry palms into a forest fire and the activated sprinkler system stained the marble so badly that a whole new floor had to be imported from Italy.

'If you'd like to sign in, sir,' the old guy said, pushing over an ornate book with a biro resting cheaply in the centre, which Alan ignored. He reached into his jacket, pulled out a fountain pen and filled in the date, time of arrival, names of visitors, name of company and name of person to see in handwriting that put the three above him to shame. It was a nice touch.

The guard turned the book round, slowly copied our names on to two fluorescent badges and handed them over. 'Seventh floor, Mr Lucas,' he said to Alan. 'Lifts are straight ahead. I'll ring and say you're on your way.'

'Thanks.' Alan checked his watch and then spent ages aligning his badge with something only he could see on his lapel. 'He'll be mighty relieved to have these documents signed and delivered, I can tell you. Right up to the last minute, it looked like we weren't going to make it. Still, that's the way it goes, isn't it? When it comes down to the wire, everybody concentrates that little bit harder and suddenly, there's your deal. Human nature, I suppose. Brinkmanship and all that. Oh, well, once more unto the breach. Good, that's my badge sorted. We'll see you later, on our way out, I suppose.'

He smiled cheerily, picked up his case again and set off for the lifts, just as two suits came up behind us to check themselves in and queue for their fluorescent badges. Out of the corner of my eye I saw the security guard making a polite with-you-in-a-minute gesture as he picked up the phone and dialled.

'It didn't work,' I hissed to Alan. 'He's phoning.' I assumed that was what the chatty nonsense was about. And riveting it was, watching my brother battle to find the common touch. I was beginning to enjoy myself.

'He won't get through,' Alan said through his teeth. 'I've got someone ringing his secretary at twelve minutes past with a complicated question about an order that doesn't exist. It should give us enough time to reach her if we hurry. We were a bit ahead of schedule at the front desk.'

'Fucking hell,' I mumbled. A thought occurred to me, rather late in the day. 'We're not robbing this place, are we?'

Alan punched the lift call button and doors to the left of us sprang open immediately. 'In your dreams,' he said harshly. 'Now put that badge out of sight in your pocket.'

I did as I was told. The lift doors closed with a soft, pneumatic hiss. They're the real test of engineering quality, doors. Doors to anything – cars, kitchen units, lifts. It's always so obvious, the ones that close softly, click discreetly, fit properly, the Mercedes-type doors. These lift doors didn't suddenly lurch together and meet with a jarring crunch like opposing rugby front rows in a scrum, they sort of purred and nestled into each other like kittens going to sleep. A single lift in this place probably cost as much as a hospital scanner.

'Don't you think the world would be a better place,' I mused aloud, 'if all the money spent on banking went to hospitals and vice versa? If all the doctors and nurses got to whizz up and down in lifts like this, so they were always calm and could concentrate properly, and all the patients could enjoy comfortable chairs, deep carpets, good food and all the things that might actually help them get better – while all the bankers had to work in big, draughty, primitive out-buildings—'

'Shut up,' Alan said, as the lift doors opened into a plush lobby containing a portrait of a self-important, podgy man with a small, wet mouth staring down at us from a gilt frame. There were two sets of double doors, one at either end of the lobby, with a sign saying 'Reception' and an arrow pointing left. Alan went right. The doors were heavy wood, probably from a non-renewable if not already extinct rainforest, and took a fair bit of pushing. Again, they fitted beautifully. The floor we found ourselves on was vast and largely open-plan, with a few partitions for those who were getting there, and a row of separate, glassed-in offices for those who'd made it. That was all I had time to notice. Alan set a cracking pace towards the first secretarial work station, where a woman with improbably long nails was staring intently at a screen and clicking a mouse.

'John Harris's office?' Alan said.

She gave us a quick glance and then pointed with one of her extended nails. 'Straight down and it's the second of the big offices on the right.'

'Thanks,' Alan said, and we were off again, not exactly in an unseemly scramble, but a lot faster than I'd usually walk through an office. I like to dawdle and watch everybody work. But this time we covered the ground in purposeful strides, avoided eye contact and reached the appropriate work station, placed protectively outside a glassed-in office with grey blinds, while the secretary was still on the phone.

'Certainly, yes . . . yes, as I said, I'll definitely look into it.' She noticed us approaching and frowned. 'Yes, of course. But there's no record of it on the computer. I've called up the order log twice. It's possible it went through another depart-ment, but . . . I'm sorry? No, I really can't see there's any point in trying again until I've checked with accounts, and I'm afraid there are people waiting in the office, so you'll just have to leave it with—'

I heard the click from a couple of yards away. Her face registered disbelief and annoyance. 'Honestly,' she said sharply, then remembered we were there and replaced the receiver with self-conscious professionalism. 'Can I help you?' She was a largish woman in her forties, wearing big, jazzy glasses and giving the impression of being well on top of her job. Which was better news for Harris than for us. We could have done with a mini-skirted YTS bimbo.

'Morning,' Alan said briskly. 'Contracts for Mr Harris. From Spinker Bull.'

This was the second deal in as many minutes she knew nothing about, and she wasn't pleased. Harris was going to get an earful. But she wasn't going to break ranks in front of us.

'Thank you. If you'd like to leave them with me.'

Alan feigned a sort of embarrassed puzzlement. Not badly, either. I've seen plenty worse on TV.

'I'm afraid we need the signatures now. It's to go straight back – the Ingham contract that's been dragging on so long.'

I looked over the secretary's shoulder at her boss's office, but couldn't see much. He wasn't peeping through the blinds.

'Mr Harris is in a board meeting,' she said, checking her watch. 'It only started quarter of an hour ago and they never break before lunch.'

This was presented with considerable back-in-control satisfaction. She even folded her hands on the desk. I could feel Alan tense beside me, his eyes fixed-focus on the secretary's mug of black coffee, calculating the odds, which were shifting remorselessly against us. He was going to back off. I knew it.

'Look, lady.' My voice sounded rougher than Alan's. I told myself that was OK – you get some wide-ish business lawyers. 'We're not motorcycle couriers. We haven't got the leathers. And we're carrying the biggest confidential contract I've ever seen, let alone worked on, which is due to come into force at twelve Greenwich Mean Time, which two of our lawyers plus a secretary have been working through the night to tie up, and which still needs one person's signature after John Harris's. So why don't we all just take a walk down to the board meeting and have a quick word with him. It'll take about fifteen seconds once we're there and might just save his job. Yours and mine, too, if we're lucky.'

I was watching Alan out of the corner of my eye. He swallowed, but the ripple in his throat was the only detectable movement. The rest of him had turned to stone. The secretary was really having a bad morning. She drew breath to say something, then changed her mind and looked round at the familiar objects on her desk – pen tray, hole punch, dictaphone – and came to a decision. She jabbed the 'divert' button on her telephone console and stood up. 'You'd better wait here.'

She skirted the front of her desk and took off the way we'd come. I kicked Alan viciously in the shins to get him moving. He seemed to be in another world. The secretary looked over her shoulder once, when she realized we were following, and gave us the sort of look normally cast at mongrels who attach themselves romantically to dog-haters in a park. But she wasn't going to risk any confrontation and potential loss of authority in front of all those colleagues whose desks we were busying past.

'When we reach the boardroom, you're on your own,' I said quietly to Alan, who nodded and continued to stare straight ahead. We marched past the double doors we'd come through and the long-nailed secretary who'd given us directions, then took a right and quick left down heavily-carpeted, peach-walled corridors with uplighters and racing prints, then found ourselves closing fast on another huge set of double doors with 'Boardroom' gilded elaborately into the wood.

Harris's secretary took the last few steps on tiptoe and put her ear to the door, waiting for a break in the conversation to knock. I nodded to Alan, nearly leaving it too late because I didn't realize he was docilely waiting for a cue. He took a step forward just as she was raising her arm for a tentative knock, ducked in front of her to reach the handle of the right hand door and then pushed it firmly open.

'What on ear—' the secretary hissed indignantly, but I was right behind her, whispering 'shhhh' and pushing her sharply, with my hand in the small of her back, into the room.

If you like rooftops, the view from the glass wall opposite was interesting, but not spectacular. The room itself was a disappointment. More undistinguished art, a truly awful oil painting of the bank's logo complete with Latin motto (the archetypal commission from hell and the ultimate betrayal of art-school idealism), a socking great slab of table that would easily have taken Thor Heyerdahl wherever it was he was trying to prove the Vikings went first, and a large white-board, propped up on an easel, with 'BULLET POINTS' written across the top in blue marker. Underneath were the words 'AMALGAMATION CONCENTRATION' and 'PENETRAT' – it was sod's law for the surprised-looking suit with the felt tip that we'd burst in just as he was getting to write the dirty one.

He was late thirties, maybe gym-preserved early forties, and the baby of the bunch. The remaining nine men were all at least a decade and a half older. The senior man present, at the head of the table, looked as if he could give God a run for his money. To his left was – inevitably – a young woman taking minutes, the only person around with no memories of VE Day. This was good news from my point of view.

Alan walked calmly over to the whiteboard by the foot of the table, smiled neutrally at the suit doing the graffiti and said, 'Thanks very much,' as if he'd just been formally introduced and invited to take over the presentation. The suit hesitated and looked around him, only to find his colleagues all hesitating and looking around them, with the exception of the senior man, who hadn't quite got it together enough to realize there was anything to hesitate about.

Alan rested his attaché case on the table and clicked open the catches. 'Sit down,' he told the suit, in the voice that had wrecked ten years of my life. He was back in the game and that was more good news. I didn't fancy taking over the presentation from his notes.

'You, too,' I said, encouraging Harris's secretary further into the room with a purposeful shove. She glanced over her shoulder crossly, then, having made her point, scuttled over to the spare chair next to the minute-taker and sat down in a bustle of female solidarity. The suit was less malleable. Deeply pissed off at being robbed of his star turn, he glowered at Alan and then at me and stayed right where he was. I balanced on the balls of my feet, again waiting for a cue from Alan, who didn't look my way.

'I'll count to five,' he said, resting his hands gently on his briefcase. The blankness of his voice suggested he'd come loaded for bear. I was also impressed by the counting routine. Those four words spoken by a child would be cute. From an adult, less so.

'Sit down, David. Stay calm.' The voice came from one of the more awake suits, almost opposite me, who clearly thought he'd walked into a *Die Hard* movie. But it was a timely intervention. Our problem youngster, much happier now the orders were coming down a recognized chain of command, gave a final glower to show he was nobody's patsy and then walked a couple of yards back to his chair, which still left him the closest of the board to Alan. I didn't like that, but short of issuing a barrage of fussy instructions along the lines of everybody move up one and then you swap with him, which would play havoc with the aura of controlled menace which I presumed we were striving for, there wasn't much I could do about it. I consoled myself by walking round the table to a wall-mounted phone, taking the receiver off the hook and then pacing back to stand with my arms folded in front of the door. It was fun, strolling behind the suits, close enough to see the tension in the back of their necks. Not one of them turned round.

Alan cleared his throat. 'We're taking any other business a little early,' he said, surveying his audience. 'My name's Alan Lucas and I'm here because John Harris seems to have a problem with meeting or even talking to me.'

Heads swivelled. It was pretty clear who John Harris was. The guy in the metal-framed spectacles trying not to look flustered.

'It's basically a technical matter,' Alan went on, after a suitable pause to allow the embarrassment to build. 'But I'll keep it simple and hope it's of interest to everyone, because it certainly should be. At any rate, it'll only take a few minutes, and if you wouldn't mind' – he turned his attention to the woman with the shorthand pad – 'I'd appreciate it if you'd carry on minuting, because some people here might like to refer back.'

Puzzled glances were exchanged round the room. Introducing yourself and asking for a written record of your presentation wasn't conventional hostage-taking behaviour. The senior man's personal assistant, a bored-looking woman with bad skin and wispy blonde hair falling in two curves round her face, looked uncertainly at him for guidance or at least to check for signs of life. He gave the briefest of nods, which may or may not have been Parkinson's, and she returned her gaze to Alan, with what looked suspiciously like gratitude for livening up her day, then sat up straight with her pen poised. A couple of the suits, clearly thinking along attention-seeking-nutter lines, began to relax. One even allowed himself a quiet smile.

'I hope we can take all the conventional threats for

granted,' Alan said, and the smile rapidly vanished. 'I'd rather not waste my time going through them, if it's all the same to you. So let's just say that while I'm speaking, I expect your attention and respect. And my twin brother' – he gestured like an air steward pointing out the emergency exits over the wings – 'is here to make sure I get it.'

Heads swivelled back towards me as I stood like a bouncer in front of the panelled doors. Twins, I could see them thinking – one the brains and one the muscle. Cute.

'I'd like to start by asking if any of you have a doctorate in science?' Alan looked encouragingly round the room, but the faces were utterly blank. You'd have thought he'd just asked if anyone spoke Farsi. 'OK,' he said after a few seconds. There was a certain tautness around his mouth. 'Well, how many of you are science graduates or have M.Scs?'

Not an eyelid flickered. Alan's right hand clenched and unclenched under his crisp white cuff as he realized what he was up against and tried to recalculate. 'Could John Harris identify himself, please?'

The guy in the specs uttered a small, coughing sound, then cleared his throat and had another go at saying 'yes'. The second attempt was better, but not much.

'You're head of technical services and you don't have a science degree.' Alan was trying to stay calm, and it wasn't working. He was making me nervous, and I wasn't the only one. Even the senior man present had picked up on something, turning his rheumy eyes thoughtfully on his colleague.

'I have a diploma,' John Harris countered desperately. 'It's mainly . . . essentially a purchasing position.'

Alan stared at him in disbelief, seemed about to say something – How the fuck d'you know what you're purchasing? was the question that occurred to me – then changed his mind and looked down at the table, shaking his head more in anger than sorrow. Christ. Who'd be a teacher? He leaned forward, took a bottle of spring water and a plastic cup off one of three trays lined up down the middle of the table and poured out a generous cool-down measure.

'I think we'd better start again,' he said grimly. He drained his cup without taking his eyes off his audience and looked round for a bin. Drinking fizzy stuff straight down was another of his little gifts. I could never understand how he managed not to choke or belch. Probably the same freakish throat muscles that produced the sonic whistle.

The bin was in the corner of the room nearest him, but still fifteen feet away. It was the sort of corporate gamble that makes a Hanson or a Goldsmith. I would never have tried it, but Alan was sufficiently brave or pissed off not to care. He flicked the cup half over his shoulder without turning, so he was facing directly away when it dropped like a stone into the bin without even touching the sides.

'Right,' he said, sensing the collective sigh of reluctant admiration and looking to build some momentum. 'Let's try an easy one. Who can tell me what make of PCs you run your bank on?'

John Harris almost fainted with the relief of hearing a question he could answer. He pulled himself together as best he could and said 'IBM' in a reedy little voice. I found myself wondering how he ever came to be on the board. He had to be somebody's nephew, but given that he was so old himself, it was hard to imagine whose. Palmerston's, maybe.

'You do indeed,' Alan said. 'Whole place is crawling with them. OK, next question. Who can tell me how many sectors are on each IBM disk track?'

John Harris's winning streak went smack into the wall. No one else looked like picking up the bonus points either, which was predictable. Alan ploughed on. 'There are nine sectors on each track,' he informed the assembled board. 'And the first sector of the first track is called the boot sector. If your PC finds an executable code in the boot sector, it runs it. That's how it loads the operating system. OK?' He smiled at the woman taking minutes, who looked as if she was beginning to feel the pace. 'Now – the funny thing about your IBM disk track is that it actually has room for ten sectors, not nine. So I want you to imagine somebody comes along with a reformatted ten-sector disk. On nine of the sectors he's put what should be there, but on the tenth sector, which he's made into another boot sector, he puts a virus. What d'you think happens?'

I was beginning to get flashbacks to French lessons when we did the subjunctive. A lot of people in the room were hoping very hard they wouldn't be picked on to answer. All except one.

'It gets neutralized by our anti-virus program.'

This affectedly languid contribution came from the suit at the front who'd been so abruptly usurped at the whiteboard. His tone lacked respect, but Alan was grateful for any feedback going.

'Good,' he said. 'I was hoping someone would say that. And you're right, of course.'

David nodded, hearing nothing that surprised him. Alan raised a cautionary finger. 'But only half the time. Don't forget, two boot sectors, one from heaven, one from hell. You've got a fifty-fifty chance of loading the right one, so when you run the virus check program, you've only got a fifty-fifty chance that it will pick up on the nightmare. Because – and this is the point I'm really keen to leave you with – no virus-check program keeps looking once it's found the boot sector.' He looked round the class, trying to gauge the comprehension level, and I did the same. It wasn't a write-off. A couple of spectacular blanks, a few frowns, quite a bit of concentration. I was pleased to see some effort going in.

'What sort of virus are you talking about?'

The question came from a plump guy right in front of me with a shower of dandruff on his shoulders and a rich, deep voice that suggested he didn't care because he was one of the few people in the room who was there on ability.

'Could be anything,' Alan said, warming to his subject. 'The one I'm working on at the moment encrypts all your data, every single keystroke, then decrypts it so you have no idea anything's wrong. It's only when you roll your famous anti-virus program that you turn all your records to mush, because you depended totally on that virus and now you've gone and destroyed it.'

Alan made a chopping motion with his hand to illustrate destruction. He was beginning to relax. When he looked down the table for another question, it wasn't long in coming. John Harris had decided to launch a comeback.

'Why should we be so terrified of a virus that doesn't even work half the time?' he drawled bravely, his fingers knotted white in front of him on the table.

'That's exactly the type of virus you should be most afraid of,' Alan said shortly. 'Think about it. How much of a problem would Aids be if it killed everyone in forty-eight hours?'

Quite a big one for the person infected, I would have thought, but Alan was thinking macro.

'Aids would be history if it was lethal in two days. It's still around because it's actually hard to catch and takes years to kill you. The most successful viruses always work badly. That way, they get passed on to more people, animals, disks or whatever they're dependent on. You die slowly, you drag more people down with you. The virus lives on.'

Interesting analogy, given his orientation. But I still had the feeling he was on the side of the virus. Even without knowing his abysmal taste in music, he came across as someone who'd cheer when the walls came tumbling down. So I wasn't surprised by the line taken by the next contributor – only by his identity. It was the senior man present, speaking with some assurance from beyond the grave.

'Mr Lucas,' he said, as the room immediately stilled, 'interesting as this is, I'm afraid the constraints of time are remorseless and we have business to conduct. If I might hurry you to a conclusion of your presentation, are we to understand, off the record, of course,' – he raised a finger and his grateful assistant put down her pen and stretched the tendons of her right hand – 'that this is no more or less than a blackmail attempt and you are threatening to introduce one of your pet viruses into our computer network?'

Fair question, I thought, if somewhat ornately put. But Alan reacted badly.

'How stupid d'you think I am, Mr Barnes?' he snapped, taking another wild risk. By all means swot up on the chairman's name, but how did he know Barnes hadn't slipped a disk playing golf and asked his deputy Fred Smullins to chair the meeting?

'I assure you I—'

'Then why assume I'm gambling my freedom on some ridiculous criminal enterprise which would have the police hammering on my door before I'd even finished cutting out the right letters from the paper for the blackmail note? Why d'you think I'm wearing a suit and not a stocking over my head? How d'you think I even knew you had a board meeting this morning?'

You didn't, you lying hound, I thought crossly – and what's more you would have bolted if I hadn't been here.

The senior man waited until he was sure he wasn't going to be interrupted again. 'Suppose you tell us, Mr Lucas,' he said quietly.

When Alan spoke again, he had his voice back under control. He must have been feeling nervous about the whole thing to rile so easily. 'This isn't about blackmail, so you can keep minuting. Sure, your system's full of holes. Your accounts, your trading floors, your loans – from what I've been able to hack into so far, it's a bloody nightmare. But you'd be very lucky to find yourself up against a blackmailer, because at least you could buy them off. It's more likely to be someone you've made redundant going out with a bang, or a secretary whose boss has ditched her, or an idiot playing a practical joke he doesn't understand, or someone offered a lot of money to run a disk for ninety seconds – because that's all it takes, Mr Barnes. Ninety seconds of malice and it's lights out, game over for you boys.'

He pulled his attaché case upright on the table and rolled his thumbs over the combinations. I unfolded my arms and tried to remember my way back to the lifts.

'Before you go, Mr Lucas,' the senior man said, as I had my hand on the doorknob. 'One last question. If you were in our shoes, what would you do?'

Alan seemed to have lost interest. Stamina was never his strong suit. For a moment, I thought he'd given up altogether on his little stunt and wasn't going to answer.

'Well,' he said eventually. 'I suppose you've got three options.' I'm not sure he'd really thought about it from their side before. 'Do nothing – my brother and I walk out and you never see us again. And you may be lucky, you may not, but if you're not it won't be anything to do with me. I've lined up a couple more guest appearances at board meetings next week. I'm pretty confident someone, somewhere will realize how important this is to them before too long.'

Two more meetings. News to me. I hoped he was bluffing.

'You could of course get on to the police alleging trespass, impersonation, false imprisonment, hostage-taking or whatever else appeals to your sense of humour, in which case obviously I'd melt down your entire PC network and have a lot of fun doing it. Or you could see sense and realize that you badly need someone like me in the tent pissing out, if nothing else so you can get back to having your board meetings in peace. So on the off chance you're interested' – he pulled a card from his front suit pocket and flicked it on to the table, where it landed face up in front of John Harris, because when you're on a roll there's nothing you can't do –

'we're probably talking a four-month contract for bomb-proofing your system plus a monthly retainer, but it's negotiable.'

He nodded crisply at me, and I opened the door. He turned for a last look at the suits. 'Think it over,' he said. 'But don't leave it too long.'

Thirteen

Ramon's was quiet – just a couple of guys in clean overalls nursing beers, with a mobile phone on the table in front of them. What Jeff needed was a jukebox with a load of traffic-noise discs to back up claims of being in the van and on our way, but roadworks have jammed everything solid. You'd need different discs to be really safe. Some DJ on the radio the other day was having a chuckle about how someone had written to the BBC complaining that it was always the same cow you heard in *The Archers*, no matter whose farm you were meant to be on. The producer owned up and apologized, and presumably sent a team of sound engineers down to Dorset for a week to interview every herd member separately. There are some sharp people out there. Sharp and sad.

Paul was behind the bar, in a lot of trouble. His eyes were glassy, he was swaying slightly and the twitch in his jaw suggested he was fighting cramp from trying not to yawn. Michael was on the other side of the bar, and it was worse than a tutorial on a hot Friday afternoon.

'. . . simply exquisite! Bosses under the ridge and on the purlins, angels flighting as terminals to the hammer beams and, behind the altar, a quite spectacular carved wooden reredos reaching up to the roof. There's simply no other Norman abbey that compares, and over the years, I don't mind telling you, I've seen . . . well, let's see, I first went over to France in—'

'Where's Jeff?' I said, coming up behind Michael at the bar and earning a look of almost manic gratitude from Paul. Michael's shoulders tensed, but he didn't look round.

'This must be the monkey looking for his organ grinder,' he said wittily, flashing a conspiratorial smile at Paul, who wisely didn't return it.

'Only one person around here who grinds his own organ,' I remarked good-humouredly. 'Pity it's not an Olympic sport. You'd be up for gold, no question.'

I was glad I hadn't forgotten my schoolboy repartee. Michael blushed angrily and Paul looked slightly edgy. 'Um . . . Jeff left a message,' he muttered. 'Said if you came in, to tell you to go over to his place. Stella's there. Something about taking out a laurel hedge. He left an envelope . . . somewhere down here . . . yeah, here it is.'

I stuffed the already folded envelope into my jeans. Michael looked on with distaste – either at the sheer blue-collar vulgarity of it all or the practical implication that I'd now have money to buy food and stay alive – while Paul looked like a boxer whose thirty-second break on the stool hadn't been nearly long enough.

'I think if Jeff were here,' I mused, hoping to impress Michael with my refined subjunctive, 'he'd want you to give me a lift out to Stella's. As you've obviously got nothing better to do this afternoon.' I treated him to my widest and most lovable smile. 'What d'you say?'

'On your bike, peasant,' he sneered, grinning again at Paul, who wasn't coping too well with this charm offensive. He looked a lot like a bunny who didn't want to go to Paris.

'Um . . . look, Mike,' I said, clapping my arm round his shoulder in a matey embrace. 'What I said just now – you shouldn't worry about it. I mean, we shouldn't be repressed about these things, we're all grown-ups.' I raised my voice slightly, so it carried to the guys in overalls. 'Masturbation isn't anything to be ashamed of. It's a natural part of human sexuality. If you haven't got a regular partner, of whatever sex, it's inevitable that tension builds up and when it does, it's just common sense to . . . take the matter in hand, as it were. I don't think there's anything to feel guil—'

The arm round his shoulder was shaken off with surprising force. 'Go to hell,' he said hotly. 'I don't know why Jeff has anything to do with you. You're just such a . . . a . . . '

Failure either of nerve or vocabulary consigned the payoff to oblivion. Michael walked quickly to the door, averting his eyes from the two workmen, who stared curiously. Even from the bar, I could see the back of his neck glowing. You could almost feel sorry for him, if he wasn't such a wanker. Literal and figurative.

'That's one you owe me,' I told Paul, who was watching Michael scurry through the door.

'Jesus,' he said in an awed voice. 'That's an hour and a half of my life gone. And what the hell's a reredos when it's at home?'

I shrugged. 'No idea. Probably some sort of sex toy. Now how about a coffee while I call a minicab? I need something if I'm going to be grubbing out hedges.'

Paul passed me the phone and started messing with filters. I had a momentary insight into what it must be like to be Jeff and have me to boss about. I could get into it.

'You look . . . ' Paul said, before he'd really thought it through – there was an awkward pause while he looked up 'like shit' in his mental thesaurus – 'Um . . . tired,' he finished lamely.

I yawned on cue. 'Up all night.' I figured if I could just keep going a while longer, I'd have the best twelve hours' sleep for ages and be back in the rhythm. The alternative was a week of disrupted jetlagged dozing, which was a bit ridiculous as I'd only travelled a few miles south and hadn't, as far as I knew, crossed any time zones. 'Nothing exciting,' I added, putting myself firmly – but only temporarily – in the Michael camp.

I ordered the cab and put too much milk in my coffee to cool it down and make it sufficiently undrinkable that I wouldn't mind leaving it.

'So, how's Lucy?' I hoped we'd put enough distance between ourselves and the topic of self abuse for the question to seem innocent.

'Oh, she phoned last night. She may be coming down at the weekend. Depends on work.'

'She's working, too?'

'Only voluntary stuff,' Paul said, guiltily aware of his own cash-in-handers from Jeff. 'Community outreach, run by the local health centre. Making contact with outgroups, as she calls them. Old people, ethnic minorities who can't speak English, single mums trapped on housing estates, people on benefit literally worried sick because they owe money to loan sharks. That sort of thing.'

I looked up from my milky slop. 'Literally worried sick' sounded like a quote to me. I scanned Paul's face, trying to work out where he was coming from on the issue of community health outreach, but he just looked back at me with his usual expression of mild embarrassment and then turned away to put some glasses in the dishwasher. I brooded darkly on whether I'd rather spend my time joining hands with society's outgroups or listening to Michael prosing on about Norman abbeys. It was a damn close-run thing. I still hadn't decided when my cab came.

Stella was already in the garden, pruning, when the minicab pulled up. The fare was more than I'd expected. I had to break into Jeff's envelope to pay. There was surprisingly little in there, which was a downer. Then again, I'd hardly done anything for him recently, so really there shouldn't have been anything in there at all.

'Taxi, no less,' Stella observed, more used to me turning up on my knees with exhaustion.

'Man of means,' I said unconvincingly.

Stella raised a cool eyebrow. 'Man who needs a shave,' she said. 'And a haircut. And what are those bruises?'

Well, bruises, of course. What else could they be except love bites from an Aspinall tiger.

'Friend of my brother's,' I explained, or rather didn't. 'Jeff not around?'

'Nope. Just me, I'm afraid. Jeff's in Wales, building an artificial log-pile holt in a nature reserve.'

'A what?'

'That fact-pack I sent off for after that programme on otters. They were appealing for volunteers. They want to attract breeding otters and to do that, apparently, you need to build a log-pile holt. Jeff's been there a couple of days.'

Bizarre. Deeply bizarre. Community outreach, listening to Michael, building starter homes for otters. Someone was trying to tell me my life was a dream palace by comparison. I shook my head in bewilderment. 'Paul said something about taking out a hedge. That one, presumably.' I pointed to a row of sturdy bushes which looked as if they might well be laurel.

Stella nodded. 'Jeff's never liked them. They were here when we came. Now he wants to start over.'

I couldn't see any reason to stop shaking my head in bewilderment. If Jeff got any greener, he'd be taking to the woods and never coming back.

'So what's he going to replace them with?'

'You.'

'Me?' Unreal. The ultimate in conspicuous consumption. Employ someone to impersonate a hedge. Who did he think I was – Gilbert and George? And what about at night when it rains?

'Yes,' Stella said patiently. 'He wants a yew hedge. The plants are turning up tomorrow, so these have to be out of the way by then. He's managed to borrow a winch and some chains. They're in the garage.'

As work went, it was probably not that different from artificial log-pile holt construction. Marginally less silly, perhaps. Stella brought out a chicken sandwich and a beer half-way through, which took the edge off the project's grim, World War I overtones as I dug a huge trench the length of the hedge and dropped down at regular intervals to check the roots. They went on for ever. Laurels take staying alive seriously.

I did what I could with a pickaxe and spade, to the consternation of a couple of neighbours, who scuttled by without making eye contact, presumably under the impression that the embryonic trench system heralded the start of a Bosnian-style civil war on the Essex border. Either that or they were just noovie snobs.

'Not very friendly around here,' I grumbled to Stella, as she bustled about with a watering can drenching pots of fuchsias. She looked me up and down – I didn't need a shave or haircut any less, and dirt was spattered across my face and clothes – hesitated, decided the job wasn't near enough done to risk a comment, and went on watering. I took the hint, anyway, and kept my eyes suitably lowered when any of the locals drifted by.

When I was happy with my earthworks – and I was surprisingly happy: mindless and extensive digging seemed to be just the ticket after the night I'd had; my muscles weren't stiffening up at all – I leaned heavily on my spade and pushed back an imaginary flat cap to scratch my head, running my fingers through a sensuous mixture of mud and grease. The trench had too many turns to be authentic Paschendaele – it was more like the tunnel networks used by the Vietcong to dodge Uncle Sam's napalm. I hauled myself up on to the grass and plodded off in search of Jeff's bondage gear.

It wasn't hard to find, all coiled up on the garage floor. Everything else was on a shelf, in a rack or on a hook. Ladders, hoses, lawnmowers, leaf-hoovers, garden shredders and a dozen gleaming aluminium tools with the labels still on, telling you what they were: fork, spade and so on. Even Bernard the Burmese's cardboard box, complete with the inevitable disgusting and unhygienic cushion, was up on a shelf, next to piles of newspaper and bottles sorted Verwoerdianly into coloureds and whites for the bottle bank. I hauled up all the chains into my arms, tucked the winch under my chin and stumbled back out towards the ditch, dropping the lot with relief as soon as I cleared the potted fuchsias.

I had a little play with the winch, to see which way the ratchet worked, then looked round for a fixed point to take the strain. Anything on the house was definitely out – it would probably have been fine, but you never know with modern stuff. I didn't want Jeff coming back to find a wittily defiant laurel and a pile of Grozny-style rubble where his home once stood.

In the end, I settled on the biggest tree around, species unknown, but which looked as if it had been there for a couple of generations at least and knew how to take care of itself. Stella brought out some homemade lemonade on a tray while I was slinging chains around, which seemed like a good excuse to take another break. She sat down on the grass, which didn't leave me much option but to follow suit, even though I was still worried that once I started relaxing it would be murder hauling myself up.

'Looks like hard work,' Stella observed, clearly satisfied Jeff was for once getting his envelope's worth.

'It is,' I said predictably, knocking back half a glass of lemonade, which was more *citron pressé* than R. Whites and definitely needed a few tablespoons of sugar. 'I don't know how I do it.' I put the glass carefully down just a bit too close to me on the grass and lay back, hoping I could knock it over when I pulled myself up without arousing suspicion or being offered a refill.

'So you went to see Maria,' Stella said, sipping her own drink with an expression of deep pleasure at all the calories it didn't contain. 'What did you think of her?'

I hadn't realized I was supposed to think about her – I thought I just had to fix her locks. Which I still hadn't done. Which I hadn't even bought. I sighed and made a resolution to sort it out as soon as I stopped putting off sorting it out.

'Well, she seemed . . . ' Skinny, not very friendly and pointlessly clever, from what I could remember. 'Nice,' I said, half impressed and half disgusted by my insipid diplomacy.

Stella looked thoughtful. 'I'll do you a favour and not pass that one on,' she said. 'Not that you actually meant it – nice is one thing Maria's never been. But I can't count the number of men I know who've been crazy about her.'

This was definitely one for my Dark Matter file, named after the surely embarrassing ninety per cent of the universe which physicists know must be there, but which they can't seem to find. I believed Stella, but I couldn't see it myself.

'She looked . . . a bit tired,' I said, to justify my lack of infatuation.

Stella nodded. 'Louis keeps her up all night,' she said knowingly. 'What d'you expect?'

Dark pouches under her eyes and nothingy sort of hair, obviously. But you'd have thought if she was being bedded that well, she'd at least be a bit more cheerful.

'Mmm,' I said, because what I really wanted to say: Sorry, I'm with Jeff on this one – his opinion, anyway, not his base instincts – would have dragged us on to dangerous ground. 'Well, I suppose I should start hauling those tree things out.' I sat up on the grass and five yards away, Bernard the Burmese raised his head off the warm earth and looked hopeful. He loved watching other people work, the spiteful little skunk.

As luck would have it my elbow brushed the half-full glass of lemonade as I pulled myself up, and tipped it over on to the grass. Bare patch there in a week or so, I thought, shuddering at the memory of bitter scraps of rind while simultaneously trying to look grief-stricken but not too thirsty. Stella wasn't fooled for a nanosecond. 'I'll get you another beer,' she said.

The minicab back took a sizeable chunk out of what remained in the envelope, which instinctively turned my stomach until I remembered it didn't have to. I guessed it would be a while before that particular reflex vanished. Stella had offered to fix some supper, but the hours were catching up on me and I was out on my feet. It was all I could do to stay awake in the cab, though the driver did his bit by speeding up to crash through every amber light he saw, then invariably losing his nerve and standing on the brakes, then swearing, then re-tuning the radio to an even more abysmal station with even more moronic ads featuring even more hysterical actors who had to mention both the product and the freephone number at least fifteen times in as many seconds, then grabbing his squawkie and yelling to base that he could be somewhere in five minutes, which he obviously couldn't unless he was planning to dump me on the roadside and hightail back the way we'd come, which I was beginning to think would be fine by me.

We made it eventually. I passed him the money over the back seat and began a long and clumsy battle to get out of the car. 'Bit stiff,' he said, presumably referring to a handle that I hadn't even managed to find yet. 'I'd put the light on for you, only the bulb went this morning.'

It was good to be home and I knew just what I needed. I didn't even bother to turn on the lights, but stumbled straight up the stairs, into my flat and through to the bathroom where I turned the hot tap on full. Then I had a rummage through all the plastic bottles, some of which went back to Opal's time. There was something by Chanel, which looked like it might be bubble bath but only had two madly sophisticated interlocking Cs and the names of a few world capitals on the outside, so I couldn't be sure. I took a chance and poured it all into the bath, hoping it wasn't moisturizer or hair tonic. Product diversification holds many terrors.

I brushed my teeth with what I knew was toothpaste, because it said 'toothpaste' right along the tube, rather than just carrying the interlocking Bs of the Boots company of Nottingham, and then peeled off my clothes, which by now were stuck to my skin with a rancid layer of sweat and grime. Leaning over to drop them in the linen box, I caught sight of my shadowy reflection in the medicine-cabinet mirror and saw I had most of a laurel tree stuck in my hair and looked like a member of Dad's Army on exercise.

The bath took ages to fill – one of those combination boilers that gives you as much hot water as you want, exactly when you want it, at around a pipetteful a minute. I was reduced to flossing my newly cleaned teeth, until I found that the angle I had to hold the floss at hurt my shoulder considerably more than tearing laurel trees out of the ground had. So that was that for another six months. I turned the cold tap of the bath warily – experience with adding milk to coffee had taught me the hard way that I was hopeless at judging liquids and temperature – and toyed with the idea of the radio. But not for long. The memory of the minicab journey was strong enough to qualify as aversion therapy. I lowered myself into the foam in reverent silence and it was one of the best feelings I could remember, lying there with my eyes half closed as the top third of the bath steadily filled up. My theory was that over the next forty minutes all the pain was going to melt away and I'd be able to formulate a strategy for the rest of my life that would combine insight, daring, initiative and sophistication in a cocktail of such brilliance that it would make your average MBA student weep with envy. The universe – at least the ten per cent of it we can actually find – was there to be mastered.

189

I'm prone to these kind of thoughts in the bath when I'm tired. I think the steam broils my brain. Usually the control-freak confidence lasts until the plug comes out and the Expelair brings the temperature down to Death Valley levels. This time, everything began to break up after about ninety seconds, when the telephone rang. In itself, not a problem – there was no way I was going to answer it. But counting the rings of a phone you're not going to pick up is distracting and doesn't help you think clearly. Nine, as it happened, probably not including the first one which bombed me out of my Roi Soleil trance. It was a downer.

But what came next was worse. Someone forced the door to my flat.

I couldn't believe it. Simply couldn't fucking believe it.

I raced through a few implausible explanations – pigeons on the roof, bats in the attic – then the phone rang again. Probably the same caller, checking they had the right number the first time. I couldn't believe two separate people felt a pressing need to talk to me on the same evening. Whoever was messing around in my flat wasn't sidetracked by this impressive evidence of my social success. I could hear furniture being moved, something being ripped and, in between phone rings, someone playing their Walkman too loud. I even recognized the tune: Meat Loaf's 'Anything for Love'.

I used the fifth ring of the phone to cover the sound of the window latch being sprung. No blood this time – the rust hadn't had time to re-oxidize. The sixth and seventh ring covered the two shoves needed to get the sash up as far as it would go. The eighth ring covered the Archimedean leap out of the bath and on to the window ledge, leaving the ninth to muffle the scrape of the sash being pushed back down. I don't know if there was a tenth ring to overdub the tearing of flesh as I misjudged the swing on to the soil stack and grated three layers of skin off my left knee. The plastic pipe shuddered and swayed. Whatever was holding the bracket where masonry screws should have been was performing beyond the call of duty. I couldn't blame it for giving up just as I was steadying myself for the drop on to Luther's kitchen roof.

I spun round in the air and came down with a crack of compacted ribs near the edge of the flat roof, still holding a pole vaulter's length of soil stack, fought desperately for any kind of grip or balance as my legs carried on down, ripping the plastic guttering off the kitchen wall, was pulled by sheer momentum backwards off the roof, realized I was heading down on to stone patio flags, tried to assume the braced paratrooper landing position, remembered I'd never been a paratrooper and consequently had no idea what the braced landing position was, which didn't matter because while I was still ruminating on the military career that never was, my feet hit the ground and drove my knees up into the tenderized remains of my chest, the soil stack I was clutching whiplashed into my face and I pitched sideways into the downpipe section of the guttering network I'd pulled down with me.

As a gymnastic routine, it scored low on style, but all the moves were there. The roof had broken my fall, along with the odd rib, and although the final drop was on to stone, at least it didn't have a rose stump at the end of it to all but sever one of my feet. My chest hurt a lot – but only when I breathed, so that was OK – Luther's patio looked like an explosion in a plumbing supplies warehouse and there was blood on my face, but I wasn't sure from where. I lay still for a few seconds, taking this in, listening to the soft patter of torn-out pointing as it drifted down into my hair. When I tried to move, it was way too early and my stomach heaved. I lay back quickly and managed to keep Stella's chicken sandwich down by sheer force of will, which I was pleased about, because I had a feeling that a patio pizza would really piss Luther off.

Talking of whom, the outside lights suddenly flicked on all the way down the garden, uplighting the lush plants and creating a tropical-paradise effect which unfortunately didn't extend to the terrace, which still looked like an explosion in a plumbing supplies warehouse, albeit an artistically lit one. The single curtain over the French windows moved eight inches from right to left as I looked at it, a catch was sprung, the sliding door moved exactly the same distance and Luther's head peered cautiously out. I'd like to be able to report that he almost fainted with surprise, but this would be some distance from the truth. He looked expressionlessly round at the broken guttering, downpipes and soil stack and finally at the bloodied heap of tenant splayed out over his flagstones.

'Is this some kind of kink?' he hissed.

I shook my head. 'Someone's in my flat.' I tried not to whimper, but it was a borderline attempt at best. Luther didn't move.

'You're trying to tell me you're gay, which is why you and Opal busted up, but the only way it works for you is if your boyfriend, the pale, skinny one, breaks into your flat while you're washing yourself for him, then you jump out the window, destroying as much of my house and garden as you can on your way down, and then you crawl back upstairs leaving a trail of blood and dirt and only then do the two of you get excited enough to enjoy some real action.'

I tried to disentangle myself from the soil stack, which was still tucked in the crook of my right arm. It came away in a smear of blood. 'Someone's in my flat,' I said, relentlessly peddling the official line as I struggled first to my knees, then shakily to my feet.

'Hold it right there!' There was no mistaking the real fear in Luther's voice. 'I got company.'

'Luther, I . . . ' As I started to plead, my legs turned not to water exactly, more to something like hair gel, which wasn't much of an improvement, and I lurched forward, grabbing the handle of the sliding door for support and sending Luther recoiling with disgust into his cosy living room. It was an unplanned but effective manoeuvre, and I made a split-second decision – well, maybe more of a four-second decision, but my brain had been sufficiently scrambled that it seemed lightning fast – to go with the flow and press home my advantage. So I took a deep breath, which was a huge mistake as it made my ribs hurt twice as much, and stumbled through the narrow gap in the sliding door, ending up a few feet inside, blinking dazedly like one of the less intelligent bulls on one of Hemingway's deathly afternoons.

Luther seemed to have gone into a trance. He was standing about six feet away, staring straight at me as if I'd turned him to stone. I was already beginning to feel better now I was inside, so I gave him an encouraging smile, tasting blood in my mouth but not finding any loose teeth, which was another boost. He didn't respond. His whole body was rigid. Then his eyes flicked to the right.

I tried to turn my head, but something wasn't working in my neck, so I ended up turning most of my upper body round like an underdressed Thunderbird puppet and then wishing very quickly and very sincerely that I hadn't.

Oh Christ. Oh shit.

Opal.

If there was one thing that got me through, it was knowing that Luther was hurting more than me. It was terrible to watch, like seeing someone go to the electric chair in Georgia. He'd spent so long trying to get us together in one room again, had probably sold his soul to the devil to make it happen, and now it had, and he hadn't been nearly specific enough, hadn't spelled out, for example, that he didn't want me lurching around semi-conscious and covered in blood, dressed only in an earring, with bits of mortar and guttering in my hair and grinning like a cretin. The devil had pulled a fast one, Luther was going to spend eternity in the flames in exchange for subjecting his daughter to this.

Luther suddenly looked like an old man.

But Opal looked just the same.

Blue jeans, faded. Thong sandals and those long, sexy toes. White blouse with just her underneath, which you could easily make out if you stared shamelessly as I always had, and it seemed much too late to change the habit. And that killer smile.

'Long time, Charlie.'

Not long enough. Another couple of hours would have been just fine. Even a couple of minutes I'd have settled for, just to grab some clothes.

'Trouble?' she added laconically. There was an unspoken rider: Or is this your usual dress code and method of leaving the house? In which case you've gone downhill even faster than I predicted when I walked out on you.

'Plenty,' I said truthfully, edging coyly behind a chair and dripping blood on the fabric. 'There's a guy in my flat.'

That brought Luther half out of his trance. He muttered something inaudible, shook his head slowly, then turned and walked out of the room. Opal and I watched him go in silence.

'He does your handwriting pretty well now,' I said, when I decided I'd been staring long enough. There was a large cricket bag at Opal's feet, half open, with pads, one glove and the handle of a bat sticking out. 'He keeps giving me letters he says you've written. They go on for ever.' Try as I might, I couldn't imagine Opal playing women's cricket.

'I did write one once. It went on for a while. But I never sent it.'

I nodded, increasingly mesmerized by the sports bag. As I saw it, I had the choice between opening a long-delayed inquest into the most important relationship of my life –

most important two relationships, in fact, but both with the same woman, separated by a disastrously misjudged few months – or being sidetracked by the props department.

'What's with the gear?' I said unhesitatingly.

Opal splayed the toes of her left foot over the handle of the bat, watching mischievously to see if she was stirring up any memories. 'Today's shoot,' she said, as I held on tight to the chair. 'To celebrate the summer tour. I get to wear the pads and gloves and a box tied on with elastic. Pictured side-on, holding the bat, with my arms across my tits because I don't show anything any more, that's in the contract. And a pale blonde called Annabel with about eight too many buttons undone on her shirt and nothing on underneath semi-transparent white trousers pretends to bowl at me. She even did a couple of times. I never realized a cricket ball was so hard.'

Once I started imagining, it was difficult to stop. I wondered which magazine had ordered the shoot. Perhaps Wisden was relaunching.

'Men are strange, Charlie,' Opal said ruminatively. 'If you want to show a black girl and a white girl with not much on, go ahead – there are worse fantasies. But you have to pretend it's all about sport, really, a humorous look at the Test series and hey, there just happen to be these two babes letting most of it hang out and stuffing the rest into what feels pretty much like fetish-wear to me. Which makes it even more exciting, only you have to make out it's just by chance that the feature inside has some sort of sex-starved title which has a double meaning and is meant to be funny and not desperate, like . . . oh, I don't know.'

'Full toss?' I suggested helpfully.

Opal shrugged. 'Whatever that means. These guys have gone for "Rampant at the Crease". Subtle or what.'

Luther shuffled back into the room with a dressing gown,

which he handed to me without a word. His sad eyes told their own story. I took the gown and pulled it on, feeling a lot more confident and poised. Remembering I had unfinished business upstairs.

'Mind if I borrow your bat?' I asked Opal, emerging bravely from behind the armchair. She looked slightly put out that her presence wasn't enough to hold me. Knowing her views on men and sport, she probably thought I was off to the nets.

'My guest,' she said wearily, and lifted her foot.

It's a strange thing, adrenalin. I couldn't remember when I'd last slept, I'd run half-way across London, been incompetently beaten up on my brother's housing estate, spent hours digging trenches and tearing up laurel trees, and rounded off an eventful enough day by abseiling down the outside of my house without a rope. And I felt good. Even better, I felt angry.

Angry at being hauled out of my bath and in effect thrown from the window. Angry at being pitched into a conversation with Opal when I hadn't prepared what I was going to say – and even if I had, it was unlikely that I'd have chosen to say it cowering behind an armchair wearing even less than Opal was paid to wear by magazines. Angry because my shoulder still hurt and my ribs hurt even more. Above all, angry because Tom was well and truly dead and I hadn't much idea what to do now.

The guy in my flat wasn't responsible for all of this. But he'd do. Sometimes, and usually just for a short while, I have a real ability to convince people who are near me that they're in the wrong place at the wrong time. I get in a mood when nothing's funny any more, I can't take a joke, I'm pissed off and glad that my hair's jet black and too long, that I haven't shaved, that I've got scary eyes and generally look like someone you'd go a long way to avoid even on the lightest of summer evenings. Sometimes I just know I'm going to make someone unhappy.

The bat was the kind I remembered from school days, with a scoop out of the back so you could hit perfectly weighted drives to all corners of the ground. It felt lighter than it had when I was fourteen. I had no trouble carrying it in my right hand as I took the stairs two at a time, not bothering to dodge the ones that creaked, and shoved open the door, which had been left carefully ajar, slamming the handle on the inside into the wall, where it gouged out a sizeable chunk of plaster. The frame shuddered.

I didn't hang around to Polyfilla. Just a quick glance round the room – bombsite: all the chair and sofa cushions cut open, rugs pulled up, the back of the TV levered off and my one plant tipped out on to the floor along with all the earth – and then three quick strides over to where the guy was just coming out of the kitchen area holding a knife in one hand and the newly-decapitated body of Fred the squeaking dog in the other.

'The fuck you think you're doing?' I said rhetorically, just because I like to hear my own voice at times like this (it soothes me and sets me up), and then swung the bat reverse-sweep and very hard at his chest. He'd started to duck, thinking I was going for his head, and now realized the bat was lined up on his face, jerked backwards and up, brought his non-knife hand forward to protect himself, which was impressive in reaction-time terms but dismal strategically, and told me straight off I was dealing with a no-hoper and shouldn't have swung so hard, only it was a little late for second thoughts. There was a gut-wrenching crack as something godawful happened to his wrist, then a pulpy thud as the bat deflected up into the side of his neck, knocking him over like a skittle and ricocheting up into the light fitting, shattering the bulb and sprinkling us both with tiny shards of glass. Another substance to add to the builder's rubble already ground into my hair. This was going to be a stiff test for my supermarket-brand shampoo.

I should have dived in and checked his pockets in case he tried anything on, but two things happened. The first was that I caught sight of a stick of bone poking through the skin above his pulped hand where his wrist should have been. The second was that he suddenly coughed, seemed to fight for breath and was then chokingly and extensively sick on one of the few stretches of Luther's carpet that I hadn't managed to cover with a rug, improving the design, perhaps, but in other ways lowering the tone considerably.

So I didn't go near him. I just watched as he half sat, half knelt in a heap against the wall, coughing quietly, his young face snow white and sweaty where it wasn't smeared with mucus and vomit. His Walkman headphones were still on his head, but not lined up with his ears. I couldn't hear any more Meat Loaf.

Maybe I wouldn't have hit him so hard if he hadn't eviscerated Julie Ray's toy dog. Which reminded me – I couldn't see where his knife was. Probably he'd just thrown up over it.

He stared down at his broken wrist, looking as if he could pass out at any moment. I stepped forward, trying to skirt the vomit, and grabbed him by the hair, forcing his head back against the wall.

'Don't think about it,' I advised. 'Just give me the number of someone who can pick you up.' I couldn't believe anyone this hopeless was out on his own.

His eyes rolled a bit as he tried to focus close up, but steadied eventually. There were some painful seconds while he tried to work out if he should just give me his name, rank and serial number. We stared at each other in the pale light drifting through from the kitchen. Something that looked like a tear glistened high on his right cheek. When it didn't move, I realized it was a small triangle of glass from the light bulb above us. I leaned forward to brush it away and he flinched.

'The number,' I said, giving up on the glass.

He managed to get his good hand into his jeans pocket and pull out a scrap of paper. When he held it out to me, his arm shook. He still hadn't said anything. I took the paper and walked over to the phone, watching him while I dialled. I didn't sit down. I'd once read an article on executive strategy which suggested your phone voice carries more authority if you're standing up. I had visions of all these corporate whizzkids standing ramrod straight in the middle of their offices, barking aggressively at each other. It seemed such a waste of all those swivel chairs.

'Sammy's,' said a male voice, slightly accented. Italian maybe. Sammy's what? I wondered. Sandwich bar, launderette, garage – all possible. Opera house, merchant bank – less likely.

'Charlie Lucas,' I said, and left it at that. A couple of units ticked on to my bill.

'So?' the voice said rudely.

'So maybe you'd like to collect your friend who's been ransacking my flat.' Another couple of units. I should have reversed the charge.

'What the fuck you talking about?'

Not only was he running up my phone bill, he had no manners.

'Listen, sweetheart – your friend's in my flat. He's sitting on the floor in his own vomit and his guitar-playing days are over because one of his hands looks like something you'd find in a butcher's. You've got ten seconds to start talking sense, before I really go to work. If you like, I'll leave the phone off the hook so you can listen. The count starts now.'

'Hey – what the fuck d'you—'

'Two seconds gone.'

'Are you crazy – we never heard of no Charlie Lu—'

'Four and counting.'

'You do what you like, we don't even know—'

'Six seconds.'

'I said I don't know who the fuck you—'

'Eight.'

'Don't you understand English, cunt? – I said we—'

'Time's up. Pleasure talking to you. Enjoy the show.'

'WAIT!'

The panic in his voice came as a relief. I was beginning to think I'd misdialled. I suppose I could have gone on to order a pastrami on rye, but it might have been a little embarrassing collecting it.

'I'm going to get someone, all right?'

I held on patiently, listening to thudding feet on stairs and urgent whispering. The guy in the corner of my room hadn't moved. He wasn't so far off the lotus position by now, but didn't look particularly spiritual. The voice that came back on the line was older, and more worried.

'Is he OK?'

Nothing like a stupid question to open the conversation. 'If he was OK, I wouldn't be calling. Right now, he's about midway between OK and amputee. I'm going to dump him on the pavement outside. You'd better send someone to fetch him.'

'They're on their way. But I'm warning you, if—'

'Shut up. I'm not interested. Just tell me why he's here in the first place, trashing half my flat, bleeding and puking over the rest. Then I won't hurt him any more.'

There was a long pause while the guy on the other end collected his thoughts.

'I knew Tom Gates,' the voice said. 'We used to drink together in the afternoons. Near the end. He talked a lot about the old times. Most of it didn't make sense – he was in a lot of pain. Some of it did. He talked about you, kept saying you had the money. Kept saying that over and over, but that was all. So I sent David round to ask a few polite questions, out of curiosity. I'm sorry if he got carried away and—'

'Spare me.' It was almost funny – all those worries Tom had about me, and in the end I hadn't said a word and he'd been holding court in a pub with his mind half blown on drugs. 'I've heard the rumours. So has everyone else. They've been going round for years, but so far you're the only person stupid enough to believe them, whoever you are.'

It wasn't worth asking. I wouldn't get the truth, and it didn't matter. If these fools knew, everybody knew. I was just lucky the first outfit to come sniffing were such clowns. Tom would have loved it, though. 'Unbelievable!' he would have snorted and gone on to roar his contempt for an education system that could only drag its criminal classes up to this sort of dismal level.

'I'm sorry, Mr ... ah ... Lucas. These weren't rumours. These were things Tom Gates was—'

'Stop wasting my time. I don't give a stuff what he was saying. Check your facts – Tom Gates was no friend of mine when he died and you should know that. Then ask yourself one simple question. If you're dying and someone you hate isn't, can you think of a better way of making their life a misery than spreading the rumour to a bunch of halfwits in a pub that your ex-buddy's got a ton of cash under the bed that he's too mean to share? Huh? Huh? And then tell me how come everyone else seems to have figured this one out except for you and your ... ' I looked at the guy in the corner for inspiration, just as his brain shut down all circuits and he toppled slowly forward, face down into his own puke, like a sitcom oldie falling asleep into his soup, only a whole lot more disgusting and not in the least funny. 'Fuck it,' I snarled into the phone. 'Do what you like. Just get this moron out of my flat.'

Fourteen

I dreamt I was in a primary-school swimming gala. Or rather, I dreamt of a primary-school swimming gala I'd been in. As far as imagination goes, my dream life is the most poverty stricken imaginable. It's little more than memory.

This time I was on the blocks, waiting for someone to shout go. It was a more than usually pointless sporting event, because a girl called Mandy Elvy was going to win by about half a length, then climb out, trot back up to the deep end and win the next race by half a length as well. Same result, whatever the stroke – except butterfly, which was a walkover because no one else fancied their chances of completing an entire length without drowning. Mandy swam it anyway, as a demonstration.

My race was the freestyle and I was off the blocks like you wouldn't believe, having calculated that my only hope was to false start by several seconds and trust no one could be bothered to call me back. I hit the pool flailing and soon had enough clear blue water behind me to make the No Turning Back group swoon with envy. I'm sure I had the small crowd on my side, too, because Mandy Elvy was – on land, at least – a lumpen and unpopular redhead, and there must have been something poignantly brave about my solo challenge.

Sadly, heroism wasn't enough. Mandy gazed in puzzlement

at the starter, shrugged, dropped the towel that was round her shoulders on to the poolside, bent down to wash out her goggles and splash water ritually over her trunk, already wet from winning the seven previous races, then straightened up, adjusted her goggles to fit snugly over her eyes and launched herself in pursuit. I doubled my workrate and splashed frenziedly like an overacting extra in a *Jaws* movie as she scythed through the water with ruthless grace and won by a third of a length.

It took me a while to register the chlorine smell hadn't evaporated with the dream. Brilliant. Someone had launched a chemical warfare attack. I closed my eyes and listened to the clump of footsteps approaching the door.

Julie Ray knocked once and peered round into the gloom. She was holding a cushion under one arm.

'I can smell chlorine,' I whispered.

She nodded matter-of-factly. 'It's grout cleaner. The only stuff strong enough for most of what's out there. You can't just Shake 'n Vac puke, you know.'

'What else is going on?'

She edged further into the room and looked around, evidently relieved it wasn't in the same state as the rest of the flat. 'Lots. I've almost finished. I had to throw your plant out, because it was all broken. And I can't reach to put a new bulb in that light. And the screws to fix the back on the telly have gone, but it still works. I'm just sewing up some of the cushions.'

'With what?'

'Stuff from Nan's sewing basket.' She registered my look of surprise. 'I came round earlier. You were asleep. I had a look around and went back for some cleaning things. I took the bat with me – I'd like to polish it up and give it to a friend at school. They're playing cricket this term.'

'What time is it?'

'Afternoon,' she said, crossing on cue to the heavy curtains and pulling them a couple of feet apart. 'Nice day. Summer. Why are you whispering?'

Presumably she'd tossed in the season in case I'd suffered a complete meltdown of my mental faculties.

'Because my chest hurts,' I whined. And to be fair, it did. When I coughed, it felt like the Alien had just burst out of it. I looked down expecting to see a steaming pile of intestines. But there wasn't even a bruise.

Julie Ray soon tired of my self-pity. 'I'm going back in there to finish. You want me to bring you anything?'

'Coffee,' I said quickly, before she disappeared. 'And something from the freezer part of the fridge to put on my knee. I think there's some peas. And maybe something to read – there's probably a paper from a few days ago that I never finished.'

Julie Ray disappeared before I had a chance to order my eggs sunny side up on rye. I managed to sit up without feeling any more pain than the average heretic under interrogation during the Inquisition and squinted doubtfully at the vertical strip of sunlight between the parted curtains. Then I remembered Fred with his head torn off and felt bad for not having said anything.

She came and went all afternoon, but never mentioned her dog. I lay there, with frozen peas on my right knee, sipping air and reading a four-day-old newspaper. When she stopped vacuuming and opened a window, I could hear Luther chatting to one of his builder mates about whether they'd need scaffolding for the repairs to the outside of the house. My opinion was probably yes, but I kept it to myself. There was a fair bit of sweeping up after that, then Julie Ray left around five, but asked if she could come round after tea to do some homework.

'Do what?' I was so taken aback, I forgot to whisper. If she'd asked to come round after tea to freebase, I could have coped better.

'Homework,' she said again, staring me down. 'I've started going to geography. I like drawing maps. And there's a boy called Toby,' she added, as if the information had been forced out of her under the most brutal cross-examination. 'He's the one I'm going to give the cricket bat to when I've oiled it. He's in the team. If that's OK?'

When she was gone, I dragged myself out of bed and crept through a haze of chlorine and polish to make another attempt at having a bath. Getting my hands up to head height nearly caused me to black out, so a hair wash wasn't on. Ditto shaving. But some of the dirt came off, and afterwards I managed to grab a packet of painkillers from the bathroom cabinet, pull on a tracksuit and shuffle as far as the re-stuffed sofa. I was never going to make it to the kitchen for a glass of water, though, so I ate the tablets dry, put my mind in neutral where it seemed happiest, and waited for Julie Ray to come back.

It wasn't a long wait. But it wasn't Julie Ray at the door, either. A couple of sharp raps and in stomped Luther before I'd even made it to the 'c' of 'come in'.

'It's time we talked,' he announced, looking round the room carefully. 'Little Missy Thing did all this repair work, I presume.' He pushed the door closed.

I nodded. 'I've been ill. In bed.' It was a long shot at the sympathy vote. In fact, it was an arrow fired at the moon. Luther didn't bother to reply. I decided on my best form of defence. 'If you had a proper lock on your front door, this wouldn't keep happening.'

'Don't get smart with me.' Luther was angrier than I'd realized. 'The only thing wrong with that lock is that your friends keep picking it and smashing up my house. Now I want to know why. Why do they keep coming round here? What's going on? Last night when Opal was leaving, she saw this car screech up with no lights to collect some bundle of rags on the pavement, only it was no bundle of rags, it was a guy. Scared her half to death. Now this isn't me being nosy or anything, but I've got a right to know what's going on in my own house.'

Luther's right index finger was pointing directly between my eyes. I motioned him to sit down, because I didn't want to shout, but the gesture came out more patronizing than I'd intended.

'I'll stay right here until I get some answers,' he huffed, condemning me to an indefinite session with my head crooked up at an awkward angle. I sighed, wishing the tablets would hurry up and work. Wishing I'd taken more.

'The guy you met a while ago. Who came here. The one who was dying. He left me some money. Only some people think it wasn't his to leave. They're giving me grief.' I spread my hands. 'That's all there is to it.'

Perhaps not quite all. Something in the region of five per cent was nearer the mark. But it was the crucial five per cent Luther was getting.

'Whose money was it?' he said, homing in on the key area I hadn't covered.

'Search me,' I said. 'But it sure as hell wasn't theirs.'

Luther hmphed and looked round the room again, wrinkling his nose. 'Smells like a swimming baths in here,' he said tetchily, taking a couple more steps towards me and sitting down on the sofa. 'Matter of fact, I wanted to talk with you anyway. Even before this . . . ' He gestured in a vague, circular motion ' . . . thing all blew up. Something I think you should know. About Opal.'

The door handle turned noisily and in clumped Julie Ray, two hardbacks and a pad of lined A4 under one arm. She and Luther eyed each other warily, but she didn't back off.

'He's ill,' she said protectively. 'He doesn't need anyone giving him a hard time.'

She meant well, but it was a mistake. Luther's eyes widened in amazement.

'Hard time? Did I hear you say hard time, Missy Thing? Because if you did, maybe you'd like to hear a bit more about the hard time I give your little friend here. D'you happen to know, for instance, when he last paid a bill? I got correspondence going with gas, electricity and water – not phone, but that's the only one – the council and two insurance companies. I'm tying 'em up in so much paper they don't know which end is up, all so he can put some money by for ... well, never you mind what for. Plus he gets the rent on this place half-price, not to mention the shed with all that wood, which is going to go up in flames one fine day and take us all with it. And what does he do in return? Nothing. Wrecks my house and expects me to tidy up after him. Well, here's one guy who's done enough tidying for one lifetime. That's it. From now on, he pays his own bills, and starting next month, he pays a decent rent. This isn't a hostel and it's about time he learned that other people weren't put on God's earth to make his life easier. That's the lesson come through to me over the last few years and I advise you to take it on quicker than me, Missy, otherwise you're going to end up just like the rest of us. And now if you'll excuse me, I've got my own life to lead and my own concerns to worry about, so I'll be getting along and leaving the two of you in peace.'

He marched past Julie Ray to the door, wrenched it open and was gone, leaving it juddering on its hinges behind him. We listened in silence to the thump of his feet on the stairs, the click of the latch on his own front door and the terminal thud of it closing. Somewhere on the roof, a pigeon cooed.

Julie Ray hesitated by the door, clutching her books. 'I think I'll come back tomorrow.'

'No, it's OK. I don't know what all that was about, but it wasn't you. Stay and draw maps if you want. I've got to get dressed and go out in a minute anyway.'

'You can't go out. You're ill.' This was her line and she was sticking to it.

'I'm not ill,' I said wearily. 'I'm just hurt. And I'm running out of time.'

She was right, though. Wedged into the corner of a taxi, wincing at every pothole, I couldn't even focus properly. Pools of amber streetlight drifted around in my field of vision, merging and splitting like oil in a kitsch bubble lamp. I was glad Tom had only made two bequests in his last will and testament, because the thought of crawling my way across London, doling out money like a low-grade Eva Perón, was grim beyond belief. And giving away money when you're not even trying to buy votes just seems unnatural. I unwrapped another couple of painkillers and crunched them down, brooding dark thoughts. The cabbie looked suspiciously at me in his rear-view mirror, but didn't say anything. Perhaps ecstasy-heads are good tippers.

The club was the sort of place I hadn't been in for years – and hadn't missed. I couldn't even see it at first and thought the cabbie had pulled a fast one and just dumped me round the corner from his favourite Soho hooker. Then I looked across the road and saw a shabby, neon-lit doorway completely filled by a guy in a dinner jacket who made Greg look like the 'before' picture in a bodybuilding advertisement. Unfortunately he picked me out as soon as I got out of the cab, with several yards of tarmac still between us. I wanted to cover them with an insouciant stroll, but when your ribs are gone, your right knee's on fire and one shoulder's higher than the other, it's not an option. The guy stroked his black tie thoughtfully as he watched me wait for a ten-minute gap in the traffic, then drag myself across the road in a hobo shuffle. Even through the pain, I could see it his way. If I ever made it on to the dancefloor, his job was gone.

Not all the pink neon on the Easy Es sign was lighting up properly, which was probably a design feature costing an extra thirty per cent – seediness and decay being essential to creating a suitably louche low-life feel. The peeling paint on the door may have been interior-designed *trompe l'oeil*, but the guy in the tux was determined that I shouldn't get near enough to find out.

'Members only,' he warned, as I stood on the pavement in front of him, my arms hugging my chest to keep it together, my lungs fighting for air. If I could only have straightened up, I'd have been a couple of inches taller than him.

'I've got some money for Solange,' I whispered, hitting with my best and only shot. Ask to see someone, you get nowhere. Say you've got money for them and the flunkey's in trouble, because turning away cash can lose you your job just as surely as letting a mutant on to the dancefloor.

'You can leave it with me.' And I'm sure I could, if I'd had it. But I just shook my head and waited, hoping Solange was one of the waitresses he was sweet on.

The stand-off was broken when he reached into his jacket for what, with my frayed nerves, I initially took to be a cosh, but realized just before diving on to the pavement and assuming the foetal position was a mobile phone. He punched in the numbers with the little finger of his left hand, which was the only one small enough to hit the buttons cleanly. 'Who are you?' he said as he dialled.

'Charlie. But say Tom Gates sent me.'

I couldn't hear the answering voice clearly, but it was male.

'Jed on the door,' said Jed on the door. 'Guy here says he's got money for Solange. Won't leave it. Says Tom Gates sent him.' The news obviously didn't mean much to the bloke on the receiving end and there was a lot of hesitation. But the word 'money' eventually swung it and some hasty instructions were relayed.

'OK,' Jed said, tucking the phone back into his pocket. 'You can go in. But go straight to the bar. There's a drink waiting for you. On the house.' He was obviously going to add something like: Don't try to dance or pick anyone up, before deciding it was redundant advice. 'Enjoy the club,' he said, moving politely away from the handrail, which I was going to need to make it down the stairs.

The music hit me when I'd limped through two sets of double doors into a strobe-filled cavern where everyone seemed to be wearing purple and white. It was distressing that even in the near blackout, I could see how much younger than me they were, and even more distressing that they could see it, too. I didn't have to push my way through to the bar – a two-lane highway opened up within seconds, with troubled groovers on either side wondering if they'd got the date wrong and this was Zimmer Night.

For someone who's sat in Greg's Mini, the volume was nothing special, and the tracks were standard Straight Outta Compton blasts, presumably about killing cops and fucking whores, or vice versa, but fortunately the lyrics were indecipherable, either because they were being yelled so fast or the discs were being spun backwards or whatever else was going down these days where the scene was hot. 'Old, old, old,' I muttered to myself as I shambled up to the bar and managed to haul myself on to a leather stool.

'I've got some money for Solange,' I muttered at the barman, a skinny alien with white-blond hair who'd either been in a big fight with his boyfriend or was wearing too much eye make-up. I don't know how he heard me – perhaps he lip-read, though even that was some trick in the gloom – but he nodded and said: 'Get you a drink?'

I had my doubts about whether anything on his shelves would blot out the pain, but a reply along the lines of: I was rather hoping you might have a little something I could inject, would have sounded too desperate. So I asked for a brandy.

'Are there many waitresses working here?' I said, as he put the brandy down on a fussy little cloth coaster. The bar top was marble, so I think he could have taken a risk, but perhaps he'd seen the state of the Parthenon these days.

'Waitresses?' he said suspiciously, as if I'd just asked if the DJ ever played 'Puppy Love'.

Well, how was I to know what they called themselves? Laptop hostesses, technobabes, comfort madonnas? But the doubts were creeping in. 'What exactly does Solange do here?'

'She owns the place.'

Oh, fair enough. I nodded knowingly, as if I'd just had confirmation of a long-held hunch, and the skinny barman shimmied off to serve someone who reminded him less of his dad. I threw down the rest of the brandy and couldn't decide whether it made me feel better or worse. The bar stool was nowhere near comfortable. I twisted this way and that, my arms still folded across my chest. And it was covered in something coarser and clammier than leather. At the height of the Empire it would probably have been elephant's scrotum, but these days it was more likely to be tofu. I kept raising my legs to unstick them from the seat until my right knee began to throb. I even thought about a dance to shake some of the pain out, but Alien Boy, who'd been watching my pitiful attempts to fidget into the groove, was swiftly over with another complimentary drink and a small packet of nuts to make sure I stayed right where I was and didn't ruin anyone else's night out.

In all, I had five brandies, and was on the stool for just under two hours. Towards the end, when the migraine had wiped out eighty per cent of my vision in one eye and thirty per cent in the other, I took some more painkillers, exciting a brief flash of interest from the barman until he saw the packet. When Solange finally appeared, I was rocking myself gently backwards and forwards on the stool, humming a nursery rhyme tune that I couldn't get out of my head. In the background – the foreground for anyone without severe brain damage – Shabba Ranks or Ice-T screamed that theirs was the longest anyone had ever seen.

I don't know how long Solange had been standing there. The alien reached over his bar and tapped me on the shoulder to get me to look up from my rocking and humming. I tried to focus with what remained of my vision, which had worsened since beads of sweat had started crabbing sideways from my temples into my eyes, and allowed myself a surge of pride that I hadn't yet thrown up. It made me significantly more presentable, I thought, if not exactly dashing.

Solange was wearing black leather trousers and a matching jacket with outsize silver buckles. She had dark hair with a fringe and a look of disdain which I told myself was typically French and nothing to do with the semi-comatose hunchback swaying on the bar stool in front of her.

'I'm going home early,' she told the barman. 'It's too quiet tonight.'

The alien nodded ruefully. The first Tube trains would be running in a couple of hours and my skull was pulsating like the inside of a speaker. It wasn't my idea of a quiet, early night. I thought I should probably say something, but the word I was looking for ('hello' I think it was) eluded me. Nor could I safely shake hands without risking a disastrous loss of balance and probably a meltdown of my internal organs with no arm to hold them in place. So I just sat on the stool and looked up at her, like a red setter that's never been quite right in the head since it was run over.

'You'd better come with me,' she said. 'It's not far.'

It seemed far to me. But I felt better towards the end of the walk than at the beginning, and better still when it began to rain. Soft, soothing summer rain which I decided, in a temporary attack of hippy-trippy rainbow insanity, was melting the pain away. Probably it was just that the painkillers and brandy had stopped combusting and trying to push the blood opposite ways through my brain.

The flat was in a mansion block round the corner from the YMCA. I'd expected some sort of airy loft, but the building smelled fusty and stale, as if several of the old lady residents bravely kept cats in secret contravention of their leases. Outside one of the doors was a pile of newspapers, neatly folded and tied up with string. Solange led the way past a couple of unconvincing-looking fire extinguishers to the single lift.

'I'll be glad to leave this place,' she said, perhaps sensing that Mr World of Interiors scuffling along behind her wasn't impressed. 'But it's hard to find anywhere central to rent.'

I nodded sympathetically, but couldn't offer up any of my own West One leasehold anecdotes, so I asked if she was French.

'Not so you'd notice,' she said. 'But technically, yes. My dad's French, but he didn't stick around for long. Jean-Claude – my partner – is the real thing. Speaks English like Inspector Clouseau. You'll meet him in a minute, if he's still up.'

She checked her watch, but the result was inconclusive. Personally, I couldn't see what on earth Jean-Claude would be doing up at this hour, unless he was determined not to miss *Farming Breakfast* on TV, but I had to remind myself that he was doubtless operating to his own generational agenda.

Solange hadn't hijacked and rerouted the lift to make it open straight into her flat, so we had to schlep several yards down the hall before we reached her front door. She turned the key softly, muttering something I didn't catch about a neighbour, and hooked up the safety chain behind me when I followed her in. There was a wonderful smell of strong coffee wafting out from the kitchen, and a gentle swell of piano-driven jazz rolling out from further inside the flat. Solange walked ahead and poked her head round a few doors, returning to inform me I wouldn't be meeting an authentic Frenchman, after all.

'He's crashed out,' she said. 'Leaving the hi-fi, the coffee percolator and all the lights on, as usual. This always happens. He says he'll wait up, but he never quite makes it. So come on in. I'm going to pour myself a cup of Jean-Claude's best. D'you want some?'

She led the way into the kitchen, heading for a shinily elaborate espresso machine. This was more than I'd bargained for. A shot of that on top of the brandy and painkillers would have my adrenal glands begging for mercy. But what the hell.

'Great – thanks,' I whispered, keen not to wake sleeping Froggy.

'It's OK – you can talk normally. Once Jean-Claude's gone, he's gone. He could sleep on runway one at Heathrow.' She poured a couple of small cups of the black stuff – the very black stuff – and handed one over. 'If it's OK by you, I'm going to take a quick shower, wash the club out of my hair. Why not go through and sit down, and when I'm feeling a bit more human, you can tell me about this money you've got.'

Whether it was OK by me or not, she was going. I just managed to say it was fine before she made it out of the door, leaving me stranded in the kitchen, feeling suddenly hungry. What I really craved was a large bowl of spaghetti, but I couldn't be sure how long her shower was going to take. And besides, they might not have parmesan. So I compromised by picking up an apple on my way out of the kitchen and taking it down a dark green corridor towards the tinkling of high-fidelity ivories.

The sitting room was dark – two table lamps, dim bulbs – and dangerously overfurnished, with huge numbers of non-identical chairs covered in scratchy and completely awful fabrics. Presumably the old lady who owned the place had been rumbled by the management company and had taken her precious Siamese off to a bungalow in Essex to be near her daughter. I picked my way carefully through to a sofa and settled down with my coffee and spaghetti-substitute.

The sofa was angled back towards a huge Nicam stereo television, which Jean-Claude had left on. A videotape was playing in the machine below, but the film was over and the screen was filled with snow. I looked round for a handset and noticed a pair of designer sunglasses and a packet of Gitanes on the coffee table, which made me smile. Only the Pernod was missing. Oh, to be that confident of national self-image, I thought, wondering why, on my occasional visits to France for Jeff, I didn't dress as a Beefeater. Perhaps if we didn't have to give Hong Kong back, I would.

I found a handset behind one of the many non-matching cushions on the sofa, but at first glance I couldn't tell if it was for the TV or video, or one of those clever ones that does both, plus the hi-fi, washing machine and electric blanket. There were about forty plus and minus buttons on it, but the symbols illustrating all the features appeared to be in Mandarin. When I looked closer I could see most of the little diagrams had been worn away, so the functions they illustrated could be called up only by daily familiarity plus impressive memory, or inspired guesswork. I was about to start punching the buttons at random, because it's really hard not to look at a huge, white, flickering screen in the corner of a darkened room, even when you know it's years since it won the Turner Prize and is way out of fashion, when the screen snow melted into the first frames of a home video.

A date a couple of years back was burned in on the bottom right of the picture, but vanished after the first few seconds. The shot was of a plain room with whitewashed walls and quarry tiles. Something about the light – its presence, probably – told me we weren't in England. A big pine double bed filled two thirds of the screen, in which a guy with tangled dark hair was lying under a single sheet asleep. Pretty convincingly asleep, too. I don't know why, but sleep seems to be a hard thing to act. Look at TV any night of the week and you'll see scores of perfectly made-up mini-series-luvvies lying decorously around on beds with their eyes lightly closed and their hair just right and they're all about as convincing as a politician saying now that the election's over it's time to unite to heal the rifts and move forward. But this guy, curled up with one arm tucked under his pillow, was enjoying his siesta for real.

The camera was to one side of the bed, angled slightly downwards as if on a tripod. The first bit of soundtrack I heard above the soft piano jazz of the hi-fi was a door opening and some muffled female giggling. It was an evocative sound, suggesting this was no eight-hour Warholian epic of a man asleep. Conditioned by those awful video-prankster programmes I began to suspect a practical joke, and tensed in anticipation of a bucket of iced water being thrown over the hapless dreamer. There was more giggling, and then two women walked into shot on the far side of the bed and smiled brightly at the camera. One of them was Solange.

She was wearing a huge baggy T-shirt which came down almost to her knees and had 'Where's the Beach?' printed on it above a cartoon surfer on a big yellow board, and she was holding what looked like a couple of dressing-gown cords in her right hand. Her friend, accomplice or paid assistant looked startlingly like her – same dark, straight hair, cut slightly shorter, same shape eyes, but (plentifully visible under not much of a white bikini) there was more of her, and she was younger. Solange handed her one of the cords and she came slightly unsteadily round the bed, shimmying playfully up to the camera, which took a lengthy but unfocused look down her cleavage.

It was pretty clear the guy on the bed was Jean-Claude. What clinched it was the time he took to wake up. I like to think that if two barely-dressed women were tying my wrists to the top of a bed, I'd come to a bit quicker – if nothing else, so that I didn't miss anything. But Jean-Claude's conscience was obviously as serene and untroubled as a Swiss lake at dawn. He grunted, he sniffed and snorted a couple of times, but slept right on until Solange leaned over and blew gently on his eyelids. Even then, the wake-up process was slow and comical. He blinked a lot and gradually focused on Solange, smiling vaguely, then tried to roll on to his side but couldn't because his arms were tied. His brows furrowed, he raised his head slightly and saw the camera, which really fazed him. He did some more bewildered blinking, trying to work out if he really was awake, then noticed the second woman coming up the side of the bed with a glass of champagne.

'Chantal?' His voice was thick and croaky. But it didn't matter – that was the only word he said.

Chantal smiled, sat down on the other side of him from Solange and tipped the champagne flute to his lips. She only let him have small sips, though, and kept pulling the glass back. Meanwhile, Solange began rolling the sheet gently down his body.

It was time to revise my bucket-of-iced-water theory. Time also to make a serious attempt to stop the tape, in the interests of basic politeness and good guestmanship. But while I was happy to concede this was towards the more benevolent end of the practical-joke spectrum, I was still far from confident about my ability to decipher the handset hieroglyphics and deeply fearful of inflicting lasting damage on the machine. So I just had to sit and watch on, as Chantal kept up the drip, drip, drip of champagne and Solange went to work with her hands.

Once he was over the initial shock, Jean-Claude woke up very fast indeed. Up being the operative word. Solange's nails and fingertips were doing the sort of damage to his composure that Helen's did to mine what seemed like a long time ago now. His hands clenched and his wrists twisted against the cords, but the girls had been practising their knots and nothing gave. Chantal treated him to a few more sips of champagne and then set the glass carefully down on the floor. As she turned back, Jean-Claude was treated to another rope trick, as Solange leaned across and used her free hand to tug sharply on the bow at the front of Chantal's bikini top, which unravelled into a few threads of white fabric, leaving Jean-Claude gazing at as fine a pair of breasts as you could ever hope to have lowered in your direction.

It was the champagne treatment again for him, as Chantal brushed one nipple, then the other, across his cheek and lips and then away, across and away, so that half the time he was sucking hungrily at air. The other half seemed to make up for it, though. I swallowed a couple of times, put my apple down and ran a finger across my top lip, which felt dry and cracked. I'd been sipping coffee as Jean-Claude sipped champagne and now it was gone and I didn't have the substitute he was so obviously enjoying. But it was when Solange licked her own lips and started planting small bites and kisses on the inside of his thighs, moving very slowly upwards, that I thought enough is enough, I really shouldn't be watching this.

But I was firmly in the grip of the Wimbledon syndrome, where it's vital neither player loses their concentration early in the set, and then even more vital that they hold their nerve in the crucial seventh game, and then even more vital than that that they hold serve or break serve to save the set and force the tiebreaker, when absolutely everything is extra-supervital and no one's even allowed to blink. In short, I wanted to see what happened next. And besides, there was no moral force behind my choice of cut-off point. I couldn't exactly tell Solange: Oh, yeah, I sort of watched up to the point when you started going down on him, and then switched off because I thought it was impolite. So I made an effort to calm down, not get anxious, and resign myself to a night in front of the telly.

Jean-Claude obviously couldn't be trusted with too much of what Solange was giving him – a few final nibbles to make sure he was ready, then she slid smoothly on top of him, tossing the hair out of her eyes and watching him closely for signs of overload, before starting to rock backwards and forwards in a gentle rhythm. Jean-Claude found himself gazing up through half-closed eyes at Chantal's breasts, swaying heavily over him in the foreground and framing Solange a little further down, with her T-shirt up around her waist.

Not that the T-shirt stayed on for long. Solange eased herself back a little and edged it up over her smaller, paler breasts and then over her head, lobbing it with a mischievous sideways glance at the camera. Had it fallen over the lens, it would have been a tragedy of epic dimensions, but fortunately it dropped well short and the camera continued to stare fixedly as Solange leaned forward and pulled Chantal gently round by the shoulder until she was lying crosswise over Jean-Claude's chest, her breasts sadly hidden. As if to compensate, Solange used her left hand to ease Chantal's bikini pants down with a series of little pushes, as Jean-Claude built up a formidable set of neck muscles straining his head forward to admire the view. Solange took Chantal's pants most of the way down to her knees, a centimetre for each stroke of her own, until her hair fell forward again over her eyes and she needed that hand to brush it back.

From the rasping noises at the back of his throat, I could tell Jean-Claude was beginning to feel the pace. I wasn't surprised. My eyeballs were starting to sweat just watching. Solange had picked up on this and slowed down on top of him. Now she slapped Chantal playfully on the behind to move her off – presumably because Jean-Claude had never been to boarding school there was no prolonged spanking – and watched as she rolled on to her back beside Jean-Claude (a fleeting and wholly enjoyable view), then turned away from him on to her side in an unmistakable invitation which he was powerless to take up until Solange gave him his passport to heaven by pushing herself off him with a final series of sharp squeezes, then leaning forward to untie his left wrist from the top of the bed. He looked up at her with awed gratitude as he turned over and used his free hand on Chantal's hips to pull her slowly back on to him. She sighed softly and he moved his hand up to knead the breasts that had been teasing him so mercilessly, then down again to pull himself deeper into her, then up again, then down, then up, until finally she caught hold of his hand and guided it down between her legs as he gave up trying to hold on and came as if he'd just been electrocuted, his back curved taut almost into a half moon and Solange, kneeling next to him on the bed, bent down to kiss his hair and whispered: '*Bonne anniversaire*,' just as the television was snapped off from over my shoulder with the right handset.

I winced and turned round slowly. Solange was sitting in an upright chair against the wall. Neither of the lamps was near her, so I couldn't see her expression.

'The tape . . . ah . . . was running,' I said feebly, then realized I was still leaning forward with my elbows on my knees. I pushed myself back on the sofa and tried to relax, but small talk didn't come easy.

'Some birthday present,' I observed. 'I . . . uh . . . I usually ask for socks myself.'

'You aim too low,' she said brusquely.

So it seemed. 'Right. Yeah. Look, I'm sorry about watching . . . um . . . ' You and your sister taking it in turns to fuck your boyfriend, basically. But how exactly to phrase it?

'Don't be. It's not the most embarrassing scene on that tape, from what I can remember. Though it's a while since we last played it. Sod's law that Jean-Claude should be skipping down memory lane the night we have unexpected company.' She yawned and looked vaguely round the room, as if she'd mislaid her cat. 'Anyway, it wasn't that generous a present. He and Chantal had always fancied each other and I had no intention of being ditched just because she's prettier than me and has bigger tits, because I know Jean-Claude, he'd just lose interest, she's not bright enough for him, and where would that leave me?'

I hoped the question was rhetorical, because there was plenty there to mull over. Not least the tantalizing revelation that I'd just sat through one of the tamer sexual vignettes on the tape. I wondered if I could perhaps ask to borrow— I pulled myself up short and tried to clear my head.

'We have until my hair dries,' she announced, staying put on the chair by the wall. She was wearing a black, wafty kaftan which reached from her neck to the ground. Her hair was loose, but without a moisture meter I couldn't begin to guess how long I had. 'Then I'm going to bed. So why don't you tell me why Tom sent you?'

I reluctantly abandoned all tape-related thoughts, but I wasn't happy being pushed around. 'Why don't you tell me why Tom went to your club?'

Solange stated the obvious wearily. 'We keep going when the pubs close. And we have better drugs. Why does anyone go clubbing?'

At this rate, we were going to be firing questions at each other all night. Or rather, morning. And Solange was probably entitled to a bit of pushing around after watching me watching her on candid camera.

'Tom left a note,' I said. 'He mentioned you. Said you'd helped him out and he wanted to leave you something. That's why I came.'

'What sort of something?'

'Money.'

'How much?'

'Well . . . ' This was the tricky part. 'He kind of left it to me.'

Solange nodded and absently combed her hair through with one hand. I wondered how it was drying. 'So you must be the guy he cracked those safe-deposit boxes with.'

Oh, terrific. Was there anyone left in Greater London who hadn't heard? Tom might just as well have acted out the whole thing on *Crimewatch*.

'Yeah, that's me.' There didn't seem much point hedging.

'It doesn't seem to have done you much good.'

Not often we see ourselves as others see us, but I had a real flash then. I knew I was in a rough patch, no question, but I'd convinced myself I was hanging in and doing OK. All she saw was a battered and shabby sleazeball oiling around offering her money.

'It hasn't been a great week,' I admitted. 'But things are going to turn.'

The classic loser's boast. She didn't even pretend to believe it and we sat in silence for a while. My stomach began to rumble, which didn't make me feel any more suave.

'You know, I used to enjoy Tom's company,' she mused. 'Not at first – at first I was embarrassed because I couldn't understand what he was saying a lot of the time, what with his regular drugs and the top-ups he bought, plus the drink. But then I realized it didn't really matter, the company was enough. And it must have taken something not just to crawl into a corner and die quietly, but to gatecrash every party you can find and keep walking up to people even when they flinch and look around and mumble some excuse to slip away for another drink. There was a lot of that at the club. But he got through to a few of us in the end. Jean-Claude for one. They used to sit in the back office at the club watching Cary Grant films through the night. Not my idea of the rave scene, but it worked for them. Some of us will really miss him.' She looked at me properly for the first time in what seemed like an age. 'And what were we getting – fifteen per cent of him? Twenty? Not much, I'd guess. Must have been a friend worth having.'

The subtext of this little speech – that the wrong half of the criminal duo had been eaten alive by secondaries – was depressingly plain. But that wasn't my fault, I kept telling myself. That was one rap I didn't have to take.

'Sure. He was more fun when he wasn't dying.'

My chest was beginning to hurt again, and yawning made it worse. My knee felt puffy even when it wasn't taking any weight. I wanted to go home. Even if I couldn't borrow the video, I wanted to go home.

'Uh . . . look – about this money. I don't know if . . . ' The sentence, which hadn't started with much promise, tailed off when I saw Solange shaking her head. Not a good sign. My first assignment, hardly Herculean, even with busted ribs, was all to hell already.

'I'm not interested,' she said.

'Well, look – why not think about it? I mean, it's not like you'll have much to do with me, if that's what you're worried about. I'll just hand over the money and go. No questions.' She was shaking her head again. 'And I'm sorry I watched when the video came on. I should have turned it off, I know. But I . . . um . . . ' Didn't, so why not just shut up about it. 'It's not from me. Tom said . . . Tom wrote that I should . . . you know . . . '

'What d'you think about the European Union?'

Grateful as I was to be rescued from my disintegrating monologue, it wasn't an easy out.

'What?' I said, smoothly playing for time.

Solange wisely decided against repeating the question, perhaps intuiting that my Euro credentials, phile or phobe, were unlikely to be underpinned by a vigorous or even vaguely coherent political philosophy.

'Jean-Claude's family made steel,' she told me. 'From way back. Only now nobody wants it, so they get a massive grant from some European deindustrialization fund to stop churning out thousands of tonnes of stuff a week that no one would buy anyway. I don't know why they didn't just go bankrupt, but it doesn't seem to work that way. If you make or grow enough of something that nobody wants, they'll pay you a fortune to stop doing it because it's all so embarrassing. So instead of being dirt poor and having to start again and do something useful for a living, Jean-Claude's family are all rolling in it and don't have to get up before midday. We're over here for a couple of years for tax reasons, and also because my dad's ill. The club's something for me to do. It's on a short lease and it's not as fashionable as it was last year, so it'll fold pretty soon and we'll go off somewhere else for a while.' She shrugged. 'So that's it, really. Nothing personal, but money's the last thing I need.'

It took me a while to absorb the information. It wasn't light outside yet, but I couldn't believe morning was far off. And I wasn't feeling bright. It was taking me at least twice as long to absorb everything, except pain.

'Well, that's . . . ah . . . good about the grant. I mean . . . ' I realized I'd just marched into the naïve and profligate Europhile camp, tent poles held triumphantly aloft. 'I mean, good for you. For Jean-Claude.' And here was the rub. How to hint at the completely unimaginable circumstance of Jean-Claude deciding to make Chantal's generous breasts a more permanent feature of his life. 'For him,' I said emphatically, and left a significant pause, signifying that I had no idea what to say next. Fortunately Solange was right there. She may or may not have been brighter than her sister, but she was having no discernible problems keeping up with me.

'It's all in my name,' she said. 'Tax again. If he walks, he pays.'

I think I managed to say 'oh' or something along those lines, but the fight had gone out of me. I knew when I was beaten. Solange smiled vaguely. 'He doesn't seem to mind,' she said. 'Anyway, he won't be moving on for a while yet. And if you'd seen the next session on the tape, you'd know why.'

Fifteen

When the going gets tough, I read about the *Titanic*. It's my all-time favourite disaster, the perfect antidote to the uplifting *Reader's Digest* school of rubbish journalism we're all subjected to day in, day out, about midair collisions missed by inches, bombs going off minutes before the arrival of convoys of school buses taking the handicapped on special outings, and huge death tolls averted by the heroism of one off-duty police officer and his paramedic dog. The mesmerizing thing about the *Titanic*, for me, is how close it came to not sinking.

If the two lookouts had seen the iceberg earlier, the ship would have been saved. If they'd seen it later, or not at all, the *Titanic* would have rammed the iceberg head on and still been OK. But going in at an angle, ripping twelve square feet of hull – just twelve square feet in a ship the size of a street – meant five watertight compartments were breached. And five was one too many. Can you imagine how the designer felt, standing on the bridge with the captain, when the news about the five compartments came through? We know what he said: 'You've got two hours.' But what was he thinking? 'Shit' wouldn't begin to cover it.

You hear a lot about the band-played-on heroism, guys changing into tuxes to die like gentlemen. But not about Lady Duff-Gordon, in a lifeboat one-third full, suggesting they shouldn't risk picking up any of the passengers struggling and screaming in the freezing water because they might be swamped. And her husband, Sir Cosmo, later presenting each crewman who'd been in the lifeboat with a five-pound cheque 'to replace lost uniforms'. And they weren't alone. The captain called through a megaphone to all the lifeboats that had left half-empty to return to pick up passengers who were otherwise going to hell. Not one boat returned.

This run-of-the-mill cowardice is refreshing, though unexceptional. But what about Elizabeth Nye, who was passed a baby boy in all the confusion and when they reached the safety of the rescue ship *Carpathia*, claimed him as her own? Stunning. In the middle of one of the greatest disasters in maritime history she tries to pull a baby snatch and the captain of the *Carpathia*, who you'd have thought had enough on his mind trying to keep the death toll below two thousand, has to adjudicate between two women, only one of whom fortunately knows that little Frankie has a strawberry birthmark on his chest. This, surely, is bad behaviour beyond the call of duty.

And little Frankie, surviving to be fought over, was one of the lucky ones. Fred and Augusta Goodwin's six children died with them. John and Annie Sage went down with all nine of their children, including baby Sidney. The roll call of the dead goes on and on. How many died on the *Herald of Free Enterprise*? Fewer than two hundred. On the *Estonia*? Maybe double that. But fifteen hundred and twenty-three people went down with the *Titanic*, including one guy who'll never be identified because he'd stolen someone else's papers. And when you're lying in bed, exhausted and in pain, and not even the sound of sirens can cheer you up because it's probably just a routine drugs bust that'll only push the price up, then reading about the *Titanic* sets things in perspective.

For what remained of the day, and through the night, I dozed and read, read and dozed, and had a bath and drank lots of water with ice in it, because I was running a temperature. I stayed off the pills, though, having gone through the best part of a packet and deciding I couldn't face sharing group therapy sessions with a bunch of second-rate film actors who once took an aspirin on the same day as they drank a spritzer, and who'd now sold their story to the Sundays under the banner of 'My Fightback from Addiction Hell'.

Julie Ray didn't call, or if she did it was while I was asleep.

Over a night and a day I'd dragged most of the freezer compartment into my bed, having made the surprising discovery, while packing my knee in peas, that having something frozen on my chest and shoulder helped as well. I ended up looking like a low-budget advert for frozen food, with greens all over my legs, a pack of three-year-old oven chips on my chest and three of Julie Ray's popsicles wedged against my neck. Bringing in the ice tray had been a mistake, though. I meant to put it on the bedside table as soon as it started to melt, but woke several hours later in a bed that would have sent nursing-home staff running to the rubber-sheet cupboard. It was time to move on.

This time round, the inventory was better. Plenty of things ached where before they'd hurt, so that was progress. There was a strange taste in my mouth, but that was probably from the visit to Solange and the consequent anxiety about what to do with the money that she didn't want because she was already the technical owner of a clutch of decommissioned steel mills in France. Give it to Maggie was the obvious move, but the thought of actually going to see her was way too daunting, so I decided to tread water for a day and catch up on a bit of DIY.

I couldn't remember if I'd made a note of how many windows there were in Maria's flat, but if I had, the scrap of paper was long gone. I tried hard to picture it as the guy in the hardware store told me the only really safe locks were those with dedicated keys, which happened to cost half as much again. But what the hell, this was my good deed for the decade. I picked up a new bradawl as well, wondering if maybe I could charge it all to Jeff.

It was another hot day on the bus routes and I was still running a temperature, despite all the frozen food. Sweat dripped steadily off my earring on to my shoulder. I hadn't shaved, either – somehow the thought of all that close control with a dodgy neck made me feel exhausted before I started. Also, the stubble was coming thicker and darker than I remembered, so I was tempted to let it roll. And my clothes were clean on, so it wasn't as if I was consigning myself irrevocably to the social dustbin. I'd even managed to brush Julie Ray's popsicles out of my hair.

Maria saw me as she came out of the newsagent's next to the bookies, and frowned. She had a point. I kept my tools in an outsize handbag that Opal had got bored with, which is fine for dragging round the house, but less suited to being carried in public, at least by me. It was heavy, too. As I plodded steadily towards her I must have looked camp, sweaty and ill. She tapped impatiently on her packet of thin cigars, but I was trudging as fast as I could.

'I brought the window locks,' I said, when I finally drew level, wondering if I could ask her to carry the tools indoors.

'Hello,' she said neutrally. 'I didn't think I'd see you again.'

She turned back towards her brown front door as I battled to compose a suitable apology for my reappearance. Unsuccessfully – my heart wasn't in it.

'Louis is with me today,' she said, pushing hard on the door instead of unlocking it and pausing as it juddered open.

I didn't actually care, and was tempted to mention this. Something along the lines of: I'm round here just to tidy up and clear my conscience, after today I'm gone, so I really don't care if one of the many men you seem bizarrely capable of attracting is paying court, though obviously I'd prefer it if you didn't get up to anything while I'm actually in the same room. Instead, I said, 'Ah.'

We walked down the dingy hallway. As soon as I saw the door with the hole kicked out of it, I remembered the bits of rough timber in Luther's shed and swore softly to myself. I probably couldn't have carried them on the bus, but at least I should have decided not to bother, rather than just forgetting.

We climbed the narrow stairs in thoughtful silence. I thought I might as well start with the sash windows over the flat roof, but didn't want to crash in on anything.

'Where's . . . um . . . Louis?' I said, as we paused on the landing.

'Asleep. In the top room – our bedroom.'

So that was OK. 'I'll just start in here. So if you want to . . .'

Maybe he worked shifts, I thought charitably, trying to suppress my raging Protestant work ethic. But an alternative explanation seemed more likely, and what I was trying to suggest was that if she wanted to slip back between the silk sheets for a post-coital cigar, that was cool, I could make my own coffee.

'I'm working on my last chapter,' she said. 'Methodology. So I'm not in a very chatty mood, I'm afraid. I'll let Louis sleep and make the most of it.'

Just what was so special about her was as mystifying as ever. Too skinny, tiny breasts and pale as a ghost. Good features, admittedly, but why scrape your hair back like that and leave the big panda circles round your eyes?

We walked through into the main room and Maria headed straight for her desk. I wasn't offered coffee. Nor did she break open the cigars, presumably so she wouldn't have to offer me one. I sighed and dumped my tools down by the right-hand sash window. The sun was shining straight in and

I didn't have any sunglasses, which didn't improve my mood. None of the surfaces on the flaking frame seemed to line up with any of the others, either. I almost commented on this, just casually, as a reflection on the woodworking standards of our age, before remembering the implicit conversation ban and biting my tongue. But I made sure to tear open the first window-lock packet as noisily as possible.

The silence lasted an hour, and at no stage could it be described as companionable. Maria simply ignored me, while I fought down the increasingly urgent desire to say vapid and annoying things (My it's hot; Did you see that documentary on the telly about otters?) or to hunt down a radio and tune it to a pop station phone-in to get some company. I didn't, of course. I just worked away, with the screwdriver slipping all over the place in the sweat that was dripping off my face. When I came to the second window I was all but kneeling on the desk in front of her, but a slight frown behind her small round spectacles was the only acknowledgement of my presence. So I made a big deal of moving the window up and down and chiselling unnecessarily to make the lock millimetre-perfect, until I got fed up with how childish I was being and decided to slip out to the newsagent's for a Coke. I didn't say where I was going, though, because by now I was really getting into this silence lark and could picture myself embracing the monastic life with robust enthusiasm.

Integrated into the universal silence I may have been, but I still didn't feel great. I held the Coke can against my forehead, then against the back of my neck, and sat for a while on the front doorstep, watching the losers shuffle in and out of the bookies. It was still a hot day, and anyone who enjoyed breathing was never going to dig it, but I don't normally sweat so relentlessly just because the temperature climbs a bit. I couldn't believe there was much more water in me. Soon I was going to be Prune Man – big pal of Tank Girl and Judge Dredd, if a little less threatening.

I drank the Coke and went back into the newsagent's for another can to press against my temples. When I was back on the step, an old guy in a cap came out of the bookies happily counting notes and headed straight for the off licence on the corner. That raised my spirits a little. He came out with a bulging carrier bag and tottered off in the direction of a slummy-looking block with mean little windows and vast silver bins, one or two of them still upright, scattered around the main doors. My spirits sank back again. I drank the Coke when it stopped feeling cool against my hair and went back inside to find Louis playing with my tools.

Rough as I was feeling I could still see pretty quickly that I'd got Louis wrong. Not so much the surly and besotted lover – I had him as dark, with a strong jaw and heavy eyebrows – but more along the lines of a very small son. I stood and stared at him for a while from the doorway. He was bringing fewer preconceptions to the encounter and stared right back. He took a while to make up his mind, then turned to his mother and said, 'Man.'

Maria had moved from her desk to the futon. She confirmed my adult male status to Louis with a nod and then volunteered, 'Charlie,' which for her bordered on the effusive. Louis considered this information gravely for a couple of seconds, then decided we'd exhausted the subject and went back to rummaging in my toolbag.

'I have to hand in tomorrow,' Maria explained. 'I thought my parents could take Louis today, but it didn't work out. That's why I'm a bit distracted.'

Try as I might, I didn't actually catch the word 'sorry', and 'distracted' wasn't the adjective I'd have chosen above all others, but I was a big enough guy not to sulk.

'I guess it must be a relief to hand in. After however many years,' I said, making a policy decision that even talking about French literature was preferable to fitting another window lock, and settling myself carefully on a cane chair. It held, surprisingly.

'It is and it isn't,' Maria said academically, as Louis carefully picked out one of my hacksaw blades and put it in his mouth. I flinched, but he didn't and neither did his mother, so I guess I was overreacting. 'My supervisor's Louis' father.'

I thought for a minute. 'James?' Sometimes I can't remember if I've had breakfast. Sometimes I can pull off a stunt like that. It's satisfying when it happens.

'That's right.'

No fulsome congratulations or swoons of surprise. My best hope was that she was secretly – very secretly – impressed.

'So is he . . . around?'

In some ways Maria was too fierce for her own good. If you were just as likely to get savaged or frozen out for an innocent question, or just for existing, you might as well pitch in with something worthwhile. Particularly if you don't want to fit more window locks.

'No,' she said flatly.

'Must be hard,' I said, choosing the vacuous over the vacuum.

Maria shrugged. 'Yes and no. A friend of mine lost her son when he was four months old. Then spent every day for weeks in his room winding up his teddy-bear mobile, until the smell of him had gone completely. Now tell me a few broken nights are the end of the world.'

Compared to death, maybe not. But I was only trying to be sympathetic.

'And my parents are good. They take Louis a lot. The other night, I was climbing the walls writing this thing up, so I just dumped him on them and took myself off to see *Les Enfants du Paradis* at the cinema. It always works. If they can make a film that magical during a war, it should take more than a thesis deadline to stop me enjoying it.'

I mulled that one over, unconvinced. Maria's strategy for coping seemed to involve contrasting her own situation with an appalling extreme – infant mortality, occupation by the Third Reich – and being grateful for small mercies. As someone who spent most of his time seething about the salaries of privatized utility chairmen, I had to admire her calm acceptance of her lot. But here I thought it was leading her astray. While the aesthete in me rejoiced that the French were able to create a masterpiece of celluloid whimsy during their darkest days, I was still troubled by the question: why the fuck weren't they out mining bridges?

'I phoned you to see if you wanted to come. You missed a treat.'

This little bombshell was detonated deadpan. Louis didn't even look up. I was left to fend for myself.

'Was this Tuesday?' I said carefully.

Maria nodded. Well, well. 'I heard the phone,' I said, then realized that sounded a little strange. 'I was . . . ' I went on, then realized I was in danger of sounding a whole lot stranger. ' . . . shinning down a drainpipe at the back of the house.'

Maria held out her hand to accept a few rawplugs that Louis was passing to her. 'How exciting,' she said.

'Not really.' Just another day at the office for a small-time thug. Maria picked up her packet of small cigars and slit the cellophane with a nail. Louis immediately tuned in and reached out a hand. She passed over a slip of paper from inside the packet and he sighed with satisfaction.

'Mingo,' he said happily.

Maria offered me one of her cigars and took my look of astonishment for confusion at Louis' vocabulary.

'It's the logo,' she explained, as I managed to decline the cigar. 'A picture of a flamingo. Poor kid – the paper's probably saturated with nicotine. What chance does he have?'

I watched Louis as he sucked his flamingo and reached back into my toolbag for a set of alun keys.

'Talking of keys,' Maria said conversationally, 'what were you in jail for? I asked Stella, but she said she'd never known. Stealing or roughing people up was her guess.'

Maybe I should have pressed on with the window locks, after all. I tested my reaction to the subject carefully, like probing a crumbling filling with my tongue. The pain I was expecting wasn't there. Even so, I gave myself some time before replying.

'They never got me for that,' I said, watching Louis drop my alun keys in dismay at their lack of menace. 'I never stole much that was worth anything and the people I roughed up were worth even less, so it worked out OK.'

Sometimes I have to laugh at myself. 'Worked out OK' sounded like I didn't quite get the grades for Cambridge and went to Durham instead, which I enjoyed so much that after getting a first I moved with my tutor to Stanford to pursue a joint research project.

'So why were you in jail?'

If she thought that inviting me to some hundred-year-old subtitled movie gave her the right to ask me these kind of questions, she was plain wrong. I tried looking back at her coolly, which was a mistake, because she just carried on looking, only several degrees cooler, as if she wasn't particularly interested but wasn't going to retreat on principle. Also, it's always a bad idea trying to out-cool someone with a cigar. They've got the props going for them.

'You want my version or their version?'

Maria considered the choice. 'The version that put you inside would seem to be the most relevant.'

'I was driving a stolen car. Left-hand drive. I was drunk. I was speeding. I hit another car head on in the middle of the road. The guy driving it died outright. The girl I was married to lost her right arm above the elbow.' I shrugged and looked at my hands. 'That's it, really. End of story. Four years.'

Maria smoked quietly. 'And you weren't hurt.'

'One broken finger. Left hand. And a headache.'

She nodded, acknowledging the vagaries of fate. 'So what's your version?'

Not different enough. Who was I kidding?

'The guy I borrowed the car from wasn't insured himself, so he had to say I stole it. That was OK – it was understood. I was right on the limit where the breathalyser can't make up its mind, only by the time it reached court there were a few more milligrams on the counter. I was certainly speeding. But the other guy was asleep and on my side of the road. I was trying to get over to his side to avoid him.' I only realized I'd been chewing my lip when I tasted blood.

'But they didn't believe you?'

'They never heard. I wasn't in the mood. What was the point?'

Maria looked as if she was just about to tell me, but stopped just in time. Very good move.

'The stuff about him drifting they couldn't miss, because of the wreckage. They gave him an official percentage of the blame. My lawyer got really excited, because when it gets above a certain figure the family can't sue for compensation.' I shook my head. Even now it seemed bizarre. 'Big deal – so they didn't get to confiscate my Walkman. Still left him without his life, Laura without most of her arm and me without Laura. There must be relationships around that can survive something like that, but ours wasn't one of them. So I had less to lose than just about anybody I knew by going down for a few years.'

I wondered if the offer of a cigar was still open. But asking would have sounded too weak. I decided to counterattack.

'So what's the story between you and James? What went wrong there?'

It was hardly fair to equate a simple split with the road-kill end to my own marriage, but Maria accepted the shift with equanimity.

'He said he never wanted children. I said if I got pregnant, I wasn't having an abortion. The usual story, except in this case, neither of us was kidding.'

The product of this Mexican stand-off pulled some black insulating tape out of his mouth and was entranced to find a tack stuck to it. 'Na,' he said delightedly to his mother, who smiled vaguely at him.

'So does he see Louis?'

She shook her head. 'The deal was we'd stay together till the birth, then split. He never wanted to see the child. And once I've handed this in, I probably won't see him again, either. End of story, as you would say.'

'It doesn't sound like he's a particularly sentimental guy.' Actually, it sounded like he was a Blade Runner replica, but you criticize people's partners – even ex-partners – at your peril.

'He's not. But at least he's honest. He knows what he wants and doesn't pretend he'll ever change.'

'And what does he want?'

'To live alone. To sleep with different women so he doesn't get bored. And to write the definitive biography of Sartre. He has thirteen thousand pages of notes so far.'

Hmm. Up to a point, I could see where he was coming from. Up to the point about Sartre, in fact. Of whom I knew little, except that he'd been so high minded that he'd managed to ignore the war.

'That's a lot of paper,' I said neutrally.

'And he almost lost it all because of us, didn't he, Louis?' Her co-accused looked up noncommittally. 'I decided to have a bath when I went into labour,' Maria explained. 'James was sweet and lit some candles, but his hands were shaking so much he dropped one. In about four minutes most of the house was on fire and the whole bathroom was about to come down on the study and all the Sartre notes. The fire brigade arrived just before he had to decide what to save. Luckily. It would have been a close call.'

'Sounds like he owed you after that,' I ventured.

She shook her head. 'Give me a break. I wasn't sixteen. I knew what I was doing and he never lied to me. Sure, I wouldn't mind a fairytale ending where the three of us live happily ever after, but it's not on offer. And I'm not dumb enough to think that making lawyer-assisted raids on his private income would make me any happier. Or Louis.'

Not the point, I countered mentally. You don't pay a grocery bill with happiness. But I decided against sharing this mercenary observation, along with its corollary, that James was one lucky sonofabitch and would have been even luckier if all his notes had been fireballed out of existence, so he could have devoted the rest of his life to enjoying his wealth and sexuality and not mired himself in the profligate and infantile rage that seems, in my grossly untutored experience, to lie at the very heart of French intellectual life.

'That's a pretty unusual—' I started to say, but was interrupted by a long, low call – 'Yooooooo-hooooooo' – coming from downstairs, followed by a nasty male laugh. Louis immediately looked at his mother, who quickly put out her cigar and stood up.

'Daaaaar-ling – time to come out and plaaaa-aaaay.'

The sing-song voice grated like chalk on a blackboard and Louis began to cry. Maria made a couple of shh-shh noises and picked him up. As they headed for the door, he was still clutching half a sheet of sandpaper.

'We usually go upstairs at this time of the day,' she said quietly to me on her way out.

I stood up too fast and my head began to spin. I steadied myself on the back of the chair. Sitting down for a few minutes had made me forget how hot and sick I was feeling. I patted my pockets hopelessly, knowing my knife wouldn't be there, thinking, So this is what all the security talk is about. Why didn't anyone tell me straight off? Because I've really lost my appetite for this kind of game.

'Just us, precious – I've closed up the shop and everyone's gone home. It's you, me and the little one, and he's not going to mind watching his mummy have a little tumble. And you can't pretend you don't want it. You must be desperate. I haven't seen a man round here for weeks.'

The first thing to hand was my woodworking chisel. I took a couple of deep breaths that didn't make me feel any better and walked softly towards the top of the stairs.

'I'm asking nicely, now. You gotta appreciate what a nice guy I am, because this isn't much of a door, honey, and one of these days I'm just going to huff and puff and blow it down. But I think you should invite me in yourself. Just give me a few special rides and we'll pretend nothing ever happened. Cub's honour. But you have to be nice to me first – extra specially nice, because there's a few things I'd like to do to you that—'

I was trying to tread carefully, but a couple of stairs creaked under my feet.

'Well, now – could this be my lucky day?'

On the whole I thought not, but this was another opinion I kept to myself as I edged down towards the door.

'And just to show you what a nice guy I am . . . here, take a look at these. I always come prepared.'

A fist came through the door – tanned, with dark hairs on the back – and the palm opened up to display half a dozen multicoloured condoms.

'Fruit flavoured, sweetheart – take your pick. We can work our way through them. You look like the kind of girl who needs a popsicle-special to get her going.'

No one had tried that line on me before, but I wasn't in the mood to be flattered. Maybe it was because I was feeling ill, but really, I can't pretend I've ever been much of a one for a fair fight, so the chances of me opening the door and saying, Now look here, were always slim. The guy shifted position, probably to look through the hole in the door. I moved while I still had a target. The chisel went through his hand and skewered it to one of the few sound panels on the door. The yelp sounded like a dog being run over. I pulled the door sharply towards me and the yelp turned into a howl.

I stepped over him into the hall, then turned round to see who I was up against. He was a heavily built guy, surprisingly young. On a good day he could have given me problems. But kneeling there with his hand chiselled to a door, the colour draining from his face in blotches and surrounded by multi-coloured condoms, it was clear that for him this wasn't a good day. I bent down until I was close enough to see the burst blood vessels in his panicky eyes.

It was Tom who taught me not to say anything. I'd always gone with the cinema convention of grabbing a guy by the throat when he's down and screaming all sorts of threats into his face. Tom said if you just stare, they'll imagine something far worse than you could ever dream up. That was point one. Point two was take a good look in case he ever turns up on your side of the street again. Point three was the hard one, but Tom said you've got no choice. Hurt someone, he said. Then scare them. Then let them catch their breath. Then really hurt them.

I straightened up and backed away, walking towards the main door on to the street. When I pulled it open, early evening light poured into the dingy hall. There was so much dust, I felt I was choking.

I stepped out on to the pavement and just managed to get my hand up to hail a cab that was almost level with me. The driver stood on his brakes and stopped a few yards down the road. By the time I caught up, I had the twenty ready to pass through the window.

'Accident and emergency,' I said. 'My mate's cut his hand

on some glass. But it's all bandaged – no blood. We'll be right out.'

Where was the nearest accident and emergency, I wondered, as I walked back through the scabby front door. They were closing them down so fast it was hard to keep track.

The guy was twisted away from me as I came in, trying to work out what to do about his hand. Either he was crying, or the dust had got to his eyes, too. I walked slowly. Partly because I was trying to work out what I was going to use as a bandage, but mainly because I knew that in about four seconds I was going to have to break his collarbone.

Sixteen

One day on, one day off. Not a great shift pattern, especially when you spend the days off lying in bed, sleeping or staring at the wall. But this time, after my taxi ride to Casualty, I knew I'd had enough. The hard, bony bits of me – ribs, knees, shoulder – were doing OK. I've always been lucky that way. But something inside was rotting and I just felt sick all the time. Sick and hot.

When the phone went for the umpteenth time, I couldn't be bothered not to answer it. Lying there listening to it ringing was pushing me close to the edge. I hauled myself off the bed and into the main room, which was just about back to normal except the television still had no back to it, I still hadn't replaced the bulb in the light I'd knocked for six, and the paintwork was another few rungs down from *House Beautiful*. I slumped down on the unevenly restuffed sofa and reached for the phone.

'The guy wants new Phantoms!' a voice yelled in my ear. 'Treads completely shot on his. They're in the back.'

'Hello,' I said cautiously, as the voice was briefly drowned out by some background workshop hammering.

'And check the belt. Christ knows what for, but I said we'd do it. Rubber fatigue, I s'pose.' There was a sudden baffled pause as he realized he wasn't hearing the ringing tone in his ear. 'Hello? Has somebody actually answered this phone?'

'Yes. I have.'

'Well, goody good, because I'm standing here looking at one huge slab of Africa Twin which belongs to you and is cluttering up my workshop, so I'm thinking to myself it's about time you paid us a visit and chugged off into the sunset.'

'Hello, Brian.' Amazing, really. I'd almost managed to forget that I'd bought myself a motorcycle. Where the hell were my priorities?

'Yeah, hello and all that. Now how about getting round here and collecting your bike?'

I settled back on the sofa and rested my head on a cushion, which was half air and half brick. There was obviously more to this upholstery business than met the eye. Through the window, I could see a tree branch drifting up and down in a soothing, wave-like motion.

'Hello? Hello? Are you still—'

'I've changed my mind.'

There was a cold sort of pause. 'Hey, look, a deal's a deal. We shook on this one, remember, and I've got cash flow to worry about and guys with families to employ, so I don't like—'

'You can keep the money. I'm just saying you can keep the bike as well. Or raffle it. Or give it to Anton. Do what you like, only count me out. I'm too old.'

If I sounded like a beaten man, it was better that way than making one comeback too many. Think of Joe Louis and Sugar Ray Robinson. Think of Ali. And weep.

'So you ain't heard about Anton?'

I didn't like the sound of this. 'No,' I said warily, dragging my mind off thoughts of my own mortality.

'Road meat. Came off last Friday. He was trying to wheelie round the whole of the Hangar Lane gyratory in the early hours. Cops saw him, so he tried to outpace them and lost it. Ricocheted off the abnormal load convoy they were escorting and into a motorway bridge. Cut up really bad. The cops took him to hospital, but—'

'How bad?'

'How bad what?'

'You said he was cut up bad.'

There was an exasperated sigh down the line. 'What are you, some kind of ghoul? He was just about as cut up as a man can be, OK? Christ, he was almost in tears. All those Isle of Man TT badges sewn on to his jacket were rubbed clean off on the tarmac. Every last one. And he's never going to be able to replace them. They were collector's items.'

I realized I'd been holding my breath and let it out. 'So he wasn't hurt?'

Another tense silence. Brian was obviously wondering if I'd had some kind of breakdown.

'Anton don't get hurt. You know that.'

'Sure – that's what I thought. Only you said about the cops and the hospital and—'

'Oh, that – yeah, right. That's the good part. When the cops realize he's OK and start asking him all these tricky questions like how come you were doing double the legal speed limit on one wheel without lights, he tells them his girlfriend's been rushed to hospital to have their baby early and he'd only just been phoned. So they pack him into the back of their car and scream him up to the nearest maternity unit, where they escort him in and tell the sister that he's the boyfriend of the woman who's been brought in early, and the sister marches him straight into the delivery room where some poor girl really is having her baby early and he's stuck there, scared out of his mind and all he can think of to say is "breathe!", and when it's all over and everyone's fine, the girl, who happens to be a single mother and is either out of her head on gas and air and doesn't know any better or is one smart cookie who thinks fast even when under a lot of pressure decides well, why not, he's got to be better than nothing – and last heard, she and the kid had moved in.'

'On Anton? Are you crazy? How long's that supposed to last?'

'Hey, don't knock it. Stranger things have happened. And Anton needs commitment in his life. He's vulnerable. All his badges have gone.'

Brian hung up long before I replaced the receiver. When I looked down, it was in my lap, the cord wrapped tight around my wrist, making the skin patchy and white. I'd been staring at the tree again, trying to decide if I felt any better or wanted to go back to bed. The answer was complicated. I didn't feel any better and I didn't want to go back to bed.

I managed to get through an entire shower without jumping out of the window, which was something of an achievement, but I still didn't feel like shaving afterwards. I told myself that holding my arm up for any length of time was just too painful. But the truth was I was beginning to fancy myself in a beard. It looked the healthiest thing about me.

I seemed to have a lot more clean clothes these days. Partly because spending every other day in bed is light on the wardrobe, partly through having Julie around. She seemed to like putting washing on, as long as it was all my clothes and didn't threaten her own grunge ensemble. I picked out some black drainpipes that I hadn't been able to fit into since – since the last time they were clean, I guess. There's nothing like violence and pain to take away your appetite. It leaves a nasty taste. I lose a lot of weight when I'm in the wars.

I picked up a white shirt which looked fresh and clean, but which turned out to be made of something alarmingly like cheesecloth. Once I'd put it on, though, I couldn't be bothered to take it off. Anyway, it went with the beard.

I thought about struggling over to Maggie's on the bus and Tube. For about a second and a half. Then I thought about not going at all until I felt better. But I wasn't confident I'd ever feel well enough to run this particular gauntlet. So I called a minicab firm and haggled them down to what was left in the last of Jeff's envelopes.

As a result, I expected the surliest guy in the team, driving a rustbucket, but it was a chatty Asian guy who turned up, dead proud of his catalytic converter.

'I'm not one of those drivers who doesn't care about the environment,' he insisted, before I'd even closed the car door. 'We've all got to play our part.'

I nodded politely, which was a mistake, because he made lots of eye contact through the rear-view mirror as he explained about the backlash against diesel. I tried to concentrate and certainly caught the drift – something to do with benzine – but I still thought minicabbing was a strange kind of job for an environmentalist. And soon after that I lost it, until he suddenly announced he had a covenant, which made him sound like Moses, or that guy in *Raiders of the Lost Ark*.

'To Friends of the Earth,' he said proudly. 'I pay something every month. And I get a newsletter. It's very informative. For instance, that tree we just passed. Behind on the left.' His eyes locked on to mine in the mirror. I sighed and twisted round awkwardly. 'Mature oak. Pumps forty gallons of water into the air every day through its leaves. Now which of us can claim to be that useful?'

He had a point. And I admired his commitment to a cause bigger than all of us. But I had a feeling that any minute he was going to start on about otters and I was going to have to tell him to shut up and drive.

We were saved by the fact that some roadworks which had been there for so long I'd come to accept them as part of the network had suddenly turned into two lanes of slow moving but otherwise unimpeded traffic. I remarked on this and then sat back as low as possible to sabotage the rear-view-mirror trajectory, while the inevitable logjams-I-have-known soliloquy rolled painlessly over my head. I spent the time trying to remember the number of the house Maggie lived in. It was in a short terrace of two-up, two-downs plus back extensions in a part of town where you settled if you valued energy and vibrancy and dynamism above not getting mugged. Maggie herself taught with flair and commitment at a multicultural school across a range of abilities. At least that was her story, in the days when I used to know her. Tom's version was that she basically taught one race – a race of very poor people – whose abilities ranged all the way from hopeless to doomed. All I could remember about Maggie's house was the burned-out car on a patch of waste ground opposite, which was a stroke of luck, because it was still there.

The cabbie seemed quite happy with his fare, which made me think I hadn't bargained hard enough. When he pulled away, he was still talking about the Westway. I hung around for a while, staring at the ash in the burned-out car, and at most of one front seat that had mysteriously survived. When I ran a finger along the metal roof frame, it came away black. As any halfwit – even one of Maggie's pupils – could have predicted. I wondered what was wrong with me and decided nothing new, I just didn't want to face Maggie in these particular circumstances.

Of course, I had a nerve calling round in the summer holidays and expecting her to be in. Isn't that when teachers are supposed to be working hardest, going into school most days, preparing coursework, reading round their subject, taking care of the gerbil and whatever else it is that makes them so uptight when you mention that they get almost as much time off as MPs and the Queen. I reminded myself sharply that I was here on business, not to debate pay and conditions, so I gave the burned-out car a goodbye rap, walked across the road and rang the bell.

Nobody answered.

I rang again. The bell was definitely working, because I could hear it inside. I waited another thirty seconds, decided against ringing a third time and tried to remember where the nearest pub was so I could celebrate my escape. Then I heard footsteps on the stairs.

Maggie was in her dressing gown, her face white and puffy with sleep. 'Yes?' she said, blinking into the light and not really focusing.

'It's me. Charlie.'

She pulled the gown tighter and started to concentrate. 'So it is.' She yawned and looked round abstractedly, clearly having no difficulty masking the rush of warmth that my reappearance in her life had generated. 'You look as rough as I feel, Charlie. What do you want?'

'To talk.' It was really my thing at the moment.

Maggie didn't move. 'So talk,' she said, which took me by surprise. Granted these weren't ideal circumstances, but Maggie and I had always got along OK. She'd never refused to let me into her house before.

'It's inside talk,' was all I could think of to say. This was already going worse than I'd expected.

Maggie looked at me tiredly. 'I'm sorry, Charlie, I don't want you in my house.'

Well, why not come right out and say it. I was taken aback at how hurt I felt. I swallowed hard and was a long way off thinking of anything else to say when Maggie made a half-hearted attempt to limit the damage.

'It's not you, Charlie. You know – it's just . . . '

It felt pretty much like me standing on the doorstep not being let in. And she couldn't even say his name.

'Tom's dead,' I told her. 'That's why I'm here.' Shades of the hard man I once was. And what a stupid place to show it. The swansong for what little judgement I ever had. 'I'm sorry. I didn't know how . . . '

But Maggie wasn't listening. She'd turned away and was walking slowly back into her house. I hesitated by the open door, wanting very much to shut it and run. It was touch and go for a while. Then I stepped inside and closed the door softly behind me.

It was a knock-through room with the kitchen tacked on the back. I could hear Maggie filling the kettle at the sink. I edged forward a few feet and looked nervously around. It didn't take long to work out why Maggie didn't want me there.

The playmat on the floor was brightly coloured, with soft gates that swung open, a tractor with blue wheels and furry farm animals all happy to bursting with their lot. To the side of it was a plastic scaffolding construction with three bug-eyed monsters dangling on swings. 'Babygym,' it said along the crossbar, though it didn't look like anything Greg had in his weights room. There was a photograph, not in a frame, propped up on the bookshelf in front of a row of paperbacks. I walked over for a closer look.

You couldn't tell, at least I couldn't tell, if it was a boy or a girl, or how old they were. I thought about Louis – I was beginning to understand what I'd heard from other people, that you get to an age when everyone you know is having kids – but it was hard to compare because Maggie's baby didn't have a hacksaw in its mouth. Plus I didn't know when the photo was taken. But say the baby was one and the photo was taken three months ago, that made fifteen months, plus another nine and a bit, say twenty-four. Two years.

'If you're counting backwards, Charlie, the answer's yes.'

I nodded slowly. Christ, what a mess.

Maggie sat down on the edge of a sofa covered in throws. 'I've put the kettle on, but I can't be bothered to make coffee. Help yourself if you like.'

I put the photo carefully back and sat down facing her in a canvas director's chair.

'No, thanks.'

So we just sat for a while, each with our thoughts. Well, Maggie with her thoughts, me with a sort of sick exhaustion which felt as if it was on a drip feed into the marrow of my bones. There was only so much of that kind of silence I could stand.

'Is . . . ah . . . I guess you were both asleep.'

'Rachel. She's called Rachel. Yes, we catch up a bit in the day. The nights aren't our best time.'

I nodded. I was getting the hang of this parenthood lark. The mother doesn't sleep, the father walks out and then either dies or writes about Sartre. No wonder the politicians are going back to basics.

Maggie hunched into her dressing gown. 'Tell me about Tom,' she said quietly. When she knew just as much as me. Just not the end bit.

I cleared my throat. 'Cancer. All over. Stomach, then everywhere. He was pretty much out of it by the end. Lots of drugs – drink as well. He stayed with Frank, but I don't think he spent much time there. He was . . . ah . . . was making new friends even then.'

'And what about Julia?'

My mind went blank. 'Julia who?' I said too fast, and by the time I'd realized, Maggie's face had closed down.

'Stop playing games, Charlie. You're not his monkey any more. And I don't care how much he left you or what he told you to say, when you're in my house, you don't lie to me, all right?'

'I'm not—'

'I asked you about Julia. If you want me to spell it out: Julia the Barons Court bimbo – a bit of pathetic alliteration that I was sad enough to need for longer than I care to admit, only now you'll doubtless tell me she's the youngest brain surgeon in London and spends her off-shift days working for Shelter.' She wiped away an angry tear. 'Well, if that's how it is, OK, I still want to know, because Tom owed me that much at least and I never got it, not one single word apart from her name, so that's something you can do for him, Charlie, you can at least put right one tiny bit of the mess he left behind when he walked off without telling me a single damn . . . '

She'd started crying harder and couldn't finish. I pulled gently on my earring, hesitated, then walked across the room, went down on my knees in front of her and took her hands, which were wet with tears, nervously in my own. This was rough terrain for me, and I'd badly lost my way. The speech I had ready, the one that Tom surely wanted me to deliver, about Julia the drop-dead gorgeous nightclub queen and sex grenade who turned his head for a few months, but who was ultimately just a nothing person in a great body and no competition for Maggie, hence the money, wouldn't come. And that left me with the truth, which really wasn't the hand I wanted to be holding when the dealing stopped.

Maggie caught her breath a few times and shuddered. 'Just tell me, Charlie. Tell me she was wonderful, tell me you were in love with her, too, tell me what the hell you like, only don't lie and don't keep me guessing.'

So that was that, and the only thing that helped me was the certainty that if I didn't say something soon, I was going to start crying, too. I still wake up sometimes in the middle of that scene – my desperate, literal dreams in bovine slow motion, with no hint of imagination, so I still mishandle everything, I'm still left telling Maggie that there was never any Julia and then, after a stunned pause, trying to hold her as best I can, still kneeling at her feet, as she goes pretty much to pieces. For the first few minutes, I kept hoping Rachel could stay asleep through all this, but then I changed my mind and hoped she'd wake up, so that at least there would be someone who needed Maggie crying for her. But in the dream, the only crying I hear is Maggie's, and it tears me apart. I always wake up when I hear the key in the lock.

'What in God's name is going on?'

The voice was deep and strong. I'd already half turned round. Maggie, who hadn't heard the door open, looked up.

We both found ourselves staring at an insignificant-looking guy with the remains of some red-blond hair which had probably been quite cute when he was eight, a couple of years before it started receding. He was an average height, vegetarianly thin, with a soft, featureless face. If it hadn't been for the voice, which he could profitably have lent out to the governor of the Bank of England, he wouldn't have amounted to much. And even with it, he could only hope to run his life on a Mr Nice Guy ticket – the decent chap who takes on another guy's kid.

Maggie pulled away and clumsily wiped her eyes on the back of her hands. 'I'm sorry,' she said hoarsely, but I wasn't sure to whom.

I'd just managed to get to my feet – with no great assurance, because the knee I'd damaged hadn't liked that scene any more than the rest of me – and take a step backwards when Mr Nice came striding over to assume his rightful place on the sofa next to Maggie, where he made a great show of putting his arms around her, stroking her hair and murmuring, 'There, there,' every now and then casting venomous glances over at the director's chair, to where I'd carefully retreated.

When Maggie had calmed down slightly and was beginning to look more embarrassed and less distraught, her partner treated me to his roughest stare yet. 'I think you've got some explaining to do,' he said, which was a devastating own goal, because we were off to a pretty rocky start and I wasn't in a punch-pulling mood. So I just shrugged, said, 'Tom's dead,' and watched his inner demons do the rest.

It was compulsive viewing. The moods passed across his face like white clouds in an azure sky. A double shot of relief, first that I wasn't in the frame except as a messenger boy, second that Tom was out of the frame for ever. Then the gnawing fear that if Maggie was this upset, it meant she'd loved Tom more than she loved him. And with that came the anger, initially with Maggie – he leaned away slightly, stopped stroking her hair – because, after all, he'd done the decent thing, more than most men would, and all she could do was break down in public over the low-life bruiser who'd knocked her up and walked out and had now obviously picked one fight too many and got what he deserved. But he couldn't afford to let that one run too long and soon leaned back in towards Maggie, because when it came down to it, he wasn't stupid, and I don't care how sensational he would have sounded in a radio production of *Othello*, he still had to face himself in the mirror and deep down he must have known that guys with evaporating hair and no features simply don't end up with women like Maggie unless they're in the right place (very close) at the right time (just after they've been messed up by another guy with a lot more class) and you just don't get a chance like that more than once in a lifetime. Which left a sackful of freefloating anger just waiting to be emptied over someone's head. How fucking predictable.

'If you've said your piece, I suggest you go.'

'Neil, please.'

'I've only just started,' I said. Which wasn't quite true – I must have been at least half-way – but it sounded good. Maggie looked over at me nervously, but let Neil do the talking.

'Then say what you have to say and get out. I think you've done enough damage for one day.'

This was so bizarrely unfair that it was almost funny. But not quite. I went very still and started calculating distances.

'Please, Charlie,' Maggie said quickly. 'This isn't easy for any of us. I know you don't mean to be . . . to be . . . '

To be what? I waited for the adjective, which never came. Maggie looked down at her bunched hands. Neil patted one of them, but it didn't uncurl.

'This is between Tom and Maggie,' I said, playing for time,

not expecting much of a result. Sure enough, Maggie shook her head slowly, without looking up.

'Not any more, Charlie.'

Which was self-evidently true, and there was nothing I could do about it. Coming back another day would have been one answer, but only in a parallel universe. In this one, I was out of time. Already, I was relying on the curvature of space to see me through, and I had a hunch it wasn't curved enough.

'OK. If that's how you want it.' I looked hard at Maggie, who didn't look as if she wanted it any way at all. 'Tom left you half his money. He asked me to give it to you.' I let it sink in. 'That's all – that's why I'm here. Doing all this damage.'

Cheap shot, but I'd earned it. I waited for a reaction, which was a long time coming.

'Tom didn't have any money,' Maggie said eventually, her voice little more than a whisper.

'Tom had a lot of money. He just couldn't touch it.'

My heart sank as I saw Neil's arm tighten protectively around Maggie's shoulder. I was beginning to doubt whether she'd ever make eye contact with me again.

'It's in cash at the moment. But if you prefer, you can give me an account number and I'll pay it in. Only I'd like to do it soon, because—'

'How did he get it?'

The predictable question, again spoken in a whisper – but by now it was something of a surprise to find anyone in the metropolis who didn't know.

'Does it matter?'

'Yes, I'm afraid it does.'

Maggie's reply was unhesitating. Maybe it was the controlling arm round her shoulders, but if I'm honest, I doubt it. I was left feeling like I was trying to steer a speeding car with four bald tyres round a hairpin bend on black ice. Everything was slipping away so fast it was hardly worth bothering.

'Don't you even want to know how much it is?'

This was desperate stuff, and Maggie didn't bother to reply. She'd also drawn the only conclusion open to her from my non-answer to her question. But at least she had the decency to face me when she spoke.

'That's not how I want to remember him, Charlie.'

She was calm now, and getting stronger. I was feeling sick and angry and falling apart. There was so much wrong with what she'd said. If she didn't want to remember Tom like that, she didn't want to remember so much of what he was, and just about everything he stood for. Or rather, against. This was personal. I didn't want her kicking over the traces of the friend I knew just because he wasn't a social worker.

'I can tell you how he wanted to be remembered, if you like. He was going to endow an annual prize. Said he was sick of watching second-rate showbiz riffraff fawning all over each other while so much genuine talent and achievement went unrecognized. He wanted an awards dinner and presentation for the year's best robbery. The Spaggiari Prize, he was going to call it.' Blank looks from Maggie and Neil, and no calls for enlightenment. I ploughed on anyway, aware that my voice was beginning to bounce off the walls. 'After Albert Spaggiari. A French paratrooper in Indo-China. When he came home, he rented a safe-deposit box at the Société Générale in Nice and worked out that the alarm system didn't respond to vibrations. He and his mates tunnelled up through the sewers over Easter. The only thing they left in the vault was a message. "Without hatred, without violence, without arms." They took about five million, which was worth something in 1976. And he died a free man twelve years later. Of cancer. Just like Tom.' I bit my lip hard. The blood was thumping in my ears. 'Maybe you'd like to endow the Spaggiari Prize with your share. I could ask around, see how it's done.'

How it's done, how it's done, how it's done. The words

echoed round the room. Or maybe it was just in my head. I started to rub my temples, and could feel the sweat under my fingertips. Maggie was looking at me with quiet pity.

'That's up to you, Charlie. You appear to be the executor.'

The legal term came close to sarcasm in the circumstances. I stroked my earring.

'What about Rachel? If Tom had known that—'

'He didn't know. He never knew. He walked out when I was still trying to decide how to tell him. So I'd rather you left Rachel out of this, if you don't mind.'

'If I don't mind?' I couldn't believe I was hearing this. 'It's not exactly the point, whether I mind, is it? I mean, what about her? It's her daddy that's dead, it's his money she should have and you're saying no she shouldn't just because you want to pretend Tom was some welfare worker who spent all his time teaching English to immigrant Bengalis. So what happens in a few years' time, when Rachel wants a new bike, or maybe to live in a decent neighbourhood or go to a school where more than a handful of other kids actually speak her language – what are you going to tell her then? Nope, we can't afford it, because all the money your daddy left you, we were just too good for it. Or are you going to say nothing at all, pretend there was no money, pretend there was no Tom, which you've more or less done already by whitewashing him, so she ends up with no daddy at all?'

I paused for breath, which I shouldn't have done, because I lost the thread, and all the stuff I thought I had lined up on my tongue turned out not to be there, after all, at least not quite, which gave Neil his chance.

'I don't know who the hell you think you are, you pathetic little fence, but I've heard enough. Rachel is my daughter and I'm going to make sure—'

'Your daughter?' What in God's name was going on here? I was so stunned I forgot to point out first, that I was at least three inches taller than him and second, that a fence sells stolen gear, he doesn't give it away.

'Are you asking to see the birth certificate?' The tone was withering, but I was in such a blind rage when I realized what he was saying that it was airgun pellets off a rhino's hide.

'I'm not talking about forms, for Christ's sake. I'm talking about blood. There's a girl upstairs whose daddy died and left her a lot of money and just because you came scavenging around after his leftovers and signed a few fucking forms doesn't give you the right to call yourself jack shit as far as I'm concerned, and the sooner you realize that and fuck off out of it, the sooner we—'

This isn't happening, I thought. I really couldn't believe Neil had stood up and was walking towards me. I looked wildly at Maggie, but missed eye contact again as she buried her face in her hands. Did he have any idea? He was probably a housing benefits clerk, or another teacher, or a male nurse. I told myself for everyone's sake, I should go easy and not hurt him too bad. I was so wound up I was scared I was going to break him in two.

He pulled me up by the front of my shirt, half turned me and slammed me back against the wall. My head went into a picture and I heard the glass break. I didn't feel much, though. While I was still warning myself not to kill him, because time was really not what I wanted to be doing for the rest of my life, he started a tug and slam routine, pulling me off the wall, driving me back into it, all the time yelling into my face a whole sequence of sentences beginning with 'Don't you dare' and 'If you ever'. A lot of them had the name Rachel in as well. By that stage I wasn't hearing too well, so I couldn't make out all the words, but the gist was definitely that I wouldn't be welcome at any of Rachel's birthday parties, with or without a present, and if I turned up again in a couple of decades wanting to marry her, he, Neil, would almost certainly object and might even boycott the wedding.

On the third or fourth slam, the frame behind my head disintegrated and a shower of splintered wood exploded off the wall and settled around my feet. Mr Nice's scalp was beginning to shine and the lids over his pale grey eyes were glowing pink. He shoved me back again into the wall and this time there was no picture behind my head, only the nail that had been holding it up, and that hurt like hell and I wasn't ready for it, so I tried to twist off the wall like Ali coming off the ropes against Foreman, only I stepped on one of the larger pieces of glass, which slid at least a foot along the carpet before it shattered, and that was enough, my legs were gone and I came down heavily on my side, which was a tough way to test how my ribs were healing, but they weren't too bad, at least in comparison to the back of my head, which felt like I imagine JFK's felt just before it landed in Jackie's lap.

'... God's sake, Neil!' Maggie's voice was shrill and ragged. I could also hear a baby crying. Rachel, right on cue.

'Get up,' Neil panted, but he was on to a loser there. I wasn't going anywhere in a hurry. I made it on to my hands and knees, just to show willing, and found myself staring down at the poster, which still had lengths of frame joined at a right angle along most of two sides. The picture was of a cold and pissed-off looking guy with a beard, standing in deep snow by a gate, thinking profound thoughts. Just in case you were in any doubt, one of them was stencilled boldly over a middle-distance frostbitten tree. I read it slowly: 'Let the lie come into the world, even dominate the world – but not through me.'

I dabbed at the back of my head and my hand came away with blood. But I hadn't checked it beforehand, and as I was on all fours in a sea of glass, the blood could have been on my hand already. It was the nearest I could manage to a comforting thought. Neil's pale fist came down to grab a handful of my shirtfront again.

'I said get up.'

This time I made more of an effort, and between us we got me back on my feet. It wasn't that wonderful to be there, because my head felt wobbly and unbalanced, and I wasn't sure where I'd be heading once Neil let go of my shirt. In the short term, though, this wasn't something I had to factor into the equation. Neil's fist had found its spiritual home. The exciting world of death-wish vigilantism had opened up for him and he was having a ball.

'Jesus – I thought you guys were meant to be tough,' he said with extravagant distaste as he dragged me in a clumsy *pas de deux* towards the door. And he had a point. I thought briefly about staging some kind of rally, for pride's sake as much as anything, but the timing was wrong. I'd come back from slow starts before, but never this slow. And only by cheating. The strange realization was also dawning, as I tried to draw on reserve tanks that turned out to be not only empty but corroded beyond repair, that I must have had a lot more pride back then as well. Neil opened the door with his free hand and told me one final time that if he ever saw me hanging round the house again etcetera etcetera, while I tried to focus on the bonnet of the Volkswagen Polo that I knew I was about to be shoved on to and get my hands up to protect my chest. Part of me – the grown-up, no pride part – said take it easy, be cool, everyone has a mix of victory and defeat on their slate, it's just another chalk mark. The rest of me felt it was a hard coming of age, a decade and a half late, to be turned over by a Citizen's Advice Bureau liaison officer with a few strands of gingery blond hair.

'Now fuck off and die like your friend,' he snarled, shoving me hard at the car, and I was so shocked I didn't even get my hands right, I couldn't believe what I'd just heard and right then was when I knew I'd lost it, whatever I'd once had, it was gone for ever, because if even half, a quarter, a third of it had been there, I would have clawed and stumbled my way back in, scraped up one of the triangles of frame glass and, time or no time, I was well past caring, opened up his neck with pleasure and watched the blood pump out.

Instead of which, I was down in the road, spitting gravel, staring past the bulbous safety bumper that was level with my head, over towards the burned-out car with its one intact seat that looked so inviting. And all I could think of was Solzhenitsyn, it was Solzhenitsyn, the guy with the beard in the poster, and he was probably looking grim because he was in despair at the lack of basic human freedoms in the former Soviet Union, rather than just being hacked off that his drive was under three feet of snow and there wasn't a gritter in sight.

Seventeen

The lifts were out of order. Or, more accurately, they weren't there at all. The shafts were empty and guys in overalls were swarming up and down ladders and calling out cable measurements to each other. They'd rigged up some powerful spotlights, which were unshielded and made my eyes hurt. The men ignored me, which was a big improvement on the last couple of hours, when hawkers of the *Big Issue* and scruffs with squeegees loitering at traffic lights had looked at me in disgust.

The sign in red apologized for the inconvenience. For me, though, it was more a question of pain. Which was why I put off the climb and hung around watching the Otis brothers doing their stuff, content not to be recoiled from but at the same time tempted to grab one of them by the sleeve and say: Oi, d'you know who I am? I'm the guy who's paying for all this. But I held off, partly out of natural reticence, partly because it wasn't strictly true (Oi, d'you know that I'm the guy who stole the cash that my brother's lover invested with ludicrous success and the rake-off is covering the installation of these lifts? Which is just as well as the council's broke and the housing corporation's little more than a holding company for Big Al), and if there was one thing I'd learned the hard way in the last few hours, it was never to let the lie come into the world through me.

When I'd watched the boys scurrying around for a while,

and nobody had offered to carry me up five flights, even though I didn't have a single carrier bag of shopping, I sighed and began the long climb myself. I was curious about how I'd get into Alan's flat without scaling the empty lift shaft, but not so curious that all the aches and pains were washed away on a tidal wave of excitement.

I eventually reached a fire door and hammered as loudly as my scabbed hands would allow – the metallic raps clattered around in my head. I leaned heavily on the wall.

'Who is it?' Alan's voice was far away and suspicious.

'Me,' I said, and then listened to the soft, sticky slap of bare feet on warm lino. Two bolts were pulled and the door opened abruptly outwards. I took a stumbling step back. Alan winced when he saw me.

'What the hell have you been doing?'

I didn't answer, because I badly needed to sit down after my climb, so I lurched past him towards the nearest of the old sofas.

'You've got blood on the back of your head,' Alan said, presumably out of genuine concern, because it wasn't as if his furniture was too precious to be dripped on.

I made it to the sofa just before my legs gave, and collapsed on to it so heavily that I could hear the frame crack. Alan went quiet and gave me some space – yards and yards of the stuff, the one luxury his apartment wasn't short of – by walking in a wide arc to the sink where he ran the cold for a while and then filled up a glass from the draining board. He peered critically at the water, decided it would do and brought it over. I'd managed to get my head forward and down, so he had to stand holding it for a couple of minutes while I decided whether or not to faint.

'Thanks,' I said eventually, when I was confident of staying conscious. Then I drank the water straight down, so Alan had to pad over to the sink and refill the glass. 'Thanks,' I said again, beginning to sound embarrassingly gushy. I recognized the problem from those occasions when you're behind someone through a whole sequence of doors. Do you thank them every time for holding one open? Or maybe just the first and last? It's almost worth elbowing them out of the way between doors so you can do your bit and not feel beholden.

'Better?' Alan asked politely.

I nodded and settled back on the sofa. 'Thanks,' I said, and could have kicked myself. There was a loud bleep from Alan's computer as it finished running one of his foxy little man-traps, but he didn't look over.

'You look beat up,' he observed, standing some way back. 'What happened?'

I wasn't in the mood to answer, so I stared around the room for a bit. A few scattered objects in a sea of industrial lino. The computer screen started scrolling a colourful geometric pattern, which drew attention to the lack of colour and geometry anywhere else in the room. Even Alan's clothes were pastel and baggy.

'How come you have so much space and nothing in it?'

Alan shrugged. 'I like space and I'm not interested in furniture. And my teapot collection's in store for safe keeping.'

The hairs on the back of my neck stood up straight and cold. I could have sworn I'd just heard a joke. I squinted uncertainly at Alan, who stonewalled to such effect that I was thrown back on answering his question.

'I got thrown against a wall with a nail in,' I said, easing up on details about the height of my assailant, his lack of hair, the probable caring and sedentary nature of his job.

'So what were you doing to these guys to piss them off so much?' Alan's assumption of multiplicity was touchingly loyal.

'There was only one of him. And I was trying to give him money. Half the money, in fact.'

Alan looked grim and unsurprised. 'So how much did he want – most or all?'

'None.'

Now he looked surprised. 'And so he threw you against a wall with a nail in it?'

'Pretty much, yeah.'

Alan turned away. 'Some people can be so touchy,' he remarked, walking over towards his kitchen area. He picked up a plastic-topped stool, sending a couple of metal trays that were propped up against it clattering to the floor, and brought it round behind the sofa. 'I don't like the look of the back of your head,' he said, venturing off again down the right wing of his room. 'Makes a change from the old days,' he added over his shoulder, 'when I didn't like the look of the front of it.'

He disappeared through his bathroom door. I sat quite still on the sofa, numb with shock. This time, there was no doubt. Alan had definitely made a joke. I listened to the fan come on automatically in the bathroom, then the sound of running water. When Alan started the long trek back, he was carrying a plastic basin of water in both hands, with a bottle of shampoo floating on the surface and a mug knocking against the sides. A towel was draped over his arm.

He put the basin down on the plastic seat of the stool. 'Sit back a bit. And tilt your head.'

I did as I was told and found myself staring at grey polystyrene tiles, numerous corners of which looked as if they'd been gnawed by gravity-defying mice. Alan lowered the towel on to my chest and pulled it up round my neck.

'I'm thinking of a perm,' I said, to cover my general embarrassment.

'That's because your brain's fallen out of the huge hole in the back of your head,' Alan said, scooping up a mugful of water and going to work. 'Which reminds me – I've got your money. In a suitcase under my bed. I'm glad you came early, because it's freaking me out. I think I hate cash as much as you hate accounts.'

If there was one thing freaking me out, it was the flow of chat. 'What's got into you?' I demanded, with perhaps inappropriate aggression. Alan wasn't fazed and continued wetting my hair.

'I'm in a good mood,' he said unnecessarily.

'Why?' Surely not just because I'd been beaten up.

I heard him put down the mug in the water and snap open the top of the shampoo bottle. 'You'd be surprised – I generally am these days. Right now it's a mix of things. You ever heard of a bank called Barings?'

'No.'

Alan sighed and worked the shampoo firmly into my scalp, skirting the bits where there was no scalp to work it into. 'You will soon. It's about to go bankrupt. You wouldn't believe what's going on.'

I wouldn't understand what's been going on, more like. Nor care. 'So what's the big deal about a bank running out of money?'

'Because it's not just any bank, little brother. That's the beauty of it. These clowns paid for the Napoleonic Wars, that's how blue chip they are. Eton, Oxbridge and the Guards over centuries, and now they're going to be sold for scrap because a plasterer's son from Watford who failed his maths A level kept playing double or quits in a Singapore derivatives market that no one in London understood.' He dug his fingers rhythmically into my scalp, hard, so I could feel his nails. 'Imagine it – you walk into a craps den and you lose a whole fucking bank. It's brilliant, Charlie, I love it. The spirit of punk will never die.' If he didn't have his hands soaked in lather and blood, I'm sure he'd have hugged himself.

'How d'you know all this?'

'Friend of Bruce's at the Bank of England. They've been tipped off, so he's been told to draft an official inquiry report explaining how none of it was in any way foreseeable or the fault of the regulatory authorities. Same as BCCI. They want the basic outline in place before the circus starts, so they can slot in a few selected facts as they become known. But you don't have to take my word for it. Just read the papers over the next few weeks. And enjoy.'

Alan had good hands. The headache that seemed to have been there on and off for a week was starting to fade. Lucky Bruce, I thought, and then worried briefly that I oughtn't to be speculating about that side of Alan's life. 'I may not be around in a week or two. I'm going away for a while. Probably to France.'

'What for?'

'To let things cool. And I've got this idea about carving stone.'

Alan mulled it over for a while. Then he cleared his throat softly. 'Can't keep running for ever, Charlie. Gotta stand and fight for something.'

To me, it felt like I'd been fighting round after round for as long as I could remember. But never for anything much – I suppose that was Alan's point.

'For something like this, you mean?' I would have made an expansive gesture with my hands to encompass his whole estate, but they were under the towel and I didn't want to risk dislodging it with the rinse still to come. Fortunately, Alan knew what I meant.

'Why not? It works for me. A few people live safer lives in better surroundings because I spend the money I don't need. That adds up to something.'

'*Si monumentum requiris . . .* ' I murmured, surprising myself.

'Yes and no. One of those petitions will work one day. There'll be a new housing officer who'll take one look at this flat, turf me out and turn it back into three. And then the lifts won't get fixed when they go wrong, and more cars will get stolen, and the graffiti will come back and the garden at the back will grow wild. It's hardly going to be a lasting monument. But for a few years, I'll have made a difference. I'm not asking for more.' I heard the mug scrape along the plastic bowl and obediently tipped my head further back. Alan cupped a hand on my forehead to shield my eyes. 'But you should. Anyone who staggers home after a pub brawl spouting Latin has a few things to sort out.'

This was poetic licence and then some. It wasn't a pub brawl, I wasn't at home and I'd managed half a well known Latin saying. 'Is this the price of a free haircut? A grow up lecture?' I started to fidget, but Alan pressed down firmly on my forehead.

'*On n'est pas là pour rigoler*,' he observed equably.

'Says who?' I asked, playing for time while I tried to work out what rigoler meant.

'De Gaulle, I think,' Alan said, which gave me the clue I needed. Not your average surf bum, in other words, so it was probably safe to assume a general thrust along the lines of life perhaps not being such a beach, after all.

I was spared having to think up a reply to the General's sparky one-liner by the towel which Alan pulled up from my chest to cover my head, having presumably decided there wasn't much more in the way of cleanliness to be gained from the one bowl of water. I pressed the towel into my face, like a tennis player between games, and enjoyed the soft, temporary darkness. When I come out from under here, I thought, listening to Alan walking back to the bathroom with his bowl full of blood and grease, I'll be grown up and full of good intentions. Even as I made it, though, this seemed a ludicrous boast. I decided to rephrase it in more realistic terms. When I come out from under here, I'll have clean hair. Apart from the bit at the back.

I stayed under the towel until I could hear Alan humming his way back towards his prehistoric stove. 'I'm going to have a hot chocolate,' he said. 'Want one?'

I emerged into the grey light to accept, and then remembered how long the operation had taken last time and thought about crawling back under the towel for a snooze. But it seemed ungrateful. 'OK,' I said. 'And I'd also like to know what's happening with the back of my head.'

'It's a scabby mess,' Alan said bluntly. 'Which is one up on a bleeding mess. D'you still mend like you used to?'

'Pretty much. But I've been pushing it lately.'

Alan poured the milk from a grubby carton into his saucepan. 'You'll probably be fine. And if you do start haemorrhaging, at least the surgeon will have some clean hair to cut through.'

I must have looked comically bewildered by this flash of the old Alan. He chuckled as he picked up his pliers and wrenched the spindle on the cooker. 'Relax. That was another joke. Your head's OK – stop being such a drama queen.'

In the circumstances, it was pretty heroic of me not to sulk. After three decades of spectacular underachievement, low-grade criminality and cheap violence, I was about to disappear into the sunset – or get caught – with a suitcase full of money, a book on marble and a hole in the back of my head. It seemed pretty dramatic to me. I'd never felt more like a luvvie in all my life.

I stared moodily at Alan, who in turn was staring at his house-clearance hob. Both of us had come to the realization simultaneously that Operation Sweet Milky Drink was likely to extend over the sort of timescale normally associated with geological shelf formations, and we'd clean run out of conversation. Both of us began to twitch. Alan glanced over at the hi-fi, which started the sweat running down my back. His priceless bootlegs may have been locked in a vault, but that still left plenty of stuff bad enough to be released. I cleared my throat loudly to derail any thought train heading in that direction, which left me the problem of what to say when Alan looked over politely.

'Ah . . . Bruce home?' was the best I could come up with.

Alan shook his head. 'Any minute. We thought you might like to stay for some supper.'

What a minefield visit. I'd completely lost the ability to read Alan. Not that it was ever much of a skill – more like a defence reflex. What did he mean, 'we'? Short of telepathy, there was no way Bruce could have known anything about my visit, let alone expressed a desire to break bread with me. And there was also the practical point. If it took this long to make a hot chocolate, when was the food going to be on the table? Not that there was one, of course.

'Takeaway,' said Alan, who clearly had no problems reading me.

'Oh, well. Sure. Thanks.'

The implications of this exchange weighed heavy on us both. Alan gazed at the milk as it battled to rise above ambient temperature. I rubbed nervously at my stubble. If Bruce's cab was caught in traffic, this was going to seem like a mighty long visit. I watched the clouds trundling purposefully across the sky and couldn't decide if they were really that grey or whether it was dirt on the windows. Perhaps Alan only had a monochrome licence for his view. I almost said something, but caught myself just in time. I was not going to be panicked into talking about clouds.

It was Alan's turn to clear his throat. A nerve in my cheek flickered. I felt like a lower-order batsman uncertain whether he's facing pace or spin.

'Don't bother answering if you don't want to. I wouldn't ask if Bruce were here. But how exactly did you get that money?'

Eighteen

You know the feeling when you're coming through Customs at the airport and you know that nobody's going to be there to meet you, it's no big deal, you weren't expecting anyone, but still, it's hard to walk past all the families shrieking and hugging and the drivers holding up bits of cardboard with the names of important people on and trudge on towards the Tube without sliding just a few feet in the direction of self-pity.

Well, imagine how it feels to come out of jail that way: through a huge, sliding door of concertinaed metal – like leaving a bus depot by the buses' exit. Why they can't let you walk out through a normal size door, Christ only knows. Instead, there's a big routine of sliding back this ridged, sludge-brown wall, just in case you wanted to drive out in the armoured personnel carrier you had on you when you were arrested. Maybe it's to make you feel small that they throw you out by the biggest door they can find.

The only thing I had going for me was that I came out the same time of year I went in. Doing years-and-a-half can play havoc with your wardrobe. Go down in a heatwave, come out in January, and straight off you've got a problem with goosebumps. It's true, you're allowed to get clothes from family and friends to come out in. But first you have to have the family and friends.

When in doubt, walk. For the first half hour you notice

everything, from the varying shades of grey of the pavements and kerbs and tarmac to the varying shades of grey of the clouds in the sky and the faces of the people. You do notice a lot of grey in this country. But I wasn't complaining. For me, it made a change from the pale blue everything, which half-way through my stretch became pale blue most things plus splashy, primary coloured other things, mainly random walls, presumably designed to cheer us up and persuade us not to riot. They only put one coat of the nursery colours on, though, so in places the blue streaked through, creating a distressed look that was madly Fulham. It wasn't enough to convince us we'd been banged up in the Conran Shop, but who's to say it didn't work? Because there were no riots while I was in. The only time we came close was when a Scottish guy three cells down, who'd spent most of his childhood and all his adult life inside, nicked a third of a can of fire-engine red paint from the dining room and the screws decided to turn out all the cells. To me, that said everything about jail. First, what the fuck is the point of nicking a third of a can of red paint? Except to make one dining-room wall more distressed than the three others, and I really don't think that's what he was aiming at. Second, just how stupid d'you have to be to think, Oh, Christ, a third of a can of paint's gone missing, it's only a matter of time before the metal lid gets turned into a lathe capable of slicing through high-tensile steel in seconds, we'd better turn out all the cells and really wind up lots of already pointlessly violent people?

This, I decided, as I walked moodily alongside cars that were travelling scarcely faster than I was, is the big problem with rehabilitation as a penal aim. Everyone around is too thick. Tom's lament about the average criminal IQ – at least, the average unsuccessful criminal's IQ – wasn't far off. Sure, there are clever cons who've masterminded frauds so complex that the jury doesn't have a hope of understanding them and ends up saying, what the hell, heads he goes down, tails he walks. But if it does land heads, they're all in Strand Open Prison, with its adjoining door to The Savoy, so lags on guilt trips can go through and rough it for a while. I was surrounded by the sort of guys who nick a third of a can of red paint as a reflex action and a whole bunch of other guys who don't see the joke.

As I walked I kept half an eye out for members of Laura's family, come to meet me with metal bars. One of her brothers in particular seemed to think at the time that striking me off his Christmas card list wasn't retribution enough. But he was younger then, and it really didn't seem likely. Tell the truth, I'd have been a lot more scared of running into Laura, trying to say something and not to stare at the empty sleeve. I'd heard she'd decided against anything plastic. Ideally, though, I didn't want to meet anybody just yet, which made my airport-arrivals whinge even more unreasonable.

I ducked into a café – the sort of place where I was one of the upmarket clientele – and bought myself a mug of tea and a bun, partly because I couldn't afford much more, partly because a bun was something I'd never had inside. Biting through the inch-thick glaze reminded me that I'd never much liked buns anyway and put the last four years into a more favourable perspective. I just about managed to finish it, give or take a hard, crusty edge, with the help of a second mug of tea and a lot of patient chewing. There was no great hurry. I aimed to check out a couple of pubs I used to haunt when the evening came round. But they weren't the sort of places that livened up early, so I had time on my hands.

When I came out of the café, the sun was out, at least intermittently, and everything looked a marginally fresher shade of grey. I decided to head for a park and find a bench where I could look at a few green things – grass, trees, that kind of stuff – and maybe even some girls. So far, they'd looked pretty beaten down and drab, pushing children or carrying shopping, most doing both. I'd never liked this part of London much. Even less than I'd liked buns.

The second time the battered white van came past, I registered three digits of the numberplate. So when it came past a third time, I knew it was the same one. By this stage, I was almost back on home turf and thinking seriously about a drink. The street was quiet. The first couple of times the van passed, it had cars following. Now, it pulled in thirty yards up the road. I stopped walking and put down my holdall. If Laura's gang were going to spring out the back with baseball bats, they'd left themselves quite a sprint.

The hazard warning lights flashed on, then off, then on again, which left me none the wiser as I've never learned Morse code. I picked up my bag and moved a few yards closer, then stopped again and looked around. No one seemed to be watching this protracted courtship ritual. There was a wrench of metal and the van's passenger door creaked open half-way, which looked about as far as it would go. Still no sign of the driver. Probably his door didn't open at all. I sighed and picked up my bag. If the back of the van was stuffed with balaclavaed thugs, I was going to have to face them sooner or later. I walked on with as much equanimity as I could fake.

Three paces behind the open passenger door, I swung my arm back and lobbed my holdall in towards the footwell, tensing on the balls of my feet for some reaction. The bag went high, hit the glove compartment and collapsed shape-lessly, half on and half off the seat. Nothing happened. No one jumped out with a baseball bat, a bouquet of flowers or a red book with 'This Is Your (Lag's) Life' stencilled in gold on it. I took a step back, unnerved by the lack of reaction, and was about to start backing off fast, minus worldly posses-sions, when a familiar and deeply irritated voice growled: 'Fuck's sake, Charlie, get in the sodding van.'

Tom pulled away from the kerb while I was still trying to close the door, which seemed to have a couple of rough welds instead of hinges. For the first couple of corners, the only way I could stay in my seat was by holding on white-knuckled to the plastic catch of the glove compartment. Then the road straightened and I managed to jam the door closed again.

'You could just have pulled alongside. Said hello.'

'People like you get nervous if vans pull up alongside them. You'd have bolted. I wanted to give you fair warning. Besides, you never know who's watching, so I wanted to keep it low-key. If I'd known you'd start mincing up and down the street doing fairy steps and then throwing your handbag around, I might have done it different.'

This seemed grossly unfair. 'It could have been anyone.'

'No, it couldn't,' Tom said, and he had a point. I folded my arms, which was the nearest I was going to get to having a safety belt on, and stared morosely through the windscreen. Eventually, Tom got the message that he'd been a little abrupt. 'You hungry?'

'Yes.'

'Good. We're heading for a drive-in McDonald's. It opened while you were away.'

The things I'd missed. 'You don't think we could perhaps try an Indian?' As soon as I'd spoken, it occurred to me that Tom might be driving around in a beaten-up old van and treating me to a burger and fries because he was broke. It was a disturbing thought. I wished I'd held my tongue.

Tom shook his head emphatically. 'No point risking that. I don't want anyone to see us together.'

It's embarrassing to recall that only then did alarm bells start ringing. It's true what they say – when you're out of the game for a while, you do slow up.

'This isn't your van, is it?'

Tom looked at me with astonishment. 'Do me a favour,' he said, clearly wondering how much of his old partner was left.

The first spots of rain appeared on the windscreen. Tom pushed a few stalks at random and eventually the wipers began smearing the glass into opacity.

'What's going on?' I said.

'I'll tell you over a milkshake.'

'Tell me now – or I jump.'

Tom sighed and turned into an industrial park crammed with electrical warehouses. A few car parks ahead gleamed the golden arches. 'Amounts to the same thing – we're here,' he said, which was a face-saver for us both. He didn't have to spill the beans early, I didn't have to fight with the door again.

I told him what I wanted to eat and then leaned forward and down as we drew up to the booth. I couldn't believe it was necessary, but it gave me the chance to shift my holdall off my left foot, which was slowly going numb.

'And two large coffees – black,' Tom said, though I hadn't asked for one. It was a sure sign that an early night wasn't on the cards. I retied one of my laces, then the other, but there wasn't much else I could do down there, so I just listened to the blood pumping in my ears until Tom had paid, put the van in first and was grinding forward towards the biggest space he could find, away from all the steamed-up Escorts rocking vigorously back and forth. It was a down-market but potent reminder of how I should have been spending my first night out, and what the blood should be pumping through. I sat up slowly, wondering why the smell of burgers made me feel both hungry and mildly sick.

Tom killed the engine and looked me straight in the eye. 'You're not thinking of going straight?'

I hesitated. 'Well . . . it's an option.'

'Bollocks. It's an option if you've got money. How much have you got?'

I took the question as rhetorical. Tom passed over my nutritionally dubious nosegay. I peered in and picked out some fries.

'Look,' Tom said persuasively, rummaging in his own bag. 'It's just a little something I've lined up for us. Small and easy, just to get you on your feet again. I'm working on a better one, but it won't come up for a few months. This is to tide you over.'

I munched steadily on my cholesterol blowout. 'I don't know . . . I mean, I only got out a few hours ago.' And I wasn't sure about an attempt on the world recidivism record.

'Exactly!' Tom said, through a mouthful of beef and ketchup. 'Nobody pulls this kind of stunt their first night out. They get drunk, they get laid – the usual stuff. It's great cover. Anyone even asks you about it, you just roll your eyes and say "Get real, I only came out that morning." It's perfect.'

I tried to concentrate, but my mind kept slipping off down the road signposted 'The Usual Stuff' – destinations drunksville and laidsville. Great places. Used to go there a lot. Hadn't been back in a while, of course.

I fished in the paper bag, brought out my coffee and balanced it on the dashboard above the glove compartment. Tom's idea of a celebration drink, I thought sourly. And hot as hell, too. I munched through a few more chips and thought about the burger. Which was preferable to eating it, I decided, rolling over the top of the bag and putting it down by the handbrake.

'You not hungry?' Tom said, pulling the bag over on to his lap before I'd had the chance to reply. 'Probably too emotional, seeing me again and all that.' He sucked noisily on his cola.

'Chips is fine,' I said wearily, trying to get comfortable on the practically foamless seat. If the choice had been between listening to Tom talk or eat, I'd have kept him primed with questions. But it wasn't an either-or deal.

'Look, I'll run it by you,' he said, chomping his way through one half of the styrofoam burger bun. 'See what you think.' He paused to wipe his mouth carefully on his napkin, which came away as red as a corpse in a splatter movie. 'There's this guy runs a small safe-deposit place up in Wood Green, near—'

'Up where?'

Tom paused to lick salt off his fingers. 'Don't knock it. The building society with the highest cash turnover in the country is in Wood Green, for your information. Plasterers aplenty, who don't use plastic and don't trust cheques. Think about it. Knightsbridge Abbey National probably turns over about seventeen pence a day in cash, because it's so vulgar. So a little safe-deposit shop in Wood Green is bound to have some useful liquidity that no one wants on their tax form.'

I wondered how soon I'd be able to get rid of the brown food bags. There was a bin a few yards away, but I couldn't see myself ever heaving my door open. 'Safe-deposit centres have good alarms. Cops cruise by them. Even in Wood Green, probably. I don't see it.'

'You don't see half of it,' Tom confirmed. 'The guy who runs the lock-up shop – Mohinder someone-or-other – has just built an extension and wants the whole place tarted up. So he calls in Frank to give him a quote, even though it's completely obvious he's going to get his cousin to do it and that Frank's just been hauled in to put downward pressure on the price.'

'Frank who?'

Tom took a bite out of what by now must have been my burger. I didn't feel cheated. 'Frank, my brother,' he said.

'I didn't know you had a brother.'

Tom looked over at me. 'It's not uncommon, Charlie. I'll tell you about him some time. For the moment, all you need to know is that he doesn't warm to Mohinder, who keeps on about how cheaply his cousin can do it and how it's going to be a dead easy job because all the lockers are going to be cleared out over the holiday weekend. Which makes sense, because he's hardly going to trust anyone else with the boxes. And while they're haggling away in Mohinder's office, Frank

278

happens to notice this tariff card for a self-storage warehouse half tucked under the phone on his desk. He puts two and two together, and when Mohinder comes back to him a couple of days later and says, surprise, surprise, that his cousin has put in a quote one third cheaper and would he like to match it, Frank says on the whole he'd rather mash his own bollocks to paste in a nutcracker, hangs up and the next time he sees me says he knows something I might be interested in.'

I sipped cautiously at my coffee, which was cooling slowly from its molten state. 'Self-storage,' I mused. 'So how d'you know which one? He probably got lots of quotes. It seems to be his thing.'

'Sure,' Tom said, lucky dipping into his bag and coming up with yet another fistful of chips. 'There's four places he could use that are convenient. I've checked them all out. This is the second nearest to him and easily the cheapest. What more d'you need to know?'

'Well . . . ' I took the question at face value. 'How we get in, for a start.'

Tom had slept. I hadn't. He could sleep anywhere. This time he'd clambered into the back of the van and stretched out on a towel. A towel, for Christ's sake. Not even a mattress. I lay down across the front seats with my head under the steering wheel, listening to the tick of the clock, watching the hands creep slowly into the early hours. After a while, Tom's snores drowned out the ticking and I sat up. I wanted something to rest my head on. Tom had said there was another towel in the glove compartment, but it turned out to be a two-inch-square rag covered in oil. I sighed and collected up all the burger debris, then slid over to the driver's door and jumped down.

The night was fresh and cold and I could feel a fine, feathery rain on my face. I picked one of the furthest bins and walked slowly over with my bags and cartons. It was satisfying to drop them in. No more blood on my hands – or ketchup. I moved away from the bin, keeping to the shadows out of habit, coming round in a wide sweep behind the van, which was one of only three vehicles in the parking lot. There was no sign of life from the other two. Either the teenagers had fallen into an exhausted sleep, or the cars hadn't started and they'd all taken the night bus home. Or it was the world's most obvious stakeout. I made a mental note – if the two cars move when we do, think again.

I was standing with my back against the side of the van, getting cold, when I heard Tom's watch alarm bleeping. It came as a relief. I swung myself up behind the wheel and then edged over to my side. Tom went through his yawning, stretching and grunting routine, which was elaborate and intense. Eventually, he clambered back over the seats and settled himself down to drive. Before he gunned the engine, he looked over at me and smiled.

'Cheer up,' he said. 'Beats work.'

The routine was so familiar, I could hardly believe I'd been away. Tom driving and talking, me watching the mirrors and twitching.

'We'll go through the vehicle entrance,' Tom said. 'It's a tall shutter door to take removal lorries. Complete crap. About as secure as a rolltop desk. There's an alarm just inside it, of all dumb places, but high up – about ten foot. I've got a ladder in the back. There's no way we'll stop it going off, but we should be able to knock it out in about five seconds, and who'll bother? The angle grinder and drill are all charged up. Brilliant things, power packs. I can't believe they're legal. But I've brought along your chisels, for old time's sake. When we get in, it's the second floor. Loads and loads of cages. Punters have to bring their own padlock. Most of them seem to bring the Squire they used on their school lockers. Mohinder's probably taken a medium-sized cage, say a hundred square feet, because the next size up is two hundred and that's a lot more expensive. We've just got to find it.'

I'd begun to feel inappropriately hungry. My stomach was growling. 'When did you check all this?'

'Wednesday. I went to a house-clearance auction and bought the first ten lots for fifty pence, loaded 'em up and drove 'em down there. Took my time about hauling them up to my little cage. Even got lost once or twice in the corridors, silly me. But there wasn't much to see. Place is full of wardrobes. It's no wonder they're not bothered about visitors.'

We passed a police car, as we always seem to, but it was parked while the cops inside made contemporaneous notes about arrests they'd made over the past six months. I hoped Tom had checked the headlights, brakelights and indicators before coming out. That used to be my job, before the State took on the responsibility for my keep. Tom put on the radio, but not for long. I remembered soothing downbeat pap being played for sad people still awake in the small hours. But this was all phone-ins encouraging the sappy no-hopers to speak from the heart about what was wrong with their lives. At cheap rate, I suppose, but even so.

'What d'you reckon the phone-ins are like in Bangladesh?' Tom mused. 'Must be a bit samey. "My rice patch is flooded and my children are starving." Time after time. Crap radio, but they've got a point. Unlike these zeros. I mean, who the hell cares if everyone in her family forgot her birthday?'

Not me, certainly, so I wasn't bothered when he retuned, found only soulful organ music on one station and a rap evangelist called Praise B on another, and snapped off the radio in disgust. We spent the next quarter of an hour in silence, as I watched familiar landmarks drift by and listened to the ladder in the back shake loose and start clattering away on the metal floor. When Tom eventually slowed to a crawl, I was as ready as I'd ever be for what turned out to be probably the least eventful criminal episode of my life.

It's always the way, isn't it. I remember once I was in a pub that was being raided, and the only thing I was doing was drinking. Even so, I found myself vaulting the bar, sprinting upstairs to the private rooms, dropping down out of the frosted bathroom window and crawling into a filthy out-house. Just to get into the spirit of things. Other times, I've made serious attempts on short- and middle-distance track records just to escape a possible caution and a few hard ploddy stares. I don't know why. I think I just get carried away. But this one, the one that set me up for life, was a stroll.

Tom hated it. He hated the luck mainly, and the lack of skill. He was working on something in the Spaggiari line – I never did find out what – which would earn him as much respect as hard cash. This was a little filler, a favour to me, a clumsy smash and grab while his mind was on other things. And then it spilled over in a way that just about wrecked the last few years of his life.

We pulled on the blue overalls and rubber gloves in the back of the van, with the engine still running. I picked up the angle grinder and decided against wearing the safety goggles Tom had thoughtfully provided. They looked grubby, and there was little enough light to see by anyway. Besides, there's a limit to how prissy you can be on these occasions. I took a final look out of the back window of the van at the rolling shutter door and checked with Tom that he thought it was a centre lock under the bottom lip.

'Has to be,' he said. 'Just slide across until you hit it. Matter of fact, we probably don't need the ladder to bust the alarm. I'll back in tight to the wall and you can jump on the roof.'

He climbed back into the driver's seat, oriented himself with the mirrors and pulled the gear lever over and back. I squeezed the catch on the back doors and quietly stepped out into the night.

Tom's prediction of five seconds was on the low side, but we did OK. Slower than a good Formula One pitstop, quicker than a bad one. The worst bit was balancing on the roof to knock out the alarm, which was wailing into my face like the hounds of hell. There was some sort of kerb, so Tom couldn't get close enough to the wall. He also had to go too far back to get the shutter door closed. I ended up leaning over and waving the drill around in my left hand, which was nowhere near comfortable. I'd have been better off with the ladder. But I've known worse. And it's such a lovely deep silence when an alarm you're working on goes quiet.

There was an open-platform lift going up the facing wall about fifty feet away, at the far end of the internal courtyard, which was wide enough for trucks to turn. Tom carried the torch, I lugged the toolbag. The platform was like the tail-lift of a lorry, except with bars round the sides. I enjoyed pushing the buttons, and could have gone up and down happily for a good while in other circumstances. When we lined up with the second floor and jolted to a halt, Tom pushed aside the plastic safety doors and then knelt down to hook them open.

'If there's trouble, I want to see it coming. Plus we might see an armoire we like.'

I assumed this was a joke, but was too wound up to appreciate it. Monica Seles seemed to enjoy her first come-back match, but she'd only been out two years.

Tom moved off down the stone-floored corridor, which smelled of industrial cleaner and reminded me of school. He seemed intent on small talk.

'So how was it inside? Come out with any good ideas? Skills? Projects?'

'No,' I muttered, wondering why he'd stuffed the bag with so many tools. Maybe we were going to have to change the van's gearbox before making our getaway.

Tom shook his head impatiently. 'I thought those places were meant to be academies of crime. How come you weren't networking and brainstorming and all that stuff?' The corridor right-angled into a huge loft space packed with silver cages, solid up to around six foot six, then with criss-crossed wire up to the ceiling.

'I wasn't in the mood.'

The cages were around the edge of the room, with a block in the middle. They looked like they should have animals in. I hoped Tom hadn't taken the wrong turning and brought us into the Rottweiler pound.

'Must have been a long sulk,' he observed, flicking his torch along the line of cages. 'Right, I reckon we look for a butcher-than-average padlock. There's a penlight somewhere in the bag. You go right, I'll go left.'

'How come you get a thousand-watt road torch and I have to stumble around with a nightlight?' I was annoyed by Tom's insinuation that I'd underachieved in prison as well as everywhere else. But for all that, it was me who found the cage. About half-way down the centre block. And it was true what he'd said about the padlocks. Most looked like they'd come from a Christmas cracker. The fat, shiny one glinting in the narrow beam was positively shrieking 'Over here!'

I grabbed the top of the solid part of the cage and pulled myself up with the tiny torch in my mouth. Having yet to discover Greg's gym, I couldn't hold myself there for long – and anyway, there wasn't much to see. A whole load of oblongs covered in dust sheets.

'Check this,' I said quietly, and waited for Tom to join me. Then I gave him a bunk-up, with one of his hefty feet in my locked hands, and he had a good peer around with the stronger torch.

'Looks good,' he said. 'Bolt cutters are in the bag.'

They were old ones, but he'd had them sharpened. The padlock snapped like a twig. Tom went in first and pulled the dust sheet off the first row of lockers. Then he stood looking at them with satisfaction, leaning forward to run his fingers carefully over the hinges. 'Angle grinder again, I think. D'you want to work left to right and I'll take the stuff out?'

Edging past Tom into the cage with the grinder was a tight squeeze. I could see a bit of care would be needed if we were to avoid sawing each other's arms off. Tom held the torch and I started on the left-hand locker, second row down, which was the most comfortable to reach. I began wishing I'd brought the goggles. In the open air is one thing, but bits of metal flying around in a pitch-black dog pound is no fun at all. Make whatever moral judgements you like, I say we earn our money.

I'd meant to go straight down the row, but I couldn't help stopping after the first one out of curiosity. Tom gently eased the door out, put it tidily on top of the locker above and shone the torch in. What I saw over his shoulder freaked me out. One C & A carrier bag. I choked violently on disgust and metal dust and started dismantling the second locker with unnecessary force. And the third. And the fourth. Fucking Wood Green, I thought savagely, punching through hinges and locks. Tom promises the world's biggest cash economy and all we're going to get is carrier bags from Shopping City. I finished off locker number five and then had to pause to pull off another dust sheet, with the howl of the grinder echoing off the metal walls and skewering through my brain. It was while I was pulling down the sheet and bunching it up that I noticed Tom hadn't moved from the first locker. He'd pulled the carrier bag out and was peering at what looked to me like a bronze life-saving certificate I'd won at school. Mandy Elvy had won a starred gold, of course, despite my best efforts to drown her.

'What's going on?' I said tetchily, feeling this was no time for nostalgia and Tom wasn't pulling his weight.

Tom poked through a few more sheets of paper, then dropped them back in the carrier bag. 'We're out of here,' he said. 'Let's go.'

'Hey! Hold on! Wait a minute.'

But he was already on the move, taking his torch with him. I was left scrabbling for my penlight, accidentally locking the angle grinder on, which started flaying strips out of the canvas toolbag and sparking off the concrete floor. With some effort, I brought myself and my matériel under control and stood there, gazing in confusion at the lockers. Tom hadn't even bothered to take the door off the second one. I reached forward tentatively, listening to his receding footsteps.

'I mean it, Charlie! I'll leave without you!'

The booming voice from somewhere over by the platform lift was louder than the alarm. I swore and pulled my hand back. 'Why not use my fucking surname as well,' I muttered, dumping the grinder in the toolbag and pulling the handles together. My fingers were beginning to sweat in the rubber gloves. I took one last regretful look around, then snapped off the penlight and dropped that in the bag too. I stumbled out of the cage and ricocheted down the corridor towards the electric hum of the lift. Once past the dogleg corner, I could see better, either because a few rays of moonlight were drifting languidly down through a skylight, or because my eyes were adjusting. I was stuck when I reached the swing doors by the lift, though, because the platform was down in the courtyard and I couldn't see the call button anywhere. Tom was half-way to the van.

I felt along the wall a few more times, both sides, but found nothing. There was a metal ladder bolted to the brickwork, standing about a foot proud of it and going right up into the roof. It wasn't much of a consolation prize, but it had the edge on jumping. I hauled the toolbag on to my shoulder and swung on to the ladder, just as Tom slammed the driver's door shut behind him. I didn't hang around, and the climb down, once I'd got the measure of the rungs, went pretty well. A few years on, if Luther had fitted something similar to the outside of his house, it would have saved me a lot of grief.

Tom had the engine running by the time I made it to the van. I slung the tools in the back and went ahead to push up the broken shutter door. He edged out into the road just as the rain started for real. I pulled the shutter carefully down, took a last look around and climbed into the back after the tools. As we pulled away, I heard a lone siren, but it never came any nearer.

'This had better be good,' I said sourly, as I climbed over on to the passenger seat. Tom was staring at the road ahead through the spattered windscreen, waiting until visibility was almost zero before starting the wipers.

'It's nowhere near good,' he growled. 'And it may be a lot worse.'

I thought about that and got nowhere. 'What's in the bag?'

'Bonds.'

'Bonds? What – premium bonds?' Alan and I had both been given one when we were kids. I think they were still in shillings. Mine, I cashed and spent in seconds. Alan's was probably financing a drop-in centre by now. 'You've just pulled us out because we've got a bagful of chances of winning twenty-five quid every couple of months? When we had it all—'

'Bearer bonds,' Tom snapped. 'Eurobonds. Dollar bonds. Call 'em what you like. Not fucking premium bonds. Jesus!'

I still couldn't see what he was so uptight about. And I liked the sound of dollar bonds, even though I had no idea what they were. 'How much?' I said pertinently.

Tom shrugged. 'I didn't count. All the ones I looked at mature in the next three months. If that goes for all of them . . . '

He did some quick mental arithmetic. When he came up

with a figure, it was all I could do not to burst into tears and suggest a sing-song. I twisted round, looking for the C & A carrier.

'Leave it,' Tom said, as if I were a toddler heading for a plug socket. He was beginning to get on my nerves.

'Who says these bits of paper are for real? They could be fakes. Or part of a board game.' Bonding, from Waddingtons.

Tom shook his head. 'They don't look like no game,' he said wearily.

'Then what's the problem? What the hell's got into you? Why are you so crabby? And what are dollar bonds anyway?'

I caught sight of a road sign and my heart sank. Tom always drove to Birmingham to dump his wheels. He said the rail connections were good. Usually, he dropped me off, but this time it looked like I was in for the duration. If only because I'd never get the passenger door open again.

'In no particular order: I'm crabby because I'm thinking. And this kind of thinking always ruins my mood. Dollar bonds are issued by companies and banks to raise money – they're Eurobonds so lots of rich people in America can get richer by dodging tax. And the problem is . . . the problem is everything. We wanted a tidy little scam to net a few grand in cash plus some toys. Everybody claims on insurance, nobody gives a damn. Instead, we've got the kind of money that people come looking for. You can lay quite a paper trail when you're loaded. Drop a hundred for a name, another hundred on the name to give you another, and a couple of hundred on the other to say what he overheard in the pub. It doesn't take long to close in when you're laying down that kind of cash.'

But they wouldn't be laying down this kind of cash, because we'd just nicked it. I thought about pointing this out to Tom, but decided against. He hated being interrupted when he was thinking. Instead, I tried to get my head comfortable on the rattling side window by cushioning it on my rubber-gloved hand.

'There's baby wipes in your door pocket,' Tom said about half an hour later. 'Better start rubbing our prints off.' And that was the last thing he said until we were more or less at the Bull Ring.

I left the van by the back door, a few hundred yards from the station. Tom had given me a handful of notes from his wallet and a lot to think about. I was still wearing my blue overalls and lugging the tools, which weren't getting any lighter. But it was the carrier bag that weighed the most.

I still couldn't believe I'd asked for it. Straight out. 'I'll take the bonds – I've got an idea.'

We were lucky it was so early and there wasn't much traffic, because Tom came close to losing control of the van. We did all three lanes, plus half the hard shoulder, in a couple of hundred yards. 'What d'you mean, an idea? You didn't even know what they were a few minutes ago.'

'Maybe not. But I know someone.'

'What sort of someone?'

I hesitated. 'Family.'

The van swerved again, and a through-the-night trucker behind us started flashing his lights. 'You haven't got any family. Except for your poofy brother, and you can't stand each other.'

'Maybe – but he owes me. That counts for more.'

'Jesus.' Tom ran his hands through his hair. This was going to mean more thinking, and he was in a bad enough mood already. It took him three more exits to straighten out his head.

'OK, you take the bonds, Charlie. Do what you have to. But make sure you're at the Pig tonight by ten, because we're going to war. I'll leave it to you to think up a reason, but I'm looking for a proper scrap, so you'd better bring a knife or else I'm just going to knock you out and no one'll even bother to remember it. And after that, we go our separate ways. For five years. Nobody sees us together, nobody connects us and we don't touch the money. Not a cent – OK?'

I swallowed hard. 'I thought this was meant to set me up. What am I supposed to do for the next five years?' My voice was dangerously close to a whine.

Tom was following signs to the station. 'Same as before, if you've any sense. Hang around the right pubs, hook up with someone who needs a little muscle, preferably not too stupid. You're bound to get offers. Don't undervalue yourself – it's a niche market. Most heavies are morons.'

It may be a city full of passion and rich in history, but downtown Birmingham isn't a great place to see in a rainy dawn. Not unless you work for Blue Circle and can salivate at the thought of all those cementation contracts. If you're an unemployed ex-con with few marketable skills and even fewer legally acceptable ones, who's just been told to put his life on hold for half a decade, it can seem a grey place indeed.

'And another thing – make sure you're seen around a lot at the beginning of next week, after our little tiff. Go into pubs, try to pick up barmaids, ask people the time, walk out of cinemas demanding a refund because you didn't realize the film was subtitled, send food back. Better still, do it some-where like Edinburgh. Because I've got a hunch Mohinder's going to have to take the lockers back on the quiet and then fake something. His insurance is never going to cover sticking them in a furniture warehouse and, more to the point, some of his customers would be really unhappy if they knew what had been going on. So if I were you I'd grab the first train north Sunday morning and take a city break.'

If the rubber gloves hadn't been saturated with sweat, metal filings and babywipe fragrance, I really think I'd have had my head in my hands by now. I'd just managed to lose a small fortune, five years of my life and the one friend I had in

a couple of hours. And now I had to go to fucking Scotland
for the weekend. The *coup de grâce*. All I could do was hope
to God the Festival wasn't on.

Nineteen

Tappety, click. Pause. Tappety, tappety, click. Longer pause. Click, click. Tappety, tappety, tappety.

I opened my eyes cautiously, but couldn't see anything for miles. That told me I was still at Alan's. On the sofa, with an unfamiliar coat over me. Somewhere off to my right, Alan was beavering away, laying software landmines around his employers' programs, then working out a path through them, then mining the path, and so on and so forth, presumably until either the hypothetical intruder or Alan himself went mad.

I was snug and comfortable, and grateful for the grimy windows and dull light, filtered to customary near extinction through the dust. Because what I also had was a thumping hangover. The first since I couldn't remember when. It felt strange to have my head hurting more than the rest of me. The front of my head, that is – not the back, where the hole was. I lay there, eyes gluey, mouth parched, cracking headache, feeling excellent. And when I turned my head, there on the floor next to my shoes was a tall glass of water.

The implications of this were not lost on me. If Alan knew I was going to need water, I must have been obviously drunk, because he wasn't one for social nuance. On the other hand, I hadn't been sick, nor revived any of the old battles of twinship that I could remember, so my account couldn't be that drastically in the red. I stretched out a hand for the water and propped myself up on an elbow. After three more quick taps, Alan turned round.

'Land of the living?' he said cheerfully.

I put the glass carefully down, half the water gone. 'Back from the dead. I'm not used to evenings like that.' Which was almost certainly true, but I couldn't be one hundred per cent sure, because I didn't seem to be able to remember much of it. 'What happened, exactly?'

Alan cast his own mind back. 'Well . . . mainly you and Bruce drank just about everything in sight and argued politics. When I came to bed, you were rubbishing the idea of a Bill of Rights, saying it would just give lawyers something to bicker over for huge fees, and mounting a no-nonsense defence of our unwritten Constitution. Apparently, you also went on to tell Bruce his country was a barely tolerated guest in the Commonwealth and infinitely less civilized than all those States which greet the Queen with tribal dancers.'

I hunched deeper into the coat, alarmed and appalled. 'What the hell do I know about our unwritten Constitution?'

Alan resisted the obvious answer. 'You did OK,' he said generously. 'You mentioned some guy called Bagehot a lot. Apart from that, I can't remember much myself. I had my mind on work. D'you want a coffee or anything?'

'No,' I said quickly. 'Thanks.' And I didn't. But I was also aware that making it would wipe out a morning's work for Alan. Besides, there was something else I wanted to know. 'Why didn't Bruce beat me up?'

The same question had obviously occurred to Alan. 'Dunno,' he said, mystified. 'He seems to have taken a shine. That's one of his most expensive coats he draped over you when you finally fell asleep. I should know, because I bought it for him.'

It was camel coloured, with a soft, silky lining. A bit effete for my taste, but great as a duvet. I swung my legs round and down and sat up. The room span crazily for a few seconds, then slowly settled down. I finished off my water and wiped the back of my hand across my mouth. 'I should get going.'

Alan stood up. 'Suitcase is behind you,' he said. 'All packed. Different currencies. Some francs.' He hesitated, looked away. 'It's not too late. You could take some, I could still transfer the rest. It's not a problem.'

I laid the coat carefully over the back of the sofa and pulled on my shoes. Then I reached for the case. It was one of those rigid plastic ones, brand new and strong enough to withstand even the most catastrophic air crash and keep your underwear intact for your relatives to claim. 'It's OK – I'll take my chances.' I sat with the case on my lap for a while, then stood up. 'I wouldn't mind a cab, though. I'll wait downstairs with the elevator boys.'

I backed away towards the fire-escape door and turned just before I reached it. 'Say thanks to Bruce.'

For what? Bruce wasn't the person I owed, and we both knew it. Alan just smiled. 'So long, little brother.'

The door at the foot of the stone staircase had been wedged open for the lift engineers to scurry between their vans and the shafts. There seemed fewer of them this morning, so either they'd picked up another contract or the work was more dangerous than I'd supposed. I knew about elevator surfing, where you lounge around smoking your first cigarette on the top of cars and hope nobody presses the top floor button, but these guys looked a little old for that, and not the sort to indulge in what, after all, would be something of a busman's holiday.

I stood to one side, out of their way, the suitcase a nonchalant couple of feet from my left leg. Basically, I wanted to throw myself on top of it shrieking 'Back off!' at anyone who even looked at me, but even I could see this wouldn't be such a good idea. So I hung around, trying to look like a guy who has a plane to catch and deals to cut across the Pond. But I was beginning to feel rumpled and grimy, which is usually a sign that I'm looking a lot worse, so I doubt anyone paying me the slightest attention would have been convinced. I glanced at the hairs on my wrist a couple of times, where employed people have watches, and pantomimed mild irritation and anxiety, before telling myself to stop bloody fidgeting and just wait.

The black cab cruised in tentatively, on the lookout for bricks being lobbed from balconies. I felt a strange surge of pride that it wouldn't happen, that my brother had it under control, even though I'd been on the receiving end of some of his community policing. I raised my arm to wave down the cab and as I did a screaming whistle exploded through the air, sending sonic waves bouncing frantically off all the walls of the estate. I looked back over my shoulder. Alan was on his balcony, proving he still had a whistle to knock Concorde off course. I think he was smiling, but at that distance I couldn't be sure.

I climbed into the cab, noticing that the driver, who assumed I was responsible for the whistle, was tense. Funny what gets you respect, I mused, giving him the name of a mainline railway station and settling back into my seat, pleased that I could resist the urge to pull the case on to my lap and hug it. Alan had some good front-line techniques, I decided, but in the end most of it came down to the stuff that was in the Samsonite. That was something that struck me about being an assisted-place kid at a reasonable school – how much sense private education makes if you've got money. You segregate your cerebral, diligent and gentle little people because you know they wouldn't last until lunchtime at the school round the corner, and what with gap years and college you can keep them out of trouble well into their twenties, when their trust funds mature and they start earning reasonable money anyway, which gives them the ultimate power over the bash street kids who are now (the lucky ones, anyway) driving skip lorries and fixing their heating, namely – toe the line or I stop the cheque. By which time, of course, they're living in good neighbourhoods away from casual street trouble. In this respect, Alan reminded me of a boxer who deliberately keeps his guard down and relies on his reflexes to stay on his feet. He wanted to be where the action was, where someone with his tastes and predilections by rights shouldn't even survive. I still don't know why. If I were a fox, I'd be happy to dodge the hounds – I wouldn't want to lead the pack.

The rattle and hum of the taxi soothed the remains of my hangover, which was already fading fast enough to suggest that the wine Bruce and I had been drinking, and Alan had been sipping, wasn't Bulgarian. Another perk of money. You get to bully people in service industries and drink decent claret. I glanced fondly at the case, feeling mellower by the second. That must be part of the appeal of taxis – the womb-like shape and the rumbling, gurgling engine that sounds like a mother's digestive system. Which together suggested the happiest person around should be a rich foetus.

The downside of letting my mind wander along these meaningless tracks, while I dreamily watched the traffic clog and unclog around me, was that I didn't remember until we were pulling up outside the station that I had no money on me. Literally on me, as opposed to boxed at my feet. I hauled the case quickly on to my lap, checked that no one was peering in through the side windows, and pressed the catches. I'd had it all planned – the trip to the gents, taking out a generous float, dropping the rest off at left luggage. Safe and anonymous. The only thing I'd forgotten was that we'd yet to attain a socialist utopia and taxis weren't free.

Nothing happened when I pressed the catches.

I blinked and pressed again. Nothing happened again. Except my heart began to thump a little louder. I looked closely at the combination locks – three digits on each of the two catches, nothing special – and saw they weren't zeroed up. In fact, they were all over the place. I flicked the numbers round with my thumbs until all the noughts lined up, trying not to catch the cabbie's eye in his mirror. Then I pressed the catches again.

Nothing happened.

I bit my lip and stared at the numbers.

'You all right back there?' the cabbie said, with a fine instinct for a fare in jeopardy.

'Yup. Sure. Keep the meter running. I'm thinking something through.'

This was going to be a touch tricky. I could ask for the cabbie's toolbox, but I didn't really want him looming over my shoulder as I screwdrivered my way into a suitcase full of cash. At the very least, it would be something he'd remember. It's one thing after another in this game. Either you're throwing your weight around, desperate to make an impression so you'll be able to prove where you were just after midnight on the thirteenth. Or you're trying to melt into the crowd and not be noticed by anyone, in which case setting up a controlled explosion of a Samsonite full of currency on a mainline railway station is almost definitely the wrong move.

'Suit yourself,' the cabbie said generously, picking his newspaper off the dashboard and spreading it over the steering wheel, presumably open at the leader page so he could stoke up on some meaty opinions. It must be an exhausting life, having to know all those streets and form all those radical views that the mainstream political parties are too timid to espouse. I wondered if they have two-part questions in the Knowledge exam – how would you get from Baker Street Tube to Flask Walk, and who is hanging too good for?

I tried to think of numbers associated with Alan. There was 131 from his Porsche registration plate, and 86 from his flat. That left one digit spare. Useless. There was 1977 from

Jubilee year when the Pistols should have been number one but weren't because of the monarchist Masonic conspiracy or whatever rubbish he insisted on believing. That left two digits. Probably the room number at the Chelsea Hotel where Sid kebabed Nancy – and I hadn't a clue. I swore under my breath and flicked the numbers at random, every so often stabbing at the catches like a pinball wizard. Six single digits – better than lottery odds, but still on the long side. By the time I got lucky, the fare would probably account for most of what was in the case.

'You got a problem?' the cabbie said, checking me out in his mirror. There was a definite edge to his voice.

'No,' I said, holding to my personal honour code, which stipulates that if a question is that stupid, whatever you say in reply isn't lying. 'I'm a mathematician. I have to work through theorems when they come to me. And I mustn't be disturbed.' I threw in the last bit just in case he'd had Stephen Hawking in his cab once.

'Only I'm already late for my coffee break,' he complained, unimpressed with the clear implication that in my head were the keys that could unlock the universe. Which was fair enough, I suppose, as I was obviously incapable of unlocking my own suitcase.

I gave up flicking the numbers round and just sat, drumming my fingers quietly on the top of the case and wondering what the hell to do next. It's embarrassing – and makes me wonder how I got an assisted place to anywhere except jail – to recall that the cabbie had to whine twice more about his coffee, by which time I'd torn my earring most of the way through the lobe, before I calmed down sufficiently to work out what should have been staring me in the face if I hadn't been so jumpy, namely that if your twin sets a six-digit combination for you with no explanation, there's only one thing it can be.

I rolled the numbers, lined them up, then pressed the

catches with moist fingertips. 'And happy birthday to you,' I muttered, as they sprang open.

The sign on the gym door, scrawled in black marker pen straight on to the wood, said 'Closed for Reeferbishment', which was probably not far off the mark, because Greg had access to some good supplies and enjoyed a toke or two in the sauna when things were quiet. Which they were now – I couldn't hear any refurbishing noises coming from inside.

I rapped hard on the wood, and flakes of red paint came away on my knuckles. The sign was bad news. I needed a weights session, even if it hurt, to clear my head. I also needed a shower. And maybe a long, slow bake in the sauna to finish off, preferably without any weed, because I usually feel airheaded enough in there with just the heat. I pummelled the door again, making it buck and shudder and shed a few more strips of topcoat, but nothing else happened. I ended up leaning my forehead wearily on the blistering paint, feeling bizarrely depressed, so when the door swung suddenly open, I pitched forward in a dazed buffalo charge at Greg's slablike chest.

'Whoa!' he said, grabbing me by the shoulders and just about keeping me upright and away from him. 'Not so fast.' He spun me round and steadied me against the side wall, glancing down at the large green carrier bag I'd kicked in as I lurched forward. 'You've come to show me your new clothes?'

'I've come to train,' I said proudly. 'They're for afterwards. How come you move so quietly?'

Greg ignored the question and closed the door behind me. 'You're out of luck. All the equipment is gone. Place is empty. New stuff doesn't arrive till tomorrow.' He shook his head sorrowfully. 'You look bad, Charlie.'

I couldn't argue with that one. Greg looked pretty much himself. Tracksuit trousers, pumped-up trainers, cheerful T-shirt (a guy in shades and a hooded duffelcoat on the front, the legend 'Unabomber has your postcode' on the back) and some dinky little towelling wristbands. Actually, they were probably headbands, but they just about made it round Greg's wrists.

'Yeah, well. Maybe I'll just take a shower, clean up a bit. If that's OK.'

Greg smiled. 'You're not hearing me, man. I said you were out of luck and I meant it. I've got no weights to play with, and all this space, so I'm doing circuits. You know, squat thrusts, two- and one-hand press-ups, burpees, sit-ups – we'll start with a hundred of them. You can hold my feet, then I'll hold yours. I've got this whole routine worked out, which now you're here I can try on you.'

'Um, Greg – I'm not sure a whole rou—'

The matey slap on my shoulder shook my bones like a depth charge. 'You know the trouble with guys like you? You have it too easy. All you're interested in is a quiet life. So I figure I'm doing you a big favour, because if it wasn't for people like me, you wouldn't even begin to understand what hurting's all about.'

Propped more or less upright on the wooden slats of the sauna, as close to coma as you can get while still registering spasmodic brain activity, I knew that Greg had me wrong. But I wasn't going to make an issue of it, because for the time being I had to concentrate on staying alive. Besides, we were still on pretty good terms, considering. One minor spat early on, just after I'd thrown up, when Greg said he'd give me a ninety-second break instead of a minute. Which was OK, except he'd wanted the ninety seconds to start immediately I began retching, rather than when I staggered back into the room from the toilets, wiping my mouth. And then a slight awkwardness towards the end, when I was curled up in a ball in the corner, sobbing for my mother, and Greg had to haul me up by my hair and remind me gently that I had no mother, or at least none that I knew, and anyway, she was almost certainly a complete neurotic, roughly my age, addicted to anti-depressants, if nothing worse, and of precious little use to anyone, let alone to the first of her by now countless giveaway children. On such empathy and encouragement were Greg's training sessions built.

'You surprise me, Charlie,' he said, leaning forward to ladle more water on to the coals. 'You can always do more than you think you can – you just need to be pushed. That was a useful session just gone. I'm glad you came by.'

'Oh, me too,' I managed to croak, my throat roasted by the gas-mark-eight air. 'Definitely.' I didn't want to sound sarcastic, but I needn't have worried. My voice was scarcely audible, even to myself. All trace of inflection had been burned out. It was a measure of the last hour and a half that I took comfort from the fact that I could still feel pain.

'You've always got some excuse about busted ribs or shoulders or your knee's gone, but you always get through with a little help, don't you? Because it's all self-belief in the end. Self-belief and how much you want it. So you shouldn't underestimate yourself – there's plenty of people out there who do worse than you.'

Even in my radically altered (for the worse) state, slumped in the far corner of the lower bench like someone who's been tipped out of a wheelchair, and with the blood-clot brain of a losing boxer, I could tell something was wrong. Greg never gushed.

'What's on your mind?' I said, sounding like Brando playing Corleone with his cheeks stuffed with cotton wool.

'Nothing,' Greg said, too quickly. Then his conscience cut in. 'Well . . . '

He was on the same side of the sauna as me, a couple of levels up. As my head lolled around at strange angles, I could see him intermittently on the edge of my peripheral vision, running his hands over his glistening, shaven scalp and looking troubled.

'Yeah, there was something I wanted to say. Meant to for a while, but . . . '

From somewhere in the gym came the thump of a door closing.

' . . . but you haven't been around much; and I didn't like to come calling. I mean, I didn't know how you'd feel and—'

'I just heard a door close.'

Greg nodded, not looking any happier. 'Cleaners could be early,' he said, without conviction. And he didn't seem in any hurry to find out. 'Thing is . . . this. What I was going to tell you – talk over with you – was . . . '

I could have sworn I heard a key turn in a locker. Greg cleared his throat loudly. 'Only I didn't want it to come from anyone else, you know. I mean, not that there's anything wrong with . . . with anything. But you know how it is.'

I hadn't the faintest idea how it was. And I could hear the gentle slap of bare feet on the changing-room floor. Whatever Greg paid his cleaners, surely they could afford shoes. The footsteps were heading our way.

'There's somebody coming,' I told Greg, feeling anxious and in no state to receive visitors. I tried to wedge myself slightly more upright against the panelled sauna walls.

'Right,' said Greg. 'Yeah. That was what I kinda had it in mind to tell—'

The door clicked open. Presumably she'd seen Greg through the small, square window, but I was too far down. She did an impressive double take when she saw me, but still recovered a whole lot quicker than I did.

'Well, well. Charlie. You never seem to have any clothes on when I see you these days.'

I nodded, slowly, aware at the margins of my vision that this cheerful greeting had not gone down well with Greg. 'Hello, Opal.'

She hesitated, half hidden behind the sauna door. 'Maybe I should leave you guys to bond or whatever it is you're up to.'

It wasn't a convincing suggestion. Leaving well alone had never been her style.

'What the hell,' she said. 'It's not as if you haven't both seen it all before.'

But in one case, rather a long time before. I watched helplessly as she walked in, turning right round to pull the door shut rather than just tugging it closed behind her, then mulling over the seating possibilities for what seemed like a generation before choosing the middle bench opposite Greg and myself and settling gingerly down on the hot wood. She pulled her knees up to her chest in a gesture that could have been seen as misguided modesty by anyone who didn't know her, and smiled in a way that not even someone who didn't know her could possibly describe as modest.

In what for me was a long and brutally hard week, this was definitely the sucker punch. The cold air Opal had let in as she pretended to dither by the door was the only thing keeping me alive. Just for once, I thought miserably, trying to be grown up and Swedish and not stare (and not even coming close), I'd like to meet up with Opal with my clothes on, at least initially, and when I hadn't just fallen out of a house or road tested Greg's new drop-and-die circuit. But this was the real world, and it wasn't going to happen. Which left me, as I saw it, a tough choice.

The dog-day afternoon approach was the sole manly option. Strangle Greg with my bare hands, then have Opal repeatedly and without mercy on the burning slats of the sauna bench. As projects go, it was morally indefensible, hysterically vindictive and mindlessly macho – all strong points in its favour. Unfortunately, it was also impractical. In my present state, if I tried anything on with Opal, let alone Greg, I'd find myself frying face down on the sauna coals. Which inclined me towards option two, namely get the hell out, and fast. Again, easier said than done, but done it had to be, because the alternative of staying sprawled in my corner, trying not to be obviously turned on by the sexiest woman I'd ever had in my bed (on the rare occasions we made it that far), who'd now seen the light and moved on to a real man, was not something I could live with for any length of time.

I had no idea how I was going to make it all the way to the sauna door. It seemed like a long time since I'd had any worthwhile control over my limbs. I decided my best – and probably only – hope lay in announcing my imminent departure and willing it to happen. Kneel down, move your lips in prayer, and you will believe. I cleared my throat.

'Gotta go,' I rasped. 'New clothes to try on.'

I broke my rule about drinking a litre of water after training and went straight on to shorts, which was a suicidal tactic that soon had me slumped in familiar sauna position on a corner seat in the pub, glassy eyed and unable to recognize the guy who'd just come up and slapped me playfully on the shoulder.

'How you doing? You look wasted.'

'Tired,' I said, trying to focus. 'Just been training with Greg.'

My friend looked slightly startled, but recovered well. 'Good for you, man. I was sorry to hear about you and sis. Guess everyone's still friends, then.'

Sis? Sis? I blinked stupidly. Christ. This was Royale.

'What you doing out?'

'Good behaviour,' he said, with a smile as dazzling as his sister's. He lowered himself into the chair opposite. 'Hey, you sure you're OK?'

I thought I was doing a fine job holding myself together. The only thing that gave me away was that I'd taken a fierce grip on his forearm as it rested on the table.

'Royale, I need a favour.'

He looked as if he might be regretting his social overture. 'Sure, Charlie,' he said uncertainly. 'Whatever.'

'I need a coffee. Make it two coffees. Black. And some water. I'll give you the money. It's right here.' I fumbled in the inside pocket of my new jacket.

'Relax, man. And stay put. I'll stand you a coffee. Be right back.'

A few people have done me bigger favours, but none so timely. He managed to persuade the new guy behind the bar to make me a thermos of coffee, which he brought back with a pint of water. Then he sat with me for an hour and a half while I dragged myself back from the completely non-functional to the merely pathetic. Towards the end of my sixth plastic thermos lid of coffee, I became confiding.

'You know, I didn't know about Opal. Opal and . . . Nobody told me. I just found out today, when I went along . . . It was . . .'

Royale nodded, eyes lowered in sympathy and embarrassment. 'Never easy, man. Never easy.' He checked his watch surreptitiously. 'Listen, Charlie, I should be moving on.' He glanced round, moved closer, looked me hard in the face, trying to decide if I was in any shape to receive information. He rejected the obvious conclusion and told me anyway. 'There's people been looking for you,' he said quietly. 'In here. At the house, bothering Dad. Asking where you are. Sort of people I can't imagine they're your friends, and if they are, maybe you should do some reconsidering.'

'*Changez vos amis*,' I said, with the lucidity of the far gone.

'What?'

'General de Gaulle. Been cropping up a lot recently. Told someone to change his friends because they didn't agree with his policy on . . . um . . . on . . . something. Can't remember. It's gone.'

Royale held my shoulders and jolted me once – hard. My head snapped back and everything spun out of focus. 'It's *your* friends I'm talking about. They're trouble. You should be careful.' I sighed sleepily and he shook me again, making me wince. I could feel a headache coming on and knew that if I could just get to bed in the next ten minutes, I could head it off at the pass. But I knew I wasn't going to be in bed for a long while yet, and when I realized I knew that, I decided I wasn't as drunk as I thought I was.

Royale pushed his chair back. 'Wait,' I managed to say, before he stood up. 'I want you to give a message to Luther.' He waited patiently while I lined up my thoughts. 'Tell him he can knock down the shed to make his rockery. But say I want to keep the flat on. For Julie. And give him this. Rent.' I reached into one of my pockets and pulled out a large wad of notes. Royale's eyes widened in panic and he pitched forward, covering my hands with his own. In a surprisingly slick operation, I pulled mine back, leaving him with the money.

'This don't look like rent to me,' Royale hissed.

'Rent and repairs,' I insisted. 'And if there's stuff over, it's for you.' I started to chuckle. 'I know how it is when you've just come out. Need a little something to set yourself up.'

Royale was biting his lip as he pulled the money towards him and buried it quickly in his jacket. 'Listen to me,' he said, as I continued laughing softly to myself. 'I'm taking this – but I'm not taking it. I'm keeping it till tomorrow and then we'll talk. Right now, it's safer with me than with you. Understand?'

I waved a hand airily. 'Whatever,' I said, as he stood up. 'And, hey – thanks, Royale.'

I was sad to see him go, but still amused by my joke about the little something to set himself up. I poured out some more coffee from the thermos, wondering if Royale had lined up a more orthodox first night than my own. Fucking Birmingham.

That was a dangerous line of thought, because it led straight back to Tom, and if I wasn't careful I'd soon be howling inconsolably like a mongrel tied up outside a supermarket. So I took a last sip of coffee and stood up with elaborate caution, using my hands for balance on the table, making sure nothing was knocked over or spilled. The operation was a welcome success, and I was sober enough as I weaved towards the door to realize that when the fresh air hit, I'd feel really drunk.

Good thinking, but wrong. The headache that had been loitering in the shadows kicked in the minute I was outside – and it was vicious. I stood there, blinking in pain and surprise. It was like the dregs of last night's hangover plus an advance on tonight's and then doubled. When I leaned against the pub wall, the bricks on my head were cool and damp. The street was quiet, and the branches of the mangy city trees rustled softly. I started off towards my flat, knowing it was the wrong thing to do, but desperate for the painkillers that I knew were in my bathroom cabinet two streets away. I honestly thought that if I turned my collar up, I could walk by the house, check it out, then dive in if nobody was around.

A few cars passed by, the headlights picking me out and then dropping me as they swept round the corner. None of them slowed down for a closer look. I picked up my pace into a stumbling, rolling trot, crossing the road a couple of times in the interests of defensive reconnaissance, which was pretty much a waste of time, firstly because my eyes seemed to be fixed focus on the distance Royale had been from me in the pub, namely three feet, and secondly because unless I happened to be directly under a streetlight, it was pitch bloody black and I couldn't see a thing.

It was just after I'd crossed the road for the third time and was within shouting distance of home that the lights on the parked car ten yards or so in front of me snapped on, full beam, bringing me to a sudden, squinting halt. I raised an arm to shield my eyes and half turned to run, knowing there was no alley around, so the side access to a house would have to do. But the lights flicked off again before I'd even moved, which isn't what happens when someone wants the key to your left-luggage locker, and I was left backed up against a privet hedge, dazed, with blood pounding in my head and my breath coming in rasps.

The soft hum of the electric window carried above the rustling of the leaves. And then her voice. 'Charlie, it's me.'

I stepped forward and walked hesitantly round the front of the bonnet, feeling my way like a blind man until I reached the passenger door. I pulled it open and lowered myself carefully on to the seat. Helen waited until I was settled, then reached across me to pull the door closed. Somehow, I'd forgotten to do that.

'What's wrong with you?' she said. Even in the dark, it seemed, the ravages were evident.

'Bad week,' I said. 'Come to a bad end.'

'And you're drunk.'

I nodded slowly. 'That as well.'

We sat in silence and it started to rain – a soft, splashy pattering on the roof and bonnet. I asked Helen if she had any painkillers and she brought some out from her handbag. I managed to swallow a few dry, and slipped the packet into my pocket. She didn't comment. The dark drops on the windscreen spread into complex patterns.

'Let me guess. You've come to say goodbye.'

Rainy Friday. When all the women in my life, who'd already moved on some time ago, queued up just to make it absolutely clear, so there could be no possible room for ambiguity, that they were gone for good.

Helen studied her hands. 'We're moving to Strasbourg. It's where most of Malcolm's work is anyway. He spends all his time on planes at the moment. They're opening up another office just to handle Commission work and they've asked him to head the team. And . . . ' She paused. Her voice dropped to a murmur. 'And we've decided to try for another child. When Malcolm isn't travelling all the time and can be at home more. When he isn't always tired.' She cleared her throat softly. 'A new start.'

I leaned my head on the glass of the side window, willing the drugs to take hold. There wasn't a single thing in what Helen had just said that I felt like picking up on. Malcolm's career in international law was a world away, while the implication that once they were happily settled into Continental life they'd be doing a lot more relaxed and happy fucking, hopefully with delightful consequences, was much too close to home. On a list of things that I really didn't want to hear, Helen had a couple of top-ten hits straight off. And how typical that just as I was beginning to feel less drunk – a detox combination of coffee, time and pain – I wished I was knocking back the shorts again.

'Well . . . ' I said, scrabbling round for the rest of the sentence. Good luck, thanks anyway, remember the good times, some day we'll meet again. But when I thought about it, Helen didn't need any luck, we probably wouldn't meet again and I couldn't reasonably ask her to remember the good times when I could hardly recall them myself, they were such a blur. A long ago blur. Which just left thanks, and I was pretty sure I'd just said that for the painkillers. So I watched the digital clock above the radio change from 9:44 to 9:45. It felt later.

'Can I buy your car?'

It was a good idea, but the timing was off. Helen looked blankly at me.

'I mean, buy it now. I've got to go away for a while. And I need a car.'

The expression on Helen's face made me wonder if I should have said a bit more about the good times, blurred or not. I hurriedly reached into my pockets and started pulling out handfuls of cash. 'I'll pay you what it's worth – more than it's worth. I just need—'

'Take the car, Charlie.' She glanced with distaste at the notes, held together with greasy rubber bands.

'No, wait a minute – look . . . ' I couldn't believe I was going through this again. 'I've got the money. More than this. I just don't want to wait till the morning to go through small ads. But I don't want charity.'

'Charlie.' Her voice was neutral, firm. 'I'm not selling my car. OK? But if it'll help you out, you're welcome to it. That's the deal. Take it or leave it.'

I shook my head in disbelief, wondering if anybody was going to accept anything from me ever again. Wondering also where the sweet sorrow was in this parting, how I'd managed with infallible reverse alchemy to turn it into something shabby and cheap. And wondering why my good ideas so often turn to dust.

'I'm sorry,' I said. 'But I really need a car.'

She nodded and pulled her handbag back on to her lap. She took out a tiny mobile phone and tapped in the number of my local minicab company from memory. That jolted some of the blurred afternoons into sharper focus, which probably wasn't such a good idea. I wanted to ask whether she knew the number by heart because the afternoons had meant something to her, or whether she just had a good memory for figures, the way some people do. But I knew I wouldn't. I heard her saying something about a breakdown, describing her car, giving the street. Her voice sounded miles away. At least from me.

'Couple of minutes,' she said, retracting the aerial and putting the phone back in her bag. 'They think I'm a lone female in distress. You'd better stay hidden.'

I nodded glumly. Getting down below the line of sight was going to bunch up some pretty tired and damaged muscles. And there was the dignity angle. Think of those classic screen goodbyes – your *Brief Encounters*, your *Casablancas*. There's a common thread running through them. The man doesn't cower in the passenger footwell of a car.

Helen smiled gently. 'So I'd better take my kiss while I can.'

That was something, I guess. And it certainly soaked up most of the two minutes. By about one minute forty my hands were on her breasts and I wanted to cancel the cab and move on to the back seat. She pushed me away, one index finger pressed to my lips, but at least she was smiling.

I had the idea of reclining the seat as far as it would go, which was a welcome alternative to the footwell option. But lying on my side, looking up at her, reminded me of being in bed and watching her dress. Then headlights swept across her face and I heard the cab chugging up behind us.

'Spare keys are in the glove compartment,' she said, and bent down to kiss me one last time. I hooked my hand round the back of her neck.

'If I'd been home when you called, instead of drinking, would you have slept with me?'

She kissed me on the nose, on both eyelids, on the forehead, then disengaged my hand and straightened up.

'Say you would,' I prompted.

She picked up her bag and smiled down at me for the last time. 'Of course I would,' she lied, and I was grateful she'd made the effort.

The door slammed shut. I listened to her footsteps, to another door opening and closing, to the engine as it revved sluggishly, pulled away and quickly began to fade. Long after it had gone, I thought I could still hear it, until a nearby siren split the night and drowned it out. I hoped police cars in Strasbourg had the same wail. It would be something to remember me by.

I pulled the seat back up and opened the glove compartment. The keys were there, along with a can of de-icer and a flimsy, free-with-every-four-gallons yellow scraper. There was nothing personal. No letters, photos, lipsticks, scarves or Everton mints. I snapped the compartment closed, shifted over to the driver's side and adjusted the mirror, which was reflecting a box of tissues on the back passenger shelf and the bulky, padded child's seat below.

I stared through the Rorschach blots on the windscreen and tapped out a soft rhythm on the steering wheel. After a while, I switched on the engine, which caught first time. Then, after indicating right and left a couple of times, I found the headlight switch as a separate button on the dash.

As I passed, I said a silent goodbye to the corner shop where I used to buy late-night milk and early-morning papers – also, occasionally, some under-the-counter, ready-rolled joints, which varied alarmingly in quality and were as overpriced as you'd expect in a late store. Skipping out when Royale had just returned to bring some much needed class and consistency to the local drug scene was going to be one of my few regrets.

Two men came out of the pub together, looked left and right down the street, then set off in the direction I'd taken. They weren't talking, they weren't cheerful, and they weren't drunk. And they probably had nothing to do with me. But I had a hard time keeping my foot steady on the accelerator as I drove past.

I eased into the anonymous headlight horde and drifted south in the patchy traffic. It felt strange driving a car that wasn't falling apart, and even stranger not riding a motorbike. I braced myself for the rite-of-passage surge of maturity that was surely my due, but all I felt was the same mindless juvenile nostalgia. Luther had angled his appeal uncompromisingly at my baser instincts. You'll never pull anyone worth having – mentioning no names of course – by tonning around like a greaser, because classy women just don't get off on being cold, uncomfortable and scared on the back of a bike, with their hair mashed up into a helmet. My God, Luther, if you could see me now, I thought, chugging around at thirty-two miles per hour in a mobile side-impact protection system fully fitted out for the growing family.

Lesson absorbed and acted upon to such a degree you'd think I was taking the piss.

It's a strange thing, though, the maturity mindset. It hardens so quickly. By the time I started looking for a meter, I was already worrying about whether the car was safe in this kind of neighbourhood and what it would do to my no claims bonus if the radio was nicked. It took significant force of will to remind myself that I was uninsured, with a criminal record, a lot of hot money and an attitude problem, and so was unlikely to be adopted by either major party as a candidate for a safe seat in the near future. To thine own self be true, I murmured, cruising appropriately to a stop on a double yellow, neatly blocking off a bus lane and obscuring the view of a zebra crossing.

This was no time to hang about. I'd done enough introspecting through windscreens to last me into the next decade, so I was out of that car and half-way across the street in one slick movement, only pausing to double back sheepishly and check the central locking had worked and I hadn't left the lights on. Turning away from the car for the second time, I noticed a tall woman with a baby strapped to her chest coming out of the door to the left of the bookies. It was a stroke of luck.

'Hi – d'you think you could keep the door open,' I said, before three things happened in quick succession. First, I remembered the door didn't close properly anyway, so I could save my breath. Second, the woman looked round, saw all she needed to see in a fraction of a second, and pulled the door sharply closed behind her. Third, the door clicked loudly, for all the world as if someone had fitted a new multi-lever Ingersoll. I sighed and slowed to a stroll, giving the woman time to move away. She stood her ground.

'D'you know if they've fixed the bell as well as the door?' I said, resigned to some small talk. 'Only I was hoping to see Maria.'

The woman had a lot of hair tumbling every which way, including some long strands over her baby's face, which would have driven me berserk. But the kid seemed to be sleeping soundly enough. 'And is she hoping to see you?' she said coldly.

Almost certainly not, was the true answer. What the fuck business is it of yours? the instinctive one. I smiled carefully.

'You never know,' I said, treading a middle path. 'Still, mustn't keep you. I expect it's past your baby's bedtime.'

Wisely, I hadn't gambled on the child's sex. With a streetlight almost directly overhead, plus random headlights and a neon fish-bar sign opposite, I could see the face clearly enough. It was puce and almost entirely featureless, like a plum dropped from a considerable height on to a concrete floor.

'Annapurna sleeps best in her sling. Sometimes it's the only way to get her off.'

The silence which followed was somewhat strained. 'Really?' I managed to say after some seconds, and then couldn't decide whether to congratulate myself on handling a tricky situation with tact and diplomacy, or berate myself for selling out and smothering the obvious natural response, namely: Annapurna's a fucking mountain.

I turned away in some confusion and pushed hard on two white doorbells, trying to remember if they'd been there before and straining to hear any buzzing noises from inside.

'It's the top one,' Annapurna's mother said. 'It's been fixed.'

Thanking her for this delayed information would have just sounded sarcastic, so I confined myself to a clipped nod, after which we resumed our stand-off, determinedly avoiding eye contact. Inside, I could hear Maria's footsteps on the stairs. Well, here we go, I thought. Not a great way to start.

Maria opened the door, saw her friend first and smiled slightly – then saw me and stopped smiling. 'Well, well,' she said. 'Hello, trouble. What do you want?'

314

When I actually thought about the question – almost certainly a mistake – I decided that what I wanted was to be somewhere far away in the sun, immediately, spending large quantities of my own money very fast. But while I was brooding on this, Annapurna's mum chipped in.

'I thought I'd stay around – you know, to check. After what happened.'

Maria nodded, perhaps with a shade of irritation. 'Thanks, Rose. But it's only Charlie. He's on my side.' She turned to study me under the municipal lighting, and her eyes narrowed. 'At least in theory.'

Rose hitched Annapurna higher up her chest. 'If you're sure,' she said doubtfully, before casting a final suspicious glance in my direction. 'May see you at the toy library, then,' she called over her shoulder as she set off into the night.

Maria said, 'Mmm,' in a way that could have meant anything. I watched Rose until I was confident she was out of earshot.

'Five minutes,' I said, finally answering Maria's question. 'That's what I want. And to know why anyone inflicts the name Annapurna on a child.'

Maria stood back to let me through. I headed for the inside door, which someone had been busy repairing since my last visit. With cheap plyboard, cut roughly to fit and then glued in. Shoddy job.

'Rose is a loyal friend,' Maria said, following me in. 'I'm not going to criticize her behind her back.'

Which effectively shut down a promising line of entertainment. I sighed and led the way up the stairs, which had considerably less to recommend it than following Maria up them. At the top, I hesitated, then walked through into the sitting room, where a battered old trunk under one of the windows caught my eye. I was pretty sure it hadn't been there before, but didn't care either way, because it looked so much more comfortable than the futon. When I sat down, though, I could feel the draught coming straight through the paper-thin curtains on to my neck.

Maria went for the futon, probably because her packet of thin cigars was balanced on the wooden back, along with a pink see-through lighter. She pulled them down on to her lap, then obviously decided she'd enjoy smoking more in five minutes when I'd gone, so put them carefully to one side.

'If you're annoyed because I never thanked you for taking care of that guy – all right, you have some justification.'

On a long list, it was probably the last thing on my mind. I started to shake my head, but she carried on. 'I know you were trying to help, but I thought you'd probably made everything worse. That he'd come back with his mates, looking for revenge as well as sport. It put me more on edge. As well as, you know, all the liberal bit about violence not solving anything. That's why I didn't get in touch.'

I shrugged. 'Doesn't matter. You're probably right that violence doesn't solve anything. But it can buy time.' Talking of which, I was keenly aware that my five minutes were ticking away. I cleared my throat, to indicate the conclusion of one topic and the broaching of another, more significant one. Then I looked round the room for inspiration, but the one thing I fastened on was the overexposed photograph of ten-year-old Maria and her cat.

'I wondered if you wanted to come to France,' I said, because I still couldn't work out how else to put it.

Maria looked more puzzled than alarmed. 'You're offering me a holiday in France?'

I shook my head. 'To live. For a while.'

'I see.' Which was almost certainly untrue, but a brave try in the circumstances. 'Why . . . ' she said slowly, 'are you going to France?'

'I need a change. It's warmer most of the year. And I want to learn to carve stone.'

I was aware that this probably seemed a little strange. But I just couldn't see a clear track through to making it seem less strange. We wrestled with our thoughts for a while in silence.

'Look . . . ' It was some consolation that Maria wasn't finding the going smooth, either. 'I don't want to sound boring and uptight about this, but I can't really see what you're going to live on.'

At least that was easy. 'I've got a suitcase full of money in a left-luggage locker. And a car outside. I'm going to get the case and head for the ports. Maybe the tunnel. Take a standby.' I replayed what I'd just said, to see if I'd left anything out. 'There's a child's car seat in the back.'

Maria nodded slowly. 'How much money fits in a suit-case?' she said, but I got the impression this was definitely a playing-for-time question. I told her anyway and, as expected, didn't get much reaction. She'd have made a lousy game-show contestant.

'D'you mind telling me how you earned it?'

Nice touch, that 'earned'. 'In principle, no. But it's a long story. I'd prefer to leave it till later.'

She nodded again. I had a hunch the key question was on its way.

'Why me?'

The fact that I was so right on timing didn't make things any easier. I ran through a couple of replies, but didn't find them convincing. 'Well,' I said, then cleared my throat and tried again. 'Well, you speak French.' So far, so incontrovert-ible. 'And I'm guessing that you don't want to stay in the Caledonian Road for ever. And maybe one day you'll want Louis to go to a school where they can afford books.' I shrugged. All good reasons, but not quite there. 'And right now . . . ' The draught on my neck was freezing it up. I dropped my head forward to loosen the muscles, in the process probably looking more pitiful even than I felt. 'And right now, I'm not doing too well on my own.'

This heartwrenching confession drew a look of mild interest from Maria, as she took her time about slipping a cigar out of the packet and lighting it. As an afterthought, she offered me one, but I wasn't in the mood for that, either.

'If Louis and I came with you,' she said, thinking it through, 'and it was a disaster and we all ended up hating each other – what then? Do we at least get the price of a ticket home and a couple of months' rent on a place like this?'

'No.' The answer was emphatic, because this was the one thing I had thought through. 'You stick it for a year. One year exactly. From five minutes ago. Then if you and Louis have had enough, you can walk out with half. Of everything.'

All she had to do was divide the number I'd just given her by two. How long could it take, even for a linguist?

'You could get company a lot cheaper from the girls down the road,' she observed finally, and such was my general state of nerves that it took me a couple of seconds to hear what she was saying. When I did, I panicked.

'Hold on . . . look. I'm not . . . I mean, it's not that kind of deal. I'm not buying company in that sense.'

'So you're asking me to uproot myself and my son, leave my family and friends behind to go and live in another country just because I know the language, and in return I don't even get laid?'

'Well, I wouldn't exactly . . . '

'I mean, the Santa routine is OK as far as it goes, but it can't be the whole story. From what Stella says, you did all right for company in the past, and you never had any money then – so what's changed all of a sudden?'

My hand had crept up to my ear, which put it firmly in the draught zone. I brought it down again, realizing too late what a catastrophic mistake it had been not bringing my lawyer along.

'Look – d'you think we could maybe negotiate on this separately?'

It was a good suggestion under pressure. Trouble was, the pressure was doubling by the second.

'Sure,' Maria said. 'But I still need some idea of where you're coming from.'

'Ah . . . how about minimum three hours, lots of dope and cunnilingus?'

Maria watched the faint wisps of smoke curling from the tip of her cigar. 'It's a start, I suppose,' she said thoughtfully.

YOU'LL NEVER BE HERE AGAIN

Mark Blackaby

WINNER OF THE BETTY TRASK PRIZE

I knew the block. I knew the floor. And when they described the view from the balcony, I was pretty sure I knew the flat . . .

Here is Paul at the breakfast table lusting fondly after his wife, when, bang, out of a clear blue sky, comes his very own Proustian moment in the unlikely shape of an estate agent's flyer.

This simple piece of paper, with its blurry photograph and blurrier prose, pitches Paul into a sudden trip down memory lane. He's still a young man (and he hates exercise), so it's more of a shortish stroll, but it's packed with incident both absurd and embarrassing.

This is the story of David, the sort of gilded youth who would give anybody a complex, and Paul, who like all the best tortoises gets there in the end. It is the story of Keith the doorman and his terminal bad luck. And it is a saga of True Love Through Hairdressing.

'Hugely entertaining debut novel, a rumbustious literary version of *Men Behaving Badly*'
Colin Donald, *The Scotsman*

'Romantic, readable and entertaining'
Joanna Trollope

£5.99   0 575 05897 8

A Gollancz Paperback